FLASHBACK

"We did a lot more than kiss."

She flashed back to that night, when she'd climbed into bed with him, pressing her icy feet to his, then her body. She remembered realising he was naked and warm and strong and hard...*God*. He'd been so utterly irresistible, she'd lost her head. And, yeah, they'd done a lot more than kiss.

"Fine. We kissed, and then I decided I should sleep with you and then walk away. Perfect, neat revenge."

"Neat, maybe. But not perfect."

His eyes were glittering with knowledge, hard won.

"Because it wasn't as easy as you thought, was it?" No, it hadn't been. Because it'd been amazing between them. So damned amazing.

First published in Great Britain 2010
Harlequin Mills & Boon Limited,
Eton House, 18-24 Paradise Road, Richmond, Surrey TW9 1SR

The Mighty Quinns: Brody © Peggy A Hoffmann 2009
Flashback © Jill Shalvis 2008

ISBN: 978 0 263 88118 9

14-0110

Harlequin Mills & Boon policy is to use papers that are natural, renewable
and recyclable products and made from wood grown in sustainable
forests. The logging and manufacturing processes conform to the legal
environmental regulations of the country of origin.

Printed and bound in Spain
by Litografia Rosés S.A., Barcelona

Available in January 2010
from Mills & Boon® Blaze®

BLAZE 2-IN-1

The Mighty Quinns: Brody
by Kate Hoffmann
&
Flashback
by Jill Shalvis

A Few Good Men
by Tori Carrington

Secret Seduction
by Lori Wilde

THE MIGHTY QUINNS: BRODY

Her eyes met his and Brody held his breath, wondering just how far he could go.

He wanted to kiss her. Hell, he'd wanted to kiss her from the moment he'd first seen her. He leaned in, hoping for a sign that she shared the attraction. Her eyes dropped to his mouth and her lips parted slightly. It was all he needed.

Bracing his hands on either side of her body, he pressed her back into the side of the SUV and brought his mouth down on hers. Her lips were soft and cool and fitted perfectly with his.

THE MIGHTY QUINNS: BRODY

BY
KATE HOFFMANN

FLASHBACK

BY
JILL SHALVIS

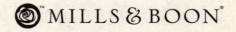

MILLS & BOON

THE MIGHTY QUINNS: BRODY

BY
KATE HOFFMANN

Kate Hoffmann has been writing for fifteen years and has published nearly sixty books. When she isn't writing, she is involved in various musical and theatrical activities in her small Wisconsin community. She enjoys sleeping late, drinking coffee and eating bonbons. She lives with her two cats, Tally and Chloe, and her computer, which shall remain nameless.

For Sarah Mayberry, fellow author and gentle reader,
who took the time to make sure this book
had "no worries."

Prologue

Queensland, Australia—January, 1994

"HOW CAN A ROCK be magic?" Callum asked, standing at the base of the huge boulder. "It's just a bloody big rock."

"Look around you, dipstick," Teague shouted from the top of the rock. "Do you see any other rocks like this around here? Gramps said it's here because it _is_ magic. You stand on top of this rock and make a wish and it comes true. Aborigines brought it here and they know a lot of magic."

"I think Gramps had a few kangaroos loose in the paddock." Callum chuckled. "I wouldn't believe everything he said."

Brody stepped up to the rock. "He did not. And I'm telling Dad you said that. It's not nice to speak ill of the dead."

"He told us there was treasure buried out here, too," Callum said. "He even told me he dug for it when he was a boy. Who would bury treasure out here?"

Brody punched Callum in the shoulder. "Give me a leg up," he said.

"No, we have to get back. Mum will have supper ready."

"I want to climb it," Brody insisted. It was hard enough always being last in line, but he hated it when Callum tried to be the boss. At least Teague liked to explore and have adventures. He treated Brody as if they were the very same age, not eighteen months apart. Callum was always the careful one, warning them off when things got too dangerous. Three years older than Brody and he might have well been forty, Brody thought.

"You'll fall and crack your noggin open," Callum warned. "And I'll get the blame, just like I always get the blame for every bad thing you morons do."

"Cal, help him up," Teague said. "It's not that high. And I'll hang on to him."

"You don't have to hang on to me," Brody said. "I'm not a baby."

Reluctantly, Callum wove his fingers together and bent down. Brody put his foot into his older brother's hands and a few moments later, Teague had dragged him to the top of the rock. "Wow," Brody said. "This is high. I bet I can see all of Queensland from here."

"You've climbed to the top of the windmills. They're much higher," Callum said as he scrambled up behind him. "And you can't see Brisbane from them. And Brisbane *is* in Queensland."

"Make a wish," Teague said. "We'll see if it works."

"I have to think," Brody said. He wanted so many things. A computer, video games, a dirt bike. But there was something he wanted more than anything. He'd never told his brothers because he knew they'd laugh. After all, there wasn't much chance he'd ever get off the station.

"Come on," Teague said. "Say it. It won't come true unless you shout it out loud."

"I want to be a footballer," Brody yelled. "I want to go to a real school and play on a real team. I want to be famous and everyone will know my name. And I want to be on the telly." To Brody's surprise, his brothers didn't laugh. In fact, they seemed to think his wish was a good one.

"That's a big wish," Callum said soberly.

"My turn," Teague said. "I know exactly what I want. I want an airplane. Or a helicopter. I want to learn how to fly. Then I can go anywhere I want, just like that. I could even fly over the ocean and see America or Africa or the South Pole."

"You could take me to my football games," Brody said.

Teague reached out and ruffled Brody's hair. "I could. But only if you give me free tickets." He stared over at Callum. "What about you?"

"I know what I want," Callum said.

"You have to say it."

Callum sat down, draping his arms over his knees as he took in the view. "How do you think this rock really got here?"

"I think it's a meteor," Brody said, sitting down beside him. "It dropped out of the sky."

Callum ran his hand over the smooth surface of the rock. "Maybe the Aborigines did move it here. Maybe it was like Stonehenge. You know, that place in England with all the rocks."

"And I think a giant prehistoric bird took a crap and it fossilized," Teague teased as he joined them. They all laughed, lying back on the rock and staring up at the cloudless sky.

Brody wrinkled his nose. "How can bird poop be magic, Teague?"

"Maybe it came from a magic bird." His brother gave him a sideways glance. "All right. It's a meteor. Or an asteroid. From another universe. Come on, Cal, you have to make your wish now."

Callum drew a deep breath. "I wish that someday I could have a place like this."

"You want a rock?" Brody asked.

"No, dickhead. A station. As big as Kerry Creek. Bigger, even. And I'd raise the best cattle in all of Queensland."

"Why would you want to live on a station?" Brody asked.

"'Cause I like it here," Callum replied.

Brody shook his head. His older brother had no imagination. Station life was horribly dull, the same thing day after day. There was never anything interesting to do. All the good stuff happened in cities like Brisbane and Sydney. Callum could have the station and Teague could have his plane. Brody knew his dream was the best.

"Dad told me he brought Mum out here when he asked her to marry him," Callum said, sitting up to scan the horizon.

Teague and Brody glanced at each other, then looked away silently. Brody wasn't sure why Callum had brought the subject up. Their parents hadn't been getting along for nearly a year now. When they weren't arguing, they were avoiding each other. Dinner was usually a shouting match or an endless meal marked by dead silence.

"I want to change my wish," Brody murmured,

sitting up beside Callum. "I wish that Mum and Dad wouldn't fight anymore. I wish they'd be like they used to be." He drew a deep breath, fighting back the tears that pressed at the corners of his eyes. "Remember when they used to kiss? When Dad would hug her so hard, she'd laugh? And they'd turn on the radio and dance around the kitchen?"

"Yeah." Teague braced his elbows behind him. "I remember that."

The first ten years of Brody's life had been spent in what he'd believed was a happy family. But then he began to be more aware of his mother's unhappiness and of his father's frustration. She hated life on the station and his father didn't know any other life *but* the station.

Callum grabbed Brody's hand and then Teague's and pressed all their hands together. "Wish it," he said, dragging them closer. "Close your eyes and wish it really hard and it will happen."

"I thought you didn't believe in the rock," Teague said.

"Do it!" Callum said. "Now."

They all closed their eyes and focused on the one wish. But somehow, Brody knew this wish didn't depend on the rock or the combined powers of the three Quinn brothers. It was up to their parents to make it come true.

When he opened his eyes, he found his brothers staring at him. Brody forced a smile, but it did nothing to relieve his fears. Something bad was going to happen, he could feel it.

He rolled over onto his stomach and slid down the side of the rock, dropping to the dusty ground with a soft thud. His horse was tethered nearby and he grabbed the reins and swung up into the saddle. As he watched his brothers jump down, Brody couldn't help but wonder whether the rock had heard them. It was just a rock. And though it didn't belong where it was, there probably wasn't anything special about it.

Pulling hard on the reins, he kicked his horse in the flanks and took off at a gallop. If his mother left the station, then he was going with her. She'd need someone to take care of her, and Brody had always been able to make her smile. She'd once whispered to him that he was her favorite. If that was true, then it was his duty to leave the station. He felt the tears tumbling from his eyes and drying on his cheeks as the wind rushed by.

The breeze caught the brim of his stockman's hat and it flew off, the string catching around his neck. Brody closed his eyes and gave the horse control over their destination. Maybe the horse wouldn't go home. Maybe it would just keep galloping, running to a place where life wasn't quite so confusing.

1

Queensland, Australia—June, 2009

HIS BODY ACHED, from the throbbing in his head to the deep, dull pain in his knee. The various twinges in between—his back, his right elbow, the fingers of his left hand—felt worse than usual. Brody Quinn wondered if he'd always wake up with a reminder of the motorcycle accident that had ruined his future or, if someday, all the pain would magically be gone.

Hell, he'd just turned twenty-six and he felt like an old man. Reaching up, he rubbed his forehead, certain of only one thing—he'd spent the previous night sitting on his arse at the Spotted Dog getting himself drunk.

The sound of an Elvis Presley tune drifted through the air and Brody knew exactly where he'd slept it off— the Bilbarra jail. The town's police chief, Angus Embley, was a huge fan of Presley, willing to debate the King's singular place in the world of music with any bloke who dared to argue the point. Right now, Elvis was only exacerbating Brody's headache.

"Angus!" he shouted. "Can you turn down the music?"

Since he'd returned home to his family's cattle station in Queensland, he'd grown rather fond of the accommodations at the local jail. Though he usually ended up behind bars for some silly reason, it saved him the long drive home or sleeping it off in his SUV. "Angus!"

"He's not here. He went out to get some breakfast."

Brody rolled over to look into the adjoining cell, startled to hear a female voice. As he rubbed his bleary eyes, he focused on a slender woman standing just a few feet away, dressed in a pretty, flowered blouse and blue jeans. Her delicate fingers were wrapped around the bars that separated them, her dark eyes intently fixed on his.

"Christ," he muttered, flopping back onto the bed. Now he'd really hit bottom, Brody mused, throwing his arm over his eyes. Getting royally pissed was one thing, but hallucinating a female prisoner was another. He was still drunk.

He closed his eyes, but the image of her swirled in his brain. Odd that he'd conjured up this particular apparition. She didn't really fit his standard of beauty. He usually preferred blue-eyed blondes with large breasts and shapely backsides and long, long legs.

This woman was slim, with deep mahogany hair that fell in a riot of curls around her face and shoulders. By his calculations, she might come up to his chin at best. And her features were…odd. Her lips were almost too lush and her cheekbones too high. And her skin was so pale and perfect that he had to wonder if she ever spent a day in the sun.

"You don't have to be embarrassed. A lot of people talk in their sleep."

Brody sat up. She had an American accent. His fantasy women never had American accents. "What?"

She stared at him from across the cell. "It was mostly just mumbling. And some snoring. And you did mention someone named Nessa."

"Vanessa," he murmured, scanning her features again. She wasn't wearing a bit of makeup, yet she looked as if she'd just stepped out of the pages of one of those fashion magazines Vanessa always had on hand. She had that fresh-scrubbed, innocent, girl-next-door look about her. Natural. Clean. He wondered if she smelled as good as she looked.

Since returning home, there hadn't been a single woman who'd piqued his interest—until now. Though she could be anywhere between sixteen and thirty, Brody reckoned if she was younger than eighteen, she wouldn't be sitting in a jail cell. It was probably safe to lust after her.

"You definitely said Nessa," she insisted. "I remember. I thought it was an odd name."

"It's short for Vanessa. She's a model and that's what they call her." Nessa was so famous, she didn't need a last name, kind of like Madonna or Sting.

"She's your girlfriend?"

"Yes." He drew a sharp breath, then cleared his throat. "No. Ex-girlfriend."

"Sorry," she said with an apologetic shrug. "I didn't mean to stir up bad memories."

"No bad memories," Brody replied, noting the hint of defensiveness in his voice. What the hell did he care what this woman thought of him—or the girls he'd dated? He swung his legs off the edge of the bed, then raked his hands through his hair. "I know why *I'm* here. What are *you* doing in a cell?"

"Just a small misunderstanding," she said, forcing a smile.

"Angus doesn't lock people up for small misunder-standings," Brody countered, pushing to his feet. "Especially not women." He crossed to stand in front of her, wrapping his fingers around the bars just above hers. "What did you do?"

"Dine and dash," she said.

"What?"

Her eyes dropped and a pretty blush stained her cheeks. "I—I skipped out on my bill at the diner down the street. And a few other meals in a few other towns. I guess my life of crime finally caught up with me. The owner called the cops and I'm in here until I find a way to work it off."

He pressed his forehead into the bars, hoping the cool iron would soothe the ache in his head. "Why don't you just pay for what you ate?"

"I would have, but I didn't have any cash. I left an IOU. And I said I'd come back and pay as soon as I found work. I guess that wasn't good enough."

Brody let his hands slide down until he was touching her, if only to prove that she was real and that he wasn't dreaming. "What happened to all your money?" he asked, fixing his attention on her face as he ran his fingers over hers. It seemed natural to touch her, even though she was a complete stranger. Oddly, she didn't seem to mind.

Her breath caught and then she sighed. "It's all gone. Desperate times call for desperate measures. I'm not a dishonest person. I was just really, really hungry."

She had the most beautiful mouth he'd ever seen, her

lips soft and full…perfect for— He fought the urge to pull her closer and take a quick taste, just to see if she'd be…different. "What's your name?"

"Payton," she murmured.

"Payton," he repeated, leaning back to take in details of her body. "Is that your last name or your first?"

"Payton Harwell," she said.

"And you're American?"

"I am."

"And you're in jail," he said, stating the obvious. She laughed softly and nodded as she glanced around. "It appears I am. At least for a while. Angus told me as soon as he finds a way for me to work off my debt, he'll let me out. I told him I could wash dishes at the diner, but the owner doesn't want me back there. I guess jobs are in short supply around here."

Brody's gaze drifted back to her face—he was oddly fascinated by her features. Had he seen her at a party or in a nightclub in Fremantle, he probably wouldn't have given her a second glance. But given time to appreciate her attributes, he couldn't seem to find a single flaw worth mentioning.

"Quinn!"

Brody glanced over his shoulder and watched as Angus strolled in, his freshly pressed uniform already rumpled after just a few hours of work. "Are you sober yet?"

"You didn't have to lock me up," Brody said, letting go of the bars.

"Brody Quinn, you started a brawl, you broke a mirror and you threw a bleedin' drink in my face, after insulting my taste in music. You didn't give me a choice." Angus braced his hands on his hips. "There'll be a fine. I figure a couple hundred should do it. And you're gonna have to pay for Buddy's mirror." Angus scratched his chin. "And I want a promise you're gonna behave yourself from now on and respect the law. Your brother's here, so pay the fine and you can go."

"Teague is here?" Brody asked.

"No, Callum is waiting. He's not so chuffed he had to make a trip into town."

"I could have driven myself home," Brody said.

"Your buddy Billy tried to take your keys last night. That's what started the fight. He flushed the keys, so Callum brought your spare." Angus reached down and unlocked the cell. "Next time you kick up a stink, I'm holding you for a week. That's a promise."

Brody turned back and looked at Payton. "You can let her out. I'll pay her fine, too."

"First you have to settle up with Miss Shelly over at the coffeeshop and then you have to find this young lady a job. Then, I'll let you pay her fine. Until you do all that, she's gonna be a guest for a bit longer."

"It's all right," Payton said in a cheerful voice. "I'm okay here. I've got a nice place to sleep and regular meals."

Brody frowned as he shook his head. It just didn't feel right leaving her locked up, even if she did want to stay. "Suit yourself," he said, rubbing at the ache in his head.

Payton gave him a little wave, but it didn't ease his qualms. Who was she? And what had brought her to Bilbarra? There were a lot of questions running through his mind without any reasonable answers.

He walked with Angus through the front office

toward the door. "Let her out, Angus," he said in a low voice. "I'll fix any mess she's made."

"I think she wants to stay for a while. I'm not sure she has anywhere else to go. I figure, I'll find her a job and at least she'll eat." He cleared his throat. "Besides, she doesn't complain about my music. She actually likes Elvis. Smart girl."

When they reached the front porch of the police station, Brody found his eldest brother, Callum, sitting in an old wooden chair, his feet propped up on the porch railing, his felt stockman's hat pulled low over his eyes.

Brody sat down next to him, bracing his elbows on his knees. "Go ahead. Get it over with. Chuck a spaz and we'll call it a day."

Callum shoved his hat back and glanced at his little brother. "Jaysus, Brody, this is the third time this month. You keep this up, you might as well live here and save yourself the trouble driving the two hours into town every weekend. At least I wouldn't worry about how you're getting home."

"It won't happen again," Brody mumbled.

"I can't spare the time. And petrol doesn't come cheap. And it's not like I don't have enough on my mind with this whole land mess boiling up again."

Callum had been a grouch for the past month, ever since Harry Fraser had filed papers in court to contest what had to be the longest-running land dispute in the history of Australia. Harry ran the neighboring station and the Frasers and the Quinns had been feuding for close to a hundred years, mostly over a strip of land that lay between the stations—land with the most productive water bore within a couple hundred kilometers.

Ownership of the property had passed back and forth over the years, dependant on the judge who heard the case. It was now the Quinns' property to lose.

"He's lost the last three times he tried. He hasn't been able to find any decent proof of his claim. What makes you think that will change now?"

"I'm still going to have to hire a bloody solicitor and they don't come cheap." Callum sighed. "And then this genealogy woman just shows up on the doorstep yesterday morning and expects me to spend all my time telling stories about our family history."

"I said I was sorry."

"You're turning into a fair wanker, you are. You could find something better to do with yourself. Like lending a hand on the station. We could use your help mustering now that Teague's practice is starting to take off. He's been taking calls almost every day. And when he's home, he spends his time doing paperwork."

"I haven't decided on a plan," Brody muttered. "But it bloody well doesn't include stockman's work. Now, can I have my keys? I've got some things to do."

"Buddy doesn't want you back at the Spotted Dog. You're going to have to find yourself another place to get pissed—" Callum paused "—or you could give up the coldies. It would save you some money."

Brody's brother Teague had been back on Kerry Creek for about a year after working as an equine vet near Brisbane. He'd taken up with Doc Daley's practice in Bilbarra, planning to buy him out so that the old man could retire. He'd saved enough in Brisbane to purchase a plane, making it possible to move about the outback quickly and efficiently.

Callum's income came directly from working Kerry Creek, the Quinn family's fifty-thousand-acre cattle station. Part of the profits went to their parents, now living in Sydney, where their mother taught school and their father had started a small landscaping business in his retirement.

And Brody, who'd once boasted a rather impressive bank account, was now unemployed, his million-dollar contract gone, many of his investments liquidated and his savings dwindling every day. He could survive another three or four years, if he lived frugally. But after that, he needed to find a decent job. Something that didn't involve kicking a football between two goalposts.

When Brody had left the station as a teenager, there'd been no other choice. He'd hated station life almost as much as his mother had. And though he'd wanted to stay with his brothers, his mother needed someone to go with her, to watch out for her. It had been a way to realize his dream of a pro-football career and he'd grabbed the chance. If it hadn't been for the accident, he'd still be living in Fremantle, enjoying his life and breaking every last scoring record for his team.

One stupid mistake and it had ended. He'd torn up his knee and spent the last year in rehab, trying to get back to form. He'd played in three games earlier in the season before the club dropped him. No new contract, no second chance, just a polite fare-thee-well.

"I'm sorry you're not doing what you want to do," Callum said, reaching out and putting his hand on Brody's shoulder. "Sometimes life is just crap. But you pick yourself up and you get on with it. And you stop being such a dickhead."

Brody gave his brother a shove, then stood up. "Give it a rest. If I needed a mother, I'd move back to Sydney and live with the one I already have." Brody grabbed his keys from Callum's hand then jogged down the front steps and out into the dusty street. "I'll catch you later."

As he walked down the main street of Bilbarra, his thoughts returned to the woman sitting in Angus's cell. "Payton," he whispered. He hadn't been attracted to any woman since Vanessa had walked out on him a year ago, frustrated by his dark moods and eager to find a bloke with a better future and a bigger bank account.

But Payton Harwell didn't know him, or football. All she cared about was a place to sleep and her next meal. And he certainly had the means to provide that.

PAYTON SIPPED at the bottle of orange juice that Angus had brought for her breakfast. She'd finished the egg sandwich first, then gobbled down the beans and bacon, enough nutrition to last her the entire day. Sooner or later, Angus would let her out and then she'd be back to scraping by for her meals. It was best to eat while she could.

She glanced over at the adjoining cell. It had been pleasant to have some company for a time, she mused. Actually, more than pleasant when the fellow prisoner was as handsome and fascinating as Brody Quinn. Payton rubbed the spot where their hands had touched, remembering the sensation that had raced through her at the contact.

She'd been in Australia for a month now and this had been the first real conversation she'd allowed herself.

She'd told him her name, but not much else. In truth, since her arrival, Payton had spent most of her time trying to figure out exactly who she was, now that she wasn't what she was supposed to be.

Until a month ago, her life had always been neatly laid out in front of her—the best schools, carefully chosen activities, the right friends, exotic vacations. As she grew older, a top-notch education and a careful search for an appropriate husband. Finally, a wonderful wedding to a successful man that her parents adored. It had been exactly the path her mother had followed, a step-by-step guide to happiness.

Payton had taken on the role of the dutiful daughter, doing all she could to please her parents and never once rebelling against their authority. Even when they'd insisted she stop riding at age seventeen after breaking her arm in a fall, Payton had agreed. She'd loved her horse, and riding had given her a wonderful sense of freedom. But she'd simply assumed that her parents knew best. If she'd had a rebellious streak, it hadn't shown itself—until a month ago. And then, it had erupted like a dormant volcano.

When it came to the moment to say "I do," Payton had turned and run. For the first time in her life, she'd made a decision for herself. Though she was twenty-five years old, her perfect life up to that point had never prepared her to deal with self-doubt. Running had been her only option.

She'd met Sam her first day at Columbia. He was the man her mother had always told her about, the man who could give her everything she'd ever want or need. He was handsome and smart, four years older, and from a wealthy

East Coast family. Her father, the scion of a banking empire, approved of his finances, and her mother, a third-generation socialite, approved of his bloodlines. And it wasn't as if there hadn't been an attraction between them. There had been…in the beginning.

An image flashed in her mind. How easily she'd forgotten Sam. All she wanted to think about now was this stranger who had touched her, this man with the penetrating gaze and the dangerous smile. A tiny thrill raced through her at the memory of his eyes raking the length of her body.

Payton leaned her head back against the concrete wall of the cell. Brody Quinn was incredibly sexy. Any woman would be attracted to a man like that. She allowed herself to speculate. Shirt on, shirt off. Completely naked and—without the bars between them, she wondered just how far she would have gone. A kiss, a quick grope, maybe more?

Payton sighed. Maybe her attraction to Brody wasn't an early midlife crisis. Maybe she was experiencing some sort of sexual schizophrenia caused by all the stress she'd been under. She'd never thought a whole lot about sex until recently. It had never been that important.

But suddenly, she found herself thinking about passion and desire, about what it truly meant to connect on a physical level with a man. Wasn't it normal for her to worry if Sam was the last man she'd ever sleep with? Shouldn't he want to touch her and make her moan with pleasure? Shouldn't sexual attraction be just as important as love and mutual respect?

There hadn't been that many men in her life—a grand total of four—so she hadn't much experience on which to rely. Two boys in high school, one in college after she and Sam had broken up for a time, and then Sam. She knew sex was supposed to be exciting and it had been, up until Sam had started working twelve- to fourteen-hour days. Suddenly, intimacy had become just another job for him, an obligation, like the bouquet of flowers he brought her every Friday evening.

In the weeks before the wedding, her mother had assured her it would all even out over time. There were meant to be highs and lows in a marriage. It kept things interesting. And heaven knows, she'd said, sex wasn't everything. She and Payton's father kept separate bedrooms and they got along just fine.

Until that moment, Payton had always assumed the arrangement was because her father snored, but once she realized her parents no longer needed each other in that way, she began to question her assumptions about a happy marriage. She wondered if her own marriage might end up more a convenient arrangement than a lifelong passion.

From that point on, Payton began to look at Sam in a different way. Every touch, every kiss, was more evidence that the passion between them was waning. Worse, she began to doubt herself. Perhaps she was just incapable of keeping a man sexually interested. Maybe it was genetic.

But that crazy attraction hadn't been missing with Brody Quinn. There had been an excitement between them, a delicious anticipation that she hadn't felt in a very long time. Her heart beat faster at the thought of him, and her breathing suddenly grew shallow. He'd been attracted to her, too, that much was obvious.

She thought back to the night before her wedding, a night spent pacing her room at the resort in Fiji. Every instinct told her to call it all off—or at least delay until she had her head on straight. But she knew what an embarrassment it would be to her parents, how upset they'd be. As an only child, so much had always been expected of her, and she'd done her best to make her parents proud. But wasn't there a point in life where she had to think about herself first?

It had taken her until the very last minute to decide to run. She'd been walking across the terrace on her father's arm, the ocean breezes ruffling her silk dress as family and friends waited on the beach. Her father had kissed her cheek and handed her over to Sam. Yet when she'd looked into Sam's eyes, Payton knew she couldn't go any further.

She tried to push the memory aside, taking another sip of orange juice as she fought back the tears that threatened. She'd run straight back to the room and grabbed her passport and a single bag. Five minutes later, she was on her way to the airport, still dressed in her white gown, ready to take the first flight off Fiji to anywhere in the world.

But a new charge on her credit card might betray her. So she'd exchanged her honeymoon ticket to Sydney for a ticket to Brisbane, assured that the airlines would keep her plans confidential. She had a visa, so it had been no problem entering the country. And once she was there, it had been even easier to lose herself.

Unfortunately, even following a strict budget, the cash she'd had with her had only gone so far. She'd heard from a woman in Brisbane that there were often jobs available for foreigners at some of the cattle and sheep stations in Queensland. They offered room and board and a decent wage—and for Payton, a place to hide out until she could bear facing her family again.

Perhaps it wouldn't be so difficult to go back, she mused. She could call her parents and explain the pressure she'd been under. Perhaps Sam might even forgive her. She drew a ragged breath. But would that stop these feelings of doubt?

Her mind flashed an image of Brody Quinn again and warmth snaked through her veins. He was dangerously handsome, his body lean and muscular, probably toned more by hard work than hours in the gym. His skin was burnished brown by the sun and his rumpled hair was streaked with blond.

But it was his eyes that she found fascinating. They were an odd color—part green, part gold—and ringed with impossibly long lashes. He didn't say much, but when he spoke, she found his accent entirely too charming. And when he looked at her, she had to wonder what he was thinking. Had he been undressing her in his head? Had he been thinking about more than just touching and kissing?

Had Angus not let him out, Payton wondered whether they might have acted on the attraction. In truth, he'd made her feel something she'd never felt before. He'd made her feel like a real woman, alive with desire and passion, not just a naive girl playing at womanhood.

Payton felt a tiny sting of regret that she hadn't accepted his offer of help. She could have used a friend in the outback, someone to show her the ropes, maybe help her find a job. Though her abilities were rather limited, she had spent the last year perfecting her skills as a gourmet cook. She could teach piano and French and Italian. She'd been an excellent rider, winning medals in dressage and show jumping. Surely there was something she could do for an honest wage.

Payton crawled off the bed and walked over to the spot where Brody had stood. She'd make a vow, here and now. From this moment forward, she'd act on her instincts. If she saw something she wanted, she'd go after it. She'd stop planning and start doing. And maybe, once she'd figured out just who she was, away from her parents and Sam, she could get on with the rest of her life.

"You finished with your breakfast?" Angus sauntered into the room, his keys jangling from a ring on his belt. He unlocked the cell door and opened it then stepped inside to collect the tray.

"Thank you," Payton said. "It was good."

He nodded. "Answer a question for me?"

Payton knew she'd have to explain at some point. What was she doing stranded in the middle of the Australian outback without a penny to her name? And what had made her think she could walk out of a restaurant without paying. "Sure. Fire away."

Angus's brow furrowed. "Have you ever been to Graceland?"

"Graceland?" The question didn't take her by surprise considering the police chief's taste in music. "No. But I hear it's supposed to be very nice. I once saw Priscilla Presley in New York, though."

"Priscilla?"

"Yes, I think she was there for Fashion Week. She was hailing a cab on Madison Avenue."

"Well, I'll be buggered! Priscilla Presley. That's almost as good as seeing Elvis." He nodded. "It's always been my dream to visit Graceland. Most folks would go to Disney World or Hollywood or one of those big tall buildings they have in New York City. Me, I'd head straight to Graceland." With a sigh, he stepped out of the cell. "Your debt has been settled, Miss Harwell. You're free to go."

"I am?" She didn't really want to leave. Not before she'd figured out her next move. But then, she had vowed to stop planning and start doing. "Who paid it?"

Angus nodded toward the door. "He's waitin' out front. You'll have to square up with him."

Frowning, Payton grabbed her bag and stuffed her belongings inside, then glanced around the cell to make sure she had everything. Whoever her mysterious benefactor was, she'd find a way to pay him back.

When she reached the porch, she saw a familiar figure waiting for her, dressed in the same faded jeans and wrinkled T-shirt he'd worn earlier. She allowed herself a tiny smile. "Are you the one who—"

Brody grabbed her bag from her hand and slung it over his shoulder. "No need to thank me," he interrupted, motioning toward the dirty Land Rover parked in front of the police station. "We criminals have to stick together, eh?"

Payton walked slowly down the steps, glancing over her shoulder to find him staring at her backside. She reached for the door of the truck, but he rested his hand on hers. "That's the driver's side, sweetheart," he said.

"Sorry," Payton murmured, the heat from his touch

sending a tingle up her arm. He followed her around to the passenger side and helped her in, resting his hand on the small of her back as she climbed up into her seat.

When he slid in behind the wheel, he looked over at her. "Where to?"

"I—I don't know," she said.

"You don't know?"

"I don't have anywhere to go."

"You're giving up your life of crime?" His dark brow arched. "You must have somewhere to go. Everyone is going somewhere."

"Not me," Payton said. "Since I'm out of cash, I can't afford to go anywhere. I need to find a job."

He nodded, then grinned. "All right. Well, I think I know a place that might need some help. As long as you're willing to work hard. What can you do?"

"Anything."

"The local brothel likes to hire talented girls. I could take you over there."

She laughed softly when she saw the smile curling his lips. He had a way of speaking, his accent broad and his voice deep, that made it hard to tell when he was teasing. "Very funny."

"You think I'm kidding? Bilbarra has a legal house of ill repute. And it stays quite busy since women are in short supply in the outback. You could make a decent wage if you were so inclined."

"I'm better with horses than I am with men," Payton said.

"Horses? Well, that sounds promising." He turned the SUV around and headed out of town on the dusty main street. As they drove, the landscape became dry and desolate, an endless vista of…nothing. This was the outback, Payton mused. And she was driving right into the middle of it with a complete stranger. "Where are we going?"

"To my place," he said.

She swallowed hard. So much for acting on instinct. "Your—your place?" Had she just made the biggest mistake of her life? He could drive them out into the middle of nowhere, chain her up and keep her as his sex slave for years and no one would ever know. But then Angus had seen them leave together and if Angus trusted this man with her safety, maybe she could, too. The idea of serving as Brody's sex slave rolled around in her mind for a moment before she shook herself. The thought was intriguing. In truth, any thought that involved Brody's naked body seemed to stick in her head.

"It's my family's place," he explained. "We have a cattle station and we raise horses, too."

"Horses!" she cried. "I'm good with horses. I can groom them and muck out the stalls and feed them…."

"Good," he said. "Then I'm sure we'll have a spot for you." He reached above the visor and pulled out a CD, then popped it into the player in the dash.

Payton watched the countryside pass as they bumped along the dirt roads. Compared to the beautiful scenery on the coast with its lush greenery and ocean views, the outback was a harsh and unforgiving environment. Only occasionally did she see signs of human habitation—a distant house or a windmill on the horizon.

When she wasn't staring out the window, Payton attempted a careful study of the man beside her. He kept his eyes fixed on the road ahead, humming along with the AC/DC songs as he navigated around bumps and potholes.

After an hour of bouncing over rutted roads, the orange juice Payton had gulped down for breakfast had worked its way through her body. "Will it be much farther?" she asked.

"Another half hour," he said.

"Is there a gas station coming up? Maybe a convenience store? Anyplace with a ladies' room?"

Brody pulled the truck to a stop, then pointed out the window. "There's a nice little shrub over there. For privacy." He shrugged. "There isn't a ladies' room between here and the station."

Reluctantly, Payton opened the door. "Don't watch," she said.

"I won't. And if a giant lizard comes wandering by, you just scoot back to the truck flat out."

Payton closed the door. "I can wait."

"The road only gets bumpier," he warned. "I'll keep an eye peeled. If I see anything approaching, I'll hit the horn."

Payton hopped out of the truck and walked gingerly through the scrub to the closest bush. It looked more like tumbleweed than a living plant, but it provided enough cover for her modesty.

She was a long way from home, a long way from marble bathrooms with gold-plated fixtures and expensive French towels. But for the first time in her life, she was in charge of her own destiny. She no longer had to please her parents, or anyone else for that matter. And though she didn't know where she'd be tomorrow or what she'd doing next week, Payton didn't care. Right now, life was one big adventure. And her traveling companion made the adventure a whole lot more interesting.

BRODY LEANED BACK against the front fender of the Land Rover as he stared out at the horizon, taking a long drink from a bottle of water he'd pulled from the Esky in the backseat. He'd been living in the civilized part of Oz for so long that he'd forgotten just how desolate the outback was.

He and his mother had left when he was fourteen. And though he'd returned for his school holidays, he was always anxious to leave again. Now, here he was, back where he started.

He heard footsteps in the gravel at the edge of the road and he turned around as Payton approached, bracing his elbows on the hood of the SUV. "Feel better?"

"Much," she said. She turned slowly, taking in the view. "It's beautiful in a rugged, bleak kind of way. You can breathe out here. The air is so clean."

"Yeah, we have plenty of clean air in Queensland. And we're a big producer of dust. Mozzies and blowies, too." She gave him an odd look. "Mosquitoes and blow flies." He offered her the bottle of water. "And where do you come from?"

She took a long drink of water, then smiled. "The East Coast. Connecticut."

"Is that near New York?"

She nodded. "Yes. Very near. My father works in Manhattan. I went to college at Columbia."

"So you're smart, then?" Smart and beautiful. A deadly combination and one he hadn't really appreciated until now. He'd never considered a brilliant mind an important part of sexual attraction. But as much as he wanted to touch her and kiss her, he also wanted to talk to her. Who was this woman? What was she doing here with him?

"I did my master's thesis on the history of anatomical study in seventeenth-century Dutch artists. I'm not sure how smart that makes me." She glanced around. "Especially out here. Unless you have an art museum filled with the works of Vermeer and Rembrandt."

"We do," he teased. "It's right behind the stables. Doesn't get a lot of visitors, though." Brody drank the last of the water. "So how does a sheila like you end up skint in a place like Bilbarra?"

"Skint?"

"No money."

"Broke," she said. "Flat broke. Probably because I didn't have a lot to start with." She paused. "I'm just a poor grad student trying to see a bit of the world."

"There's not a lot to see in the outback," he said.

"You don't think the scenery out here is spectacular?" Payton asked, pointing to a low range of hills in the distance. "It's wild, untamed. Dangerous. I like that. Don't you?"

He stared down at her face, taking in the simple perfection of her features. "It's gotten a lot nicer since you arrived."

Her eyes met his and Brody held his breath, wondering just how far he could go. He wanted to kiss her. Hell, he'd wanted to kiss her from the moment he'd first seen her. He leaned in, hoping for a sign that she shared the attraction. Her eyes dropped to his mouth and her lips parted slightly. It was all he needed.

Bracing his hands on either side of her body, he pressed her back into the side of the SUV and brought his mouth down on hers. Her lips were soft and cool and fit perfectly with his.

Brody's tongue traced the crease between them before she opened and let him taste her. At first, he thought she might end it all quickly, but then, Payton reached up and ran her fingers through the hair at his nape, sending a shiver through his body and a flood of warmth to his crotch.

The kiss turned intense, fierce and filled with need. God, she was incredible, he thought as his hands skimmed down her arms, then clutched at the hem of her shirt. It had been a while since he'd touched a woman, but he hadn't remembered it being this good. He smoothed his palms beneath her shirt, up her torso to cup her breast. Payton arched toward him, a tiny sigh slipping from her throat.

Brody had seduced his fair share of women, but he'd always tempered his attraction with an underlying suspicion. What did they really want from him? Were they merely interested in bedding a famous footballer? Or did they imagine themselves catching a husband who had the money to provide a fancy lifestyle?

There were no worries with Payton. To her, he was just the guy who'd bailed her out of jail and found her a job. He could let down his guard, at least for a little while. In truth, for the first time in his adult life, he could enjoy a woman without any inhibitions.

When he finally drew back, he found her face flushed and her lips damp. "We should probably go," he said, certain that there would be much more to come. Once he got her to the station, she'd be there for a time. He could afford to seduce her properly.

Her eyes fluttered open and she drew a deep breath. "Yes," she said softly. "Yes, we should."

Brody reached around her and opened the door. But before she could crawl back inside, he stole another kiss, lingering over her lips until he was satisfied that they'd both had enough. He liked kissing her. She had a mouth that was made for that particular pastime.

They drove on for another ten minutes before they spoke again. She cleared her throat and Brody turned to look at her, noting the pretty blush that stained her cheeks. "What?" he asked.

"Nothing," she said.

"You have something you want to say?"

She shook her head. "No."

"Do you regret what just happened?"

She drew another breath and then twisted to face him. "I hope you don't think I just go around kissing strangers, because I don't. It's just that I..." Payton paused. "No, I don't regret it. It was...nice."

"Onya," he replied, satisfied with "nice." Next time it happened, it would be better than nice. Brody grinned. There would be a next time. And a time after that...

"Onya?"

"Good onya," Brody corrected. "Ah...good for you."

"Right, good for me," she said, nodding. "I mean, on me. Good on me."

"No, it doesn't work that way." He grinned.

She smiled and shrugged. "Then, good onya. On you."

"No worries, then?" he said, knowing full well that his kiss was more than welcome.

"No worries," she replied.

Brody chuckled. "And feel free to perv on me whenever you like. Because I wouldn't mind if that happened again. Between us. But I should warn you off on the other blokes."

"Blokes?"

"It's mostly men on the station. There's just our cook and housekeeper, Mary. You'll be the only other woman. The boys on Kerry Creek are root rats of the first order, so keep a watch out for them. They go through women like water." All of a sudden Brody regretted his decision to bring Payton out to the station. He should have flown them both straight back to Fremantle, to his comfortable apartment with the big soft bed and the river views.

Though Callum and Teague weren't quite as bad as the rest of the jackaroos, his brothers wouldn't be immune to Payton's beauty. Women were in short supply in the bush and Brody intended to keep her all to himself. He'd have to find a way to make that clear to his brothers before they got any ideas about seducing her.

"Root rats," she said. "I suppose I could guess at the meaning of that." She sighed. "Are there a lot of root rats where we're going?"

"Yeah," Brody said. "But if any bloke cracks on you, just speak up. I'll sort him out."

"If any guy comes on to me, you'll punch his lights out?"

"That too," Brody said, chuckling. "Don't worry, you'll be safe. I'll watch out for you."

She'd be safe from the other blokes, but could he

guarantee she'd be safe from him? Right now, his thoughts weren't so much focused on protecting her as they were on seducing her. And he couldn't help but wonder what was going through her pretty head.

2

"WILL YOU EXCUSE US for a moment?"

Payton nodded, sitting primly on the edge of her chair as Brody and his brother Callum stepped out of the cluttered office. They didn't go far and their whispered discussion in the hallway soon became loud enough for her to hear.

"And who was whinging about all the work to be done just a few hours ago?" Brody accused. "She claims she knows horses and isn't above mucking out the stables. If she takes care of that, then you've got more help mustering."

"You met her in the jail," Callum shot back. "That might give you a clue to her character."

"She's just down on her luck," Brody said. "She needs a job. I'll vouch for her. If you catch her stealing, I'll haul her back to Bilbarra without a word."

"And what about you?" Callum asked. "If I give her a job, what are you going to do? Just lay about the house all day feeling sorry for yourself?"

"I reckon I'll give you a hand," Brody said. "I've got nothing better to do."

There was a long silence and she heard a curse, though she wasn't sure who it came from. A moment later, the two brothers reappeared in the door. "Brody tells me you're good with horses. You'll be expected to put in a full day."

"I really need this job. I'll work hard, I promise," Payton said. It was the truth, though she didn't want to sound too desperate. This station was the perfect place for her, a good spot to stay until she figured out her next step. She'd have a place to sleep and three decent meals a day. She'd have a job to occupy her time. And then there was Brody. "You won't regret this."

"All right. You can stay in the south bunkhouse," Callum said. "It's got a proper dunny and shower. But you'll have to share it with Gemma."

"Who's Gemma?" Brody asked, frowning.

"The genealogist," Callum explained. "Gemma Moynihan. She's from Ireland, doing some sort of research on the Quinn family. I told her she could stay until she finished her work here."

"No worries," Payton said, adopting the local language. "The bunkhouse will be great."

"All right," Callum said. "You'll start in the stables and you'll lend a hand in the kitchen when Mary needs help. You slack off and you'll earn yourself a ride back to Bilbarra. You work hard and I'll pay you a fair wage."

Payton nodded, relieved that he'd agreed to Brody's plan. It was the first real job she'd ever held and she was determined not to mess up. Her new life began here and now and Payton couldn't help but be a bit excited at the prospect.

Callum glanced at his brother. "Brody will show you around and get you settled. If you have any questions, ask him."

The elder Quinn brother strode out of the office and Brody followed after him. "I'll give her a day. Two at the outside," Payton heard Callum say.

When Brody returned, she pasted a smile on her face. "He's wrong. I'll work hard."

Brody reached out and took her hand, turning it over so he could examine her palm. Running his thumb over the soft skin, he slowly smiled. "You'll need a pair of gloves," he said. "And a proper hat."

Payton laced her fingers through his and gave his hand a squeeze. "Thank you for this. I won't disappoint you."

He hooked his finger beneath her chin, forcing her gaze up to his. At first, she hoped he might kiss her again, but then he must have thought better of it. "No worries. I can't imagine that ever happening."

"No worries," she repeated.

Brody picked up her bag and motioned her toward the door. "Come on. I'll show you what's what. We'll see the homestead first. Maybe Mary will make us a bite."

As they walked through the beautifully furnished room that Brody called the parlor, Payton's attention was caught by a huge oil painting hanging over the fireplace. She walked up to examine it more closely. "This is a beautiful portrait," she said.

"We call him the old man," Brody explained as he stepped up beside her. "His name is Crevan Quinn. He was the first Quinn in Australia. Came on a convict ship when he was nineteen."

"He was a convict?"

Brody nodded. "A bit of a thief, a pickpocket they

say. He had the portrait painted for his seventieth birthday, in the late 1800s. Went all the way to Sydney to sit for it. And then he died the day after it was finished. It's hung in this house ever since. His only son was my great-great-grandfather."

"Backler. I've never heard of the artist," she said. "It's quite lovely."

Brody gave her a dubious look.

"The technique," she said. "The layering of color." She stared at the subject, a man with wild white hair, huge muttonchops and a fierce expression.

"Good thing his looks don't run in the family," Brody said.

"His penchant for crime does," Payton teased.

With that, Brody grabbed her around the waist and gently pushed her back against the mantel. His hand cupped her cheek and he looked down into her eyes. Payton held her breath, caught by the desire in his gaze.

"And where would you be right now if it weren't for my criminal activities?"

"Or mine," she countered. "I'd be without a job and with no prospects for finding one."

"I think that deserves a kiss, don't you?"

"I suppose I could spare one. But don't get greedy."

She pushed up onto her toes and kissed him, not waiting for Brody to make the first move. She liked the taste of him, the way his hands felt on her body. His touch made her feel alive, as if she was doing something far too dangerous for her own good. It was exhilarating and frightening all at once.

Payton looped her fingers in the waistband of his jeans and pulled his hips against hers. He groaned softly as the kiss deepened and their bodies melted into each other. Her hands slipped beneath his T-shirt and she ran her nails up his spine and back down again.

She'd never been so aggressive with a man, but with Brody, all her inhibitions seemed to fall away. There were no rules when she kissed him. Here in Australia, she'd live every day as if it were her last, with no regrets and nothing left undone.

Suddenly, he pushed himself away from her. He sucked in a sharp breath and Payton could see he was trying to regain his self-control. She glanced down and noticed the bulge in the front of his jeans. His reaction pleased her.

"Later," he assured her. He picked up her bag, then grabbed her hand and pulled her along to the front door of the house.

They ran into a man jogging up the front steps and he stopped and pulled off his hat, glancing back and forth between Payton and Brody, before noticing their linked hands. "Hello," he said.

"Teague, this is Payton Harwell. Payton, this is my brother Teague."

He held out his hand and Payton was forced to let go of Brody's to shake it. "Pleasure," he said with a wide grin.

"She's going to be working with the horses," Brody said.

"Good onya," Teague replied. "That's where I'll be working for the next few days. You have much experience with stock ponies?"

Payton shook her head, grateful for the welcome but worried that she might not prove herself useful. "No.

But I've been around horses since I was six or seven. Show jumpers. But horses are horses. They all have four legs and a tail, right?"

Teague chuckled, as if pleased with her little joke. "Yeah. They usually do. So I guess I can't give you any of our three-legged ponies."

Payton's eyes went wide.

"Crocs," Teague said, a serious expression on his face. "They'll eat the legs right off a pony if you let them. One leg we can deal with. But a two-legged stock pony just doesn't work."

"Oh, no," Payton said. "That's horrible. Can't you—"

"Don't be a dipstick, Teague." Brody shook his head.

An older woman appeared at the screen door. "Doc Daley is on the phone," she said to Teague, motioning him inside. "Says it's an emergency and he's tied up in surgery this afternoon."

Teague frowned, shaking his head. "Probably another croc attack," he said. "Another three-legged pony. Mary, have you met Brody's new friend?"

The woman stepped out onto the porch, a smile twitching at the corners of her mouth. She wiped her hands on her apron, then smoothed a strand of gray hair from her temple. "Well, now. It is a pleasure to meet you, dear. I'm Mary Hastings. No matter what these Quinn boys tell you, I'm the one in charge here."

Payton shook her outstretched hand. "Payton Harwell."

"Ah, an American. We seem to be attracting an interesting group of ladies. First, an Irish lass and now a Yank. If you need anything, you come to me, dear. We girls have to stick together." She leaned forward and lowered her voice. "And don't believe a word about those three-legged ponies. These boys get too cheeky."

Teague grabbed Mary around the waist and planted a kiss on her cheek. "And don't you love it? Don't worry, Mary, you're still my girl."

Brody took Payton's hand and led her off the porch. "Come on, I'll show you the bunkhouse."

"It was a pleasure meeting you," Payton said, waving at Teague and Mary.

"See ya later, Payton," Teague called.

"When you're settled, you come back to the kitchen for tea," Mary called.

They walked together to the south bunkhouse, a low building set near a small grove of trees and a neatly tilled vegetable garden. "That's Mary's garden," he said. "You might want to avoid walking by when she's working. She'll have you pulling weeds all day long."

"She's nice," Payton said.

"After my mum left the station, my dad hired her. She's kept the house running."

"Are your parents divorced?"

He shook his head. "Nope. They're living together in Sydney. But there was a time when they were separated, my dad here and Mum in the city. Station life is hard, especially for women."

Payton gave him a sideways glance, wondering if he was warning her off. She was just looking for a job. She didn't intend to spend the rest of her life in the Australian outback. "I can imagine," she replied.

Brody opened the front door of the bunkhouse, then stepped back to let her enter. Payton found the interior simple but clean. In one corner of the room, several overstuffed chairs were gathered around a small iron stove. There was a scarred desk beneath one of the windows and a dry sink beneath another, complete with bowl and pitcher. An old wardrobe stood near the backdoor. Each of the three walls held a bunk bed, crudely constructed of rough planks and a pair of mattresses. One of the lower bunks was made up with a colorful quilt and two pillows.

"That must be where the genealogy lady is sleeping," Brody said. "Bedding is in the chest at the end of the bunk. The dunny is out back, through that door."

"The dunny."

"The toilet. There's a shower back there, too." He walked over to the wardrobe and rummaged through the contents until he found a pair of gloves and an old felt hat, like the one his brother Teague wore.

Brody set the hat on her head and handed her the gloves. "There you go," he said, tugging on the brim. "Pretty spiffy."

"I'd like to get to work," she said.

"You don't have to. It's your first day. Take some time and settle in. We'll have some lunch."

"No, I'm ready to start," she insisted, well aware that she'd have to prove herself to Callum.

"You're not really dressed properly. We'll need to find you something to wear."

"I don't really have anything else along," Payton said, glancing down at the peasant blouse and jeans she'd bought in Brisbane. "Just a few dresses. This will have to do for now. I'll find something later."

"All right," he said with a shrug. "Let's go."

They walked out of the bunkhouse and through the

dusty yard. The station was almost like a small village. Brody pointed out each paddock and barn and shed, telling her what function it served. There were two more bunkhouses for the stockmen and a small cottage for the head stockman.

The stables consisted of a long building with stalls along one side and tack, feed and supplies stored on the opposite side. "We breed stock ponies here, so we keep a lot of mares. We break the ponies and then sell them to stations all around Queensland. Kerry Creek ponies fetch a good price."

Payton pulled on her gloves and braced her hands on her hips. "All right. Well, I'd better jump right in." She spotted a pitchfork in a corner and grabbed it. "I guess I'll see you later."

He seemed to be a bit surprised that she was blowing him off so quickly. Though Payton found him wildly attractive, she needed to keep this job and first impressions would count. If she had to ignore her desires for a few hours, it was a small price to pay.

"We eat dinner at six this time of year. I'll come and fetch you."

"That's all right," Payton said. "I'll find my way."

He turned and walked out of the stable. Payton folded her hands over the end of the pitchfork and watched his retreat. Her girlfriends had always told her how hot Sam was and she'd never quite understood what they meant. Sam was handsome, but Brody Quinn was hot. He oozed masculinity from every pore.

She tried to imagine him without the T-shirt, without the jeans, without any clothes at all. A shiver skittered down her spine and she felt her pulse quicken. Sleeping with the boss was never a good thing. But was Brody her boss or was Callum?

Payton made a mental note to find out as soon as she could. For now, she had a bed and free meals and something to occupy her time—along with a man who made her heart race and her body tingle. What more did she need?

LIKE EVERYONE ELSE at Kerry Creek, Brody had worked the station from the time he'd been able to walk. He'd started in the garden with his mother, then moved to the stables and on to working with the stock as soon as he could ride. But he'd spent most of his teen years in the city, and once he'd signed his first pro contract, he'd made only occasional visits to Queensland, stopping in before a holiday spent surfing or diving on the Great Barrier Reef.

His brothers teased him, insisting that city life had made him soft. Maybe it had. But now that he was living on the station again, it was all coming back to him. He'd spent the afternoon repairing fences with the newest jackaroo, a kid named Davey Thompson, who'd wandered in a few months before to join his older brother, Skip, on the station.

Davey had kept up a constant stream of chatter, moving from women to music to cars and back again. One thing was quite clear. He was glad to have moved up in the pecking order, his stable job handed off to Payton, who was now the lowest in seniority.

"That new girl, she's a pretty sheila," he said as he picked up a roll of barbed wire. "She has nice hair. All long and curly."

"You just steer clear of her," Brody warned.

"What? She's your girl?"

"As far as you're concerned, yes," Brody said. "She's my girl."

"No worries," Davey replied with a grin. "But does she have a sister? If she does, I wouldn't mind an introduction."

They worked until sunset, hauling their gear with quad bikes rather than on horseback. Since his father had left the station to join his mother in Sydney four years ago, Callum had taken steps to modernize the operation and his ideas had made the work at least a bit more enjoyable.

Brody and Davey unloaded the gear from the ATVs, then headed to the big house for dinner. Mary fed everyone at the large table in the kitchen, preparing the heartiest meal at the end of the workday. Brody took time to wash up at the outdoor sink before going inside.

He'd expected to see Payton there, waiting for him, but she wasn't seated at the table. The other new arrival was the genealogist from Ireland. He'd expected some gray-haired lady with sensible shoes and little reading glasses perched on her nose. Instead, he found himself smiling at a woman almost as beautiful as Payton.

"Gemma Moynihan," she said in a lilting Irish accent. "And you must be Brody. I can see the family resemblance."

"Gemma," Brody repeated. He glanced over at his brother Callum, only to find him staring at them both, a tense expression on his face. It was easy to see why Cal had been on edge. His oldest brother had always been obsessed with the station. But the choice to work or to spend time with Gemma the genealogist was probably causing him to seriously question his work ethic.

"Have you met Payton?" Brody asked, suppressing a grin.

"Yes, I have," Gemma said.

"Is she coming in to eat?"

"I don't know. She was lying in her bunk when I left. She looked knackered."

"Maybe I should take her something," Brody suggested, stepping away from the table.

This brought amused glances from the rest of the stockmen, but Brody didn't care. He grabbed a plate and loaded it with beef and potatoes, covering the entire meal with a portion of gravy. Grabbing utensils and a couple of beers, he headed out to the ladies' bunkhouse.

He found Payton curled up on her bunk sound asleep. He set the meal on the floor beside the bed, then pulled up a chair, straddling it. Reaching out, Brody brushed a strand of hair from her eyes. Her lashes fluttered and she gazed up at him.

"Morning," he said.

Payton pushed up on her elbow looking worried. "Is it morning already?"

He laughed. "No. I brought you some dinner. Are you all right?"

She sat up, wincing as she moved. "Yes. I'm fine. I'm just not used to shoveling horse poop for four hours." She groaned, rubbing her shoulder. "I was just going to lie down for a minute, and I must have fallen asleep."

"Come here," Brody said, swinging the chair around and patting the seat.

When she was seated, he handed her the plate, then stepped behind her and began to massage her sore shoulders. "Oh, that's nice," she said, tipping her head back and closing her eyes. Her silky curls fell across his hands. "Right there."

He rubbed a little harder at her nape, brushing her hair over her shoulder. "Here?"

"Mmm," she said.

"Eat your dinner before it gets cold."

She glanced down at the plate, then scooped up a forkful of beef and potatoes. "This is good," she said as she chewed. "I didn't realize how hungry I was. Don't you want some?"

"You eat," he said. "I'll go back and get another plate."

She reached down and grabbed a bottle of beer, then attempted to twist off the cap. When she couldn't, she handed it to him. "What did you do today?"

"Repaired fences," Brody said.

"What time does work start in the morning?"

"The stockmen are usually up at dawn. But you could probably sleep later, if you like. The stables aren't going anywhere."

"No, I'll get up with everyone else."

"I don't reckon Cal expects you to put in stockman's hours."

"What else is there to do except work and eat and sleep?" Payton asked.

Brody bent over her shoulder and sent her a devilish grin. "I can think of a few things," he whispered.

She filled a fork with food, then held it up to him, and he took a bite of her dinner. "Other than that, what do you do with your free time?"

"We're five hours from the nearest movie theater in Brisbane, but we've got DVDs to watch. Cal favors westerns, I like gangster movies and Teague prefers science fiction." He paused. "We've got a pool," he added. "Sometimes we go swimming when the weather is warm."

"I didn't see a pool."

"It's not a swimming pool, more like a watering hole. And Cal put in a hot tub out back. That's nice now that the nights are a bit cooler."

"Oh, that sounds like heaven," she said.

"Finish your supper and we'll go for a dip."

"I don't have a swimsuit."

"You won't need one," Brody said.

"I'm sure that will create a good impression," she replied.

To his surprise, she finished the entire plate in ten short minutes, then drank her beer and his. Through it all, she asked questions about the station and he did his best to answer. She'd just assumed he'd worked the station his whole life, and he wasn't going to tell her differently, at least not yet.

He had his secrets, but Payton Harwell had her own. When he asked for details about her life in the States, she always gave him some airy-fairy answer. After fifteen minutes of questioning, he realized he didn't know much more than he'd learned on their ride to the station. But the more beer she drank, the more forthcoming she became.

"Let's go," he said, anxious to spend some time in a location more conducive to seduction. "The hot water will make you feel better."

"Later," she said. "I just want to lie down for a bit."

She crawled back into her bunk and patted the spot beside her. "Just for a minute. Then we'll go."

Brody crawled into the tiny bunk, and he had to wrap his arms around her just to keep from falling on the floor. He smoothed his hands over her hair and she looked up at him and smiled. "Who are you, Payton Harwell?" he murmured.

"I don't know," she said with a soft sigh. "If you figure it out, be sure to fill me in."

He bent closer and kissed her, this time allowing himself to relax and enjoy the experience. His hands roamed over her body, slipping beneath the waistband of her jeans to cup her backside. Brody pulled her beneath him, his shaft growing harder as the kiss deepened.

His hips pressed into hers and he slowly began to move, creating a delicious friction. He remembered the first time he'd done this with a girl and the rather surprising results. But thankfully, he'd managed to acquire a bit more self-control over the years. Still, the feel of her beneath him, her leg pulled up alongside his, teased at that control. Brody knew Gemma might be back at any second, but he didn't care.

Payton slipped her hand beneath the hem of his shirt. She smoothed her palms up his chest, then trailed her fingertips down his belly. He groaned softly when she slid her hand lower, across the front of his jeans, then back again. Somehow, it all seemed more intense, more pleasurable, with clothing between them and the chance of discovery.

He pulled her shirt over her shoulder, exposing a delicious curve of flesh. Pressing his mouth to the base of her neck, he slowly worked his way down, to the tops of her breasts, left exposed by her lacy bra.

He slid lower along her body, his lips teasing at her nipple through the lace and satin. Payton furrowed her fingers through his hair and he sucked gently, until she moaned in response.

He fought the urge to strip off all their clothes, knowing they didn't have much privacy in a shared bunkhouse. Perhaps Gemma would be occupied with Callum for the rest of the evening. Maybe she'd choose to spend the night in his bed instead of her own. But their privacy was cut short when he heard the front door open.

"Sorry," Gemma called. "I'll come back later."

When the door closed behind Gemma, he drew back and looked into Payton's eyes. She forced a smile. "Maybe you should go," she said.

"Maybe you should come with me," he suggested. He curled up against her, nuzzling his face into the curve of her neck. "I have a very large bed in my room. And a strong lock on the door. We won't be disturbed."

"We won't get any sleep, either," Payton said.

"That's the point, isn't it?"

She sighed softly and he waited for her decision. But after a minute or two, Brody realized that she'd fallen asleep. Her breathing had grown soft and even and the arm resting on his hip had gone limp.

He bit back a curse, then pressed a kiss to her forehead. She stirred for a moment, her eyes fluttering. "I'm going to go. You need your sleep. I'll see you in the morning."

"Morning," she sighed.

Reluctantly, he untangled himself from her embrace, rolled off the bed and tugged his shirt down. He turned to look at Payton, her dark hair fanned out over the pillow, her hand curled over her face.

If he wasn't such a gentleman, he'd pick her up, carry her to his bedroom and make love to her all night long. But he had time. And when it happened, they'd both be awake and completely aware of what they were doing. It would be good between them. Maybe better than it had ever been with any other woman.

For that, Brody was willing to wait.

PAYTON GRABBED the hoof pick, then pushed the horse up against the side of the stall with her shoulder. Lifting the gelding's front leg, she held its hoof between her thighs and began to clean out the debris between the frog and the bars.

Unlike the horses she rode for show, the horses on the station didn't spend much time in the stable. They were brought in after a day's work and then quickly groomed and sent out to a large paddock where they were fed. The ground was dry and the stable kept clean, so there was no need for a farrier and horseshoes.

The Kerry Creek horses were a sturdy lot, most gentle and accommodating—the furthest thing from the pampered, high-spirited show horses she'd learned to ride. Brody had informed her that the stockmen were responsible for the daily care of their own mounts, but she was expected to care for the remainder in the paddock and the stables—nearly forty by her count.

These included mares that were in foal and the colts who were yet to be broken, along with at least ten extra stock ponies. She'd also spend part of each day in the tack room, keeping the stockmen's saddles and bridles in good working order. And with what time was left over, she'd turn her attention to mixing feed and keeping the stables tidy.

The dry season was the busiest of all on a cattle station. The stockmen were getting ready to bring the cattle in for the yearly mustering, setting off to the far corners of the station to gather the herd, sometimes staying out three or four days. The new calves would be examined, vaccinated, tagged and branded with the *K* that signified Kerry Creek station.

The horses that were part of the breeding operation were pastured closer to the homestead where they could be watched closely and brought inside as their time grew near. Foals that were dropped outside could be easy prey for dingoes.

"You look like you know what you're doing."

Payton glanced up to see Brody's brother Teague standing just outside the stall, his shoulder braced against a post, his arms crossed over his chest. Like Brody and Callum, he was gorgeous. But unlike Brody, he didn't send shivers of desire coursing through her body, nor did she spend hours thinking about kissing him.

She shoved the sleeves of her oversize work shirt above her elbows, then nodded. "It's a whole different kind of horse," she said with a smile. "They have a wonderful temperament."

"That's the way we breed them and train them," he said. "And for stamina and strength and agility. They need to be able to last all day long. Sometimes all week."

Payton continued her work. "What are the bloodlines?"

"Originally thoroughbreds and Arabians with some Welsh mountain and Timor pony thrown in."

"When do they foal?"

"They tend to start in September and go through the first of the year. Usually right after mustering ends, we start in with foaling."

"Davey said the colt in the next stall has been sold. He's beautiful."

"He's going to be trained as a show horse. Some of our horses are used for polocrosse. And some for camp-drafting."

Payton set the horse's hoof onto the concrete floor and straightened, brushing her hair out of her eyes. "What's that?"

"Besides Aussie-rules football, polocrosse and campdrafting are the only native Aussie sports. Polo-crosse is a mix of polo, lacrosse and netball. And I reckon campdrafting is kind of like your rodeo riding. The horse and rider cut a calf from the herd, then they have to maneuver it around a series of posts."

"I'd like to see that," she said.

"I'll take you sometime," Teague promised. "There's a campdrafting event in Muttaburra in August if you're still around."

"I'd like to try it."

"Then I'll teach you."

"Teach her what?"

Brody appeared at his brother's side. He was dressed in traditional stockman's attire, a work shirt, canvas jacket, jeans. He wore a felt hat on his head and his hands were clad in well-worn leather gloves. She hadn't seen him since the previous evening and she'd forgotten just how beautiful he was.

"Hey, little brother. Where have you been?"

"I went out with Davey to fix the windmill in the high pasture."

Teague clapped his brother on the back. "Good to see you putting in an honest day's work." He touched the brim of his hat and nodded at Payton. "I've got a call. I'll see you later, Payton. Maybe you can give me a hand tomorrow morning. I've got vaccinations to do on the yearlings."

"Sure," Payton said. "I'd be happy to help."

He nodded again. "I think I'll like having you here." Teague turned to Brody, arching an eyebrow and examining him critically. "Have you had all your shots?"

Payton watched Brody's jaw grow tense. As the youngest brother, he probably had to put up with a greater share of the teasing. "Don't mind Teague," Brody said as his brother turned and walked away. "He has a bad habit of yabbering to anyone who'll listen."

"So, is Teague in charge of the horse-breeding operation?"

"When he's around. He's a vet."

"A veterinarian? Really?"

Brody nodded. "He's usually flying from station to station. He spends a few days at home, then takes off again. He's the brilliant one in the family."

"He's nice," Payton murmured. She met Brody's gaze and her breath stopped in her throat. It was all there, the desire, the need and even a tiny hint of jealousy. She drew a ragged breath as he crossed the short distance between them to pull her into his arms.

Payton had tried to put all of this out of her head. From the moment she woke up that morning she'd been waiting to touch him, to taste him. It had been eight hours of sheer torture and now she felt the tension in her body release as their mouths met.

The more she saw of him, the more difficult it was to resist him. And yet, that didn't frighten or confuse her. She didn't need to figure out the consequences of her every action and reaction. She could kiss Brody and that was all it was, a kiss. It felt good to cast aside her penchant for planning and just go with the flow.

But how long could that last? How long before a simple fling turned into something more complicated? Her feelings for him were already so intense, her desire undeniable. She'd promised herself that she'd be guided by her instincts, and every instinct told her to enjoy their time together. They didn't need to make promises to each other. This was enough.

He cupped her face in his palms and drew her deeply into the kiss, as if desperate to possess her. Payton was stunned at how easy it was to stoke his need. There was no hesitation, nothing she held back. Though she barely knew Brody, she felt a connection with him that she'd never shared with a man before.

He pulled her out of the stall, his hands tight around her waist. Stumbling back, they fell into a pile of straw, their mouths still frantically searching for the perfect manifestation of their need. He tossed his hat aside, then tugged off his gloves, his hands immediately moving to cup her backside. Though Payton knew their privacy in the stable wasn't certain, she didn't care. All that mattered was his touch, his fingers tearing at her shirt until he exposed the curve of her shoulder.

His teeth grazed her skin and Payton tipped her head back, inviting him to take more. There were moments when she acted on instinct, as if this woman had always been buried deep inside her and was just waiting to get out. And then, at other times, she felt like a teenager, fumbling her way though her first sexual experience.

He excited her and frightened her all at once. And yet, she pushed aside her fears, rushing headlong into her desire, aching to experience release. Payton tugged at his jacket, pulling it over his arms until she could unbutton his shirt.

"Too many clothes," she murmured as she brushed aside the shirt and placed a kiss in the center of his chest. He was so magnificent, she mused, his skin deeply tanned and his body finely muscled. Her lips found one of his nipples and she circled it with her tongue.

Brody ran his fingers through her hair, sighing her name softly as if urging her on. Slowly, Payton worked her way lower, trailing kisses over his abdomen. But before she could go farther, she heard the clip-clop of hooves on the concrete floor of the stable.

She looked up to find Callum standing just inside the stable door, his horse's reins dangling from his fingers. With a soft cry, Payton scrambled to her feet, brushing the straw from her clothes and trying to adjust her shirt. Callum arched a brow as he looked down at Brody. "I can come back later," he said slowly.

Brody shook his head, cursing. "No. Feel free. We were just…talking."

"Oh, is that what they call it?" Callum asked. He pulled his horse along until he stopped in front of Payton. "Is my brother bothering you? If he is, you can just tell him to leave."

Callum was always so serious that Payton couldn't tell if he was angry or just teasing. She gave him an apologetic smile. "It—it won't happen again," she said. "I'm sorry."

Callum reached up and plucked a piece of straw from her hair and handed it to her, a grin quirking at the corners of his mouth. Payton felt her cheeks warm and she took the reins from his hand. "I'll take care of your horse," she mumbled.

Tugging at the bit, she pulled the horse along the length of the stable, hoping to get as far away from the two brothers as possible. She would not keep this job for long if she continued to show such a blatant disrespect for her employer.

And she needed this job! She wasn't ready to go home. The thought of facing her family and Sam was just too much for her right now. Here, on the station, she felt useful, which made her far happier than she'd been in a very long time.

But was it the work that made her happy or was it her growing infatuation with Brody Quinn? She'd be deluding herself if she ignored his part in this. Glancing back, she caught sight of Callum and Brody, deep in conversation, Callum gesturing with his gloved hands and Brody watching him with an indolent expression.

She barely knew the Quinn brothers, but the family dynamics were quite evident. Callum was the caretaker, the responsible brother whose only focus was the success of the station. Teague was the charmer, the smart, funny one with the ready smile and witty conversation.

And Brody…well, he was a little more difficult to define. He seemed to be the rebel of the family, a bit of an outsider. Payton couldn't understand why he stayed on the station when it was so obvious that it wasn't his favorite place to be.

She tied Callum's horse up to a nearby post and began to remove the saddle. When she straightened from unbuckling the cinch, she found Brody standing behind her. He gently turned her around to face him, then bent lower and kissed her.

"Sorry about that," he said, reaching out to smooth his hand over her hair.

"We can't do that again," she said, looking up at him. "I need this job, Brody."

"You're not going to lose your job," he said. "Cal doesn't care. He's so preoccupied with Gemma, he doesn't have time to worry about us."

"*I* care." Turning back to Callum's mount, she pulled the saddle off and set it on a bale of straw. "I like working here. And I need to pay you back for taking care of my debts."

"Cal can't complain about what you do when you're finished working, can he?"

"No," she said, setting the saddle pad on top of the saddle. "I guess not."

"All right, then. We'll just have to confine ourselves to the hours before breakfast and after dinner. And we're going to have to find a place that offers some privacy." He grabbed the saddle and hoisted it over his shoulder. "Why don't you let me take care of Cal's horse and you can finish what you were doing earlier. Then we'll go eat."

"You don't have to help me."

"Yes I do," Brody said. "Because the sooner you finish, the sooner I'll have you all to myself."

Perhaps he was right. As long as she finished her work, Callum couldn't begrudge her evenings spent with Brody. "Okay."

Her second day of work had been as exhausting as her first. But the prospect of spending time alone with Brody gave her a sudden surge of energy. She'd fallen asleep in his arms last night then woken up to an empty bed. She wasn't about to do that two nights in a row. "It's a date."

"Good." He grabbed the blanket and headed toward the tack room.

Payton watched him, smiling to herself. There was something so attractive about a man who actually worked for a living, a man who used his body the way it was meant to be used—for hard labor…and seduction. Brody was dirty and sweaty, yet she wanted him more than she'd ever wanted a man in her life.

3

BRODY DROPPED the phone into the cradle, then pushed back in Callum's desk chair, linking his hands behind his head. He hadn't bothered to pick up his messages on his mobile phone since reception in Bilbarra and at the station was nonexistent. But remotely checking the voice mail of his home phone at his apartment in Fremantle had brought an interesting development.

Cursing softly, he closed his eyes, a tightly held breath escaping his chest. When he'd left Fremantle, the team doctors had assured him there was no chance he would ever play football again. But now, a doctor in Los Angeles had developed a surgery that offered a way to reconstruct his bum knee.

Why now, why after he'd resigned himself to his fate? Why even tempt him with the possibility of regaining everything he'd lost? Brody knew it would be a long shot at best. And even if the surgery was successful, there'd be months, maybe a year or two, of rehab. Was he really willing to put in the time, just for another chance to play?

He didn't really have a choice. Brody had never been cut out for station life. The problem was he didn't have any options beyond football and stockman's work. He could invest in a business before he retired, but he wasn't sure what he wanted to buy. Or he could go to university and learn something new, but he was too old to go back to being a student.

"You never were one to plan ahead," he muttered to himself.

"Hey, dinner is on the table," Callum said, poking his head in the door. "Best be quick or Davey'll snag the seat next to your girl."

"She isn't my girl," Brody said, running his hand through his hair.

Callum shrugged. "I'm sure the boys will be happy to hear that. They've been carrying on like pork chops since she and Gemma arrived."

"All right, she *is* my girl. For now. And I expect that pretty Irish thing won't be spending much time with the boys, either. I see the way you stare at her. Explain to me again what she's doing here?"

"Research," Callum said. "She's working for some distant relative of ours on a family history. I guess one branch of the family left Ireland for the States and another branch came here. She's been going over all the old records for the station."

"What does that have to do with family history?" Brody asked.

"I don't know." He drew a deep breath. "I don't really care. As long as it keeps her here."

"Maybe she really fancies Teague. He's always been the looker in the family."

"Teague's got something else going," Callum murmured. "I was up early this morning and I saw him come in just before sunrise. There's not an available woman, besides Gemma, Payton and Mary, within fifty kilometers of this station, but he sure looked well satisfied."

"Maybe he's clearing the cobwebs at the brothel, or with a married lady," Brody said.

Callum shook his head. "Teague wouldn't do that. He's too bloody honorable. And why would he when he can usually have any woman he wants?" Callum paused. "I'm just worried he—"

"What?" Brody asked.

"I heard Hayley Fraser's back on her grandfather's station. Teague's always been a bit jelly kneed when it comes to her. First love and all that."

"Marrying Teague off to Hayley would solve all your problems." Brody teased. "The Frasers would be family, and family don't sue family." He pushed away from the desk. "If that's who he's messing with, he should be encouraged, don't you think?"

Callum cursed softly. "And maybe Fraser is using his granddaughter to mess with us," he shot back. "Did you ever consider that? Maybe he thinks if he can't get the land in court, he'll get it another way."

"How?"

"I don't know. Blackmail. Extortion. Fraser will go after that land any way he can. I just hope Teague doesn't get caught in the crossfire."

"Come on, Cal, you're talking crazy now. This feud has gone on for so long that nobody can see straight."

"I'm not going to surrender to Harry Fraser," Cal said. "That land belongs to the Quinns and we're not going to lose it while I'm in charge." He nodded his head. "Come on, dinner is ready. Mary won't wait."

Brody stared after him, then slowly stood. There were times when Brody wondered how Cal handled all the pressures of running the station. So many people depended on him. His parents took a share of the station income. Then there were the stockmen who expected to be paid. Teague's practice wouldn't make decent money for a few years, so he traded vet services for room and board. And now Brody was sponging off Callum. From now on, he'd make a better effort to pull his own weight.

The kitchen was already noisy when Brody walked in, filled with the usual dinner guests—the stockmen, Teague and Mary, and now Gemma and Payton.

With women at the table, the conversation had become much more civilized. Brody dislodged one of the jackaroos from the chair next to Payton, then sat down beside her. Unlike the majority of the men, Brody unfolded his serviette and placed it on his lap instead of stuffing it down the front of his shirt.

"What exactly is a B and S?" Gemma asked.

"Bachelors and Spinsters Ball," Teague explained as he grabbed a piece of bread and slathered it with butter. "All the unmarried people get together for a weekend of silliness. If you're not an Aussie, I don't think I'd recommend it. Foreigners might not have the fortitude to survive the weekend."

"But it sounds like fun," Payton said, leaning forward and bracing her elbows on the table. "I always loved balls and dances and cotill—" She stopped short, as if she'd suddenly revealed too much. Forcing a smile, she continued, "Is it formal or semiformal?"

"Tell her, Teague," Brody insisted, chuckling to

himself. Though Payton hadn't said much, she had revealed something of value this time out. She'd either enjoyed a high-class upbringing or she was a professional princess. He'd never known a single person who'd been to a real ball.

"It's not really a ball, the way you're thinking," Teague explained. "And by silliness, I mean debauchery."

"It's more like a big outdoor party," Callum explained.

Teague nodded. "There's music and drinking and… well, the whole idea is to get pissed, have a good time and hopefully enjoy a shag at the end of the night."

Gemma and Payton looked at each other, shocked expressions on their faces. "Have sex?" Payton asked.

Teague nodded. "Yeah, I guess that's the point. Lots of blokes bring their swag along for just that purpose. Life gets real lonely in the outback."

"What is swag?" Gemma asked. "Money? Do you pay for sex?"

"It's a sleeping roll," Brody explained. "Camping gear. Believe me, you don't want to go to the B and S. It gets feral."

"Filthy is a better word for it," Mary said as she set a bowl of peas next to Brody. She took her spot at the far end of the table. "If you don't want to get dirty or pawed, I wouldn't recommend it. And the loos are disgusting."

"I heard they're going to do something about that," Callum commented. "The organizers reckon they'll get a better class of sheilas if they guarantee clean toilets. They're going to hire someone to keep them tidy."

"I remember last year, Jack made his own loo with

a milk crate and a dunny seat," Teague said. "All the girls were wild for it. He'd let 'em use it, then try to charm them out of their grundies. Such a player, our Jack."

The lanky stockman shook his head, his long hair falling into his eyes. "I won't be able to compete with trailer toilets," Jack said glumly.

"It might be fun," Payton said. She turned to Gemma. "What do you think? When in Australia, do as the Aussies do?"

Gemma laughed. "We'd have to get something nice to wear."

"I have dresses," Payton said. "I need work clothes. I can't wear Davey's castoffs forever. Not that I don't appreciate the loan," she said, giving the kid a warm smile.

"I have to fly to Brisbane in a few days. I could take you shopping," Teague offered.

"Hang on there," Callum interrupted. "Gemma and Payton are not going to Bachelors and Spinsters."

"We won't participate," Gemma said. "We'll just go to…observe. Think of it as sightseeing. Or anthropological research."

"If you want to see the real sights of Australia, I'll take you," Teague said. "Queensland is beautiful from the air."

"There's an idea," Callum said. "You'd be much safer in a plane piloted by our brother than at Bachelors and Spinsters."

Brody slipped his hand beneath the table and smoothed his palm along Payton's thigh. "We could always send Mary to the ball. It's about time she got off this station and had a bit of fun. There are plenty of blokes who'd fancy a dance with our Mary."

The older woman's cheeks turned bright red and she hushed the laughter around the table. "Maybe I will," she said, giving them all a haughty expression. "I'd venture to say I could outdance all you boys."

The rest of the dinner conversation focused on the sights that every visitor in Australia needed to see, the Bachelors and Spinsters forgotten. Everyone at the table had an opinion about the finest tourist sights, both in and outside of Queensland. By the time they'd finished dessert, Teague had a long list, starting with a trip to Brisbane.

As Mary began to clear the table, Brody pushed back, then slid Payton's chair out for her. The rest of the hands looked at him in disbelief. "What are you all gawking at? Some of us here have good manners," Brody said.

The men quickly scrambled to their feet and rushed to Gemma's chair, but Callum waved them off. In truth, Brody's actions had nothing to do with manners. He wanted Payton all to himself and the faster that happened the better. But she seemed determined to keep him waiting.

"I'm going to help Mary clean up," she said, taking his plate and hers.

"Go along with you now. I have all the help I can handle," Mary said. "Davey promised to lend a hand."

Brody squeezed her elbow and pulled her along, out the backdoor to the porch that ran the width of the house. He found a dark corner and pushed her back against the house, then kissed her long and hard, his hands trapping her arms on either side of her head, his hips pressing into hers.

"I've been wanting to do that since I sat down next to you." He groaned.

Payton clutched the front of his shirt, then pushed up onto her toes and kissed him back. "Me, too," she said breathlessly. "I know where we can go. Someplace private."

This time, she pulled *him* along. They headed toward the stables, now dark and silent. When they got inside, Payton fumbled around in the gloom. "There's a flashlight here somewhere."

Brody grabbed it from a shelf above her head and flipped it on, holding it under his chin. "It's called a torch," he said.

Payton held out her hand and he gave it to her. They made their way down the length of the stable to an empty stall. She slid the door open and stepped inside. To Brody's surprise, she'd laid blankets over a mound of straw and arranged a few bales for seating.

"You did this?"

Payton nodded. "When you left to take the phone call. I figured we wouldn't have any privacy in the bunkhouse with Gemma there."

"And what do you plan to do with me once you've lured me inside?" he teased.

"I think we should get to know each other a little better," she said. She caught the front of his shirt and pulled him toward her. "There's so much I don't know about you. So many questions I have to ask."

"You want to talk?"

She nodded.

"I don't know anything about you," he said, smiling down at her. "Tell me something. Anything"

"My birthday is August tenth," she said. "I'm going to be twenty-six."

"Something more interesting," he demanded, his breath warm against her mouth.

"I broke my arm when I fell off my horse. I was seventeen. I had to have surgery." She pointed to her elbow. "I have a scar."

He ran his fingers through her hair and she closed her eyes and tipped her head back. "Something more intimate," he urged, pressing his lips to her throat.

"I lost my virginity in a stable. The Grand Prix in 2001. A month before I broke my arm. I was seduced by a Brazilian stable hand with the most beautiful blue eyes."

"Funny," Brody replied. "I lost mine in the back of my mother's car after footy practice. I was fifteen and she was older. Eighteen, if I recall."

Payton worked at the buttons of his shirt and when they were all undone, she looked up at him. "What else?"

Brody chuckled. "I think we can leave the questions until later."

"So you know what you're doing?" she whispered.

Somehow, he found her question incredibly intriguing. "Yes," he replied as she slid his shirt over his shoulders. "I know exactly what I'm doing. Do you?"

She nodded. "Close the door."

Brody moved to do as she asked, then froze. Hell, he didn't know what he was doing. He hadn't even bothered to bring along protection. "Sorry," he said, turning to face her. "Wait here. I'll be right back."

He tugged his shirt back on, then took the torch from her hand. He jogged back to the house and when he got to the kitchen, he found Mary sitting alone at the table, reading a magazine and sipping a cup of coffee.

"Back so soon?" she asked.

"It's a little chilly out. I need to get a jacket for Payton. Wouldn't want her to catch a cold."

"You're a gentleman," she said, glancing up. "And I hope you'll use a condom. Safe sex and all."

Brody stopped short. Mary had slipped into the role of mother to Callum and Teague after their own mother had moved off the station. And now that Brody had returned, she'd welcomed him as a surrogate son and was equally as protective. "Yes, I won't forget that. Not that it's any of your business."

After retrieving the condoms and a jacket from his room, Brody jogged back out to the stables. He found Payton standing at the stable door waiting.

"What was so impor—" She stopped when he held up the string of three condoms. "Oh. Well, that's probably a good idea."

He drew her into his arms and they stumbled toward the stall. After they stepped inside, Payton pulled the door closed. The light from the torch, when reflected off the walls of the stable, was just enough to see by. Suddenly, he felt nervous, just as he had the first time he'd been with a girl.

This was silly. There had been plenty of women in his life since then. But none of them had ever affected him the way Payton did. Was it because she was still a stranger? That couldn't be it. Or was it because she seemed more exotic, different from the women he usually took to his bed?

She was well educated, he knew that much about her. Though she chose to work in a stable, Brody suspected that she'd probably never done a hard day's work in her life before arriving at the station. And there was the sense that Payton Harwell was the kind of woman who wouldn't give a guy like him a second glance out in the real world. She was seriously out of his league.

So why was she here, trying to seduce him? What did she really want from him beyond having a shag? Brody stood in front of her and cupped her cheek in his hand. Was it just an undeniable sexual attraction they shared? Or was it more?

He'd find some of his answers in her touch, in the feel of her body. And the rest, he'd leave for later. Spanning her waist with his hands, he pulled her body against his, then reached down and drew her leg up along his hip.

Her breath caught in her throat as he stared down into her eyes. Burying her fingers in his hair, she fixed her gaze on his mouth. "Well, then," she murmured, "I guess we're both ready now."

PAYTON ARCHED against the stable wall, reveling in the feel of Brody's hands on her body. It was so simple to want him. She didn't even think before falling into his arms. Maybe there was something in the water here in Australia. Or maybe it was just the man, Payton mused.

Something had changed inside her. For such a long time, she'd tiptoed through life, afraid to make a mistake, fearful that she might disappoint her parents. She'd been their only child, her difficult birth the cause of her mother's inability to have another baby. So there'd been a lot of pressure for her to be perfect.

But from the moment she'd hopped on that flight in Fiji, she'd felt a burden lift from her shoulders. Her parents would never forgive her, so there was no use trying to appease them. She could be whoever she wanted to be now. And she wanted to be wild and passionate, a woman who took chances and lived life.

She looked up into Brody's eyes. This was what she wanted, and not just his gorgeous face or his beautiful body, his penetrating gaze or his playful smile. He was what a real man was supposed to be—strong, confident and just a little bit dangerous. His muscles were hard and his hands rough.

Was that what she'd been looking for? Payton wondered. A man who had the power to possess her completely? Except for that very first time, she'd never made love outside the confines of a bedroom. But here she was, in a stable again, anxious to shed her clothes and feel him move inside her.

Here, everything seemed so much more real, more intense. She didn't feel sheltered and protected anymore. Instead, she'd become wild and uninhibited, like this land and the people around her, taking pleasure in the simplicity of everyday life—and everyday desires. This was her chance to start again. The ties to her past were gradually fraying.

Drawing a deep breath, Payton kissed him, this time making certain he understood her need. She slowly let her leg drop down along his hip, until she stood squarely in front of him. Then she tore at the buttons of his shirt.

He was as anxious as she was to get rid of the garment and a moment later, it lay on the straw at their feet. Payton ran her trembling hands from his shoulders to his belly and back up again. Then, she leaned forward and pressed a kiss to his warm skin, just below his shoulder.

What began gently gradually turned desperate. With every kiss, every caress, Payton wanted him more. He found the hem of her shirt and tugged it up, the fabric bunched in his fists as his hips pinned hers against the side of the stall. Slowly, Brody sank lower until his mouth was on her bare belly.

Payton's fingers furrowed through his hair and his lips trailed higher. He pulled at the lacy bra she wore and when his mouth captured her nipple, Payton cried out in surprise. A wave of sensation washed over her and for a moment, she wasn't sure she could stand.

Holding her tight, Brody tumbled them onto the blankets, pulling her on top of him. His fingers worked at the elastic that held her hair in check, freeing it to fall like a curtain around them both, and then he yanked her shirt over her head.

Payton sat up, straddling his hips, and ran her hand through her hair. Reaching behind her, she unhooked her bra and shrugged out of it. A tiny smile played at the corners of her mouth as she saw his expression shift.

"God, you are beautiful," he murmured, smoothing a hand over her shoulder to cup her breast. He rubbed her nipple to a hard peak and Payton closed her eyes. She didn't want to wait any longer. He could seduce her slowly some other time. Right now, she needed to satisfy a craving deep inside of her.

Payton pushed to her feet, standing over him, her gaze fixed on his. She kicked off her shoes, then slowly shimmied out of her jeans. There wasn't any hesitation or any insecurity. She knew exactly the effect she had on him.

She reached out for him and pulled him up beside

her. Her fingers worked at his belt and then his zipper and when he was standing in just his boxers, Payton let out a soft sigh. "That's better," she said.

He reached out and wrapped his arm around her waist, pulling her against his body. Brody's mouth came down on hers, his kiss deep and demanding. His hands skimmed over her. He knew exactly where to touch to make her ache with desire.

They fell back onto the blankets, Brody rolling her beneath him until his body was stretched out over hers, his hips cradled between her thighs. The delicious sensation of his weight sent a shiver through her limbs.

There were a lot of things Brody said that Payton didn't quite understand. They came from different worlds, and yet their desire for each other needed no translation. Her pulse racing, his hands searching, the anticipation growing between them until it was almost too much to bear.

As he moved above her, his shaft hard between them, Payton remembered her first time and the strange mix of fear and desire and excitement she'd felt. It was like that now with Brody, as if she were just a teenager, still in possession of her virginity.

She sensed this experience wouldn't be like anything she'd ever had before. He was different. But even more important, she was different. Something inside her had changed the moment she'd run away from her wedding. And it was time to see exactly what it was.

However, Brody seemed intent on taking his time. He smoothed his hands over her bare skin, sending shivers of sensation coursing through her body. His lips drifted lower until he drew her nipple into his mouth again.

Payton couldn't take it anymore. Holding him close, she rolled on top of him. Then she straddled his hips, feeling the hard ridge of his cock between them.

"We can do it that way, too." He grinned.

She reached for the condoms lying on the blanket next to them. His erection pressed out against the cotton fabric of his boxers, but she didn't take the time to pull them off. The need to feel him inside her had overwhelmed any thought of seduction.

After tugging the waistband down, she sheathed him, then drew her panties aside. A moment later, Payton slowly sank down on top of him, closing her eyes and holding her breath until he'd buried himself completely. She'd never taken control like this, but she knew exactly what she wanted and how it would feel.

Liberated, she thought as she slowly released her breath. Sex had always been an obligation with Sam, but now it was a basic need, a desire so strong that she'd lost any sense of propriety.

When she opened her eyes again, he was staring at her, passion burning in his gaze. "Don't move," he warned.

"I have to move," she replied with a slow smile. "That's the way it works. At least where I come from." She rose on her knees, then slowly lowered herself again.

"Oh, God, this is not going to last long if you can't follow directions."

Payton leaned forward and kissed him softly. "What is it they say? Just lie back and think of queen and country?"

Brody grabbed her hips and held her still. "Australia is a constitutional democracy," he said.

"I don't care," Payton replied as she rocked forward, ignoring his plea. "We can discuss politics later."

What began slowly and purposefully soon dissolved into a frantic need to satisfy. Brody wasn't as close as he claimed and drove into her again and again, their bodies straining.

Payton felt the beginnings of her release grow inside her, the urge to surrender more intense than she'd ever experienced in the past. She closed her eyes and focused on the feel of him, the wonderful sensations that their coupling created in her body.

His hand touched her face and he drew her down again until their lips and tongues met. It was the kiss that sent her spiraling over the edge. The orgasm came as a complete surprise at first and then Payton was forced to let go, to surrender to the powerful shudders and spasms. She collapsed on top of him, and a moment later Brody found his own release, driving deep inside her, his body tense and then trembling.

They lay together for a long time, gasping for breath, neither one of them speaking. Payton wasn't sure what to say. Thanks were probably in order, considering she'd never experienced an orgasm so powerful. But then, this was only their first attempt. What would subsequent seductions bring?

"That's never happened before."

He gently pushed against her shoulders until their eyes could meet. "You're kidding, right?"

She felt a warm blush creep up her cheeks. If she was liberated enough to make love to a man she barely knew, then she should be able to express her desires. "I mean, it's happened, but not in that way."

He stared at her, a perplexed expression on his face. "Well, that's good, then."

"Yes," she said, smiling. "Maybe we could do it again?"

Brody chuckled. "I think we might have to wait just a bit."

"A bit? What is that in Australian? Because in American that means a minute at the most." She reached down and ran her fingers along his still-rigid shaft, pulling the condom off along the way.

Brody groaned as he clenched his teeth. "A minute. Maybe two." His breath caught in his throat. "Maybe less, if you're very gentle."

BRODY WASN'T SURE of the time. It was late. After midnight. He and Payton had chosen conversation over sex and she was curled up against him, her leg thrown over his hips and her cheek resting on his outstretched arm.

The batteries on the first torch had faded, but Brody had run out and gotten another. For now, they relaxed in complete darkness. Though he loved to look at her, he was just as content to communicate through touch. Her body was made for his hands, her skin so soft and her curves like a landscape to explore.

"We'd probably be more comfortable in my bed," he said, smoothing his hand over her tangled hair.

"We can't," she said.

"Why? There's nothing wrong with what we're doing."

"I know. I'm not ashamed. It's just…"

"What?"

"I'm an employee here and I should probably try to behave myself." She pushed up and grabbed the torch, then shined it on his face. "Besides, this is much more exciting, don't you think?"

"Exciting, maybe." Brody chuckled, holding up his hand. "But not nearly as comfortable." He rolled to his side and pulled a piece of straw from the blanket beneath him.

She sat up beside him and brushed her hair over her shoulder. With a lazy caress, she smoothed her hand over his belly. "When I saw you in the cell next to me, I thought about what you'd look like without your clothes."

Brody gasped, a laugh slipping from his lips. "Really?"

She nodded. "You look different than what I imagined."

"Different bad or different good?"

"Good," she said. Her fingers drifted lower, running along the length of his thigh. He watched, surprised at how such an innocent action could so easily stir his desire. He loved the feel of her hands on his body. As far as he was concerned, she could take whatever she wanted from him. He was willing and quite able to satisfy whatever need might arise.

Her fingers paused when she reached his knee and Brody sucked in a sharp breath. He knew it was ugly. The scars were still sharply defined, to the eye and to the touch. "What happened?" she asked.

He didn't want to tell the story again, especially not to her. It had been a foolish mistake that had changed the entire course of his life. But then, that course had led to her, hadn't it?

"I tore up my knee in a motorcycle accident," he said. "It's not nearly as bad as it looks. It happened a long time ago. I barely even think about it anymore." At least that was the truth, he mused.

She bent over him, her hair tickling his thigh, then pressed her lips to the scar. "There. All better."

Brody chuckled softly. "Yes. That does make things feel much better."

She pushed up on her hands and knees and crawled on top of him. In the soft light from the torch, Payton looked like some ancient goddess, her perfect skin gleaming like marble. He could imagine how a woman like her could drive men into battle for her favors. He was already lost and he'd only known her a few days.

"Any other interesting scars?"

"What exactly are you looking for? Defects?"

She picked up the torch again and shined the light on the tattoo on his right biceps. "What is this?" She rubbed her fingers over the inked skin.

"Nothing, really. Just something tribal."

"I have a tattoo," she said.

Brody pushed up on his elbow, stunned by the admission. "Where?"

She pointed to her ankle and he took the torch from her and held it there. "I don't see anything."

"There. It's that red dot right there."

"That's not a tattoo, that's a freckle."

"No, it was supposed to be a tattoo. But I chickened out after just a few seconds."

"Because it hurt?"

"No. Because I was afraid of what my parents might say. And my—" She smiled. "My boyfriend." She shook her head. "There were a lot of things I thought about doing and then never followed through on. Spontaneity was not something that was encouraged by my family."

"Tell me about this boyfriend," he said.

"That was a long time ago."

"What would they think of you now, lying here naked in a stable with me?"

"They'd probably have me committed."

Brody reached out and picked up her hand, then pressed it to his lips. "I wouldn't let them take you," he said. "You'd be safe with me."

A winsome smiled touched her lips. "I'm not sure *safe* is the right word."

Brody leaned forward and pulled her into a long, lingering kiss. "Will you spend the night with me?" he whispered.

"Here?"

"Wherever you want. Here is good."

"Gemma is probably going to wonder where I am."

"I think Callum is keeping her occupied," Brody assured her.

"The same way you're keeping me occupied?"

He shook his head. "I expect my brother has his own talents. He's—" Brody stopped short when a sound from outside the stall caught his attention. He reached over and switched off the torch, then pressed a finger to Payton's lips.

"What is it?" she whispered.

"Someone is out there."

The sound of horse's hooves on concrete echoed through the silence and Brody got to his feet and moved to the door of the stall. A moment later a light flicked on in the tack room, illuminating the interior of the stable enough to see who had intruded.

Payton stepped to his side, wrapped in one of the wool blankets, and peered out through the bars on the top edge of the stable door. "Who is it?"

"Teague," Brody whispered.

"What's he doing?"

"I think he's saddling his horse."

"Where is he going to ride in the dark?"

"Hell if I know," Brody said. He might guess where his brother was going. Hayley Fraser was back on Wallaroo Station. One plus one equaled two.

Brody thought about what Callum had said earlier. Family loyalty aside, whatever Teague was up to was his business and no one else's. Just like what went on between Payton and him didn't involve his brothers. They were adults now, and they made their own choices. "He's probably riding out to check on the herd," Brody said.

"Alone?"

"Yeah. Why not?"

They listened until the stable was once again silent, the light from the tack room left burning by his brother. Then Brody turned and tugged the blanket off of her. She squirmed playfully as he ran his free hand from her belly to her breast. "We're alone again," he said.

"We should get some sleep," Payton murmured.

Brody groaned as he kissed his way to her nipple. Teasing it to a peak with his tongue, he tried to convince her that sleep was the last thing on his mind. But when she ran her fingers through his hair and pulled his gaze up to hers, he realized just how tired she was. Her eyelids fluttered and she bit back a yawn.

"You're right," he said. "We both have to work tomorrow." Why the hell had he decided to bring her here? Brody wondered. If she hadn't taken this job, then they'd be free to do exactly what they wanted with their time. He should have bought them both a ticket to

Fremantle and they could have spent a week in his apartment. Or he could have found some private getaway where they'd be waited on hand and foot.

Instead, he'd brought her to the station, where they had to sneak around and hide in a horse stall to find some privacy. "You know, the weekend is coming up. You don't have to work on the weekend."

"What? Do you send the horses off to a spa on Saturday and Sunday?" she inquired with a raised brow. "They still need to be fed and groomed."

"But someone else can do that," Brody said.

"It's my job," she replied.

He drew a deep breath and sighed. "There has to be some benefit to sleeping with the owner's brother, don't you think?"

She slipped from his embrace and began to collect her clothes, scattered over the straw-covered floor. "There are a lot of benefits. But I'm not sure unlimited vacation time is one of them."

Brody wrapped his arms around her waist and pulled her back against him. "But aren't you interested in seeing some of Australia while you're here? Isn't that why you came? I'm sure Callum can get one of the jackaroos to take your job for a while."

She shook her head. "Not now. Maybe after I've worked here longer."

Brody understood her worry. After all, when he met her, she'd been reduced to petty crime just to survive. Here, she had a place to sleep, three meals a day and a paycheck at the end of each week. Security trumped great sex, at least for now.

"All right." He took Payton's clothes from her hands

and grudgingly helped her dress. Though she'd removed her clothes as quickly as possible, Brody didn't rush putting them back on, taking the chance to touch her one last time. When he finished, he pulled his jeans on, before slipping his bare feet into his boots. He didn't want to bother with the rest, tossing the remaining clothes over his arm.

"Come on, I'll walk you back to the bunkhouse."

Payton shook her head. "No. Wait here for a few minutes. I can walk back on my own." She pushed up onto her toes and gave him a sweet, lingering kiss. "I'll see you tomorrow," she whispered.

"Abso-bloody-lutely." He captured her mouth again with a deep and possessive kiss of his own.

"All right," she said, running her hands over his bare chest. "Tomorrow."

She turned and hurried out of the stable. Brody watched her as she disappeared into the dark. They'd only known each other for a few days, but he'd already twisted his life around hers. Living on the station had become almost tolerable and working the stock just a way to mark time until he could be with her again.

Brody knew the fascination would probably fade. It always had in the past with other women. There was something about Payton, though, that made him believe it might be different this time.

But was it her with her sweet smile and gentle touch? Or was it him? Had he finally let go of his former life and begun to look forward to what the future held?

4

A BEAD OF PERSPIRATION fell into Payton's eye and she straightened and brushed her arm over her damp forehead. Her back ached from the day's work—mucking out the stables and moving bales of straw into the freshly cleaned stalls. Setting the pitchfork against the rough wooden wall, she stretched her hands above her head and twisted to work the kinks out of her back.

"A dip in the hot tub would soothe those sore muscles," Teague said.

"Sounds good," Payton replied. "Maybe after dinner."

He stared at her for a long moment. "You know, you don't have to work quite so hard. Callum is already impressed. You do twice as much work as all of the jackaroos who've had the job before you."

"What exactly is a jackaroo?"

"Just another name for a stockman. Technically, you're a jillaroo since you're of the female variety."

She smiled. "I like that. I have a title. Maybe I should get some business cards printed. Payton Harwell, Jillaroo."

"Really, I'm serious. No one is going to fire you. And if you're trying to impress Brody, don't bother. He's never been one to enjoy station work."

"Why is that?"

Teague shrugged. "From the moment he could express an opinion, he wanted off the station. He's more like our mum than our dad. He finds it sheer drudgery."

"So, why does he stay?"

"I expect because you're here. Before you came, he spent most of his time in Bilbarra."

"No, I mean, why did he stay as an adult?"

"He didn't. He left the same time our mum did. Moved with her to Sydney when he was fourteen. After that, he only spent holidays here. He hasn't told you this?"

Payton shook her head. "We haven't really talked about our pasts. I guess we've been focusing on the present." She pulled off her gloves, then sat down on a nearby bale of straw. "So he's just here visiting?"

"He's been back for a while. Since his accident—"

"His motorcycle accident?"

Teague nodded. "Since his accident, he hasn't been able to play and he got dropped by his club."

"Club?"

"He hasn't told you much at all," Teague said. "Football club. He was a professional footballer. Aussie rules. He played for a club in Fremantle for the past five years. But he tore up his knee in the accident."

"I've seen the scar," she murmured. "He just brushed it off like it had happened years ago."

"He was in the hospital for a month and in a cast for six. He's lucky to be alive."

"I wonder why he didn't tell me?"

"He doesn't like to talk about it. The accident ended his career. Just when he was starting to play really well, too. And I suppose he thought it didn't make any difference." He sat down beside her. "Does it?"

"No. The scar doesn't bother me. Why would it? It's just that—" She shook her head.

"What?"

"I guess we don't know each other very well. At least not in that sense."

Teague shrugged. "Believe me, it isn't any easier when you know everything about each other. Maybe you and Brody are better off. Less…baggage?"

"Maybe." What Teague said might be true. She and Sam had known each other for years and the passion between them had faded to nothing more than a dull glow. But with Brody, there was fire, flames shooting up into the sky every time their bodies came together. Maybe all the things she didn't know just kept it more exciting.

"I'm flying into Brisbane day after tomorrow. Do you and Gemma want to ride along? You'd mentioned you wanted to shop."

"I have to work," she said.

"We'll be back before dark. I can't land on the station after sunset. And I'm sure some of the guys will take over your duties for a day."

"I don't have any money."

"Payday is Friday," Teague countered. "And I'd be happy to loan you a dollar or two if you're short."

"I couldn't ask you to do that."

"Hey, I think you're a trustworthy sort."

"Then you haven't heard of my criminal past," she said, laughing. "I met your bother in jail."

"Callum mentioned something about that. I guess we've all done things in the past that we wished we could change." He stood, then held out his hand to help her up. "Can I ask you something? From a woman's point of view?"

"Sure," she said.

"Do you think it's possible to forgive past mistakes? I mean, if things get royally stuffed up, is it possible to begin again?"

"I don't know," Payton said. She'd wondered the same thing. "I'm not sure you can ever go back and fix the mistakes you've made. You can just go forward and promise not to make them again."

He nodded, then smiled. "Yeah, I see what you mean." He drew a deep breath. "Listen, if it's all right with you, can we vaccinate those yearlings next week? I've got somewhere I need to be."

"I'm not going anywhere," she said. "Except to Brisbane, if you still plan to take us."

"That I do," he said as he strolled out of the stable. Brody passed him as he wandered in with his horse. Glancing back over his shoulder, he sent his brother an irritated frown, then turned to Payton. "What did he want?"

"He just stopped by to say hello," she said. "We were going to vaccinate the yearlings, but then something else came up." She slipped her gloves on. "He's going to fly Gemma and me to Brisbane on Saturday."

"And what are you and Gemma going to do in Brisbane?"

"Shop. I need to buy some work clothes," she said, glancing down at Davey's jeans and shirt. "And maybe we'll have some lunch and get a pedicure and a manicure. I'd like to get my hair cut, too. I feel like I need a change. This hair just gets in the way."

Brody rested his hands on her shoulders and dropped

a quick kiss on her lips. "But I like the way you look right now." He rubbed a stray strand between his fingers. "And I'm fond of your hair."

Pulling her against him, he kissed her again, this time more passionately. A shiver skittered through her body and she felt her desire warm. It didn't take much to make her want to pull him into a stall and tear off their clothes. "We could go to Brisbane together," he suggested. "Maybe spend the day at the beach instead. Do some surfing."

"It's really a girls' day out," she said. "I'm sure you can get along without me for a day, can't you?"

"I don't know," he teased.

"We'll spend the evening together. I'll be back before dark. Teague said he can't land once it's dark."

"Which means he'll probably find a way to keep you both in Brisbane for the night," he said cynically.

She shook her head. "I don't think so. I think Teague has something else going on."

"Why is that?"

"He asked my advice. Something about starting over again."

Brody sucked in a sharp breath. "Oh, hell. That can only mean one thing. Hayley Fraser. I figured that's where he was off to last night. Callum is going to be mad as a meat-ax."

A giggle slipped from Payton's lips.

"What?" Brody asked.

"How could a meat-ax get angry? And what is a meat-ax?"

"I don't know. What would you say?"

"Mad as a…wet hen?" She laughed. "All right. Yours is much better."

"Wet hen," he muttered. "That's just lame. Who would be afraid of a wet hen?"

"Why will Callum be angry?"

"There's a lot of history between our family and the Frasers. It has to do with a piece of land that Hayley's grandfather claims my great-grandfather stole from the Frasers. We've been fighting about it for years."

"A family feud. Like the Hatfields and McCoys." She paused. "The Montagues and Capulets."

"Yeah, I think Teague and Hayley fancied themselves Romeo and Juliet back when they were teenagers. They were obsessed with each other, to the point where my mum and dad thought they might run away and get married. Then Teague went off to university and a few months later, Hayley ran away. After that, he never mentioned her name again."

"What happened?"

Brody shrugged. "I don't know. Teague doesn't talk about it. He was really messed up for a while."

"So if they're Romeo and Juliet, who are we?" she asked. "Bonnie and Clyde?"

He grinned. "I loved that movie. And we did meet in jail."

"They died in the end of the movie. Riddled with bullets, I think."

"So you're expecting a happy ending for us? I can't think of a movie that ended happily. *Casablanca.* No, that one really didn't—how about—no, that one ended badly, too."

"Breakfast at Tiffany's," she murmured. A happy ending? Payton hadn't thought about the future at all. It was silly to think that she and Brody would share

anything beyond her time in Australia. "Life isn't a movie. It's not...perfect." She reached out and took the reins of his horse. "And I have work to do."

"Time for a break," he said. He circled her waist with his hands and lifted her until she could swing her leg over his horse, then handed her a small canvas bag. "Come on. Let's go for a ride."

Brody hooked his foot in the stirrup and settled behind her, taking the reins from her hands and slipping his arm around her waist.

"I haven't been on a horse in years," she said. "Where are we going?"

"I fancy a swim. And there's dinner in that sack."

"I don't have a suit."

"Then you can sit on the shore and watch for crocs."

He gave the horse a kick and guided it out of the stable. They rode in silence past the outbuildings and toward a small grove of trees in the distance. The sun was low in the late-afternoon sky but the air was still warm. Winter in Queensland was more like summer in Maine—the nights cool, sometimes chilly, and the days comfortably warm.

"Won't the water be cold?"

"The pond is pretty shallow," he said.

"Are there really alligators?"

"No. We don't have alligators, we don't have crocodiles, either. They're not common in this part of Queensland. Teague was just being cheeky with you." He paused. "Although, I suppose they could wander in here without us really knowing."

"Snakes, crocodiles, spiders. It's kind of easy to get hurt here."

He nuzzled his face into her neck. "I'll protect you."

"Who will protect you?"

They reached the pond a few minutes later. It wasn't like any pond Payton had ever seen. The water was brown, like the soil around it, and a pipe led from the pond to a nearby windmill. She studied the shoreline, searching for anything that moved. "How long can a crocodile hold its breath?"

"An hour, maybe more," Brody said. "The salt-water crocs are the bad ones. Freshwater crocs aren't nearly as nasty. And if they were here, they'd be on the shore, warming themselves in the sun."

He slid off the horse, then helped her down, before wrapping the reins around a nearby branch. Taking her hand, Brody led her to the edge of the water. Then he slowly began to remove his clothes.

"I really wish you wouldn't go in," she said.

"I've been swimming in this pond since I was a kid. Believe me, it's safe."

"And I think I'll just watch for a while," she said.

He kicked off his boots and socks, then slipped his jeans over his hips. A moment later, he was naked. Payton held her breath as she watched him walk to the water. He really was a beautiful man, every muscle in his body perfectly toned.

Desire raced through her body and her fingers clenched at the thought of touching him. Suddenly, crocodiles didn't seem like such a big deal. Not compared to swimming naked with Brody. As he sank into the water, Payton removed her jacket and dropped it to the ground. A moment later, she pulled off her shoes.

"My parents used to take me to the beach when we

went on vacation," she said. "And they'd never let me go in the water."

"Why not?"

"My mother was afraid of sharks. And my father was afraid I'd drown, even though I'd taken swimming lessons for years." Payton shook her head. "They spent so much energy protecting me from alligators that weren't there."

"Crocodiles," he said.

When she skimmed her jeans down over her thighs, he smiled. And when she was left in just her underwear, he slowly stood. She walked to the water's edge. "Take it all off," he said softly.

Payton drew a ragged breath. They'd been naked together last night, in the shadows of the stable. But it felt just a little bit naughty out in the open. Still, her desire for him was strange and powerful, a force she didn't want to deny.

The water was cold on her skin and she groaned as it slowly moved up her body. Then, holding her breath, she slipped beneath the surface and popped up in front of him. "It's freezing!" she cried.

He pulled her into his arms. "You'll be warm soon," he said, letting his hands drift over her body.

"I've never done this before. I've always thought it would be fun to swim naked, but I've never had the opportunity." As he wrapped her legs around his hips, she leaned back, letting her hair fan out in the water. "It feels nice on my sore muscles."

"You work too hard."

"That's what Teague was telling me," she said as she floated on the surface of the pond.

"And what else was Teague telling you?" Brody asked, an edge to his inquiry.

"Nothing." She didn't want to tell Brody that she'd had an interesting conversation with his older brother, that he'd told her things Brody hadn't bothered to mention. Even now, as she looked into his eyes, Payton saw him differently.

He wasn't just an object of her desire anymore. He was a man with a real life, a life that hadn't gone exactly as planned. But then, her life wasn't exactly a fairy-tale, either. Payton smiled.

She felt his eyes on her naked body and a moment later his hands smoothed over her breasts and down her belly. The sensation was like nothing she'd ever felt before. His touch was warm yet cold, fleeting yet so stirring. Every sensation seemed magnified by the water, her skin slick and prickled with goose bumps.

When he touched her between the legs, a tiny moan slipped from her throat. His caress was so light, so skilled that Payton felt the rise of her need almost immediately. Her eyes still closed, she gave herself over to the feeling. The water lapped around her body, her skin chilly in the late-afternoon air.

She still couldn't understand how easy it was with Brody. She wanted him and he wanted her. They satisfied each other in the most basic way, driven purely by sexual desire. And yet, there was an intimacy growing between them, a trust that seemed strengthened by their passion.

He slipped a finger inside her and she felt herself losing control. And then, a heartbeat later, Payton dissolved into spasms of pleasure. She arched back as the orgasm rocked her body and for a moment, she sank beneath the surface.

But then Brody grabbed her and pulled her up against his chest. Payton coughed and sputtered. She wrapped her arms around his neck, her heart slamming. Another shudder shook her body and he held her tight.

"Are you all right?" Brody asked, brushing the wet hair away from her face.

She nodded, wiping the water from her eyes. Then she began to giggle and couldn't seem to stop. The things Brody did to her were scandalous—she felt wicked when she was with him. Payton kissed him hard. "I think you're more dangerous than the crocodiles. But what a wonderful way to go."

THERE WERE TIMES—though not many—when Brody truly did appreciate the beauty of the outback. He stared up at the inky-black sky, picking out the constellations that he recognized as the moon slowly rose. "Look," he said, pointing to a shooting star. "Quick, make a wish." He drew Payton closer, his arm wrapped around her shoulders. "Got it?"

She nodded as she lay beside him on his bedroll. "The stars are different here."

He pointed into the darkness. "There's the Southern Cross. And the Milky Way."

"No Big Dipper. Or Orion."

"We have Orion," he said. "In the summer. Orion is upside down here. Standing on his head." He rolled onto his side to face her. "It's not much, but it's all the station has to offer for entertainment."

"The swim and the sunset and the stars were perfect," Payton said softly.

"Better than all those balls and cotillions you used to go to?"

"Much better," she said, turning to face him. "And I didn't go to that many balls. Well, maybe I did. But my mother was into those kinds of things. High society and all that. Her one goal in life was to find me a good husband."

"And now you're here in low society with me."

She shook her head. "I'm exactly where I want to be."

"And how long will you be here?" Brody asked, twirling a strand of her hair around his finger.

"I hadn't thought about it. I came in on a tourist visa, so I have three months." She shook her head. "I like it here. I'm not leaving anytime soon."

He drew a deep breath. "Don't you think about going home? To your family and friends?"

She turned her attention back to the stars and Brody sensed she was avoiding his question. She seemed to be reluctant to talk about what had brought her to Oz. He suspected she wasn't just a student touring the country. If she came from a wealthy family, what was she doing working for slave wages on a cattle station? And why had she run out of money so quickly?

"You don't belong here," he said.

"I don't have anyplace else to be right now," Payton replied.

"I don't believe that. What are you running away from, Payton?"

"Nothing," she said. She glanced over at him. "Really. Nothing."

"Talk to me," Brody said, suddenly desperate to know more. Sooner or later, the sex wouldn't be enough. And if there was nothing else to hold her here, to keep her in Australia, she'd leave.

"There's nothing to say," she insisted. "And what difference does it make, anyway?"

He'd always been realistic about his relationships with women. He'd been an enthusiastic lover, romantic when the time called for it, and supportive if required. But he'd never surrendered his heart, never allowed himself to get too close.

Yet the intimacies he'd shared with Payton made him want more. He needed to know who she was and where she came from. He longed to know how she felt about him. Why was she here and how long would she stay?

"Fine," he muttered. "And I suppose I shouldn't be surprised if I wake up one day and you've just moved on."

"I wouldn't do that," she said. "I'd say goodbye."

"Well, that's nice to know." Brody couldn't keep the sarcasm from his tone. He pushed to his feet and walked over to the edge of the pond, the moonlight gleaming on the water. He grabbed a small pebble and threw it into the pond, hearing the *plunk* before the ripples glimmered in the dark.

He closed his eyes when he felt her hand on his back. "I don't understand what you want," she said.

"I don't know what I want." He turned and pulled her into his embrace. How could he answer that? All he knew was he didn't want to hold anything back. He wanted honesty and openness and complete surrender. But then, he hadn't been honest with her. Perhaps that's where it would have to start.

The problem with his story was it really didn't make him look good. He hadn't planned well for his future, he'd bet everything on a successful football career. And then, in one incredible act of stupidity, he'd blown it all.

"We should go back," he said. "It's starting to get really cold and I don't want to you catch a chill."

He rolled up his swag and retied it onto the back of his saddle, then took her hand and led her over to his horse.

She looked up at him and forced a smile. "Thank you for bringing me here. It was fun."

Grasping her waist, Brody helped her up into the saddle. After he mounted, he turned the horse toward the house. Payton leaned back against him and he turned his face into her damp hair, inhaling her scent.

"Stay with me," he said.

"I'm not going to leave."

"I mean tonight. Stay with me tonight."

"Not tonight," she said.

"I want you with me," he said. "I don't like sneaking around. We're not doing anything wrong, why do you act as if we are?"

"Because it's just between us right now," she said. "Nothing can mess it up if it's just us. I've known you for three days, Brody. We should at least try to take a few things slowly, don't you think?"

This was exactly why he couldn't be friends with a woman. He didn't understand the reasoning. It was all right to have sex in the stable, but not in his bed. Everyone on the station knew what was going on between them, but pretending that nothing was happening made more sense.

Arguing with her wouldn't help, he mused. If he

wanted more from her, then he'd just have to wait until she was ready to give him more. When they reached the bunkhouse, he helped her down and gave her a quick kiss. "I'll see you tomorrow," he murmured.

She nodded. "Tomorrow."

He turned away and led his horse toward the stable. As he passed by the house, he saw Callum sitting on the back porch, a beer in his hand, his feet kicked up on the railing. "Where were you?" Callum asked.

"I went for a swim with Payton," Brody said. He swung off his horse and wrapped the reins around the post at the bottom of the steps. "Do you have another one of those?"

Callum reached down and picked up a bottle. "You have to go fetch the next round," he said.

Brody twisted off the cap, then sat down in the chair beside Callum's. He took a long drink of the beer and belched.

"Nice," Callum said. "A bit more choke and you would have started."

"Thank you," Brody muttered.

"Funny how you're on your best behavior around Payton and then you revert to typical Brody."

"And you don't put on airs when you're with Gemma?" He paused. "And why aren't you with Gemma? How come you're all alone here, crying into your beer?"

"She's shut herself in the library. I can't understand what's taking her all this time. It's not like we're royalty. But she's going over every single journal and account book in there."

"What does that have to do with our family history?"

"Don't ask me," Callum said.

"She's pretty. Not as pretty as Payton, but pretty."

"I beg to differ," Callum said. "Gemma is much prettier."

"Payton told me she spoke with Teague today. He was talking like he'd started things up with Hayley Fraser again. And he took off in the middle of the night last night on horseback."

"Shit," Callum said. "When I heard she was back, I wondered if he was going to see her again. What do you think she's up to?"

"You never liked her, did you?"

Callum shrugged. "She put Teague through hell the first time they were together. He has a blind spot when it comes to her."

"Maybe that's our problem," Brody mused. "We've never had a blind spot when it comes to a woman. Maybe we're missing out on something."

Callum took a drink of his beer. "Maybe." He pulled his feet off the railing and stood. "I'm going to go check on Gemma. See if she might need some help." He stepped over Brody's outstretched legs and walked back inside the house.

Brody glanced over at the light shining from the window of the bunkhouse. If Gemma was in the library then that meant Payton was alone in the bunkhouse. He drank the last of his beer as he wandered off the porch toward the light.

When he rapped on the door, there was no answer from inside, but he heard the sound of running water and walked around the corner of the bunkhouse to the rough wooden shower. He pulled the door open and stepped inside, slipping his hands around Payton's waist.

She screamed, but he stopped the sound with his kiss, his tongue delving into her damp mouth until her surprise was subdued.

She brushed her soapy hair from her eyes and looked at him. "Your clothes are getting all wet," she said.

His fingers skimmed over her naked body, deliberately tempting her. "I just wanted to say good-night." He leaned forward, his lips barely touching hers.

"I thought you did that already," Payton said.

"I wanted to leave you with something a bit more memorable," he said. His hands slid around to cup her backside and he pulled her hips against his, making his desire completely evident.

Brody's mouth found Payton's again and he felt her melt against him. "If you want more, I'm in the first room at the top of the stairs." With that, Brody stepped out of the shower. "Good night, Payton. Sleep tight."

She didn't return the courtesy. He imagined that she was considering his offer. But Brody really didn't expect her to follow through. Not tonight. But maybe tomorrow night. A grin curved the corners of his mouth. He could be bloody persuasive when he wanted.

THOUGH SHE WAS EXHAUSTED, Payton couldn't sleep. Her head spun with thoughts of Brody. She wanted to go to him, to crawl into his bed and into his arms and just fall asleep with him beside her. The need was so acute it had become an ache.

Cursing softly, she tossed aside the bedcovers and swung her legs off the edge of the bunk. Gemma had come in an hour before and Payton had assumed she was asleep, but then she spoke.

"Can't sleep?" she called from across the room.

"No. You can't, either?"

"No."

A moment later, the light on Gemma's headboard came on. She sat up, crossing her legs in front of her, then ran her hand through her thick auburn hair. "Would you care to talk?" she asked. "I'm a good listener. All my friends tell me so."

"It's complicated," Payton replied.

"I can handle complicated. Is it Brody? You two seem to be...attracted."

"That's putting it mildly," Payton said. She crawled out of bed and crossed the room, then sat down on the edge of Gemma's bunk. "Can you keep a secret?"

"Of course."

"A month ago this last Saturday, I was putting on my wedding gown in Fiji and getting ready to walk across the beach and get married."

Gemma gasped. "Oh, goodness. What happened?"

"I got scared and ran away." She frowned, searching for the words to explain her actions. "I just wasn't sure he was the man I wanted to spend the rest of my life with. There was no...fire. Do you know what I mean?"

Gemma nodded. "Yes," she said. "I know precisely what you mean."

"So I grabbed a few things, stuffed them in my bag, exchanged my honeymoon ticket for a flight to Brisbane and...disappeared into the outback."

"And here you are," Gemma said.

"Yes."

"Have you called your family?"

Payton shook her head. "I left a message at the hotel

in Fiji after I landed in Australia. I said I'd call them soon, but they're going to be so angry with me that I don't even want to think about that now. The embarrassment and the expense of the wedding. The gossip will be awful."

"What of your fiancé?"

"I can't imagine what he's thinking. I'm sure he doesn't want anything more to do with me. Not that I want him to. I made my choice and I can live with it."

"Well, there it is, then," Gemma said cheerfully. "As Callum would say, no worries."

"Oh, I have plenty to worry about. Like this thing with Brody. I'm sure it's just a reaction to what I did. I was a little…repressed and now I'm testing my boundaries. And the attraction will probably fade soon. But then, I'm not sure I want it to." Payton paused. "He's like a rebound guy, but I think he might be more."

"A rebound guy?" Gemma said. "I understand. But wouldn't any man who came after your fiancé be a rebound guy? So, in theory, it would be better to go out with some git after you break up so you don't waste a good bloke as a rebound guy."

"I suppose that would be sensible. So you think I'm wasting Brody?"

"Or perhaps, you could consider the possibility that fate has put this man in your path and the reason you ran away from your wedding is that you were really meant to be with him all along."

"No," Payton said, the notion too absurd to consider. "You think so?"

"I think it's silly to try to figure out a relationship before it's really begun. Maybe you should just let it happen."

Payton considered Gemma's point, then slowly

stood. "Thank you," she said. She walked over to her bunk and grabbed her jacket from where it hung on the bedpost. "I'm just going to visit Brody for a few minutes. Don't wait up for me."

"I won't," Gemma said with a sly smile.

Payton slipped her shoes on and pulled the jacket over her T-shirt and flannel pajama bottoms. The night was chilly as she ran from the bunkhouse to the main house. Mary had left a light burning over the sink in the kitchen, but the house was silent. Tiptoeing through the kitchen, she headed toward the stairs. But when she reached the top, she was faced with two choices.

Brody had said his bedroom was the first door at the top of the stairs, but she couldn't remember if he'd said on the right or the left. She reached for the door on the right and opened it carefully. To her relief, she found a linen closet stacked with towels.

Drawing a deep breath, she opened the opposite door and slipped inside. The bedside lamp still burned and Brody's hand rested on a sports magazine that he had been reading before he fell asleep. He slept in a tangle of blankets, his chest bare and his hair tousled.

Payton slowly undressed, dropping her clothes on the floor. When she was naked, she stepped to the side of the bed and gently moved the magazine from beneath his hand. He looked so relaxed, almost boyish. His brow, usually furrowed into an intense expression, was now smooth, and his lips, so perfectly sculpted, were parted slightly.

Payton carefully pulled the covers back and slipped into bed beside him. He awoke with a start and stared at her for a long moment before he comprehended what was going on. Then, with a soft sigh, he rolled her beneath him and kissed her.

There was no need for words. They communicated with taste and touch, with soft moans and quickened breathing. Payton slid her hand down and wrapped her fingers around his rigid cock and at the same moment, he found the damp spot between her legs.

All the while, as they teased each other closer to the edge, he kissed her gently, murmuring her name and telling her how good it felt to touch her. At first, Payton was a bit inhibited talking about such things. But then, she let her insecurities go and began to take part in the highly charged conversation.

She could feel his body tense as she brought him closer, his breath coming in short gasps. Carefully, Payton drew him back from the edge, becoming more skillful with every caress. Brody took his cues from her and did the same until they were both almost frantic for release, writhing against each other, their limbs tangled in the sheets.

And when her need finally overwhelmed her, Payton knew that it was exactly what she was searching for. He surrendered a moment later, her hand becoming slick with his orgasm.

Brody's mouth found hers and he kissed her gently. Such a simple thing, Payton mused. And yet, every time they surrendered to each other, she felt the bond between them growing. It wasn't just sex. They were discovering each other and with each new experience, Payton found herself wanting more.

"Are you going to stay?" he asked, his lips brushing against hers as he spoke.

Payton nodded. It would be easy enough to sneak out before morning. But then, why even bother to deny what was happening between them? They were both free to enjoy each other. They were both consenting adults. Any shame she might have felt about sleeping with a man she barely knew was just residual guilt left over from leading a rather sheltered life.

She wasn't the same Payton who had flown to Fiji for her wedding. She wasn't even the same Payton who had run away in the middle of the ceremony. Every day she was on her own, she was learning more and more about the woman she really was inside.

She'd spent so much time in familiar surroundings, safe among family and friends, her every need met, her every worry soothed, that she hadn't really bothered to question who she was or what she wanted. But now, each day was a choice, a choice to go backward or to move forward.

"You're not a dream, are you?" Brody whispered, running his fingers through her hair.

"No," she said.

"You won't be gone the next time I open my eyes?"

"No."

Satisfied, Brody pulled her against his body, tucking her backside into his lap and wrapping his arms around her. His lips pressed to her nape and Payton closed her eyes, a warm feeling of contentment washing over her.

The world she'd once known seemed like another lifetime. She was happy here in Brody's arms. And whether it lasted a day or a year, she wouldn't question it again, for perhaps Gemma had been right. Perhaps fate had brought them together.

5

BRODY PARKED the Land Rover in front of Shelly's coffeeshop, waiting for the dust on Bilbarra's main street to settle before stepping out of the truck. He had just enough time for a late lunch before heading back to the station.

Gemma and Payton had taken off with Teague at sunrise for their girls' day out in Brisbane. To keep his mind off Payton, Brody had driven into Bilbarra to pick up a part for one of the windmills that had gone down the previous week.

But the long ride in had left him plenty of time to think about the past five days. It had only been five days since he'd first set eyes on Payton. Hard to believe considering what had passed between them. It wasn't just the desire, Brody thought. He'd felt that way about other women, at least in the beginning. But he found himself focused on different matters when it came to Payton—like how long she'd stay and whether she had any reason to go home.

They seemed to fit so perfectly, understanding each other's needs without even having to speak, focusing on the present instead of the future. He needed a woman like that, a woman who wouldn't insist on plans and promises.

She'd spent the last three nights in his bed, though she hadn't been brave enough to face the group at the breakfast table. Instead, she'd slipped out in the hour before dawn, while the house still slept.

Oddly enough, his brothers wouldn't have even noticed her comings and goings. Teague hadn't bothered to come home the past two nights, only just turning up to grab a shower and change clothes. And Callum had his own preoccupations, disappearing with Gemma the night before last and returning the next morning.

It was strange that all three of them were suddenly involved when not one of them had bothered with dating for months. He headed toward the post office, but a shout stopped him in the middle of the street.

"Brody Quinn!"

Brody turned to see Angus Embley lumbering after him, his tie undone and his hair standing on end.

"I haven't done anything wrong," Brody said, holding up his hands in mock surrender.

"I've been wanting to speak with you," Angus said. He motioned Brody toward police headquarters and Brody jogged across the street, joining him on the porch. "Why have you been dodging my calls?"

"I'm sorry," Brody said. "I was just planning to go over to the Spotted Dog and pay Buddy for that mirror I broke last weekend."

"I'm not worried about Buddy's damn mirror. I'm on the organizing committee for Bachelors and Spinsters and we're going to hold an auction this year. You're the only celebrity we've got in Bilbarra besides Hayley Fraser and I don't think we can convince her to participate. You'd fetch a pretty penny. All the proceeds go to the library book fund. And you don't have to sleep with anyone, just have dinner together."

Though every unmarried person within a two-hundred-mile radius looked forward to the annual Bilbarra "ball," Brody and his brothers suddenly had three very good reasons not to attend—Payton, Gemma and Hayley. "I heard Hayley was back on Wallaroo Station," Brody mentioned, hoping for some additional news.

Angus looked surprised. "Really." He appeared to weigh his options for a moment, then shook his head. "Naw. She's a big telly star. She's probably got a whole building full of people telling her what she can and can't do."

"I think I'm going to have to pass," Brody said.

"Hey, there is something else." Angus braced his arm on the porch post. "There's a private detective hanging about."

"Looking for me?"

Angus chuckled. "One would think that might be a good bet. But he's looking for that lady you bailed out of my jail. Payton Harwell. What did you do with her after you bailed her out?"

Brody considered his answer for a long moment. He could trust Angus, but the man was an officer of the law. If Payton was a fugitive, Angus might not have a choice in taking sides. Brody shrugged. "I gave her some money and sent her on her way. She said she was headed back to Brisbane. That's the last I saw of her."

Angus frowned. "There's a reward for information. Ten thousand American."

"What did she do?"

"He wouldn't say. You could ask him yourself. He was looking to have a bit of lunch, so I pointed him toward the coffeeshop. He may still be there."

"Thanks," Brody said, starting off down the street.

Hell, this was all he needed. He was lucky he hadn't brought Payton to town with him. He'd been concerned about her flying to Brisbane with Teague, but she seemed almost anxious to get off the station and spend time shopping with Gemma. The testosterone-heavy atmosphere on the station did require time away occasionally.

If she was running from something—or someone—then who could say when she'd just up and disappear again? Maybe she planned to use the trip to Brisbane to make her escape. He shook his head. She'd promised to say goodbye before she left. He'd have to take her at her word.

The bell above the door of the coffeeshop jingled as he stepped inside. "Hey there, Shelly!" Brody slid onto one of the stools at the counter and picked up a menu.

Shelly Farris wiped her hands on a towel and strolled over to him. "Brody Quinn. What brings you into town on a weekday?"

Brody set the menu down and watched as she poured him a cup. "I'm picking up a few parts for Callum. I thought I'd check up on you. See if you made any of my favorite meat pies today."

"We have steak mince, steak and mushroom, and a few of our breakfast pies left."

"I'll have a steak mince," Brody said. "Make them takeaway." He closed the menu and glanced over his shoulder. There was only one other customer in the place. "Tourist?" he asked, nodding in the man's direction.

Shelly shook her head. "No. Private investigator. Looking for that girl who stiffed me on the bill last week. The bill you paid. I don't think you did society any favors there."

"Why? What did he tell you?"

"Nothing. Only that he's offering a reward for information. I couldn't give him more than what I just told you. Do you know where she is?"

Brody shook his head. "No, how would I? I was just doing a good deed."

Shelly disappeared into the kitchen to get his order while Brody sipped his coffee. If he wanted to know more about Payton Harwell, all he had to do was ask. But by asking, he might create undue suspicion. Still, idle curiosity wasn't out of the ordinary.

He slipped off the stool and wandered over to the booth where the middle-aged man sat, a half-eaten Lamington on his plate. "Don't like the dessert?" Brody asked.

The man glanced up from the study of his mobile phone. "What?" He looked at his plate and smiled. "No. It was great. Can I get my check?"

"I don't work here," Brody said.

"Oh, sorry."

When the man made a move to leave, Brody sat down on the opposite side of the booth. "I hear you're looking for someone."

"Yes. Yes, I am." He reached into a leather folder and pulled out a photo, then set it down in front of Brody. "Do you know her?"

Brody nodded. "I do. We were incarcerated together."

His eyebrow shot up. "I knew she spent some time in the local jail, but I didn't know you were with her when she was arrested."

"I wasn't," Brody said. "We just happened to be confined at the same time. I paid her fine and settled her accounts. Why are you looking for her?"

"It's a private matter," he said. "Do you know where she is?"

"Did she break the law?"

"As I said, it's a private matter. But there is a reward for information leading to her location, if you know something."

"I bailed her out and then dropped her on the road out of town. I think she said she was going to make her way down to Sydney," Brody lied. "I told her she could probably catch a ride on one of the road trains that pass through."

"Road trains?"

"It's a semitruck that pulls a string of trailers. They pass through Bilbarra occasionally, hauling feed and building supplies." He leaned back and stretched his arms out to rest on the edge of the bench. "She could be anywhere by now."

"Yes, well, thank you," the man said. "That's the most I've found to go on. She didn't say anything about where she might be staying or whether she met up with any friends?"

Brody pretended to ponder the question for a moment, then shook his head. "Nope. She just wanted to get out of town."

The investigator threw a wad of cash onto the table, then held out his hand. "Your lunch is on me," he said. "Thanks for the information."

"No worries," Brody said. "I hope you find her." He watched as the man walked out the front door then went back to his spot at the counter. When Shelly returned with his meat pies, he pointed to the empty booth. "He's buying me lunch."

"Well, there's a clever boy. What did you tell him?"

Brody scooped up the pies wrapped in paper, and took a big bite out of one of them. "Not much," he said as he chewed. "But I got a free lunch out of it." He headed toward the door.

"Where are you going?" Shelly asked, disappointment tingeing her tone. "I just rang my husband to stop by. Arnie's got himself mixed up in some silly football scheme with the boys over at the Spotted Dog and he needs advice on his footy picks. He's been losing twenty dollars a week to those fools."

"I'm out of the game," Brody said, pointing to his knee. "I'm trying my best to forget footy."

"You were one of the best, Brody Quinn," Shelly called.

As Brody strode down the street, he inhaled the two meat pies. He was tempted to stop by the Spotted Dog for a beer to wash them down, then realized he'd been banished from the place until further notice. Instead, he decided to stop at the local library. A quick Internet search might turn up a few clues on Payton and her past…and maybe even outline her crimes.

The public library was attached to the small school in Bilbarra. Though nearly all of the children who lived on cattle and sheep stations took their classes by computer, those who lived within a short drive of Bilbarra attended a regular school. Some of the advanced classes were still taught online, but there were two teachers that guided the thirty or forty students through their studies, and the town librarian to see to their literary needs.

When he walked into the library, a trio of young boys gathered at a large table. One of the boys recognized him immediately and quickly informed his friends. The librarian, Mrs. Willey, looked up at the commotion, then smiled. "See there," she said. "Everyone uses the library, even football legends."

Brody grinned. "She's right, you know. The library is one of my favorite spots in all the world. Read more books!" He stopped at the counter. "There," he muttered. "I've done my duty as a role model, ma'am. Now, I was wondering if I could use a computer with Internet access."

"Certainly," Mrs. Willey said. "Use any one of those three along the wall. But I'll have you know, accessing adult material is prohibited and will result in the suspension of your privileges."

He caught her teasing smile and chuckled. "There'll be none of that," he said. "I'm here to look up some recipes."

He sat down and keyed in his favorite search engine then typed Payton's first and last name. Brody paused before he hit Enter, wondering what he'd find. Maybe it would be something he didn't like, something he'd rather not know. And shouldn't he wait for Payton to tell him about her past? Real relationships were supposed to be about trust.

He had to know all the facts before he could protect

her, Brody rationalized. If she was in trouble, he'd do everything in his power to help her. "So I have to know," he said as he hit the keys.

"Payton Harwell," he read. "Over one thousand hits?" Brody clicked on the first one and found her name mentioned as the winner of a horse show. But right below that was a startling headline: Payton Harwell to Wed Heir to Whitman Fortune.

He clicked on the article and an instant later, a photo of Payton and her fiancé appeared. He scanned through the text beneath it and stopped at the wedding date. "The couple will be married on the island of Fiji in late April with close friends and relatives in attendance. The bride will wear a gown by designer Sophia Carone."

Late April? If Payton had been married in late April and he'd met her the first of June, then her marriage hadn't lasted more than a month. "Oh, shit," Brody muttered. Had he been having a naughty on a nightly basis with a married woman?

There weren't many rules in Brody's book when it came to sex, but not bedding another man's wife was one of them. After witnessing the problems in his parents' marriage, he'd vowed never to be involved in breaking up a family. Besides, there had always been plenty of single women willing to jump into bed with him, he'd had no need to do it with the married sort.

He leaned back in his chair and studied the photo. They looked happy, their arms wrapped around each other, smiling for the photographer. Worse, they looked as if they belonged together, living in some fancy mansion in New York with servants to tend to their every need.

Well, at least she wasn't a criminal, Brody mused. She was simply a runaway wife. He paused. Or maybe a runaway bride. There was no proof that she'd ever gone through with the wedding. Maybe she'd arrived in Fiji and decided marriage just wasn't for her.

"Is there anything I can help you with?"

Brody quickly clicked back to the search engine, then glanced over his shoulder at Mrs. Willey. "No. Nothing. Just catching up on a few of my old friends." He stood, shoving his hands into the pockets of his jeans. "Thanks. I'm in a bit of a hurry right now, but I'll stop by soon and pick up some books."

"You do that," she said with a wide smile. "Be sure to come on a school day if you can. I'm sure the students would love to talk to you."

Brody strode out the front door of the library into the midday sun. He headed back to the Land Rover, parked near the coffeeshop. He'd have to decide just how to discuss his discovery with Payton. Though his rule regarding married women still stood, it seemed rather pointless to avoid sex now that that horse was already out of the barn.

Hell, the only way to avoid wanting her was to leave Queensland altogether. He could no more control his desire for Payton Harwell than he could stop breathing.

THE PLANE TOUCHED DOWN as the afternoon sun hovered near the western horizon. Payton peered out the window, catching sight of one of the station's utes, the name she'd learned to call the pick-up trucks that nearly everyone drove. She saw Callum leaning against the truck as the plane taxied to the near end of the runway, but Brody was nowhere to be seen.

When Teague had turned off the single engine, Callum approached and opened the door. He helped Payton out, grabbing shopping bags as she jumped lightly from the plane. He then turned back to wrap his hands around Gemma's waist. Payton watched as their gazes met and he gave her a quick kiss.

Though Gemma hadn't said anything about her relationship with the eldest Quinn, it was clear to everyone that something was going on. Callum didn't smile much, but he always seemed to be smiling when Gemma was present.

Callum helped Teague secure the plane before all four of them hopped into the truck and headed toward the house. Payton had hoped to find Brody standing on the porch or lounging on her bunk, but she was disappointed.

"He took off about a half hour ago," Callum said. "On horseback, toward the west. I'm sure he'll be back soon."

Payton forced a smile. She'd been looking forward to seeing Brody all day. She'd bought a sexy new swimsuit for the hot tub and some lacy underwear that she was certain he'd appreciate. Her nails and toes looked perfect and her hair smelled like fruit. In short, she was almost irresistible.

She set her bags inside the door of the bunkhouse then turned and jogged down the front steps. "I'm going to ride out and meet him," she said.

"It's getting dark," Callum warned.

"Don't worry, I won't go far. I can see the lights of the station from pretty far away."

She ran to the stables and found a gentle mount, then quickly saddled the horse. She tied a bedroll on the back in case she and Brody decided to make a stop at the swimming hole again. Then, after swinging her leg over the saddle, she steered the horse out of the stable and into the waning light.

Though she'd ridden to the pond with Brody the other night, this was the first time she'd been on a horse alone since her fall nine years before. "Like riding a bike," she said, settling into the rhythm.

She urged the horse into a relaxed gallop, letting the wind whip her hair into a riot of curls. It was still easy to see where she was going, the last rays of the sun shining on the red dirt of the outback.

As she rode, her thoughts wandered to Brody, to spending the evening alone with him. Brisbane had been so busy and exciting that she'd wished he'd been there to share it with her. Maybe next weekend they could go together, as he'd suggested. They could spend some time at the beach or find a comfy hotel room and revel in absolute privacy.

As the sun dropped lower, the air became chilly and Payton drew her horse to a stop. She scanned the landscape for Brody, but it was difficult to see. Tugging gently on the reins, she turned the horse around. Her breath caught in her throat. She couldn't see the station anymore.

Rubbing her eyes, she squinted into the distance, searching for the lights that would guide her back. Slowly, she realized she'd ridden too far, lost in her thoughts and unaware of the passing time. Everything looked the same. Starting off in the direction she'd come from, Payton kicked the horse into a gallop again.

But a moment later, the horse stumbled in an unseen gully and she found herself thrown forward.

Payton hit the ground with a hard thud, knocking the wind out of her. Groaning, she lay back in the dirt and took a quick inventory. Her limbs were still intact, no broken bones, just wounded pride. Levering to her feet, she brushed the dirt off her jeans and remounted, but as soon as she spurred the horse forward, she could feel the animal favor its right foreleg.

Sliding off again, she bent down and ran her hands over his leg. "What happened?" she cooed. There was no swelling and no broken bones. She's seen enough stumbles in her show-jumping career to suspect that it was probably just a bruise. Though riding was possible, there was no need to put the horse under any more stress. She mentally calculated the distance and figured she probably had at least an hour's walk.

Payton stared up at the stars, trying to remember what she'd seen in the night sky. The last traces of the day were visible on the horizon, so she grasped the reins and began to walk the opposite way, east, toward the station.

The outback looked deceptively flat, yet as she walked, she realized that a gentle rise could easily hide things in the distance. She tried to keep moving in a straight line, finding a cluster of stars to keep over her right shoulder. But it was difficult to maintain her bearings in the dark. In the end, she decided to give her horse its head. He knew how to get home better than she did.

But, to her surprise, the horse didn't lead her back to the station. Instead, she found herself standing at a low iron gate. She hadn't come through any fence on her way out, but the horse seemed to know what it was doing. "Do I trust the horse or do I trust myself?"

In the end, she opened the gate and led the horse through. A few seconds later, she noticed the outline of a small building, just barely visible in the growing moonlight. Obviously, the horse had been to the spot in the recent past. "What is this?"

The front door was unlocked, but she could see nothing in the black interior. Closing her eyes, she felt around with her hands, stumbling over what felt like beds along the walls. She wandered back to the porch, then noticed a lantern hanging beside the door and a tin box of matches nailed below it.

The match flared and she lit the lantern, then walked back into the small shack. It was obvious it was some kind of remote bunkhouse, though it seemed to be awfully close to Kerry Creek to be of much use. She found a couple more lanterns and, after lighting them, took the first one out onto the porch to serve as a sign that she was there.

Someone would come looking for her sooner or later. And if they didn't come tonight, she'd simply wait until the morning and then head toward the sunrise. Payton walked over to her horse and took off his saddle, dropping it onto the front steps of the shack.

She folded the saddle blanket and threw it on top. Then she carefully tethered the horse to a hitching rail in front of the cabin before stepping inside.

The interior of the cabin was cozy and almost as comfortable as the bunkhouse, though a bit dustier. From what she could tell, the place had been used recently. There was a stack of firewood next to the cast-iron stove and canned food in the small cupboard above the dry sink. She picked through the assortment and found a can of nuts.

A shelf of paperback novels, mostly mysteries, caught Payton's attention and she chose one and sat down at the small wooden table. Though it was hard to read in the flickering light, she managed to finish a few pages before her eyes grew tired. With a frustrated sigh, she laid her head down on the table and closed her eyes.

She wasn't sure whether she'd fallen asleep or not, but a loud crash brought her upright. She saw a shadow in the doorway and screamed. But a moment later, Brody stepped into the light.

He crossed the room in a few long strides, grabbed her arms and yanked her into his embrace. "What the hell were you thinking?" he muttered. "I got back to the station and they said you'd left on horseback."

"I was just going to ride out to meet you and then my horse came up lame. I thought he'd lead me back to the stable, but he came here."

"You're on Fraser land," Brody said. He pressed a kiss to the top of her head and then took a deep breath. "Do you know how dangerous it is out here? You can walk for a day and not see anything familiar."

"That's why I decided to stay here."

"The first smart move you made all day." He cupped her face in his hands and kissed her, his mouth harsh and demanding, as if he was exacting punishment for what she'd done.

But he didn't stop there. He tore off his jacket and tossed it aside, then began to work at the buttons of her shirt. When he wasn't removing her clothes, he was stripping out of his, and within a minute, they were both naked.

Payton wasn't sure what to say. She knew he was angry and maybe a bit shaken, but he seemed to need reassurance that she was safe. He buried his face in the curve of her neck, his hands skimming over her body as if to prove to himself she was unhurt.

Brody turned her around in his arms. Payton knew what was coming, but she wasn't prepared for the intensity of his need. "I don't have protection," he murmured.

"It's all right," Payton said, arching against him. She'd taken care of birth control a long time ago, choosing a method that was both constant and convenient. She wanted to experience him without any barriers, to feel just him inside her.

He buried himself deep in a single thrust, then held her, drawing a deep breath. She wriggled against him, silently pleading for him to move, but he held her still until he regained control.

He began slowly at first, with a delicious rhythm that she couldn't deny. Her mind whirled with a maelstrom of sensation and she felt herself losing touch with reality. Every stroke brought her closer to completion.

Payton moved with him, sending him even deeper. Every movement felt like perfection, as though their bodies were made to do just this. His fingers grasped her hips as she urged him on, so close to release that she was afraid they might both collapse onto the floor before they were through.

Brody moaned and she knew he was close. But then, suddenly he stopped. "Say it," he murmured. "Tell me you'll never leave me."

At first, she wasn't sure what he meant. Did he just want to hear the words, or was he demanding the promise behind them. In the end, Payton didn't really care. If he wanted her to stay, she would, for as long as this passion lasted. "I won't," she said. "I promise."

"Promise me," he said, his voice raw as he moved again.

"I promise."

Satisfied, he brought them both closer and closer. And then, in a blinding instant, Payton cried out and dissolved into powerful spasms of pleasure. He was there with her, his body shuddering with every stroke.

Brody sighed as he kissed her nape, his teeth grazing her skin. When he stumbled, Payton steadied them both, their bodies still joined. "I think we should sit down," she said.

"No," he murmured. "I want to stay just like this."

"All right," she said, reaching back to wrap her arm around his neck. She shifted and he groaned, slipping out of her.

Brody moved over to one of the bunks and gently lowered her onto the rough wool blanket. Then he stretched out beside her. Goose bumps prickled her skin and she pulled the edges of the blanket up around them both. "It's not as comfy as your bed," she said. "But it will do."

"We're trespassing. Considering the feud between the Frasers and the Quinns, we might end up shot, or in jail."

"It was worth it," she teased.

"No more adventures in the outback for you."

"I'll just take you with me." She closed her eyes and snuggled against him. At that moment, Payton couldn't imagine ever doing without this passion. Or without this man. What that meant, she wasn't sure. But it did mean something.

"TEAGUE?"

Brody awoke to the sound of a woman's voice. The door creaked and he pushed up on his elbow, squinting against the sunlight that shone through the door, Payton still sound asleep beside him. "Brody," he said.

He heard hurried footsteps on the front steps, then carefully rolled out of bed and tugged his jeans on. When he got outside, Brody found Hayley Fraser mounting her horse.

"Wait," he called, raking his hand through his tousled hair.

She paused, watching him warily from atop her horse. Brody hadn't seen Hayley in ages, not since she and Teague were teenagers. But he had seen photos of her in magazines and on television. Teague's ex-girlfriend had become one of Australia's most popular young actresses. She had a part on a television show that almost everyone in Oz watched every Thursday evening, and there were rumors that she was about to make a move to Hollywood.

"What are you doing here?" she asked, her wavy blond hair blowing in the morning breeze.

"We needed a place to sleep. This was close by. Was Teague supposed to meet you here?"

"No," she said, an edge of defensiveness in her voice. "Why would you think that?"

"It was almost as if you were expecting him," Brody said.

"I saw the Kerry Creek horses and I thought it

might be him. But I was mistaken. Sorry. I didn't mean to wake you."

She looked even more beautiful than she did on television. But instead of being dressed in some sexy outfit, with her hair fixed up, she wore jeans, a canvas jacket and a stockman's hat. "Should I tell Teague you were looking for him?"

"Why?" She shook her head. "No. You don't need to tell him anything."

Brody felt a hand on his arm and he turned to see Payton standing beside him, wrapped in the wool blanket. "Morning," she said, nodding to Hayley.

"Payton, this is Hayley Fraser," Brody said. "Her family owns this place. Hayley, Payton Harwell."

Payton smiled. "Thank you for letting us stay here. I got lost last night and wasn't really prepared to sleep outside."

Hayley nodded, her expression cool and guarded. She'd never really warmed to anyone else in the Quinn family or anyone connected with them. In truth, Brody's parents had discouraged a relationship to the point where they forbade Teague from seeing her. At the time, both Callum and Brody had sided with their parents. But Teague had never bothered to follow their advice. And he probably wouldn't now.

"I—I have to go," Hayley murmured. "Stay as long as you like. I won't say anything to my grandfather."

She wheeled her horse around and kicked it into a gallop, the dust creating a cloud behind her. Brody and Payton watched as she rode off. Brody glanced down at Payton, then slipped his arm around her shoulders. "That was odd," he said.

"She seemed nice."

Brody laughed. "What is it with you Americans?"

"Us Americans?" Payton looked around. "There's only one American here. Are you speaking of me?"

"Yes. Why do you always have such a positive attitude about everything? Everything is always…nice. Even if it isn't, you smile and pretend it is. Why don't you just say what you think? Hayley Fraser is a bitch."

"I don't even know her. Why would I think that?" Her brow creased into a frown and she shook her head. "And why are you such a grouch?"

"See, there you go. I *am* being a grouch." He turned and walked inside, grabbing his clothes scattered across the floor. "At least you said what you thought."

"My mother always told me if I couldn't say something nice, I shouldn't say anything at all. It's hard for me to forget those little lessons."

"People aren't always perfect," he said.

"I know that. I'm not naive. But I prefer to see the positive qualities rather than dwelling on the negative."

"Like the way you look at me?" Brody asked.

Payton sat down on the edge of the bunk and began to idly pick lint off the blanket, smoothing her hand over the rough wool every now and then. "You've been very nice—I mean, you've been generous and kind and understanding. You got me out of jail, you gave me a place to live and—"

"I sleep with you. I make you moan with pleasure, I touch your body like—"

"All right. You do have a nasty sarcastic streak that comes out when you haven't had enough sleep. You're not perfect. And neither am I. So can we leave it at that?"

Was that it? Brody's jaw twitched as he tried to control his temper. He'd been so happy to find her last night he hadn't even thought about what he'd learned from the Internet. She'd run away from her family and the man she was supposed to love and for some reason, she'd decided to hide out with him.

But sooner or later, she'd get sick of life on the station, just like his mother. She'd realize she'd made a mistake and she'd be gone, back to her comfortable life with her rich husband and his fancy job. So why hadn't she told him the truth about her past?

Maybe for the same reason he hadn't told her about his past—he wasn't proud of who he'd been, or of some of the things he'd done.

"Get dressed," he said. "We need to get back. Cal will be wondering where we are."

"If there's something you want to know, all you have to do is ask," she said.

"No." He shook his head.

"I'll tell you anything."

That was the problem. Did he really want to know all the details of her relationship with a man she loved enough to marry? Did he want her making comparisons between the two of them? He ought to be happy for the time they had together and just leave it at that. Brody certainly couldn't offer her the kind of life that Sam Whitman could.

"I'm fine," he said, forcing a smile. "You're right. I'm just cranky." He walked across the room and stood in front of her.

"Don't act like such a dickhead," she muttered, sending him a sulky look.

Brody laughed, taking a step back. "Well, there you go again. I see you're learning the lingo. You could tell me not to be such a drongo."

"That, too." She drew a deep breath. "What is that?"

"A dimwit," he said. "An idiot for not appreciating you. A fool for taking my bad mood out on you." He held out his hand and when she placed her fingers in his, he gently pulled her to her feet. "So, what are we going to do with our day today?"

"I have to work in the stables. I was gone all yesterday."

"I'll help you finish."

"I bought a swimsuit, so we could hang out in the hot tub. And I bought some new underwear. I might even model it for you."

"I'm feeling my mood getting much lighter," he said. "What color?"

"Is your mood?"

"No. What color is the underwear?"

"Black," she said.

He wrapped his hands around her waist drawing her body against his. "I like black underwear."

"Every man likes black underwear."

He bent down and brushed a kiss across her lips. "You know, we could stay here a little longer. At least we have some privacy."

A tiny smile curled the corners of her mouth. "For a little while," she suggested. "But only if we go back to bed."

With a low growl, he pushed her backward until they both tumbled onto the narrow bunk. "Maybe if I have a bit more sleep I won't be so cranky."

He felt her hand on the front of his jeans. "I know exactly how to make you feel better."

"Then I'll put myself in your capable hands—or hand."

6

THE MIDDAY SUN shone in a cloudless sky. Payton stood on the fence at the edge of the paddock and watched as Callum demonstrated the fine art of campdrafting. He'd declared a holiday from all work in honor of the queen's birthday—June 8. Brody had explained that it wasn't Queen Elizabeth's real birthday, but no one seemed to care about that small technicality. A holiday was a day off, something they all needed.

The stockmen had decided a barbecue was in order and had set up an afternoon of lighthearted competition between station employees followed by a sumptuous meal. They'd begun with a brief course on one of Australia's original sports, showing Gemma and Payton how campdrafting worked.

A calf was let out of a pen into the paddock and the rider carefully herded the calf around a series of obstacles, barrels and posts. Each rider was timed and the fastest to get the calf through the obstacle course would win a cherry pie that Mary had baked for the event.

Gemma and Payton watched from behind the fence, cheering on each stockman and wildly applauding their efforts against Brody and Callum. Though Payton had only known Gemma for a week, it was easy to like her.

She was witty and audacious, yet very levelheaded, someone Payton could turn to for advice. They'd taken to meeting up midafternoon for tea with Mary, the three of them enjoying freshly baked biscuits and a cuppa, as Gemma had called it.

To the surprise of everyone, Teague had turned up halfway through the competition with Hayley Fraser in tow. At first, she'd caused quite a stir among the men. Payton had informed Gemma that, according to Brody, Hayley was a popular television star in Australia and a huge celebrity. But the extra attention seemed to only make Hayley more uncomfortable and she chose to stand alone while she watched Teague compete with his brothers.

"She looks miserable," Payton said to Gemma. "I'm going to go talk to her."

"Callum certainly hasn't done much to make her feel welcome," Gemma commented. "Men can be so thickheaded."

Payton grabbed Gemma's arm. "Come on, let's go teach those boys a little bit about hospitality."

They walked over to Hayley and stood on either side of her, their arms braced on the top bar of the fence. "You know what I love about this," Gemma chirped in her charming Irish accent. "I love the chaps. A man wearing chaps just sets my imagination to working overtime."

"Why is that?" Payton asked, playing along.

"I just can't help but think about what those things would look like without the jeans underneath." She glanced over at Payton and pulled a silly face. Payton burst out laughing and Hayley couldn't help herself. A giggle erupted from her throat and she bit her bottom lip to stop herself.

"I was thinking exactly the same thing," Hayley said. "Why do I find those things so sexy?"

"It's the leather," Gemma said. "It's so…"

"Dangerous?" Payton asked.

"Smooth," Hayley said.

"Naughty," Gemma added. "I mean, I can understand how a man would enjoy lacy underwear on a woman. For me, a man in leather just gets me all tingly."

The trio stood and silently watched as Teague maneuvered a calf through the maze of posts and barrels, the rest of the stockmen shouting directions from across the paddock.

"Thanks," Hayley said.

Payton turned to face her. "For what?"

"For making it easier. I know how Brody and Callum feel about me and I don't think they were too chuffed to see me turn up here."

"Whatever is going on in their heads has nothing to do with us," Gemma assured her.

"Sistahs before mistahs," Payton said decisively. They both looked at her as if she'd suddenly begun speaking Armenian. "Sisters before misters. Girlfriends should come before boyfriends."

"Oh," Gemma said. "Yes. I completely agree."

"Do you ride?" Gemma asked Hayley.

"Like the wind," she said with a grin. "What about you?"

"No. If they did this on bicycles I might give it a go. But horses scare the bleedin' bloomers off me. And I don't care for the way they smell either." She sighed.

"Still, I wish I knew how to ride. Callum seems to be more comfortable on a horse than on his feet."

"I could teach you," Payton said.

"Me, too," Hayley offered.

Gemma smiled. "Callum offered, but I didn't want to look like a muppet in front of him, so I begged off. But as long as I'm here, I wouldn't mind trying."

"It's a date then," Hayley said. "Payton can bring you out to the shack. I'll organize a lunch and then we can ride back together."

The idea of making plans together seemed to solidify their new friendship and as they watched the boys, they chatted amiably.

"What do you think they're talking about?" Gemma asked, nodding in the direction of the three Quinn brothers. The men sat on their horses, staring across the paddock.

"Maybe they think we're plotting against them," Payton said.

Brody was the first to approach. He smiled as he drew his horse to a stop. "Ladies," he said, tipping his hat. "Are you having a lovely time?"

Payton smiled seductively. "Absolutely," she said.

"What are you doing over here all on your own?"

"Discussing our love of chaps," Gemma said. "With or without jeans. If I might be so bold, which do you prefer?"

Her question took him by surprise and he grinned. "That's between me and my horse." He turned to Payton. "Would you ladies like to give it a go? I'm sure the boys would love to see you jump into the competition. And there are prizes to be had for the winners."

"I'll try," Payton said.

"Me, too." Hayley crawled over the fence and started in Teague's direction.

"I'm afraid I'll have to sit this one out," Gemma said.

"Come on," Brody insisted. "Callum will ride with you. You can steer and he'll work the pedals."

Gemma grinned. "All right."

Payton helped her over the fence and they strode across the paddock, Brody riding beside them. When they got to the boys, Brody suggested that they all compete in pairs to make the game more equitable. The girls would hold the reins while the boys held the girls and used the stirrups.

As the eldest, Callum went first, settling Gemma on the saddle in front of him and wrapping his arm around her waist while his other hand gripped the saddle horn. Brody and Payton watched from a spot at the fence as Davey released a calf from the pen.

He stood behind her, his chin resting on her shoulder, his hand on her hip. "So what were you girls really talking about?" he asked, his voice soft against her ear.

"Sex," she said.

"Really?"

"That's all girls talk about when they're together. We were comparing the three of you."

"And how did I fare?" he asked.

"Oh, I spoke very highly of you," Payton teased.

His hand slowly moved forward on her hip until it was pressed flat on her lower abdomen, right above the waistband of her jeans. "Did you tell them how good I am at making you moan?" His fingertips drifted a bit lower.

"Stop," Payton said. "Everyone is watching."

"No one is watching," Brody countered.

She closed her eyes and moaned softly. How was it possible that he could set her nerves on fire with a simple touch? They were both fully dressed, standing amidst a group of people, and all she could think about was his hand dipping into her pants.

"How far will you go, Payton? Can I make you come just by talking to you?"

"Don't even try," she said.

"I'll wager I can. Dare me."

"Brody, I—" He shoved his hand a bit farther beneath her waistband and she sucked in a sharp breath. "All right. You probably could. But that doesn't mean I want you to. Not here."

"Where?" he murmured.

"Your room."

"Hey!" Brody called. "We're going to grab some more coldies. Who wants one?" He took the time to count the takers then turned to Payton. "Come on, you can give me a hand."

They started off toward the house without attracting any attention. When they reached the porch, Brody pressed his finger to his lips, then poked his head inside the door. Though the smell of fresh-baked bread drifted out, Mary was elsewhere. He took Payton's hand and dragged her through the kitchen, then up the stairs, taking them two at a time.

When they were both inside his room, Brody slammed the door behind them and began to unbutton her jeans. Payton fumbled with the belt holding his chaps, but let go when he bent over to pull off her shoes. Her jeans and panties followed and by the time he stood, he was completely aroused, his erection pressing against the faded denim.

Getting him undressed was too much effort and in the end, she unbuckled his belt and pulled his jeans down around his hips. He picked her up and carried her to the bed.

In one exquisite movement, he slid inside her, her body ready for him, so wet with desire. From the moment he moved, Payton felt herself dancing near the edge. This wasn't a slow, easy seduction but a desperate attempt to possess each other.

She clutched at his shoulders, her mouth pressed against his throat. "Oh," she cried. "Oh, yes."

"Tell me you want it," he said, his voice raw with passion.

"I do," Payton said, her own desperation growing.

She felt her orgasm building, fueled by the almost violent nature of their bodies arching against each other. Every thrust became magnificent torture, pushing her closer to the edge and then drawing her back again. Payton let her mind drift, focusing on the spot where they were joined.

And then, she was there, her release shattering reality. Wave after wave of pleasure coursed through her and she felt him surrender to his own orgasm. He kept moving inside her until he couldn't move anymore. Then Brody rolled onto his back, carrying her with him.

The entire encounter had only lasted a few minutes, but Payton had never experienced anything quite so powerful. She'd wanted him so much that her desire had overwhelmed all rational thought. He owned her body and he was quickly taking possession of her soul.

"We're bad," he whispered.

"I know," Payton said. "I think it was the chaps."

Brody laughed out loud, wrapping his arm around her neck and rolling her onto her side. He faced her, his hand lazily trailing through her hair. "So all I have to do to get you into bed is wear leather?"

"I think you already know the answer to that question."

"Tell me anyway."

"You just have to touch me," Payton said softly. "That's all it takes."

He smiled boyishly, then stole another kiss. "I'll remember that." Pausing, he ran his finger along her jaw and met her gaze. "There is one thing. We haven't been using protection, and at the shack you said—"

"It's all right. There won't be any surprises."

"Good," he said. "I mean, not that surprises are always bad, but I'm not sure we're ready for that."

Sam had been obsessed about birth control, insisting that Payton find a method that would protect them both without fail. They'd been engaged and they'd always planned to have children, so Payton wondered why he'd been so adamant. Sam had acted as if an unplanned pregnancy would've been a disaster. Why hadn't she ever questioned him making such a decision about her body?

"Payton?"

She blinked, startled from her thoughts. What had brought Sam to mind? She hadn't thought of him in…days.

Brody was staring at her, a frown on his face. "What's wrong?"

Payton shook her head. "Nothing. We should probably get back outside. The boys will want their beers."

Brody levered to his feet, then held out his hand. He patiently helped her dress, patting her backside once she was completely clothed again. But as he turned for the door, Payton noticed a purple mark on his neck.

"Oh, no," she said, reaching up for his chin and tipping his head up. "Did I do that?"

"What?"

She laughed. "I think I gave you a hickey."

"What's that?" Brody asked.

She pulled him over to the mirror above his dresser and pointed to the spot on his neck.

"A love bite," he said, examining it closely. "I haven't had one of those since I was a teenager."

"Sorry."

He shrugged. "I like it. I like knowing I can make you do such things to me."

She stared at his reflection in the mirror and smiled. "I think we're both in trouble," she said.

He nodded. "I think you might be right."

"Brody!"

They both turned to see a horse approaching at a fast gallop. Davey pulled the horse to a stop, nearly running into Brody. "What the hell are you about?" Brody shouted.

"Callum," he said, gasping for breath.

"What's wrong? Is he all right?"

"Yeah. Yeah, he's fine. He needs you back at the house. Right now. He said just you, not Payton. Just you. He made that very clear."

Brody frowned. "Well, I'm not going to leave Payton out here on her own," he said.

"No, I'm to help her out," Davey said. "Go ahead. I'll carry on."

Brody regarded the young kid suspiciously. Why was it so important for Payton to stay behind? What the hell was Callum up to? He maneuvered his horse next to Payton's, then reached out and placed his hand on her cheek. "I'll be back in a bit." Brody leaned over and dropped a kiss on her lips. "Don't let Davey boss you around."

She smiled. "I won't. I'll see you later."

Brody kicked his horse into a gallop and headed toward the house. This had damn well better be an emergency. The ride back to the homestead was almost fifteen minutes. As he rode, Brody's thoughts rewound over the past few days. He and Payton had settled into a life of sorts.

She'd managed to charm Davey into working the stables for the day while she worked the station with Brody. They enjoyed the long ride together and Payton had been fascinated with discovering new plants and animals in the outback. She'd nearly fallen off her horse when she'd spotted her first kangaroo.

He liked having her with him, and Callum hadn't seemed to mind that they'd paired up. After greasing two of the windmills, they'd eaten some lunch, then set off to ride the fence lines. Payton had quickly learned how to handle herself on a stock pony, eagerly taking tips from Brody when he offered.

Still, her fascination with station life worried him. Was she happy here or was she just avoiding her real life with Sam Whitman? He needed answers, yet he couldn't bring himself to ask the question. Was she married? And if she was, did it make a difference anymore? He wasn't sure that it did for him. Not now.

Brody had been considering his options, specifically another surgery on his knee. He was still covered under the team's insurance and he really didn't have anything to lose, except a month or two off his feet and at least a year spent in rehab. He cursed softly. The more time he spent with Payton, the more confused he became about his future.

He'd always trusted his gut instinct when it came to any decision, and his gut had never steered him wrong—until the accident. The rain had made the roads slick and he'd already been late for practice, caught up in an argument with Nessa. He hadn't been paying attention and had taken a turn far too fast. As he went down, his only thought had been that he ought to have trusted his gut and taken the Land Rover to work.

Right now, every instinct told him that Payton belonged in his life, that he should to do everything in his power to keep her there. So why couldn't he just say that to her? Why couldn't he tell her how he felt? Brody had never doubted himself until now. Maybe his feelings weren't as strong as they seemed. Or maybe, this was something more than just infatuation.

As he rode past the horse paddock and into the yard, he saw Callum standing on the back porch, pacing nervously. He waited for Brody to come to a stop before jogging down the steps. Brody hopped off, gathering the reins in his hand.

"Come on," Callum murmured.

"What's up?"

"Teague is in the house. There's a private investigator here looking for Payton."

"Shit," Brody muttered. "How did he find her?"

"You know about him?"

"Yeah, he was in Bilbarra trying to track her down. I talked to him. I thought I sent him off to Sydney to look for her."

"Well, he's a little bit smarter than you reckoned," Callum said. "Payton used her credit card at David Jones in Brisbane. And Teague bought something right after her with his card. The clerk mentioned that they were together, so that's why he's here. Teague is feeding him some story, but I'm not sure if he's swallowing it."

Brody frowned. Payton had spent time in jail for dining and dashing. Why had she suddenly chosen to use a credit card? Had she wanted to be found? Was she looking for an excuse to leave? Or was she unaware that a detective had been sent to find her? "We have to get her out of here," Brody muttered.

"What the hell has she done?" Callum asked.

"I don't know." Brody cursed softly. "She was supposed to get married in April. She ran out on her wedding. And I'd assume her fiancé or her husband wants her back, since he sent someone to fetch her. Bit of a problem there since I don't want to give her back."

"Brody, she's an adult. She should make these decisions for herself. If she wants to stay, she can just tell the guy to get lost."

"And what if she doesn't?" Brody asks. "What if she decides to leave with him?"

"Then that's her choice. You can't keep her here if she doesn't want to stay."

"She may want to stay," Brody countered. "Only she isn't ready to admit it yet. She might need more time."

"Did you ever think about asking her straight out?"

"I'm not going to ask her unless I'm sure she'll give me the right answer."

"Bloody hell, Brody, just talk to the girl."

"I will," Brody promised. "Soon. But right now, I have to get her off the station. I'll go back and get her and we'll ride to the airstrip. I need you to go to the bunkhouse and gather up her things and put them in your ute. Teague can meet us out there."

"Are you sure you want to do this?" Callum asked.

The backdoor squeaked and Teague stepped outside. The moment he saw Brody, he grabbed him by the arm and pulled him around the side of the house. "What the hell is going—"

"Don't ask," Brody said. "I'll explain it all later. Can you get away or is this guy going to follow you wherever you go?"

"I think I can lose him. Why?"

"I need you to fly Payton and me to Brisbane. I'm going to go and get her and we'll meet you at the airstrip. Callum is going to put her things in his ute. Whenever you can, get away and meet us there."

"All right," Teague said, nodding. "I better get back in there. He thinks I'm making coffee."

Brody jumped on his horse and turned it away from the house. "We'll be at the airstrip in a half hour," he said. "Don't let him follow you."

The ride in had taken twice as long as the ride back. He rode as hard and as fast as he'd ever ridden, as if his life depended upon it. In the end, his life did depend upon Payton. He'd grown attached to her and he couldn't imagine losing her, especially to another man.

He found them where he'd left them, working on a broken gate that led to the east horse pasture. Davey was holding the gate off the ground while Payton twisted the turnbuckle. They both stopped what they were doing and watched as he approached.

"Get on your horse," he told Payton. "Come on, we have to go."

"What's wrong?" she asked.

"I'll tell you after we get to the airstrip."

"Why are we going to the airstrip?"

"Payton, don't ask any questions. Just get on your horse and let's ride."

She studied him for a long moment, then handed Davey the spanner she was holding. Snagging her jacket from where she'd thrown it over the gate, she kept her gaze fixed on him. Then, in an easy motion, she put her foot in the stirrup and swung her leg over the saddle.

Brody didn't take the time to explain any further. He simply wheeled his mount around and took off, hoping she'd follow. A few seconds later, she caught up to him and they rode through the scrub, a cloud of dust forming behind them.

Their horses were winded by the time they reached the airstrip. Brody dismounted and then helped Payton do the same. He slapped both horses on the rump and sent them running, knowing they'd find their way back to the stables on their own.

"Are you going to explain what we're doing here?" Payton asked.

"First, you have to tell me something. And I want you to be completely honest, because I'll be able to tell if you're lying to me."

"All right," she said softly.

Brody grabbed her by the arms and pulled her toward him, his mouth coming down on hers. He softened the kiss immediately, hoping that it would serve as a last attempt to prove his feelings for her. Then he drew back and took a deep breath. "Are you married? Did you go through with your wedding or did you walk out before you said 'I do'?"

Her mouth dropped open and she stared at him in utter shock. "How do you know about—"

"Just answer the question. Are you married?"

"I…" She paused, as if she wasn't sure how to answer him. "No. Of course not. If I were married, I'd be with my husband. I certainly wouldn't be sleeping with you. How did you know about my wedding?"

"We have the Internet here, too."

She took a moment, then shook her head. "You Googled me?"

"Yes. And a private investigator tracked you here," he replied. "You used your credit card in Brisbane and he figured out where you were."

She groaned, closing her eyes and shaking her head. "I knew I shouldn't have used the card. I didn't use it earlier for food. But I thought since I was flying right back to the station, it wouldn't make a difference. They wouldn't be able to find me even if they were watching the card."

"Turns out Teague bought something at the same time and he used his card. They figured out you two were together." He rubbed her forearms. "I think you should tell me what's going on, Payton. Tell me about Sam Whitman."

She sucked in a sharp breath and looked at him, her eyes wide. "You know about— But, how—"

"It doesn't matter. Just tell me what happened."

She drew a deep breath. "I ran out on the wedding before we got to the vows." She took his hand. "I should have told you. But I wanted to leave that part of my life behind."

"Why did you run?"

She shrugged. "I'm not sure. I just had this feeling that I was making a huge mistake. I honestly can't say what it was. I'm not an impetuous person, but I had this—" She put her hand on her stomach.

"Gut feeling?"

"Yes," she said, as if his explanation suddenly made perfect sense of her actions.

"So what does your gut tell you to do now?" Brody asked. "We can ride back to the house and you can talk to this guy. Or we can leave. Teague will fly us to Brisbane and from there we'll catch a flight to Perth."

"Perth?"

"I have an apartment in Fremantle, just across the river. We can hang out until the investigator leaves."

She considered the offer for a long moment. "And then what?" she asked. "I can't avoid my family forever."

"Then we'll go back to the station right now and you can call them."

He waited as she weighed her options, hoping and praying that she'd choose to leave with him. He knew he'd have to let her go sooner or later, but he wasn't ready. He'd take another day, another week, as much time as he could get.

"I don't know what I want," she said.

He'd asked her if she was married and he'd gotten the right answer. But the second question had gone unasked. Was she still in love with her fiancé? The words were on the tip of his tongue, but he was afraid of what she might say. Right now, he'd rather not know.

He reached up and cupped her face in his hands. "Come with me to Fremantle," he said. Leaning forward, he kissed her again, softly, a silent plea.

"All right," she said. "For a little while. We'll go to Fremantle."

Brody released a tightly held breath and yanked her into his arms. He had a few more days, a week even. And this time, he wasn't going to waste it. He'd savor every second he spent with her. They'd walk on the beach and make love all night and sleep until noon and then do it all over again the next day. And, maybe, she'd decide she never wanted to leave at all.

BY THE TIME they landed at the airport in Perth, Payton had filled in the details of her story, from her parents' high expectations, to her belief that Sam was the man she was supposed to marry. And then she told him about her sudden decision to break free from the path that had been laid out for her. Until that moment, she'd simply deferred to her parents and her fiancé.

It felt good to pick apart her life, to examine her motives and try to make sense of them. And it almost gave her enough courage to call her parents and apologize for everything that she'd put them through. But after a half day's work on the station and two separate plane trips, she was exhausted. The thought of making that phone call twisted her stomach into knots.

"I know what you're thinking." She sighed, avoiding his gaze as they walked from the plane.

He held her hand, his fingers laced through hers. "No, you don't," Brody said.

"You think I'm…naive. Spineless. And maybe I am—or was. But I'm not that way anymore."

He pulled her to a stop, forcing her to face him. "Are you under the impression that this has changed the way I feel about you?" Brody asked.

"It hasn't?"

He shook his head. "No. Not at all."

They took a cab from the airport to Brody's apartment. Payton was curious about what she'd find on the other side of the front door. The building was luxurious, with its richly appointed lobby and thickly carpeted hallways. Brody hadn't told her much about his life off the station. What she knew had come from Teague—a career in football, the accident that had ruined his knee and a retreat back to the station.

He reached for the front door, then paused. "I don't remember what it looks like inside," he said, forcing a smile. "It's been a while since I've been home and I had to let my cleaning lady go." He shoved the key into the lock. "Maybe I should just check it out."

"It's all right," Payton said. "I've been working in a stable. Unless you have a dozen horses in there, nothing is going to freak me out."

Brody chuckled. "All right." The door swung open

and he stepped aside to let her enter first. She walked inside slowly, taking in the details of the interior.

It was a beautiful apartment, sleek and modern. A wall of windows overlooked the water and filled the apartment with light. It was furnished sparsely yet fashionably.

Payton wandered over to the windows and took in the view of a wide river and the city on the other side. "It's wonderful," she said. "So different from the station."

"One of the guys on the team gave me the name of his decorator. I didn't pick this stuff out myself. I would have been content with a couch and telly and a bed."

She stared up at a painting hanging on the wall above the sofa. "Very nice. So, is this what football buys?"

Brody smiled. "That's what football bought. Footy doesn't buy anything anymore."

"It's difficult to imagine you doing that. Dressed in all that gear."

"Aussie rules is not like American football," he said. "We don't wear anything but a shirt, shorts and shoes. It's more like rugby than what you think of as football." He paused. "So you know how I found out about your wedding. How did you find out about my busted career?"

"Your brother Teague. He said you were good, but that your motorcycle accident ended your career."

Brody nodded. "I was. I was the top scorer on our team. But that doesn't really matter anymore. Now some other bloke is the top scorer on the team. And I'm just a guy who spends his time working a cattle station in Queensland."

"There's nothing wrong with that," she said.

"It's not the same as being famous."

Payton ran her hands through her hair. "I'm still dirty from work. Can I take a shower?"

Brody took her bag off his shoulder. "The bathroom is through the bedroom," he said, pointing to a door in the far wall. "I'll show you."

She followed him into the bedroom and he set her bag on the bed, then turned and helped her out of her jacket. He smoothed his hands over her shoulders and nuzzled his nose in her hair. "It's nice to have you here," he said. "All to myself."

Payton leaned back against his chest and drew his arms around her. "It is funny how things work out. We've both lived such different lives, and then they touched for a moment in that jail cell. If you hadn't drunk so much beer or I'd paid for my meal, we would never have met. Gemma thinks it was fate."

"Maybe it was."

Payton turned in his arms and then pushed up on her toes and kissed him. She slipped her arms around his neck and drew him more deeply into the kiss, loving the way he tasted, the way his mouth fit so perfectly with hers. Just a simple kiss was all it took to ignite her desire.

She reached up and tugged his jacket down over his arms, then moved to work on the buttons of his shirt. They'd undressed each other so many times that it had become second nature to them. There was no longer any hesitation or embarrassment. They felt more comfortable out of their clothes than in them.

When they were both naked, he took her hand and led her into the bathroom. The shower was surrounded by glass block from floor to ceiling. He opened a door and stepped inside, turning the water on and then helping her inside when it was the proper temperature.

It was a shower made for a man who came home with bruises and sore muscles: a variety of shower-heads angled in all different directions. The door kept the steam inside and before long, the moisture created a fog around them both.

His hands smoothed over her body and she closed her eyes and enjoyed his caress. He turned her around and pulled her against him, his growing erection pressing against her backside. His palms slowly ran the length of her torso, from her breasts to her belly and then to the juncture of her thighs.

He delved between the soft folds of her sex and when he found the spot, began to touch her in a way he knew so well. Payton arched back, wrapping her arm around his neck and pulling him into another kiss.

But he wasn't content to just touch her. His mouth moved over her shoulder, his tongue tracing a path to the curve of her neck. Brody gently urged her to sit on the low bench at the center of the shower. And then he knelt in front of her, spreading her legs and continuing the seduction with his tongue.

Payton had always felt this was the most intimate ex-pression of desire and until now, they'd both been sat-isfied with other things. But Payton let go of the last shred of inhibition, surrendering to Brody, the shudders rocking her body. And as she surrendered to him, she realized that this was no longer just physical. She'd grown to need him in so many other ways.

She felt tears press at the corners of her eyes, but when he met her gaze she forced a smile. How could she ever consider living without him? He'd become part of her life, the new life that she'd found in Australia.

But was she really ready to walk away from her past, from her family and everything she'd known, to stay here with him? Payton reached up and brushed his wet hair from his eyes. She didn't need to tell him how she felt. It was understood between them, communicated by smiles and sighs and soft kisses in the dark.

Brody drew her slowly to her feet and then led her out of the shower. Her release only made her exhaustion more acute and when he wrapped her in a thick cotton towel, Payton closed her eyes and leaned against him for support.

They ended up on the bed, Brody stretched out beside her, his fingers gently stroking her cheek. "Tell me about him," he said softly. "Why did you love him?"

"That's a question," she said. "I'm not sure I have an answer."

"Try," he said. "Please?"

"I thought he was right for me. And I knew my parents would love him. I always tried to do what I thought they wanted me to. I was a very good girl."

"But there must have been something about this guy," Brody said.

"We were together so long, I guess I forgot what it was that attracted me in the first place. He was supposed to be perfect for me."

Brody was silent for a long moment, then drew a deep breath. "Do you still love him?"

"I'm not sure I ever did," Payton said. "At least not the way a woman should love the man she marries."

He seemed to take comfort in that answer. But did it make a difference? She was here, with him, running away from all her problems. She hadn't thought about how this might end between them. It was so simple to believe they would just continue, without any difficulties. They were living off the high of their infatuation. Real life hadn't intruded yet. But it would soon enough.

7

"PADDLE, PADDLE, PADDLE!" Brody shouted. He gave the surfboard a final shove, sending Payton off into the set of small waves on Cottesloe Beach. They'd practiced on the beach first and then he'd caught a few waves with her in front of him on his board. But she was determined to do it on her own.

"Pop up!" he called.

To Brody's surprise, she nimbly got to her feet. Steadying herself, she slowly straightened, her arms out to the side. Brody shouted as she rode the wave. There wasn't much that Payton couldn't do once she set her mind to something.

She stayed on her feet all the way to the shore, hopping off the board just before she hit the beach. She looked at him, waving and jumping up and down in excitement. Then she turned the board around and paddled back out to him.

The weather was perfect for a winter day in June. The sun was shining but the water was a bit chilly, so they both wore wet suits. Brody had made a gift of the surfboard and wet suit, hoping that they'd be staying in Fremantle long enough to enjoy them.

Life was certainly simpler here than it had been at

the station. Their days and nights belonged entirely to them. They strolled the streets, stopping to eat or browse through a shop when they wanted. They went to the movies and a concert in the park and rented bicycles to tour old Fremantle.

Brody had planned a trip to Rottnest Island for the next week, booking a room in the old hotel in case they wanted to spend a few hours alone together during the day. Though he knew she might decide to leave at any time, he wanted to believe she'd still be with him in a week.

They kept themselves busy during the day, but it was the nights that Brody found most satisfying. Blessed with absolute privacy, they had the time to explore the limits of their passion. Sex ranged from a silly romp, to a frantic drive for release, to a slow, methodical seduction—and all in one day.

"Did you see me?"

"I did," Brody said as she paddled up to him. "You were great."

"I was! It was so much fun. I want to try a bigger wave."

"All right, hang on. I'll just put in your order." He looked up at the sky. "Can we have some bigger waves, please?"

She splashed water in his face. "I meant, we should go to another beach with bigger waves."

He splashed her back, then reached out and grabbed her, both of them tumbling off their surfboards. Treading water, Brody pulled her into his arms and kissed her, his mouth searching for hers through the saltwater that dripped from her hair.

There was nothing more satisfying, he mused as he teased at her tongue. The fact that he could kiss and touch her whenever he chose to was something he had come to appreciate. In truth, he couldn't imagine doing without it.

He drew back and looked down into her eyes. Droplets of water clung to her lashes. "We'll find some bigger waves tomorrow," he said. He helped her back onto her board, then straddled his. "We need to get you in to shore and put some sunscreen on your face. You're starting to burn."

"Let me try one more wave. Then we can go."

"Only if you kiss me again," he said.

She leaned into him, her feet dangling off the sides of her board, and placed a quick kiss on his lips.

He frowned. "You can do better."

With a dramatic sigh, she leaned in again and this time, treated him to a full-on tongue kiss, her mouth warm against his. She knew exactly how he liked to be kissed and she used that knowledge to her advantage. When she drew back, she arched her eyebrow.

"All right," he agreed. "One more wave. I'm not going to give you a push this time. I'm just going to tell you when to go."

She lined her board up, watching over her shoulder as the next set rolled in. "Tell me when," she said.

"Go," he said. "Paddle hard. Paddle!"

This time, she got up right away. But she was so excited that she threw her arms over her head and disrupted her balance. She wobbled and then tumbled off the board into the water. Brody waited for her to come up and when she didn't, he paddled over to her board, cutting through the water in strong, even strokes.

By the time he reached her, she was up and

coughing water, clinging to the edge of the board. "Are you all right?"

She nodded. "Water up my nose." She coughed again. "That was bad."

"You shouldn't have put your hands up," he said. "You were doing so well." He held her board as she climbed back on. When they reached the shore, he helped her tuck her board under her arm before walking onto the beach.

"It's getting late," he said. "We should get some lunch." He jammed the surfboards into the sand, then peeled his wet suit down around his waist.

Payton took a deep breath and turned her face up to the sun. "I love it here. It's just like California. Only no earthquakes."

"I wish it was spring," he said. "We could go bush-walking and see the wildflowers. Western Australia is known for that. Miles and miles of flowers."

"Maybe we can," she said.

Brody knew it was just an offhand reply, that her words contained no promises. They hadn't made any plans or given any pledges to each other, beyond the promise of unbridled passion in the bedroom. He didn't want to think about that now. Instead, he was determined to show her exactly how much fun life was with him here in Oz.

"What do you want to do with the rest of the day?"

"I want to enjoy the good weather." She glanced over at him. "I noticed there's a football game this weekend. Could we go?"

"Why would you want to do that?"

"I'm just curious to see what you used to do for a living."

"I don't know," he said, shaking his head. "I haven't been to a game since I got dropped from the club."

"It's all right," she said. "If you don't want to, we don't have to."

He thought about her request for a few seconds. Denying her anything was impossible. And what did he have to lose? It might be fun to explain the game to her. There was nothing quite like Aussie football. "All right. I'm going to call and see if I can get us some decent seats."

She grinned. "Good."

"Any other requests?"

"I heard there was a nude beach around here."

"Yes," he said. "Swanbourne Beach."

"I've never been to a nude beach. I think I should try it at least once. I was really good at skinny-dipping, so I think I'd do well at the nude beach."

"You do realize you'd have to take off your clothes and go naked in front of strangers, don't you?"

"Yes. That's the point. I've never done that. I'm trying new things. Trusting my instincts. And it might feel good, liberating, don't you think?" She reached out and ran a finger down his chest. "It'll be fun."

"No," Brody said emphatically. "I'm not taking you to Swanbourne. You can go on your own if you like, but I'm not going."

"Prude," she teased. "You have a very nice body. And you're well endowed. There's nothing to be ashamed of."

"That's not it. You know exactly what happens to me when you get naked. And I'm not going to walk around the beach with a throb in my knob."

"I'd find that visual very entertaining," she said. She glanced down and fixed her gaze on his crotch.

"Stop," he said.

"What? I'm not doing anything."

"Stop it. You're going to get me all worked up."

"I'm not doing anything," she repeated in a voice filled with mock innocence.

"There's no extra room in this wet suit," he said. "So just knock it off."

She looked up at him and gave him a devilish smile. "I have such amazing powers," she said. "I surprise even myself."

He pulled her against him, wrapping his arm around her neck in a playful headlock. "Why don't we go home and you can give me a demonstration of your powers."

"I'd be happy to," she said. "I think it's important that I share my powers with as many people as I can."

"Now you've gone too far," he said, kissing the top of her head. "There will be no sharing."

They gathered their things and walked back to the car, Payton's hand tucked in his. It had been another perfect day, he mused as they strapped their boards on the BMW's roof rack. Brody couldn't imagine life getting any better than this.

PAYTON CLUTCHED the program in her hands as they walked through the crowds of fans to their seats. Brody's appearance seemed to cause quite a stir among those in attendance and he was stopped again and again with requests for autographs and photos. Payton waited patiently, watching as he handled each request with surprising grace and enthusiasm, giving special attention to the younger fans.

She hadn't realized how famous he was and she

found herself regretting her request to come. It couldn't be easy to answer all the questions about his injury, about the chances of him playing again, about the plays that everyone remembered him making.

When he finally pulled himself away from the fans, she held on to his arm and gave it a squeeze. "I'm sorry," she said.

"For what?"

"For asking you to come here. I didn't realize how difficult it might be for you. It was selfish of me."

"No," he said. "Actually, I'm doing all right. I thought it would be a bit dodgy, but it's not that bad."

They found their seats and settled in. Payton took a good look around, then turned to him. "All right, give me the scoop."

"You want ice cream?" he asked.

"No, the scoop. The skinny. The 4-1-1. Tell me what I need to know."

"Oh, all right. Well, this is the Subiaco Oval. And that's the team, my former team, out there warming up."

"The field is round," Payton said.

"Oval."

"I like the outfits," she added, observing the players on the field. "Not as hot as chaps, but pretty sexy. Nice short shorts. And sleeveless jerseys to show off the muscles." In truth, she could imagine Brody running around in that uniform. "Maybe you could take out your old outfit when we get home and we could play footballer and the surfer girl."

Brody laughed, glancing around to see if anyone had heard. "Better yet, I'll buy you a guernsey, you wear it and nothing else, and I'll show you some of my moves."

"A guernsey. Is that like a jumper or a cardie?"

"Jumper," he said. "Cardie has buttons down the front."

"And what is the team called?" she asked.

"Their official name is the Fremantle Football Club, but everyone calls them the Dockers. See, they have an anchor on their jumpers."

She nodded. "So, what's the deal? How do they get points?"

She listened as he explained the rules. Eighteen players on a side. The aim was to kick the ball through the poles on each end of the field. They could throw, kick and pass the ball to move it downfield, but they weren't supposed to hold on to it. When they kicked the ball through the center pair of four posts the team scored six points. But Payton became hopelessly confused when Brody tried to explain something called a "behind."

The game began and the crowd immediately grew noisy. She'd never been to an American football game, but she couldn't imagine more of a party atmosphere than she was experiencing now. There was music and cheering and dancing in the stands, along with a lot of beer. And incredibly dangerous activity on the field.

The players wore no padding or helmets, yet they seemed to slam into each other on a regular basis. Men were thrown to the ground and bloodied by flying elbows and knees. Payton was grateful that Brody was sitting safely next to her. She couldn't imagine watching him and not worrying herself sick.

Brody cheered the team, shouting out his displeasure at good plays by the opposition. As the game went on, he continued to explain the intricacies of the plays and by the time it ended, Payton actually could follow each play as it developed on the field.

The Dockers lost, but Brody didn't appear to be too upset by the result. In truth, he seemed to be quite happy that they'd come. Payton wrapped her arm around his waist as they walked out of the stadium.

"Brody Quinn!"

They stopped and Brody turned, then smiled as an older gentleman approached them dressed in a polo shirt with the Fremantle team logo stitched on the chest.

"Simon. How are you?"

"I'm well. You look grand. Healthy. Keeping fit, I see."

"Trying," Brody said, rubbing his abdomen. He turned to Payton. "Simon, this is Payton Harwell. Payton, this is the team doctor, Simon Purvis. He helped me through my rehab."

Simon held out his hand and Payton took it. "Pleasure," he said. "Did you enjoy the game?"

"I did," Payton said. "It's a little rougher than I expected, but it was fun to watch."

"We're a tough lot here in Oz." Simon grinned. "So, you're from America. I recognize the accent."

"I am," Payton said.

"Where do you call home?"

"Connecticut. Though I live in Manhattan. New York City?"

"Ah. New York Giants. New York Jets. Interesting. Almost bizarre, that."

"What?" Brody asked.

"I just met a scout for the Americans. For their NFL. He's come looking for kickers. I wasn't about to send any of our guys to see him. But you might want to give him a tingle, Brody."

"No," Brody said. "I'm in no condition to play."

"There's the thing," Simon said. "It's a different game. At least for kickers and punters. All you have to do is kick. They put the ball down and you kick it through the posts. Or you drop-kick it. They call that punting. Once or twice, they might knock you down, but if they touch you while you're kicking, it's a penalty. Brody, you've got a way with that foot of yours. It would be a shame to see it go to waste."

Payton turned to Brody, trying to read his expression. But she could see nothing that indicated how he felt. She expected him to be happy, or at least curious about the possibility. "I don't know. I was going to look into that surgery you told me about, but I'm not sure I—"

"You might not need the surgery," Simon said. "You don't have to carry the ball. There's no cutting or quick direction shifts. You might have to tackle, but that's really not your job." He paused. "I can ring him up, if you like. I'm sure he'd be interested in seeing you."

"I'll think about it," Brody said.

"Don't think too long," Simon warned. "He's only going to be here for a few weeks and then he's back to the States."

Brody shook Simon's hand, and as they walked back to the car, he was strangely silent. Payton wasn't sure whether he wanted her opinion on the matter, and decided to wait for him to speak first. But when he didn't, she decided to start the conversation. "That was interesting," she said. "But what is a tingle? And why do you have to give this guy one?"

"A phone call," he explained. "You know, there have been a couple of Aussies that have gone over to play in America. One was a kicker. He did pretty well."

"Do you want to play again?"

"Sure. But Aussie football is what I do."

"Have you ever seen an American game?"

"The Super Bowl once or twice. I never really paid much attention." He shook his head. "It's a crazy idea. They're not going to want anything to do with me once they see my knee."

"Maybe you could wear long pants. And show them how you can kick first, before you tell them about your injury."

Brody chuckled. "That might work. But the first thing they're going to ask is whether I've been seriously injured."

"It wouldn't hurt to talk to the guy," Payton said.

Brody opened the door of the car for her and helped her inside. "I'll think about it."

As they made their way out of the parking lot, Brody was lost in his thoughts. He held her hand, his fingers woven through hers, and every now and then, he brought her hand up to his lips and kissed it, as if to remind himself she was still there.

Payton drew a deep breath and then relaxed back into the seat. She wasn't quite sure how she felt about the possibility of him moving to the States. Here in Australia, she was the visitor. If things didn't work out, she could always leave. But having Brody in the U.S. seemed like such a serious shift in their relationship.

It was silly to worry over it now, though. When she

had to make a choice, she'd make a choice. And until then, she intended to enjoy her time with Brody.

BRODY STARED at the ceiling above the bed in the early-morning light. Sleep hadn't come easily for him, though he and Payton had exhausted themselves making love before she'd curled up in his arms and drifted off.

Instead, his head was filled with thoughts about the day's revelations. His life had taken so many sharp turns lately, he shouldn't be surprised at this one. Playing in America would give him a chance to get his life set up again. He'd be working, making a decent salary. He could save his money, instead of blowing it on expensive toys and exotic vacations. He'd have something to offer Payton then. But the chances of getting a job in the U.S. were slim, especially considering his injury.

Brody rolled over onto his side and stared at her. Her hand was curled next to her face, her hair tumbled over her shoulder. He still thought she was the most beautiful woman he'd ever met. There were moments when he believed he'd never be able to do without her, that waking up with her by his side and falling asleep with her in his arms was the only thing that mattered.

He reached out and smoothed his hand over her hip, her skin like silk beneath his fingertips. How was it that she suited him so perfectly? Whether they were living on the station or here in Fremantle, their lives seemed to mesh flawlessly.

He'd had his share of high-maintenance women—girls like Vanessa, who'd demanded far too much and offered far too little. They'd been extras in his life, like fast cars and expensive electronics, something to acquire and then grow bored with over time.

But he'd never felt as if he'd acquired Payton. She'd appeared in his life one day and decided to stay. He was well aware that she might choose to leave at any time. He wasn't in control of this relationship, she was. And maybe that's what kept the boredom at bay.

He was almost afraid to believe they might make it work. He'd always assumed he'd find the right woman, but he'd imagined it would happen at a distant point in the future, not now. She was the right woman. Brody was fairly certain of that.

So what was required to keep her? He needed a way to support them both, to give her a comfortable lifestyle. Without a job, he could give her four or five years. With a job, maybe a lifetime. And he needed to make sure her fiancé was out of her life for good. He ought to encourage her to contact her parents and smooth out the problems there. And then he needed to plead his case to her family.

Hell, they'd probably be suspicious of him from the start. He didn't come from some blueblood line with money coming out of his arse. He was a working-class bloke without a proper education. But he had one thing going for him—there wasn't another man in the world who loved Payton more than he did.

He drew a deep breath. He loved her. It was that simple. Brody gasped, stunned by the revelation. *Love* was the only way to describe how he felt.

But how did she feel? Payton had been silent on that issue. She seemed content to just go along as they were—lovers, friends, companions. She lived in the present, avoiding any discussion of what was to come.

Why was that? Brody wondered. Was it because she thought their relationship had no future? Or was it because she didn't want to face returning to her fiancé and family? If she truly loved him, she would have given him some hint by now. Every other woman he'd known was ready to profess love after the second date.

Maybe he just didn't measure up. Maybe she was biding her time until some other man caught her eye. Brody rolled over on his back and pressed his palm to his chest, aware of the ache in his heart. He'd never loved a woman before, so he'd never risked getting hurt. For the first time in his life, he was afraid. What if she didn't want him? Would he ever be able to forget her and move on?

He sat up and swung his legs over the edge of the bed, and pushed himself to his feet. Raking his hands through his hair, he wandered over to the windows and stared out at the river and the lights twinkling from the opposite side.

If he was going to make this work, he needed a plan. Hell, Callum was the planner in the family. Maybe he ought to go to his older brother for advice. Worst-case scenario, he could always work the station. They'd have a home and Payton seemed to enjoy living there. Best case, he'd find a job that allowed them to live wherever they wanted, on the station, in Fremantle, in Manhattan, if they chose.

Sighing softly, Brody walked out of the bedroom and into the kitchen. He grabbed a jug of orange juice and unscrewed the top, then took a long drink. Suddenly, he was wide awake, his mind spinning with the possibilities. If he couldn't play, maybe he could coach. Or he could be an analyst for one of the networks. Or a sports presenter on the local news.

Brody strode into the living room and picked up the remote, then flipped through the stations until he came to ESPN Australia. The network played mostly American sports, but there was a nightly program that focused on Aussie sports. He could talk football and rugby and make a paycheck doing it. And if ESPN didn't want him, perhaps he might convince someone to hire him at Seven Network.

He leaned back into the sofa and closed his eyes. His coaches and friends had all told him he could find a career outside football, but he'd been too stubborn to listen to them, too angry about his injury to even consider the alternatives. But now he had a reason to get serious about his future.

He switched the telly over to a DVD of his rookie season, listening to the analysts as they described the action. His attention shifted to the twenty-year-old kid in the green guernsey. It was hard to believe he'd ever been that young. Though it was only six years ago, it seemed like a lifetime.

"What are you doing out here?"

He turned to see Payton standing in the bedroom doorway. She'd pulled on the Dockers jumper he'd bought her at the game and she looked irresistible in it, her hair a riot of curls around her face.

"Just watching some telly," he said. He patted the sofa cushion next to him and she crossed the room and curled up beside him.

"Is this your team?" she asked.

"Yep. See, there I am. Number fifteen. Watch. I'll

score a goal." He waited, knowing every play by heart. This was the game when he'd broken the season scoring record for rookies. "There. There it is."

"Yay for you," Payton said, patting his belly. "Good onya."

He wrapped his arm around her neck and pulled her closer, pressing a kiss into her fragrant hair. "I want you to stay with me," he murmured.

"I'm not sleepy," she said, mistaking his request.

"No, I mean, I want you to stay with me. I want you to live with me, here, in Australia. I don't want you to go back to the States." He'd made the same request back at the shack that night she got lost in the bush. But then, he'd just wanted reassurance. Now, he wanted to focus on the future.

She pushed back and looked up into his eyes, her brow creased in an intense frown. "I'm not going anywhere."

"Promise me," he said. "I don't want to wake up some morning and find you gone. I want to make this work."

She sighed softly, then glanced away. "I'm here because I want to be, Brody. If I didn't want to be here, I'd tell you."

"Would you? You ran out on your wedding. You didn't tell your fiancé that you didn't want to be there."

"That was different," Payton said.

"How? Tell me how."

"I—I…" She paused for a moment, then shook her head. "I should have been brave enough to tell him the truth. I don't have any excuses for that. But I'm different now. I'm not afraid to speak up for myself, for what I want. I promise, I'll tell you if I want to leave."

It wasn't the promise he was looking for, but it was as good as he was going to get. Brody would have to be satisfied that it was enough. And yet he wasn't. Until Payton faced her family and her ex-fiancé, he'd always be looking over his shoulder, waiting for someone to turn up and lure her back to the States.

Did he really want to live with that kind of doubt? A sensible, secure guy would tell her to go back and clear up the mess she'd made and then return to him, free of any entanglements. But Brody had never cared for any woman the way he cared for Payton. And he didn't want to let her out of his sight for a moment, much less send her toddling back to Mr. Moneybags.

"Do you ever think about him?" Brody asked.

"Sam?"

Sam. There. She'd said his name. How many times had she said that name? How many times with love in her eyes and how many times with passion in her touch? She had a whole history with this man, a life that Brody knew nothing about.

"Never mind." He pushed to his feet. "I don't need to know. I really don't want to know." He raked his hands through his hair again, suddenly feeling a bit vulnerable, standing in front of her stark naked. This was exactly why he couldn't allow himself to believe in a future with Payton.

She might be able to handle it, but he'd surely find a way to fuck it up. "I'm going to go for a run," he said.

"But, it isn't even light out."

Brody shrugged. "It will be by the time I get back."

"I could come with you."

"No. I just need to clear my head." He walked back

to the bedroom and put on a pair of shorts and a T-shirt, then grabbed his trainers from the closet floor. When he returned to the living room, she was sitting where he'd left her, her knees pulled up beneath the oversize jumper.

"I'll be back in an hour," he said. "Why don't you get a little more sleep and then we'll go to breakfast."

Brody slipped out of the door before she could reply to his suggestion, then strode down the hall to the lift. He stepped inside, releasing a tightly held breath as the doors closed in front of him.

There was no sense trying to plan his future right now. Until he found work, it would be best to keep his feelings for Payton in check. He could enjoy their time together, enjoy the passion they shared, but anything beyond that would be a risk.

8

PAYTON STROLLED slowly through the Fremantle Market, searching for inspiration for the evening meal. She'd already purchased prawns at the fish market on the harbor and now she was studying the vegetables that filled the stalls.

Though they'd only been in Fremantle for a week and a half, she'd already settled into life with Brody. They'd spent their days touring the city and surfing and trying new restaurants. Yesterday, they'd sailed a friend's boat to Rottnest Island and ridden bicycles over the picturesque roads. Brody had even rented a room at the old hotel where they had their lunch and enjoyed a "nap" before continuing their tour.

Payton smiled to herself. Though they'd stripped off their clothes before crawling into bed, neither one of them had had any intention of sleeping. Instead, they'd spent a lazy hour kissing and touching before they made love.

It had been a wonderful day filled with long walks and quiet conversation. Brody was a complicated man, troubled by his own doubts and worries. He'd confessed that he was toying with the idea of calling the NFL scout and talking to him about a job.

Though she could sense his tension over scheduling

a tryout, Payton tried to reassure him that even if it didn't work out, it didn't represent a failure. In the end, Brody made the call.

The NFL scout had arranged to meet him at the Oval tomorrow. Brody had nearly canceled, but she'd convinced him she would be there when he came home, exactly as she was when he left, whether the tryout was a success or not.

The more she got to know Brody, the more she realized how vulnerable he was when it came to his emotions. He seemed so self-assured on the outside, but inside, he was a tangle of insecurities. There were moments when she caught him watching her, times when she woke up and he was clutching her hand so tightly it hurt. Was he really that afraid of losing her?

Though Payton had left a mess in Fiji, she didn't have any plans to return home. She would have to call at some point and had resolved to do that by the end of the week. The private investigator was probably still searching for her and it wouldn't do to waste more of her parents' money or cause them any more worry.

By now, they should be comfortable with the fact that she wouldn't be coming home anytime soon. They'd have accepted the notion that Sam would not be her husband and that she would not be living a comfortable life in Connecticut, raising their grandchildren and attending charity events.

She shook her head, a tiny shudder running through her at the thought. How close to that life had she come? If she'd pushed aside her fears and married Sam, it would have been her future—everything all planned out in front of her.

But her life with Brody was exciting. Every day was a new adventure. And though he worried about his career, Payton was truly convinced that she could live anywhere with him and be happy. She loved working at the station. And she loved Fremantle, too. But most of her affection for both places had come from being with Brody.

Payton strolled over to a vegetable stall and chose some colorful sweet peppers and fingerling potatoes. She waited for the vendor to put them in a bag for her. Then she moved on to the nearest fruit stall and picked out some red oranges, knowing they would make a wonderful tangy-sweet sauce for the prawns. At the last second, she picked up a kilo of strawberries for dessert.

It wasn't a long walk back to Brody's apartment and the weather was pleasant. She'd bought only enough for the evening meal and didn't mind carrying the bags.

As she approached Brody's building, she noticed a dark sedan parked across the street. A man was standing against the front fender, his arms crossed over his chest. He saw her almost immediately and Payton's breath caught as he removed his glasses.

"Sam," she whispered to herself. Her heart slammed against her rib cage as he slowly crossed the street to where she stood. She blinked, hoping that she was seeing things, but as he came closer, Payton knew he wasn't a figment of her imagination.

"Hello, Payton," he said. He reached out and grabbed her elbow, then brushed a kiss on her cheek.

"Hello, Sam. What are you doing here?"

He gave her a cool look, his icy blue eyes cutting through her. "What do you think, Payton?"

She opened her mouth, then snapped it shut. She didn't know what to say.

"Don't worry," he muttered. "I'll wait for your answer. I'm used to that."

His words dripped with sarcasm. She hadn't realized until now, but that was one of things she truly hated about Sam. When he was angry, he got nasty. She'd always just accepted it as part of his nature, but now she realized there were men who didn't feel it necessary to patronize the women they loved.

"I'd assume you're looking for me," she said, keeping her voice calm and detached. "How did you find me?"

"Your parents and I hired a private investigator. They thought you might have had a—a breakdown."

She bit back a laugh. "I'm mentally sound," she said. "I'm not crazy."

"The investigator tracked that Quinn fellow here after he figured out you'd left the station with him. He's spent the last few days following you. You've had quite a vacation. Or maybe we should call it a honeymoon?"

Payton glanced around. She and Brody had been so caught up in each other, they hadn't even noticed someone following them. "Why don't you just say what you came to say, Sam. I understand you're angry and I'm sorry for any embarrassment I caused. But you have to realize I saved us both a lot of heartache."

This seemed to soften his prickly facade. "Did you ever love me?"

"I think I did," she said, knowing it was probably a lie. "But I also think I was getting married to please my parents. They wanted me to be settled and happy and I never thought about what I really wanted."

"And this is it? Some guy you just met? I've read the report on him, Payton. Come on, you can't seriously be thinking of staying here with him. He's just some washed-up jock."

"I don't know what will happen tomorrow or the next day. But I'm happy right now, Sam. Happier than I've been in a long time."

"Payton, be practical. You don't belong here. You're thousands of miles from everything you know—your family and your friends. I forgive you. You made a mistake, but it's nothing that can't be fixed. We can begin again."

"I did make a mistake," she admitted. "I should have been honest about my feelings and my fears. I should have told you how I felt long before our wedding day."

"You got cold feet. Lots of women go through that. But give it a little more time and you'll realize who really loves you. And then you'll come home."

"Sam, I don't—"

He reached out and pressed his finger to her lips. "Don't. Just think about what I've said, Payton. I'm staying in Perth for the next three days. I think we should take some time to talk. To see if we can smooth out this wrinkle."

Wrinkle, Payton mused. She ran away from their wedding and took up with another man and Sam considered it a wrinkle. "I don't think we have anything to talk about."

"I'm at the Intercontinental. Room 1250. I'll be waiting for your call." With that, he turned and walked back to his car. Payton stared after him, wanting to shout out her anger. How dare he assume that she'd change her mind? She wasn't some feebleminded doormat who could be convinced by his mere appearance.

Sam could wait all he wanted, but she wasn't going to change her mind. She'd call her parents tonight and tell them exactly that. And then she'd tell them to talk some sense into her ex-fiancé. But first, she'd tell Brody about Sam's sudden appearance. Knowing Sam and his inability to accept losing at anything, she could expect another visit. She would not allow Brody to be caught off guard.

When she returned to Brody's apartment, she found him sitting on the sofa, examining his knee. He glanced up as she walked inside and she noticed the worried expression etched across his face.

"Is everything all right?" she asked. From the looks of things, now was not the time to bring up her ex-fiancé. That could wait until tomorrow, after the tryout.

"Sure," he said. He pushed to his feet and crossed to her, taking the bags from her hands. "Dinner?"

"Yes. I'm cooking something special. A good-luck meal. I figured it's about time to show you my true talents in the kitchen."

"You have talents in the kitchen too?" he teased, his mood shifting quickly. "I knew you were great in the bathroom, the bedroom and the living room. But the kitchen wasn't something I'd considered."

"I'm a very good cook," she explained.

He peered inside the bags, then pulled out the strawberries she'd purchased. Payton reached for them. "Those are for dessert," she said.

"Can't we have dessert first?" He took one from the bag and bit into it, then held it in front of her mouth.

Slowly, he drew the fruit across her lower lip. She ran her tongue over the sweet juice and smiled.

With a quick move, she bit down on the strawberry, then pulled him into a long, deep kiss. The taste of the berry exploded in her mouth, and Payton wasn't sure that she'd ever tasted something quite so wonderful.

The kiss went on forever, their hands moving over each other's body, so familiar yet still so exciting. He spanned her waist with his hands, then lifted her onto the granite countertop. The short shirt she wore bunched high on her thighs and he slipped his hand between her legs and began to caress her.

Payton knew his touch, yet every time he seduced her, he found a new way to take her to the heights of pleasure. He pushed her back until she was lying across the cool granite. Then he pulled her panties off and trailed kisses along the insides of her thighs.

She knew what was coming and waited, knowing the exquisite sensations his tongue could elicit. And then, he was there, sucking gently, making her writhe with the need for release.

She'd meant to tell him about Sam, but as her pleasure began to escalate, all thoughts of her former life dissolved. She was here with Brody now, and what they were doing was perfect. Nothing could possibly spoil it.

BRODY WINCED as he pushed up from a crouch and ran the width of the field. Though he was in pretty good shape, he hadn't really run full out since before his accident. When he reached the far side of the field, he gulped in a deep breath, then turned and ran back.

The scout scribbled something in his notebook, then nodded. "I understand your injury prevents lateral movement."

"Not prevents," Brody said. "Hampers. I'm just not as quick as I was. But it doesn't affect my kicking. You saw that. I put ten of them through the posts from fifty meters. I can do ten more. Hey, I can kick all day and I won't miss."

"But you'll have to run and tackle," he said. "And even though we have a rule against roughing the kicker, you will get knocked down. That knee isn't going to take much abuse."

"I know I can do this," Brody said. "Just give me a chance. I'll come to the States. I'll kick in your football stadium. I'll play for free."

The scout considered Brody's offer, then nodded his head. "You're a hell of a kicker. But I'm worried about the knee. The strength just isn't quite there. But you do some serious work and that might change. You should be running every day and doing some intense weight training. The NFL preseason starts the end of July. If a team is in need of a kicker, they'll be looking before the regular season begins in September." He held out his business card. "You call me after a month and we'll see where you're at."

Brody stared down at the card. "All right. I can do that. Thanks for taking the time."

"Good luck, son. I hope I hear from you."

Brody walked toward the exit, resigned to the fact that he'd given it his best try. Hell, he'd kicked well. No one could quarrel with that. But his knee wasn't what it should be. Even he knew it. He drew a deep breath, trying to push back the disappointment.

Though it wasn't good news, it wasn't really bad. He had a chance, if he put in a little work. He still had access to the team's training facilities and their physical therapists. Given a month, maybe he could gain more strength.

As he walked through the tunnel to the car park, he saw Payton standing in the entrance, her slender form outlined by the morning sun. She smiled and he felt his spirits rise. Even if the world was falling apart at his feet, she could still make him feel like a hero.

"How did it go?" she asked as he took her hand in his.

"I kicked well," he said. "But he didn't like the look of my knee."

"Well, you expected that," she said.

"He said I should work harder on rehab and then give him a call in a month."

"Are you going to do that?" she asked.

Brody shrugged. "I don't know. Maybe. It would give me more options." He smiled. "I can kick the damn ball. At least the next time one of their kickers goes down, he'll be thinking of me."

They drove back to his apartment, his mind distracted by the traffic. Every now and then, he caught Payton glancing over at him. He wanted to tell her how he was feeling—the frustration and the doubts—but his problems were his own. This afternoon, they'd find something to do that would take his mind off his troubles. And tomorrow, he'd figure out a plan.

As they drove up to the apartment, he reached out and took her hand. "Why don't we go surfing this afternoon." He looked over at her to see her gaze fixed on a car parked across the street from his building.

"What's wrong?"

"Keep driving," she said.

"Why? We need to get our gear if we're going surfing."

"Just keep going."

He did as he was told. After a few blocks, Brody drove in to an empty parking spot and pulled the truck out of gear. Then he turned to her. "Would you like to tell me what's going on?"

She gnawed at her lower lip, avoiding his eyes. "Yesterday, after I came back from the market, I saw Sam. My ex. He was parked in front of your apartment building waiting for me."

Brody felt as if he'd been hit in the gut. This didn't make sense. "You talked to Sam?"

She nodded, then risked a glance over at him. "I wanted to tell you yesterday, but you had the tryout today and I didn't want you to be upset. Besides, when I got home we got distracted and I guess I just forgot."

"You forgot?"

"Well, not exactly. It wasn't the right time."

"Which is it, Payton?"

She cursed softly. "What difference does it make? I'm telling you now. He asked if I'd come home. I told him no."

"Then what's he still doing here?"

"I guess he thinks I might change my mind."

Brody's fingers tightened on the steering wheel, his knuckles turning white. "And will you change your mind?"

"No," Payton insisted. "I don't want to marry him. I told him that. But he doesn't like to lose. And he certainly doesn't like to be embarrassed. He and my parents seem to think I've had some sort of mental breakdown and that if I just get a little help, I'll regain my senses."

"We're going back," Brody said. "I'll talk to the guy. I'll tell him to back off."

"No," Payton said. "This is my problem. I'll—"

"It's my problem now. He's screwing with *my* life."

"I know where he's staying. I'll call him tonight and tell him to go home. And I'll call my parents and let them know I'm going to stay in Australia for now."

Brody didn't like leaving it up to Payton. She'd obviously tried to convince Sam the first time they'd talked and it hadn't worked. Either Sam wasn't listening or she hadn't been forceful enough. But there would be no denying Brody's argument—either the guy would leave Fremantle immediately, or Brody would give him a thick ear.

"So what does this mean? We can't go back to the apartment?"

"Why don't we go get some lunch and maybe he'll be gone when we return." She reached out and pried his hand off the wheel, then laced her fingers through his. "As you've probably noticed, I'm not very good with confrontation."

"What are you talking about? You've told me off plenty of times."

"It's different with my family and with Sam. They make me feel—" Payton searched for the word "—small. They make me feel small."

He turned to look at her, noticing the uneasy expression on her face. Hell, he never wanted to do anything that made her feel that way. "You're one of the strongest, most determined people I know," he said. "Don't let them do that to you. Think of everything you've done over the past weeks."

Brody paused, carefully considering his next suggestion. He was tired of all the wondering—did she love him, would she stay, how did she really feel about Sam? There were too many unanswered questions that she had to settle once and for all. "I think you should go see him," Brody said.

"Really?"

"Why not? He was an important person in your life. Hell, you were going to marry him. Maybe he just needs some...what do they call that?"

"Closure?" she suggested.

"Right. Closure."

A long silence grew between them. "All right," she said softly. "If that's what you want, I'll go see him tomorrow."

It wasn't exactly what he wanted. But it was the quickest way to get to what he wanted. And for that, he was willing to take a risk. He'd give Sam Whitman one last chance to plead his case and if he didn't leave after that, Brody would personally escort him to the airport.

He wasn't about to let Payton go. At least, not without a good fight.

"WHAT DO YOU THINK?"

Brody frowned, staring down at the assortment of towels. He winced, then ran his hand through his hair. Payton could see the confusion in his eyes, but she suspected it had nothing to do with his choice of towels.

Payton had called Sam and agreed to meet him the

next morning. Since she'd made the decision, she and Brody hadn't spoken of it. In truth, she'd carefully avoided the subject. But she could see that it was killing Brody. He'd been hovering over her all day, obviously wanting to ask her what she would say, but afraid to bring up the subject.

"Ah…well, they're towels," he said. "I've never really had an opinion on towels. They're just sort of there when I need them." He nodded. "That's what I think."

"I mean the colors. Your bathroom is so neutral."

"Is it? What does that mean?"

He was going to make this difficult, Payton mused. She'd wondered if buying new towels for him was really a good idea. But she wanted to contribute something to the home they'd made together, even if it did mean spending a bit of his money. "Neutral means there's a lack of color."

"And color is good?"

"Yes. Now, do you like the ice blue or the burnt sienna? These are both masculine colors, but one is cool and the other is warm. I like the burnt sienna."

"Then I like that one, too. Don't I have towels?"

"Yes. But they're a little worn. And they're kind of mismatched. I just thought these would be pretty. And they're really soft. One hundred percent Egyptian cotton." He nodded mutely. Frustrated, Payton picked up the towels and shoved them back into the bag. "Never mind. I'll return them."

"No, no. Don't do that. I like them. I like the burnt sienna. And the blue, too. Maybe we could keep both. One color for summer and one for winter. Cool and warm, right?"

Payton gave him a grudging smile. "I just thought I could make your apartment look a little more homey."

"It doesn't look homey?"

She shook her head. "No. It looks like a bachelor's apartment. It's very nice, but very sterile. And if we're going to live here together, then I want it to be like a home."

A slow smile curled his lips. "A home. With me and you."

"Yes. I like it here."

"Is there anything else that needs fixing?" he asked.

"Well, the kitchen could use some nice towels. And a few accessories, maybe a bowl for the island, for fresh fruit. And some nice wineglasses to put in the china cabinet. Those refrigerator magnets have to go."

Brody chuckled softly. Then he dragged her into his arms, kissing her squarely on the mouth. "Do whatever you want," he said. "As long as you're staying, you can paint the place pink. And if you need more money, just ask."

She'd been thinking about exactly that subject. She wanted to contribute, to help pay for their living expenses. "I'm going to try to find a job," she said. "And to get a job, I suspect I'll need a work visa."

"We can think about that later. I have cash enough to last for a while."

"No, I want to contribute," she said.

"Then let's find out about a work visa." Brody reached out and removed the towels from the bag, stacking them up on the coffee table. "We'll go first thing tomorrow morning."

Payton forced a smile. "I'm going to see Sam

tomorrow morning. Remember?" She studied his expression. He didn't look happy. But then, he hadn't been very happy since Sam had appeared in Fremantle.

"We should go try out these towels," she said. "Let's take a shower."

Brody shook his head. "You think that if you seduce me, I'll stop worrying about him?"

"There's no need to worry," she assured him. "Brody, I'm decorating your apartment. I wouldn't do that unless I was planning to stay."

"He's leaving tomorrow?"

"That's what he said," Payton replied.

"Good. Then, day after, we can stop talking about him." He pushed her back on the sofa and crawled on top of her, rubbing his nose against hers. "Do you have a nice dress?"

"Not really."

"Then, go out and buy one. We're going out to a swank place tomorrow night for dinner. It's my birthday."

"It's your birthday? Why didn't you tell me?" Payton asked. "I'll make a cake. We'll have presents and a celebration."

"I just want to take my girl out," Brody said.

His girl. She liked the sound of that. It wasn't too serious. Yet, it did suggest a real relationship, one that was more than casual. "I'm not sure where to go to find something."

"There's a David Jones in the mall in Perth. It's the same store you went to in Brisbane."

"They have really pretty dresses there." She kissed him. "I'll go this afternoon. You can come and help me pick something out."

"Surprise me," he said. Brody brushed the hair out of her eyes. "When is your birthday?"

"August tenth," she said. "I was born twelve minutes before midnight."

Payton realized they didn't know the little details about each other's lives. Maybe it was time to find out. "What's your favorite color?" she asked.

"Neutral," he teased. "No, it was blue. But now, it's this really pretty shade of pink." Brody smiled. "Exactly the color of your lips."

Payton groaned inwardly. Her attempt to learn more about him was swiftly turning into a full-out seduction. But then, they had plenty of time to go over the silly little details. "What is your favorite sexual fantasy?" she asked.

He laughed sharply. "How did we go from colors to sexual fantasies?"

Payton shrugged. "Just curious."

He thought about his answer for a long time, then smiled. "There is this one. I'm asleep and I'm having this dream that there's a woman in bed with me. And she's doing all kinds of wonderful things with her lips and her tongue. And I open my eyes and it's not a dream."

"Has it ever happened before?" Payton asked.

"No," he said.

"Your birthday is coming up. That could be arranged, you know."

"Arranged? Only if you're the woman I'm waking up to. I'd reckon that would be a bonzer prezzy."

"Bonzer is good?"

"Very good. Great. Incredible. The best."

"Hmm. That's a lot to live up to. Maybe I should just buy you a bonzer watch. Or a bonzer shirt."

"Do not tease me," he said. "It's my birthday. And as my girl, it's your job to treat me special."

Payton giggled. "It's not your birthday yet." Now that she'd decided to stay, she had every intention of making all Brody's fantasies come true. Life—and sex—with Brody would be one long adventure.

9

THE BUZZER ON the security system startled Brody. Payton had left less than an hour ago to shop for a dress for tomorrow's birthday celebration. He hadn't expected her to return until just before dinner.

He pushed the button and leaned in. "Did you forget your key?"

There was a long pause on the other end. "I'm looking for Brody Quinn."

"And who might you be?" Brody asked.

"Sam. Sam Whitman."

Brody stepped back from the intercom, then cursed softly. What the hell was this? Payton had assured him that she'd called Sam and told him she would see him in the morning. Either he was a very impatient man or he wanted to talk to Brody directly.

Brody drew a deep breath. "She's not here," he said.

"I'm here to talk to you," Sam said. "Man to man."

Brody shook his head, then opened the front door and walked to the lift. If this guy wanted to talk, they'd talk. But Brody was going to have much more to say than "get the hell out of our lives." As he rode the lift down to the lobby, he carefully schooled his temper. The last thing he wanted to do was punch the guy. There was no need to get physical. But he was prepared to take it that far if the situation warranted.

He'd seen the photo of Sam on the Internet and knew what to expect. But when he walked into the lobby, Brody was surprised at how slight he was. In a bar brawl, Sam Whitman wouldn't last a minute.

To Brody's delight, Whitman seemed to be a bit intimidated by Brody's size. Brody had at least ten centimeters on him and a good fifteen kilos. "What do you want?" he demanded.

"I have some things to say about Payton."

"She plans to stay here with me. She was going to stop by your hotel tomorrow morning and let you know."

Sam paused, as if considering his next comment carefully. "You don't find it unusual that she'd abandon her family and friends? Without a second thought?"

"No," Brody lied. "Not after the way you treated her. She has a right to make her own decisions."

"I think we both have to be honest," Sam said. "Maybe I didn't give her the attention she needed. And I'll admit, I might have focused on work too much. But I can give her a very comfortable life. From what I know of you, you can't."

Brody quelled a surge of temper. He knew it was the only advantage that Sam Whitman had on him. And Whitman obviously wasn't afraid to use it.

"I have some opportunities," Brody said. "Besides, we can always live on the station with my family. Payton loves it there."

"For how long?" Sam asked. "How long until the novelty wears off and she grows tired of being isolated from everything she knows and loves?"

He was saying the same things Brody had said to himself. "Do you honestly think you can buy her back?"

"No. But I believe if you really love her, you'll consider what's best for her. I believe if you're selfish enough to keep her here, you'll pay the price later. And by isolating her from her family and friends, you're allowing her to avoid the consequences of her actions." Sam reached into his jacket pocket and pulled out a leather wallet, then withdrew an envelope from it. "This is an airline ticket and enough cash to get her home."

"What makes you think I'll give this to her?"

"Because you want to know as much as I do," Sam said. "You love her enough not to leave any stone unturned. Send her home. If she comes back to you, you'll know she's made her choice." He held out his hand. "May the best man win."

Brody bit back a curse. This guy was arrogant and condescending and in need of a good beat-down. But he was also right. If Brody did want to keep Payton in his life permanently, then she'd have to face up to her past mistakes. It was better to lose her now than later.

He reached out and shook Sam's hand, then nodded. "She loves me," he said.

"Then I guess you have nothing to worry about. Tell her good-bye. And I'll see her back home."

With that, Sam turned on his heel and walked out of the lobby. He watched as Sam jogged across the street and got into his car. Then Brody glanced down at the airline ticket. He ought to just toss it in the rubbish and forget it ever existed.

Why not? He could accept the risk that it would all explode in his face at some point. He'd have more time to convince Payton she'd made the best choice by staying. But Sam was right on one point. It was probably better to know how she really felt, before investing his heart in a relationship that was doomed from the start.

Brody walked back to the lift and pushed the button, then stepped inside after the doors opened. A single shot at an NFL career wasn't enough. If he wanted to compete with Sam Whitman's millions, he had to look at other options.

The moment he got back to his apartment, Brody found his phone and dialed the Dockers' office. When the receptionist answered, Brody asked to speak to John Cook. When the assistant coach got on the line, Brody drew a deep breath and said a silent prayer.

"John. Brody Quinn here. Say, I was wondering if you still had the name of that bloke at Seven Network. You know, the one you thought might be able to find a spot for me an analyst?"

To Brody's surprise, Cook had the number at hand and encouraged Brody to make the call. They chatted for a few minutes about Brody's knee and the possibility of surgery, but Brody cut the conversation short and hung up. After a half hour, he had a list of seven contacts for a wide range of jobs, from school coach to equipment salesman.

He stared at the phone for a long time, trying to put his thoughts in order. Then he tossed the phone on the sofa and stood up. This was far too important to bungle. The NFL would pay the best, but television was more secure. He'd follow Callum's advice and write everything down first, the pros and cons of all his options.

Brody found a pad of paper, sat down at the table and carefully wrote out the skills that he possessed. He'd always been the club's best student of the game. He read the opposition like no other player and could talk at length about a player's strengths and weaknesses. He had a good mind for statistics and remembered almost everything he read. He didn't stammer or mumble and his teammates had often teased him about his pretty face. And he was considered quite charming.

"What more is there?" Brody asked himself, staring at the list. He owned a suit and tie and a decent pair of shoes. He wrote that down, though he assumed if he got a job in the business world, he'd need a better wardrobe. He started a list for the NFL job and even made one for getting back into Aussie football.

Brody heard the front door open and turned to see Payton walking in. Their eyes met and for a moment, Brody forgot to breathe. He still found himself amazed that she'd wandered into his life. How the hell had he gotten so lucky?

"You're home early," he said, glancing over at the plane ticket he'd left on the table.

She held up a sheaf of papers. "I stopped by the immigration office on my way back from shopping. I have to fill out all this paperwork and then call back for an appointment." Payton dropped her shopping bags on the floor, then sat down on his lap and slipped her arms around his neck. "What happens if they don't let me stay? What if they force me to go home?"

"Maybe you need to go home," he said. The moment the words slipped out of his mouth, he wanted to take them back. Why would he encourage her to leave? Was he compelled to test her feelings for him? Brody took the plane ticket from the table and held it out to her.

"What's that?"

"A ticket home," he said. "Sam dropped by. I guess he got tired of waiting for you and decided to talk to me."

Her expression turned angry. "I left a message that I was coming to see him tomorrow. He always has to control everything. God, I hate that about him. I'm not going home. And I'm not going to talk to him again. I'll just return the ticket. Or better yet, exchange it for tickets we can use together."

"I think you should go home. Payton, I don't want to constantly be looking over my shoulder, waiting for him to turn up again like he did today. You need to clean up the mess you left behind and then, if you still want to, come back. But this is always going to be hanging between us, Payton. I'm always going to wonder if I'll wake up someday and you'll be gone."

She bit on her lower lip, her eyes filling with tears. "So you want me to leave?"

"Of course not. But if you're going to stay, I want you to stay forever. And if you don't smooth things out with your family, you're always going to regret that. Do it now. Make amends. And then come home to me."

A long silence grew between them as she considered his suggestion. "You're right," she finally said. "This whole thing has been hanging over us like a dark cloud. I know what I want and I shouldn't be afraid to tell them." Payton cupped his face in her hands and stared into his eyes. "I'll go back day after tomorrow," she said. "After we've celebrated your birthday. And I'll call my parents and let them know I'm coming home." Payton leaned forward and gave him a fierce kiss. "I will come back. You can count on it."

Brody's pulse leaped. He cupped her face in his hands and molded her mouth to his. How would he live without this? After a day or two, he'd be ready to hop a flight to the States and drag her back.

But he'd have to be strong and hope that she would return and stay for good. Brody slipped his arm beneath her knees and stood, then slowly walked toward the bedroom, their mouths still caught in a deep kiss.

As he lowered her onto his bed, they broke apart for a moment. He stared down into her beautiful face and tried to memorize all the tiny details that he'd begun to take for granted. He didn't even have a photo of her. But then, perhaps that was for the best.

He could believe she'd existed in a dream, that what they'd shared hadn't been real. If she didn't return, he'd continue with the fantasy. And if she did, reality would be better than anything he could have ever imagined.

They undressed each other slowly, taking the time to touch each inch of exposed skin. There were so many spots on her body he'd lingered over, spots made just for his lips or his tongue or his touch. In his eyes, she was perfection and there would never be another woman like her.

And when they finally came together in a long, delicious possession, he was already regretting what he'd done. He should have burned the ticket, should have trusted his instincts and kept her with him.

He thrust deep and held her close, desperate to seal the bond they shared. Again and again, they moved together and when their release finally came, Brody knew just one thing was certain. He loved Payton and if giving her up meant assuring her happiness, he'd do it in a heartbeat.

JFK WAS CROWDED with summer tourists, the concourse a maze of luggage and late passengers. Her flight from Perth had been a marathon affair, though passed in the comfort of first class. She'd boarded a Qantas flight almost thirty-five hours ago and had changed planes in Melbourne and Los Angeles. At this point, she could barely summon the energy to lift her bag onto her shoulder, much less marshal the resolve to face her parents.

But her trip was far from over. Before she'd left Perth, she'd booked her return flight and a night at an airport hotel, putting the charges on her credit card. One last thing her father would pay for before she was completely on her own. She was due to get right back on the plane in another twenty-four hours. In all, she'd be apart from Brody for three and a half days—enough time to realize she could never stay away longer.

They'd had a wonderful birthday celebration, though it was laced with the bittersweet knowledge that they'd soon be miles apart. After returning from the restaurant, they'd stripped out of their fancy clothes and made love all night long.

When it was time for her to leave, he'd reluctantly let her go. He'd decided to call a cab, rather than drive her to the airport himself, and Payton was glad for it. Emotional goodbyes would have been too difficult to handle. She was determined to get her problems solved and then return. Neither one of them would have time to be sad.

Payton wondered why she'd even bothered to leave. She didn't need to see Sam again. As for her parents, she could have invited them to Fremantle for a visit and a chance to meet the man she loved.

Payton stopped short, causing a traffic problem on the concourse. She hadn't admitted it to herself until now, but she was in love with Brody. It had taken thirty-five hours in and out of the air for her to come to that realization, but at least she was dead certain of it. She loved Brody Quinn and deep down inside, she knew he loved her, as well.

"So what am I doing here?" she muttered, staring at her surroundings. Payton hoisted her bag back up on her shoulder and started off again. "Closure," she murmured.

How wonderful would it be to return to Brody without a single thing hanging over their heads? She smiled to herself as she walked, thinking about the last time she'd seen him. He'd stood in the doorway of his apartment building, watching her get into the cab. He'd looked so sad, almost as if he didn't believe he'd ever see her again. She'd prove him wrong.

Her parents had promised to meet her outside the security checkpoint and as she neared the spot, Payton said a silent prayer that they'd kept their promise. As she worked her way through the crowd, she caught sight of Sam. He waved at her and she started toward him. He met her halfway, then grabbed her bag.

"I thought my parents would meet me."

"They're waiting in the Red Carpet Club just down the concourse. I wanted to talk to you first."

"I don't have anything to say to you, Sam."

"I have something to say to you," he said. He took her elbow and steered her over to a row of chairs set against the wall. "Sit."

Payton gave him a withering look. She wouldn't be ordered around like some naughty pet.

"Please, sit down," Sam amended, motioning to the chair. "I have something I need to tell you before you talk to your parents."

She frowned, taking in the stricken expression on Sam's face. Payton had never seen him so worried. Her stomach lurched. "What is it? Are my parents all right? Has something happened? Did someone die?"

"No," Sam said. He sat down, then pulled her down beside him. "It's me."

"You're dying?" Payton asked.

A wry smile touched his lips. "Metaphorically, yes." Sam drew a deep breath, then met her gaze. "For the past three years, I've been carrying on an affair with my executive assistant. Your father found out about it and I'm sure your parents will bring it up. They think that's why you ran out on the wedding."

Payton stared at him, his words a jumble in her mind. "You were having an affair? You were cheating on me? And my father knew about it?"

"Yes. To all three questions. I know how you must feel and I can only beg for your forgiveness and spend the rest of my life making this up to you. It's over. It's been over for a month now and—"

"Wait," Payton said, holding up her hand. "A month? You mean, it was still going on while we were in—" She stopped, stunned by the realization. "She was there. In Fiji. Emily was there. We invited her to our wedding. Oh, my God. You were planning to carry on after we were married?"

"I know this must be a shock, but I can assure you that—"

Payton shook her head, a laugh bubbling up inside her. "I knew something was wrong. I trusted my instincts and I was right." She stood and picked up her bag from the floor, slinging it over her shoulder. "Do you want to know what I feel, Sam?" She shrugged. "Nothing. I feel nothing. I thought I loved you, but I know now that what we had wasn't love. It was obligation. And I'm fine with this."

He jumped up and reached for her arm, but Payton avoided his grasp. "Unfortunately, you won't be taking over Daddy's bank, but I'm sure you'll find comfort in the fact that you can keep sleeping with Emily." Payton held out her hand. "Goodbye, Sam. Have a nice life."

He took her hand and gave it a weak shake. Then, Payton turned on her heel and headed down the concourse. As she walked, she tried to make sense of what Sam had told her. Her parents had known about his affair and they'd still gone ahead with the wedding plans. How was that possible?

When she reached the first-class lounge, she stood in the doorway, her gaze falling on the handsome couple sitting at a nearby table. They spotted her at the same time and her mother rushed up to her, arms thrown open. She gathered Payton in a frantic embrace, hugging her tightly. "You're home," she cried. "Thank God. I was beginning to wonder if I'd ever see you again."

A moment later, her father appeared at her side and patted her on the shoulder. "There, there. Well, I'm happy to see you've come to your senses, Payton. Come on, let's get out of here. We have a car waiting."

"No," Payton said.

Her father arched his brow. "No? How do you propose we get home?"

Payton straightened her spine and took a deep breath. "I'm not going home, Daddy. Not tonight."

Her mother gave Payton's arm a gentle squeeze. "Oh, George. She's going to Sam's, of course. Darling, we couldn't be happier. You know how much we adore Sam. And he loves you. Just wait, this whole terrible embarrassment will be forgotten in no time."

"Mother, I'm not going to Sam's." She took her mother's hand and pulled her along with her toward their table. "I think we should order some wine, sit down and talk. I have something I need to tell you."

"She's pregnant." Her mother pressed a hand to her heart and closed her eyes. Her father held her elbow to keep her upright.

"I'm not pregnant!" Payton groaned. "Why would you think that?"

"Sam said you were—oh, how did he say it, George?"

"Shacked up, Margie," her father said. "He said Payton was shacked up with some unemployed soccer player."

"Football," Payton said. "Aussie rules football. Mother, Father, sit down," she ordered. It was time they started treating her like an adult and not some eager child always willing to please. This conversation would be between three reasonable adults—or one reasonable adult trying to calm two irrational-overbearing adults. She drew a steadying breath. "I'll be right back."

She strode up to the bar, ordered three glasses of Merlot and paid with one of the twenties that Sam had given her. Then she carried the wine to the table and sat down.

"Why are we staying here?" her mother asked. "Why don't we go home and have a drink? I'm sure the quality of this wine isn't up to the standards of what we have in our wine cellar." She took a sip and wrinkled her nose. "Just as I suspected."

"This is ridiculous." Her father pushed away from the table. "You're coming home with us right now, Payton. You are going to get a good night's sleep and then we are going to figure out how you can make this all up to Sam."

She shook her head. "I don't love him. And neither should you. He cheated on me. You knew and you were going to let me marry him all the same. You two spent a lifetime trying to protect me and then, when I really needed you the most, you were ready to walk away, to let me marry a man who didn't love me."

"Sam assured me the affair was over," her father said. "And that it wouldn't happen again."

"Well, he wasn't telling you the truth. Thank God, I figured it out."

"When did you find out?" her mother asked.

"A few minutes ago," Payton said. "But I knew something was wrong for a long time. I felt it in the weeks before the wedding. And in Fiji. That's why I ran." An image of Brody flashed in her mind and she smiled. "And I'm lucky I did. Because I've met a man I can really love and trust, a man who wants me and not the bank I'll inherit. I have to live my life now on my own. And I'm going to do that in Australia. With Brody."

"What is she saying, George?" her mother asked.

"She's just distraught. You need help," her father

said, turning to Payton. "We can get you help. A nice quiet place to get some perspective."

Payton giggled softly. "Daddy, I don't need help. I'm perfectly sane and I'm happier than I've ever been. And I hope someday you'll come to visit me. I'd love for you to meet Brody. He's a wonderful man. Or maybe, we'll come here for a visit. Brody might have a tryout with a football team later this summer." She gulped down the rest of her wine, then stood, satisfied that she'd said everything that needed saying.

Though she ought to have been angrier over her parents' deception, there wasn't really a point. Everything they'd done had led to Brody and that was all that mattered. She rounded the table and kissed them both on the cheek. "I have to go now. I think I might be able to catch the flight back tonight if I hurry."

"You only just got here," her father said.

"And now I have to go," Payton replied, picking up her bag. "I love you both. And don't worry, I know exactly what I'm doing."

She walked to the doorway of the bar, then turned and waved at her stunned parents. It was enough for them to see that she was healthy and happy. They'd get over her broken engagement and their disappointment that Sam wouldn't be a part of the family. And they'd find a way to explain the embarrassment of the wedding. And maybe someday they would meet Brody and understand why she loved him.

As much as she wanted to feel regret while walking away from them, Payton couldn't. She was returning to the man she loved, to a land she was learning to love and to a life that would be built on love. She wasn't frightened or nervous or anything but bliss-fully happy.

She checked the signs at the end of the concourse and headed toward the Qantas desk. If she hurried, she could hop the 7:10 flight to Australia, a full day before her scheduled return. Then, in about thirty hours, she'd be back in Brody's life—and in his arms—for good.

"DAVEY, GRAB ME that spanner." Brody crawled halfway down the windmill and waited as the kid searched the ground at his feet. "Next to my saddlebags."

He picked up a tool. "This one?"

"No, the big one."

Davey finally found the tool, then climbed up the ladder and handed it to Brody. They'd been working together all day, greasing and adjusting the six windmills close to the station. Tomorrow they'd catch the ones on the outlying pastures, traveling by ATV rather than horse.

Brody had decided to return to the station after just one day alone in Fremantle. The apartment seemed so empty without Payton there and he found himself spending every waking minute thinking about her. He could rehab his knee as easily on the station as he could in Fremantle, and he'd have work to occupy his mind the rest of the day. Station work was difficult and ex-hausting—and exactly what he needed.

He wasn't sure when Payton would return. She'd promised to call once everything had been settled, but he expected she'd spend at least a week or two in the States before she left again. He'd decided to go on as if she wasn't going to return. Then, everything after that—if there was anything—would be like a gift.

Brody climbed back up to the top of the windmill, the spanner tucked into his jacket pocket and the grease gun still clutched in his hand. As he went through the maintenance routine, he heard the sound of a plane overhead and glanced up to see Teague coming in from the east.

He hadn't seen Teague at all since his return and Callum had ridden out an hour after Gemma had left a day ago, heading into the outback with his horse, his pack and his rifle. He'd left Skip in charge of preparations for the mustering, a sure sign that he was upset. Now that Teague was back, Brody would get some answers. He had tried not to dwell on his brothers' love lives. Thinking about their happiness only made his life seem emptier.

"What is he doing?" Davey asked.

Brody glanced over his shoulder to see Teague circling the plane. "I don't know." He watched as Teague made a wide sweep around the windmill, wiggling his wings before he headed toward the airstrip.

Brody finished his work, then carefully surveyed the landscape from his perch high above the ground. He used to love this view when he was a kid. He always thought if he just looked hard enough, he could see the real world in the distance. Now he took some comfort in the fact that he was isolated from that world.

If things didn't work out the way he'd planned, then he'd return to the station for good and make his life here in Queensland. He'd always have a place with his brothers and there was some comfort in that.

"Are we done?" Davey called.

"Yeah," Brody replied. "Pack it up. It's getting late. We should start back if we want to make it by dinner."

Davey gathered the tools, then strapped the pouch to his horse. By the time Brody joined him, Davey was mounted and ready to ride. There was no keeping him from a meal. Davey kicked his horse into a gallop, but Brody decided to take a slower pace.

"Come on," Davey shouted over his shoulder, pulling his horse up to wait.

"Go ahead," Brody called. "I want to enjoy the ride."

"Suit yourself. But Mary's got pork chops tonight. If you don't sit down on time, the rest of the boys will eat all the potatoes."

He waved Davey off and watched as the kid took off in a cloud of dust. Brody wasn't anxious to get back to the dinner table. Since he'd returned, he'd been grabbing a plate and eating by himself, too preoccupied to socialize. Mary and the jackaroos had given him a wide berth and he'd been grateful for it.

As he rode toward the house, he noticed the Fraser shack in the distance. His mind wandered back to the night he'd spent there with Payton. Everything had been so new with them then, so exciting. Only a few weeks had passed since, but it seemed like a lifetime.

He wondered what Payton was doing, trying to calculate the time difference between New York and Queensland. There was almost a twelve-hour difference, so it was the middle of the night there. Was she sleeping alone or had Sam convinced her to return to his bed?

Brody cursed beneath his breath, brushing the image from his mind. He wanted to believe that thoughts of him filled her mind, that she missed what they had together, that she ached for him the way he ached for her. Sleep hadn't come easily since she'd gone.

He fixed his gaze on the horizon and let the horse navigate. It felt good to think about her, to rewind every encounter and enjoy them all over again. They'd been wonderful together, both in and out of bed. He closed his eyes and tipped his face up, the sun warm on his back, exhaustion setting in.

Maybe he'd sleep tonight, he mused. Perhaps his bed wouldn't seem so cold and empty. It had to happen sooner or later. The loneliness would fade and he'd get his life back—pitiful as it was.

When he opened his eyes again, he noticed a rider approaching from the direction of the homestead. He squinted to see in the late-afternoon light, trying to make out who it was. Slowly, he realized it was a woman. Hayley?

Suddenly, the rider pulled to a stop and jumped off the horse. Brody's breath caught in his chest. He blinked hard, wondering if he was imagining her, like a mirage in the middle of the desert. He kicked his horse into a trot and covered the distance between them.

As he approached, she pulled off her stockman's hat and her curly hair fell down around her shoulders. Brody smiled. If this was a dream, then he planned to enjoy it.

He reined in his horse before he reached her, then slid down to stand beside it. For a long time, they stood facing each other, neither one of them moving. And then, at the very same moment, they covered the distance between them in just a few seconds.

Payton launched herself into his arms and he picked her up and spun her around. She felt real, warm and soft, the scent of her hair filling his head. "Is it really you?"

"I think so," Payton said. "I can't have changed that much in four days."

He set her down and stepped back to look into her eyes. "You're more beautiful, I think. Is that possible?" Brody took her face in his hands and kissed her, his tongue delving into her mouth and savoring her taste. "Did you even go home?"

Payton nodded. "I did. I saw Sam and my parents and I turned around and came back. When I got to New York, I realized it was the last place in the world I wanted to be. You shouldn't have made me leave, but I'm glad I put that part of my life to rest."

"I won't do that again," Brody said. "God, I missed you. How did you get here?"

"Teague picked me up. When I got to Fremantle and you weren't there, I figured you might have come back to the station. I flew to Brisbane and then called Teague and he came to get me. I thought it might be nice to surprise you."

"Nice," he said. "I like *nice* now. Coming back to me is definitely nice."

"I may have to leave again if they don't extend my visa. But maybe, we can go to New York for a visit."

"Or for that football tryout. I'm going to give that a go. And if it doesn't work out, I have some other interesting prospects."

She pushed up onto her toes and kissed him softly. "I don't care what you do or where we live. I don't ever want to be away from you again. I—I think I might love you."

Brody chuckled softly. For now, he was happy with a vague statement of love. He could wait for her feelings to grow stronger. "I think I might love you, too. A lot."

He grabbed her hand, then pulled it to his lips. "So, what are we going to do with ourselves?"

"Mary's making dinner. We could eat and then go for a swim."

"Aren't you tired? You've been on a plane for the better part of four days."

"About seventy hours," she said. "I've taken off and landed sixteen times."

"Then I definitely think you need to get to bed. Right now. For your own health. And mine." He glanced over his shoulder. "We could head over to the shack and spend the night there."

"But we're not lost. And that would be trespassing."

Brody smoothed his thumb over her lower lip. "This all started with a life of crime. I think we can live dangerously."

Payton threw her arms around his neck. "Forget about nice. I'm really starting to enjoy dangerous."

He wrapped his hands around her waist and set her back on her horse, then remounted. As they rode toward the sunset, Brody wondered at how his life had changed so much in such a short time. There were no answers to his questions, and maybe there never would be. But Payton was here, with him, from half a world away.

This hadn't been his dream, but it was now. And it was better than any dream he could have ever imagined for himself.

* * * * *

FLASHBACK

BY
JILL SHALVIS

USA TODAY bestselling author **Jill Shalvis** is happily writing her next book from her neck of the Sierras. You can find her romances wherever books are sold, or visit her on the web at www.jillshalvis.com/blog.

1

THE FIRE BELL RANG for the fourth time since midnight, interrupting Aidan Donnelly in the middle of a great dream in which he was having some fairly creative, acrobatic sex with a gorgeous blonde. The last thing he wanted was to be shaken awake, but apparently sex, imaginary or otherwise, wasn't on his card for the evening.

He was on the last few hours of a double shift from hell. The loudspeaker mounted in one corner of the bunk room was going off, telling him and his crew that they would not be going home in one short hour after all, but back into the field on yet another emergency call.

Putting the blonde back where she belonged, in the file in his brain labeled Hot Erotic Fantasy, Aidan got up to the tune of a bunch of moans and groans from his crew.

So close. He'd been so close to three desperately needed days off....

Across the room Eddie kicked aside the latest issue of *Time,* which had an entire company of firefighters on the cover. "A lot of good being the sexiest occupation does us," the firefighter grumbled, "when we're too exhausted to take advantage of it."

"Some of us don't need beauty sleep." This from Sam, Eddie's partner. "Like, say, Mr. 2008 here." He slid a look Aidan's way, but Aidan found himself too tired to rise to the bait.

Through no fault of his own, he'd been named Santa Rey's hottest firefighter for 2008. This dubious honor came along with another—being put on the cover of Santa Rey's annual firefighter's calendar. "I told you, I didn't submit my name."

Eddie grinned in the middle of dressing. "No, we did, Mr. 2008."

Aidan gave him a shove, and Eddie fell back to the mattress, snorting out a laugh as he staggered upright again and grabbed his boots. "Yeah, like being that pretty is a hindrance."

"I am not pretty."

No one answered him in words as they pulled on their gear, but several made kissy noises as they headed toward their rigs. Still groggy, and definitely out of sorts, Aidan took the shotgun position next to Ty, his temporary partner, on loan from a neighboring firehouse, since his usual partner Zach was still off on medical leave.

Eddie and Sam grabbed their seats, as well as Cristina and Aaron, another on-loan firefighter, and they were all off into the dark night—or more accurately, the dark predawn morning—following the ambulance, which had pulled out first. The air was thick with dew, and salty from the ocean only one block over. For now the temperature was cool enough, but by midday the California August heat would be in full bloom, and they'd all be dying. Aidan got on the radio to talk to dispatch. "It's an explosion," he told the others grimly.

"Where?" Ty asked.

"The docks." Which could be anywhere from the shipping area, to the houseboats filled with year-round residents. "Only one boat's on fire, but several others are threatened by the flames, with no word on what caused the explosion."

Behind him, Eddie swore softly, and Aidan's thoughts echoed the sentiment. Explosions were trickier than a regular fire, and far more unpredictable.

"Are they calling for backup?" Sam asked.

They needed it. Firehouse Thirty-Four was sorely overworked and dangerously exhausted going into the high fire season. They'd had a rough month. Aidan's partner and best friend Zach had been injured after digging into the mysterious arsons that had plagued Santa Rey. Mysterious arsons that were now linked to one of their own.

Blake Stafford.

Just the thought brought a stab of fresh pain to Aidan's chest. Now Zach was off duty and Blake was dead, leaving them all devastated.

Cristina was especially devastated, and with good reason. She'd been Blake's partner, and the closest to him. She'd suffered like hell over his loss, and also over the arsons he'd been accused of committing.

She blamed herself, Aidan knew, which was ridiculous. She couldn't have stopped Blake.

As it turned out, none of them could have stopped him.

Aidan considered himself pretty damn tough and just about one-hundred-percent impenetrable, but losing Blake had been heart-wrenching. He missed him, and hated what he'd been accused of. He didn't want to believe Blake was dead, and he sure as hell didn't want to believe Blake guilty of arson, and the resulting death of a small boy—none of them did, but the evidence was there. He could hardly even stand thinking about it—classic denial, Aidan knew, but it was working for him. "Dispatch's sending rigs from Stations Thirty-Three and Thirty-Five."

No one said anything to this, but they were all thinking the same thing—it'd take those stations at least ten extra minutes to get on scene from their locations—and the sense of dread only increased as they pulled up to the docks.

Turned out that the fire wasn't at the shipping docks, but where the smaller, privately owned boats were moored at four long docks, each with ten bays. Possibly forty boats in total, many of them occupied.

Chaos reined in the predawn. Their senior officer was usually first on scene, setting up a command center, but he was coming from another fire and was five minutes behind them. The sky was still dark, with no moon, and the visibility wasn't helped by the thick plumes of black smoke choking the air out of their lungs. Flames leaped fifty feet into the air, coming from a boat halfway down the second of the four docks. Aidan took a quick count, and his stomach tightened with fear. There were boats on either side of the flaming vessel, and more on the opposite side of the dock.

Not good.

As they accessed their equipment and laid out lines, three police squad cars tore into the lot, followed by the command squad, all of whom leaped to work evacuating the surrounding docks. Aidan and company needed to contain the flames, but the explosion burned outrageously hot. He could feel that mind-numbing heat from a hundred feet back. With the chief now on scene, barking orders through their radios, Aidan and the others moved with their hoses, their objective to keep the flames from spreading to any of the other boats. They were halfway there when it came.

A sharp, terrified scream.

The sound raised the hair on the back of Aidan's neck, and he dropped everything to run toward the burning boat, Ty right behind him.

The scream came again, clearly female, and Aidan sped up. No one knew better than a firefighter what it was like to be surrounded by flames, to have them lick at you, toy with you. It was sheer, horrifying terror.

They had to get to her first.

Behind them came Sam, Eddie, Cristina and Aaron, directing water on the flames to clear Aidan and Ty's path down the dock toward the boat. Twenty feet, then ten, and that's when he saw her. A woman standing on the deck of the burning boat, wobbling, the flames at her back.

"Jump!" he yelled, wondering why she didn't just make the short leap to the dock—she could have made a run for safety. "*Jump*—"

Another explosion rocked them all. Aidan skidded to a halt, spinning away and crouching down as debris flew up into the air to match the intensifying flames. The chief was shouting into the radio, demanding a head count. Aidan lifted his head and checked in as he took in the sights. The boat was still there. With his heart in his throat, he searched for a visual on the woman—

There. In the same spot she'd been before, still on the deck but on the floor now, holding her head. *Goddammit.* He got to his feet, took a few running steps, and dove onto the boat.

She nearly jumped out of her skin when he landed next to her. "It's okay." He dropped to his knees at her side to try to get a good look and see how badly she was injured, but the smoke had choked out any light from the docks and she was nothing but a slight shadow. A slight shadow who was hunched over and coughing uncontrollably.

"The boat," she managed. "It k-keeps b-blowing up—"

"Can you stand?"

"Yes. I—" She let out a sound that tugged at his memory, but he pushed that aside when she nodded. She got up with his help, twisting away from him to stare up at the flames shooting up the mast and sails. "Ohmigod…"

He pulled her closer to his side, intending to jump with her to the dock and the hell off this inferno, but several things hit him at once.

The name of the boat painted across the outside of the cabin, flickering in and out of view between the flames. *Blake's Girl*.

No. It couldn't be. Then came something of far more immediate concern—the rumbling and shuddering of the deck beneath their feet. "We have to move."

"No. No, please," she gasped. "You have to save the boat."

"Us first." He couldn't have put together a more coherent sentence because of all that was going through his head. *Blake's Girl...*

Blake's boat. God, he'd all but forgotten that Blake had owned a boat.

Then there was the woman in his arms, facing away from him, but invoking that niggling sense of familiarity. There was something about her wild blond curls, about the sound of her voice—

The warning signals in his brain peaked at once. In just the past thirty seconds, the flames had doubled in strength and heat. The deck beneath their feet trembled and quivered with latent simmering violence.

They were going to blow sky high. Whipping toward the dock he got another nasty surprise—the flames had covered their safe exit.

On the other side of those monstrous flames stood Ty, Eddie and Sam, hoses in hand, battling the fire from their angle, which wasn't going to help Aidan and his victim in time. Cristina was there, too, with Aaron, and even in the dark he sensed their urgency, their utter determination to keep him safe.

They'd so recently lost one of their own; there was no way they were going to let it happen again.

"Ohmigod," the woman at his side gasped, staring, as if mesmerized, at the sight of the flames closing in on them.

She wasn't the only one suddenly mesmerized, and for one startling heartbeat, Aidan went utterly still, as for the first time he caught a full glimpse of her.

He knew that profile.

He knew her. *"Kenzie?"*

At the sound of her name on his lips, uttered in a low, hoarse, surprised voice, her head whipped toward his, eyes wide. Her wavy blond hair framed a pale face streaked with dirt and some blood, but was still beautiful, hauntingly so.

She was Mackenzie Stafford, Blake's sister. Kenzie to those who knew and loved her, Sissy Hope to the millions of viewers who watched her on the soap opera *Hope's Passion*.

She was not a stranger to Aidan, but not because of her television stardom. He knew her personally.

Very personally. "Kenzie."

"I can't—I can't hear you."

People never expected fire to be noisy, but it was. The flames crackled and roared at near ear-splitting decibels as they devoured everything in their path.

Including them if they didn't move, a knowledge

that was enough to pull his head out of his ass and get with the program. Old lover or not, he still had to get her out of there alive. But she was looking at him through Blake's eyes, and his heart and gut wrenched hard. There was maybe twenty feet of water between *Blake's Girl* and the next boat, which was starting to smoke as well, and would undoubtedly catch on fire any second. It didn't matter. They had no choice. "Kenzie, when I say so, I want you to hold your breath."

"D—do I know you?"

He wore a helmet and all his equipment, and in the dark, not to mention the complete and utter chaos around them, there was no way she could see him clearly. Still, he had to admit it stung. "It's me, Aidan. Hold your breath now, on my count."

"Aidan, my God."

"Ready?"

"The boat's going to go, every inch of it, isn't it?"

Yep, including the few square inches they were standing on. In fact, it was going to go much more quickly than he'd have liked. Since they couldn't get to the dock, it was into the ocean for them, where they'd wait for rescue.

"No," she said, shaking her head. "There's got to be another way."

Unfortunately there wasn't, and he quickly stripped out of his jacket and gear because the protection they offered wouldn't be worth the seventy-five pounds of extra weight while treading water and holding up Kenzie to boot. At least she was conscious. She didn't appear to have on any shoes, or anything particularly heavy on her person, all of which were points in her favor. "On three, okay? Remember to hold your breath."

"I don't think—"

"Perfect. Go with that. One—" He nudged her in front of him, pushing her to the railing.

"Aidan—"

"Two—"

"Are you crazy?"

"Three."

"Hell, no. I'm not going into the—"

He dropped her into the water, and she screamed all the way down.

2

KENZIE HIT THE ICY OCEAN, and as she took in a huge mouthful of water, she realized she'd forgotten to hold her breath, a thought that was completely eradicated when *Blake's Girl* exploded into the early dawn.

In the brilliant kaleidoscope, she barely registered the splash next to her, or the two strong arms that came around her, supporting her as flying pieces of burning debris hit the water all around them.

Aidan. My God, Aidan… That it was him boggled her mind. She tried to remind him that she could swim on her own, but the shock of the cold water sapped both her voice and the air in her lungs, and also hampered the working of her brain.

She'd never experienced anything like it. Never in her life had she been so hot and so frozen at the same time. The heat came from the flames, so high above them now that she was in the water, but no less terrifying. And yet, an icy cold had taken over her limbs, making movement all but impossible, weighing her down, sitting on her chest, sucking the last of the precious air from her overtaxed lungs.

Someone was screaming, and Kenzie envied their ability to draw air into their lungs because her own felt as constricted as if she had a boa slowly squeezing the life out of her.

The scream came again.

Huh?

It sounded sort of like her.

And then she realized, as if from a great distance, that it *was* her screaming, which meant that somehow she was breathing. Okay, that was good. So was the man holding her in the water, tucking her head against him, shielding her from the pieces falling out of the sky at his own risk. Without him, she'd have gone down like a heavy stone and she knew it.

"Shh," he was murmuring. "I've got you. It's okay, Kenzie, it's going to be okay…."

She was hurt, but not so hurt as to stop the memories bombarding her at the sound of his voice. How could she not have *instantly* recognized him?

He was the first man who'd ever broken her heart.

He'd ditched his helmet and she could see his face now. He didn't look happy to see her, and honestly, on that point, if he hadn't been saving her sorry ass, they'd have been perfectly in sync. "Aidan." She could see the fire reflected in his eyes. *Blake's Girl* was really blazing now. "My God, we almost—"

"I know." His short, dark hair was plastered to his head. Water ran in rivulets down his face, which was starkly pale. His long, inky-black eyelashes were spiky, and he had a cut above one eyebrow that was oozing blood. In spite of all of that, she had the most ridiculous thought: *wow,* he looked good all fierce and intense and wet.

Aidan Donnelly, first real boyfriend. First…everything…. She could hardly believe it, certainly couldn't process it, so she craned her neck, staring at the boat that looked like one big firecracker. "It just blew, and I—"

"Kenzie—"

"—I mean one minute I'm sitting there missing my brother, and the next…"

He looked into her eyes, his cool and composed. "It's going to be okay, but I need you to—"

"And it blew. I was just sitting there, surrounded by his things, missing him, and then *boom*. My Choos are probably halfway to China by now. I really liked those Choos."

"Kenzie," he said in a tone of authoritative calm. "I need you to listen to me now. Can you do that?"

She could take a gulp of air. But listening? The jury was still out on that one. Her ears were ringing. And the water was so damn cold. In fact, she was shaking and hadn't even realized it, shudders that wracked her entire body and rattled her teeth.

"Hold onto me, Kenzie. That's all you have to do, okay? Just hold onto me."

Right. Hold onto him. She'd grown up here in Santa Rey, and once upon a time she'd held onto him plenty. She'd held onto him, laughed with him, slept with him…

Actually, there'd never been much sleeping involved between them, a thought which brought an avalanche of others. Him fresh out of the firefighters' academy and possessing a body that had made her drool, not to mention the knowledge of how to use that body to make hers go wild…

But that had been what, six years ago? Hell, she could barely think, much else handle any math at the moment, so she couldn't be sure.

He was towing her out, away from the boat and any danger of falling debris, while shouting something to two firefighters on the other side of the burning vessel, both of whom had hoses on the fire.

She'd been in a fire before. On the set of her soap opera, *Hope's Passion,* before it'd been cancelled. But that was under carefully controlled circumstances. This wasn't a TV show with lines for her to follow. This was the real thing, with no makeup department standing by to color in pretend injuries, dammit.

She'd have loved a script right about now, with a happy ending, please.

At least she was still breathing.

Hard to beat that.

Blake's Girl hadn't gotten so lucky.

Neither had Blake. Oh, yeah, *there* was the familiar rush of pain, slicing right through the numbness from the cold water, lancing her heart—the pain that had been with her since she'd learned Blake was dead. Making it worse, adding confusion and anger to her grief was the fact that he'd been accused of being an arsonist and murderer.

God, Blake...

Another chunk of burning debris fell from the still flaming boat, and she imagined it was something of Blake's, something she'd never see again. Or maybe it was her own suitcase, or her laptop, which wasn't a big loss in the scheme of things, but it held the scripts she'd been writing...

At least if she died, she would no longer be a freshly unemployed soap star.

It was so damn ironic—she'd never been able to come home when Blake had been alive because she'd been too busy working. Then days after he'd died, her soap had been cancelled. Now she could drive up all she wanted, and he was gone.... Her first trip home in forever and it had been to see after his things, things that were now smoldering in the water around her.

"Don't give up on me," Aidan said. His eyes focused ahead on where he was swimming to, some point invisible to her. It was too dark to see their color clearly but she knew them to be a light brown with flecks of green that danced when he laughed.

He wasn't laughing now.

Nope.

He glanced at her, then resumed swimming straight and sure, moving them away from the flames, which also meant away from any warmth, while she did as he'd asked and just held on. She could do nothing but. Like old times...

Why did it have to be *him,* the guy who'd crushed

her heart, stomped on her pride and then walked away from her without a backward glance?

Did *he* hurt over the loss of Blake?

Did *he* believe the lies?

Because that thought, and all the others that came with it, came close to defrosting her, she shoved them aside. The blessed numbness was working for her. She hadn't come to Santa Rey in the past six years, but Blake had visited her in L.A. on the set, whenever he could, and on top of his visits, they'd been in frequent contact by e-mail, texting and phone calls, and had remained close despite their physical distance. He was the only family she'd had.

And now he was gone.

Forever gone.

"Kenzie? You still with me?" Aidan's lean jaw was tight with tension and was scruffy, as if he hadn't had time to shave in a day or two. Or four.

"Unfortunately." She'd like to be anywhere but "with" him. She could feel his longer, stronger legs moving, bumping into hers, and it made her irrationally mad. She didn't want help, not from him, but when she wriggled free to prove herself fine, she went down like a stone. Straight beneath the surface of the icy water, where she promptly did the stupid thing of opening her mouth to breathe and got a lungful of extremely cold salt water for her efforts.

Thankfully, she was immediately hauled back up again and pulled against a hard chest, one hand fisted in the back of her shirt, the other arm across the backs of her thighs in a grip that could have rivaled Superman's.

Firefighter to victim.

Not ex-boyfriend to ex-girlfriend.

And wasn't that just the problem? Once upon a time he *really* had had her, only he'd been the one to let go. He'd done it, he'd said, because of their respective careers and because he didn't like hiding their relationship from his friend Blake, but she knew the truth. It was because he'd decided she'd been falling in love with him and he hadn't been ready for love, so he'd shooed her away and had moved on.

She'd hated him for that for a good long time, for not giving himself a chance to feel what she'd felt, and, yeah, he'd been right—she *had* been more than halfway in love with him. It'd taken a while, but eventually her anger had drained, and she'd acknowledged that he'd been right to break it off with her before she'd gotten even more hurt…. But that hadn't eased her pain at the time.

Maybe she should consider herself lucky they were doing this reintroduction in an official capacity—him on the job, and her being just one in a blur of people he rescued. Less personal.

"Stop fighting me." His voice cut through the shocking noise of the night: the sirens, the shouting of the other firefighters and personnel, the ever-present, horrifying crackling of the flames, the small waves smacking into each other, waves that would be cresting over her head if it wasn't for Aidan's holding her with what appeared to be little to no effort. "I've got you."

"I don't want you to have me."

"Okay, roger that. But at the moment you don't have a choice."

"Of all the firefighters in this damn town…"

She thought she caught a flash of a grim smile. So he was no more thrilled than she was. He wasn't even looking directly at her, his attention instead focused on the boat behind her, and the dock behind that, reminding her that not only was he saving her hide, he was simultaneously looking for other people who needed help.

"I was alone on the boat," she told him.

"What were you doing?"

"Saying good-bye to Blake."

Sorrow, regret, and anguish all briefly flashed in his eyes. "Kenzie—"

"He didn't do those things you're all accusing him of, Aidan."

She had his attention now, all of it, and she'd forgotten the potency of having Aidan Donnelly giving her one-hundred-percent of his focus. *"He didn't."*

"Did he say something, anything to you at all, before he died?"

Died… Hearing the words from his mouth made Blake's death all the more real, as did being back here in her hometown, and it hit her hard. Throat so tight that she couldn't speak, she shook her head. No, Blake hadn't said anything at all, which made her feel even worse. "It wasn't him who set those fires. I know it."

"Kenzie," he said very gently, but she didn't want to hear it, didn't want to hear anything he said, so she shook her head again and closed her eyes, which brought an unexpected and horrifying sense of vertigo, making her clutch at him. "I want out."

"I know. They're coming for us right now."

That was good. Because something was definitely wrong. Her vision was getting fuzzy. Her brain was getting fuzzier. Scared and a little overwhelmed, she pressed her face into the crook of his neck, her nose to his throat, the position hauntingly familiar and at once flooding her with memories.

She'd been here before.

Okay, not here, not in the water, freezing, scared, but she'd been held by him, had pressed her face against his warm flesh and inhaled him in, absorbing the way he held her close, as if he'd never let anything happen to her.

He smelled the same, a scent she'd never quite managed to forget, and it was messing with her brain in spite of the fact that she'd just survived an explosion, a nighttime swim in the freezing ocean, and an uncomfortable reunion with the one and only guy she'd ever let break her heart.

Dammit. She blamed Blake. *Blake…*

"Kenzie." Aidan gave her a little shake. "Stay with me now."

No, thanks…

"Open your eyes," he demanded. "Come on, Kenzie. Stay awake, stay with me."

As opposed to giving in to the delicious lethargy slowly taking over? *Nah…* "Too tired."

"I know, but you can do this. You can do anything, remember?"

She nearly smiled at the reminder of her own personal motto, but then remembered who was talking. Yeah, she'd once believed that she could do anything, with him at her side.

He'd proved her wrong.

Oh, boy. Her eyes *were* closing. It'd be so easy to let them, to just drift off and not feel the cold anymore, but even in her fuzziness, she knew that was bad, so with great effort, she pried her eyes open.

And her gaze landed on him. The last time she'd seen him, she'd been so young. *They'd* been so young. She'd just turned twenty-two, been signed by a Los Angeles agent, and had landed her first small walk-on role. He'd been two years older, fit and gorgeous, and on top of his world as a young firefighter.

Plastered against him, her hands clenched on his biceps, her legs entwined with his, her chest up against him the way it was, she could feel that he was still fit.

Very fit.

And thanks to the flames and also the spotlights from the guys on the dock keeping track of them, she also knew that he was still gorgeous. If he hadn't cut her loose without a backward glance, she'd be happy to see him.

Very happy.

A group of firefighters had made their way through the flames to the end of the neighboring dock, and had secured it with criss-crossing lines of water. One of them leaped into the ocean, and with long, sure strokes swam toward them.

"Here," he called out to Aidan, holding out an arm for Kenzie.

"I've got her," Aidan said.

But Kenzie had had enough, of Aidan and his capable, strong arms, of his scent and especially of the memories. So she reached out for the second firefighter, going into his arms without looking back, arms that had never held her before, arms that didn't know her, arms that didn't evoke the past.

Even though she wanted to, she wouldn't look back.

3

By the time Aidan hauled himself out of the water, Ty had handed Kenzie off to the EMTs. Dustin and Brooke took her away from the flames and straight to their ambulance.

Good.

Chilled, drenched to the skin, Aidan made his way through the organized mayhem to his rig, where he stripped down and pulled on dry gear, the questions coming hard and fast in his head.

What the hell had Kenzie been doing there? Odd timing, given that in all these years, she'd not shown up in Santa Rey, not once. At least that he was aware of. Blake had never mentioned any visits, but then again, why would he? He'd had no idea that Aidan had dated his baby sister, and then walked away rather than engage his heart. They'd never told him, knowing he wouldn't have liked it.

Nope, Kenzie hadn't been back, not even for Blake's memorial service, and yet suddenly here she was, on Blake's boat, a boat that just happened to blow sky high once she'd set foot on it.

Odd coincidence.

During the time the two of them had been in the water together, the sky had lightened. Dawn had arrived. The chief had put an explosives team in place, and had a plan to contain the fire. Aidan needed to get back into the thick of it, but first he had to see Kenzie and make sure for himself that she was okay. She'd had a head laceration and multiple cuts and wounds, and that had been before he'd tossed her into the water.

He looked through the horde of people working the flames—Eddie and Sam, Aaron, Ty and Cristina, plus the guys from Thirty-Three, all on hoses and past the explosives experts surveying the still burning shell of *Blake's Girl* to where the ambulance was parked.

Kenzie was seated at the back of the opened rig between Dustin and Brooke. She was dripping everywhere, her clothes revealing what he already knew, that she was petite and in possession of a set of mouthwatering curves that had gotten only more mouthwatering in the past few years. She wore layered tees, the top one pink, ribbed and long-sleeved, unbuttoned to her waist, the one beneath white with pink polka-dots, opened to just between her breasts, both soaked through and suctioned to her body enough to expose her bra, which was also pink, lace and quite sheer.

He'd been a firefighter for years and he'd rescued countless victims, many female, some of whom had been as wet as Kenzie, and never, not one single goddamn time, had he ever stopped in the middle of a job to notice their breasts.

It was his first clue that he was in trouble, deep trouble—but when it came to Kenzie, that was nothing new. He chose to ignore his observation for now, for as long as he possibly could. His gaze dropped past her shirt with shocking difficulty, to a pair of button-fly jeans low on her hips, also dangerous territory because he'd always loved her legs, especially how bendy they could get....

Don't go there.

She shoved her hair out of her face, which still looked far too pale, even a little green, although that didn't take away from her beauty. Once upon a time she'd been a gorgeous study of sexy, frou-frou feminine mystery to him.

Some things never changed.

As if she felt his gaze, she looked up, and from fifty feet, between which were other firefighters, equipment and general chaos, she found him.

Between them the air seemed to snap, crackle, pop.

Six years ago, the thought of a long-distance relationship had been as alien to him as a close-distance relationship, and he'd told himself he had no choice but to break things off, even though that had really just been an excuse.

He'd broken things off because she'd scared him, she'd scared him deep. And apparently, given the hard kick his heart gave his ribs, she still did.

She'd been able to get inside him, make him feel things that hadn't been welcome, and, yeah, he'd run like a little girl.

He felt like running now.

But this time it was Kenzie who turned away. Dustin unfolded a blanket and wrapped it around her shoulders, while Brooke checked her pupils, then dabbed at the various cuts on her face.

Kenzie sat still, eyes closed now, looking starkly pale but alive.

Alive was good.

She huddled beneath the blanket, cradling a wrist, nodding to something Brooke asked her. Aidan knew that Brooke and Dustin, both close friends, would take good care of her. They took good care of everyone, which meant that Kenzie was in the very best hands.

Still in the thick of the organized chaos around him, Aidan took a second to let his gaze sweep over her. She really did seem as okay as he could hope for, and he told himself to turn away.

He was good at that. After all, he'd learned to do so at a young age from his own family, who'd shuffled him around more than a deck of cards on poker night. Yeah, he was good at walking away. Or at least good at pretending he didn't care when others walked away from him.

And after all, he'd done the same to her.

God, he'd been cruel to her all those years ago. Not that he'd meant to be. Going through the academy had been a life lesson for him. He *could* belong to a "family." He *could* make long-lasting friends. He *could* love someone with all his heart.

But loving his fellow firefighters like the brothers they'd become was one thing.

Loving Kenzie had been another entirely.

Since she'd left, he'd seen her only on TV. As a rule, he didn't watch soaps. He didn't watch much TV at all, actually. If he wasn't working, he was renovating the fixer-upper house he'd bought last year, emphasis on *fixer-upper.* If he wasn't doing that, he was playing basketball, or something else that didn't cost any money because the fixer-upper had eaten his savings.

But there'd been the occasional night where he'd sat himself in front of a game and caught a promo for Kenzie's soap. There'd also been the few times at the station where one of the guys had flipped on the TV during her show.

Three times exactly—and yeah, he remembered each and every one. The first had been five years ago, and she'd been wearing the teeniest, tiniest, blackest, stringiest bikini in the history of teeny-tiny black string bikinis, her hair piled haphazardly on top of her head with a few wild curls escaping, looking outrageously sexy as she'd seduced her on-screen lover. It'd taken him a few attempts to get the channel changed, and even then it hadn't mattered. That bikini had stuck with him for a good long while.

The second time had been a few Christmases back. She'd been wearing a siren-red, slinky evening dress designed to drive men absolutely wild. She'd been standing beneath some mistletoe, looking up at some "stud of the month." Aidan hadn't been any quicker with the remote that time, and had watched the entire, agonizing kiss.

The third time had been for the daytime Emmys. She'd accepted her award, thanking Blake for always believing in her, and then had thanked some guy named Chad.

Chad.

What kind of a name was Chad?

And where was Chad now, huh? Certainly not hauling her off a burning boat and saving her cute little ass. Guys named Chad probably only swam when playing water polo.

In the ambulance, Dustin said something to Kenzie, and she opened her eyes, flashing a very brief smile, but it was enough.

She was okay.

Aidan forced himself to move, to get back to the job at hand, and it was a big one. The explosions had caught the boats on either side of *Blake's Girl,* escalating the danger and damages. They had the dock evacuated, and as the sun streaked the sky, they were working past containment, working to get the flames one-hundred-percent out.

With one last look at Kenzie, Aidan entered the fray.

IT TOOK HOURS.

Aidan and his crew piled into their rigs just as the lunch crowd began to clutter the streets of Santa Rey. If he closed his eyes, he could still feel the imprint of Kenzie in his arms. He'd held onto her for what, three minutes tops? And yet she'd filled his head and his senses, and for those one-hundred-and-eighty seconds, time had slipped away, making him feel like that twenty-four-year-old punk he'd once been.

He'd been with Kenzie for one glorious summer, and she'd wanted to stay with him, which should have been flattering. She'd wanted to wear his ring and have a house and a white picket fence.

And his children.

But it hadn't been flattering at all. It'd been terrifying.

So he'd acted like a stupid, shortsighted guy. There was no prettying that up, or changing the memory. Fact was fact. He'd gotten a great job, and he'd had the world at his feet, including, he'd discovered, lots of women who found his chosen profession incredibly sexy.

He'd not been mature enough to realize what he already had; he'd been a first-class asshole. He'd sent Kenzie away, pretended not to look back and had filled his life with firefighting, women, basketball, woodworking, more women...

A hand clasped his shoulder. "Hey, Mr. 2008. Home sweet home."

"Shut up." They'd pulled into the station. He hopped out of the rig and went straight to Dustin, who was cleaning out the ambulance. "The victim? How is she?"

Cristina poked her head out from the station kitchen. "Hey, guys, there's food—" At the sight of Dustin, who she'd gone out with several times before unceremoniously discarding him without explanation, she broke off. "Oh. *You're* here."

Dustin looked at her drily. "What, is the food only for the staff that you *haven't* slept with and dumped?"

Aidan winced at the awkward silence, and if he wasn't in such a desperate hurry to hear about Kenzie, he might have refereed for the two of them, because if anyone needed refereeing, it was these two. "The vic," he said again to Dustin.

"Sorry," Dustin said, turning back to him. "She's not bad, thanks to your quick thinking. A few second-degree burns, possible broken wrist, some lacerations."

"Her head trauma—"

"No concussion."

"Stitches?" he demanded, causing Dustin to take a quick glance at Cristina, who raised an eyebrow.

Aidan knew he was bad off when the two of them could share a worried look over him.

"No stitches," Dustin said. "You okay?"

"Yeah." Aidan took his first deep breath in hours, which prompted another long look between Dustin and Cristina.

"You sure?" Cristina asked.

Jesus. "*Yes.*" Leaving them alone to work through their issues, he headed inside the station. After he'd showered, cleaned up and clocked out, he got into his truck and debated with himself.

Home and oblivion were attractive choices.

Or he could go to the hospital, see Kenzie and get a question or two answered.

Not quite as attractive, because nothing about sitting with Kenzie and looking into her soulful eyes was going to be simple. Nope, that was a guaranteed trip to Heartbreak City.

Home, then, where he wouldn't have to do anything but fall facedown into his bed. Yeah, sounded good. He put his truck in gear.

And drove to the hospital.

KENZIE OPENED HER EYES and stared at a white ceiling. She was on a cot in the emergency room, her cuts and burns all cleaned and bandaged, her wrist wrapped, her head stitched back on—okay, so it'd only needed butterfly bandages. Now she was being "observed," although for what, she had no idea.

At least she was warm again, or getting there. She had three blankets piled on top of her, which helped, and a hospital gown, which didn't.

She'd just seen the fire investigator, Mr. Tommy Ramirez. Tommy was short, dark, and quite to the point. The point being that he'd found it extremely odd that she'd been on Blake's boat at the time of its explosion.

She did, too, considering she'd only gotten to town that night. Closing her eyes, she frowned. She also found it odd that he was wasting his time questioning her instead of investigating the real perpetrator of the arsons, because her brother was *innocent*. No way had Blake set all those awful fires they were trying to pin on him. Blake, sweet, quiet, loving Blake, the brother who'd been there for her when their parents had died fifteen years ago, when they'd gone through foster care, when she'd wanted to go off to Hollywood. He'd never have hurt a fly much less purposely hurt another human being. And endanger a child?

Never.

God, she hated hospitals. They smelled like fear and pain and helplessness, and all of them combined reminded her of her own uncertain childhood. She wished she was back on the L.A. set of *Hope's Passion,* acting the part of the victim instead of really being one. Comfort food would help. Maybe a box of donuts—

From the other side of her cubicle curtain came a rustling, and then the hair at the back of her neck suddenly stood up, as if she was being watched. Opening her eyes, she blinked the room into focus. Everything was white and...*blurry*. But not so much so that she missed the back of a guy's head as he ran off and out of sight. "Hey!"

He hadn't been wearing scrubs but a red T-shirt, so he couldn't have been hospital staff. Who'd come to see her and then leave without a word? She struggled to think but she was so tired, and a little woozy still, and when she let her eyes drift shut, she ended up dozing off...

"NOT THE SAME TYPE of point of origin as the other fires."

Kenzie opened her eyes and turned her head, taking in the curtain, now pulled all the way closed around her cot. She was a woman who liked change, who in fact thrived on it, but she had to say, she didn't like this change. Not at all.

How much time had passed?

"So you're saying what, Tommy, that the chief has you on a gag order?"

Oh, boy. She didn't need to peek around the curtain to know *that* voice. That voice had once been the stuff of her daydreams, of her greatest fantasies. That voice had used to melt her bones away and rev her engines.

Aidan.

"I'm not saying anything," Tommy said. "Except what I told Zach weeks ago. I'm on this. It's a kid glove case. So you need to back off."

"I want to see Kenzie when she wakes up."

He'd been the one who'd looked in on her? She didn't know how she felt about that. Had he seen her sleeping? Had she been snoring?

Why hadn't he come back when she called out?

"Tell me this much at least," Aidan said, presumably still to Tommy. "Did either you or the chief even know Blake had a boat?"

"No, but I was waiting on a full investigative report from the county, and it would have shown up on there."

"And then you would've what, seized the property as evidence?"

"Yes, of course. To search it, just like we've done with his house. All the current evidence regarding the case points to Blake being in on the arson."

In on the arson. Kenzie absorbed the odd choice of words. Did he mean that he thought there could be more than one arsonist?

"So who beat you to the boat, Tommy? Who wanted to make sure there was no chance of extracting any evidence from it?"

The answer actually gave Kenzie hope—because it

meant that someone *else* could possibly be proven to be responsible for the arsons, maybe even someone who'd framed Blake.

"There's been at least seven highly destructive fires," Tommy said. "Adding up to millions of dollars in damages. The chief's ass is on the line, and so is mine. If Blake was still alive, he'd be behind bars. That he's not doesn't change anything. The investigation is ongoing."

"But it's possible he was working with someone," came Aidan's voice. "Is that what you're saying?"

"No comment."

"Do you know who?"

"No comment."

"You know something's off, Tommy, or you wouldn't be here."

"Yes," the investigator agreed tightly. "Something is off, and…"

Their voices lowered to a whisper. She leaned toward the curtain, but they were talking so quietly now she couldn't hear anything but…her name. Definitely, she'd heard her name.

Why were they talking about her?

She scooted even closer to the edge of the cot and cocked an ear, but still couldn't hear anything. *Dammit!* Blake couldn't have done any of those things they'd accused him of. She knew it, and she was going to prove it herself if necessary, starting with eavesdropping on this conversation. Tommy said something Kenzie couldn't quite catch, so she leaned even further, and—

Fell off the cot to the floor. *"Ouch."*

At the commotion, the curtain whipped open. She tried to push herself upright but with one wrist useless and the other pinned beneath her, she was pretty much a beached fish. A nearly naked beached fish, with her butt facing a crowd of three: Tommy, the nurse and, oh, perfect—Aidan. She could see the tabloids now: Ex-Soap Star Mackenzie Caught Panty-less. "Ouch," she said again and rolled to her back, gasping when the cold linoleum hit her bare backside. She sighed just as someone dropped to his knees at her side, and then Aidan's face swam into her vision.

"Are you okay?" he demanded.

Sure. Sure, she was okay. If she didn't think about the fact that she'd just mooned him.

"Here." After helping him get her back on the cot, the nurse fussed a moment, checking all of Kenzie's various injuries. Luckily, Tommy had backed out of the room, vanishing, for now at least.

"What the hell were you doing?" Aidan demanded when the nurse left them alone, too.

"Oh, a little of this, a little of that—" Realizing her gown was twisted very high up on her thighs—which, of course, was nothing to what he'd just seen—she grabbed her blanket and tried to cover herself up. A little like closing the barn door after the horse had escaped, she knew, but she was mortified. Except the movement made her want to throw up, and she reached up, holding her head tightly.

"Here." He took over the task of covering her,

quickly extricating his hands when he was done, not quite meeting her gaze as he sat at her side.

Awkward moment… "So," she said. "What are you doing here?"

"Looking in on you."

Yep. And he'd gotten to look in on far more than he'd probably intended.

"Are you all right?" he asked.

"Depends on your definition of *all right*."

At that, his eyes cut to hers and he sighed, scrubbing a hand over his face, his fingers rasping over the growth there. He looked and sounded exhausted. "I'm sorry, Kenzie."

"For what? That I just mooned you, or that I'm here at all?"

Aidan got to his feet, pulling the curtain shut again to give them privacy, privacy that she wasn't sure she wanted.

He'd changed his clothes. He wore a pair of jeans now, loose on his long legs, low on his hips, with a long-sleeved shirt unbuttoned over a gray T-shirt that seemed to emphasize his broad shoulders and tough, athletic build. "Your shirt isn't red," she said slowly.

"What?"

"Before, somebody in a red shirt was looking at me."

"When?"

"I don't know." She rubbed her temples. "I'm out of it."

"It was a tough night."

"Yeah." But *he* didn't look like he'd just worked his

ass off and managed to save her life to boot; he looked casual, relaxed.

Cool as a cucumber.

And so hauntingly familiar, not to mention gorgeous, that she couldn't keep her eyes on him. How unfair was it that he'd gotten even better-looking with age? "Thanks for stopping by, Aidan, but you can see I'm fine. You can go."

He looked doubtful.

"Seriously. I'm really okay."

She almost had him, she could tell, but then she ruined it by shivering.

Without a word, he grabbed another blanket and settled it over her. She appreciated his sense of duty, but what she would appreciate even more would be his vanishing.

Or her.

Yeah, that might be better. If she could just vanish on the spot. *Poof.* "Okay, now I'm good, thanks. Really."

"Really?"

"Yes. I mean you can't even look at me, so—"

Lifting his head, he met her eyes, his hot enough to singe her skin.

"Oh," she breathed, feeling her heart kick, hard.

"I can't look at you?" he repeated in low disbelief. "Are you kidding me? Kenzie, I can't do anything *but* look at you."

4

At Aidan's words, Kenzie's breath caught and held. She didn't know how to take him, especially the way he was looking at her, as if maybe he could see all the way through her, to her heart and soul, right to the very center of her being, where all the hurt was so carefully bottled up.

She'd gotten over him. Years ago. She really had. She'd gotten over how he'd once made her laugh, made her think, made her happy…

Made her come…

No way could he possibly reach her now. Not with that hard body, not with the look in his eyes and definitely not with the memories.

Okay, maybe the memories got to her, just a little bit. For one glorious summer, he'd been the best part of her life—before he'd walked away without so much as a glance back, that is.

Good. There was her anger, which would hopefully negate the fact that he was standing right here in the flesh looking good enough to…well… That thought made her want to sweat. But apparently she could be both over him and turned on by him at the same time, which confused her to say the least. She had no idea what that was about. No idea at all.

None.

She'd moved on years ago from that young, sweet, innocent girl. Now she was a woman with a backbone of sheer steel that had gotten her through some tough times.

She knew people tended to look at her carefully cultivated outer package—thank you, stylist to the stars—an outer package that was petite and willowy, even fragile-looking, and completely underestimate her.

But on the inside she was one-hundred-percent survivor, thank you very much. She'd lived through losing her parents early, through a happy-as-it-could-be teenage-hood with just Blake. She'd lived through being in the public eye, through the ups and downs of TV fame and most recently, through the death of her brother. All of that would have cracked most women, but she wasn't easily cracked.

She would get to the bottom of this mess, no matter what she had to do in order to get there. *No matter what.* Even if she had to use her beauty, her checking account, her damn body.

She would do it.

Whatever it took.

For Blake.

"I heard you talking to the investigator," she said softly.

Aidan's eyes met hers, and she wished like hell she

could read his mind. But she couldn't, and he didn't say another word to help.

"I think he's wondering if I'm guilty of something."

He just looked at her some more.

"The only thing I'm guilty of is knowing that he hasn't done his job if he thinks Blake did those things."

At that, his face softened, and regret filled his eyes, along with a grimness that had her shaking her head before he even spoke.

"Don't say it," she warned, not willing to hear it, not from him. Not from anyone. Not when she was this close to a breakdown. A grief breakdown. "Don't." She *knew* Blake, goddammit. She did. She didn't remember much about her parents before they'd died in a car crash, but she remembered Blake. Every bit of him. He was the boy who'd held her hand every time they'd had to move to a new foster home. He was the teenager who'd punched a boy in the face when he'd hurt her, he was the man who'd believed in her enough to work double shifts to pay for her publicity shots so she could pursue her acting dream.

He could *never* have committed arson. She'd have sworn Aidan would have known that as well, but apparently she was wrong.

"There's evidence—" he began, but she shook her head.

"Circumstantial." She swallowed hard but a lump of emotion, the one that had been there since Blake's death, remained. "I see that you're no better a friend than you were a boyfriend."

He opened his mouth, but before he could respond, the nurse pulled aside the curtain and entered the cubicle, followed by a doctor. "Everyone out," the nurse ordered.

"I'm the only one here," Aidan said.

"So get out," the nurse responded sweetly.

Kenzie closed her eyes and lay back. She didn't look at Aidan again; in fact, she didn't open her eyes until she heard the rustling of the curtain, signaling he'd left.

Which was fine. Perfect, really. Because she'd sure as hell rather be alone than look into his eyes and see things she didn't want to see.

AIDAN EXITED the emergency room, feeling like a class-A jerk. Though how that was possible, what with his saving her life and all, he had no idea....

Okay, he knew.

She'd seen the look in his eyes; she'd understood something she hadn't wanted to understand—that he knew Blake was involved with those arson fires.

Aidan felt torn up about it, sick over it, but facts were facts. Blake had been placed at the scene of each arson by various witnesses. He had been depressed since losing Lynn, his partner before Cristina, in a fire the year before. His home had been seized and searched, and in his garage they'd found a stack of wire mesh trash cans, similar to the ones identified as the point of origin in each of the arsons.

Most damning, Aidan's partner, Zach, had also seen

him holding a blowtorch just moments after Zach's house had been set on fire, with Zach and Brooke inside. Zach had almost died there.

And Blake *had* died there, perhaps deliberately. He'd died, leaving all of them, Zach, Aidan and the other firefighters, even Tracy, the woman he'd had such a crush on, everyone, destroyed.

Kenzie was in denial. He got that. She was angry. He got that, too. She needed someone to vent that anger at, to place it on, and he'd been handy enough.

I see that you're no better a friend than you were a boyfriend.

Yeah, that had been a direct hit. Having her look at him as if *he* was the bad guy had really gotten to him, especially considering he still had the scrapes and bruises from saving her.

The late afternoon sun was sinking fast, cooling off the day. Having been up for two straight days now, he desperately needed sleep. He could close his eyes standing up right there in the hospital lot, and not wake up if a cyclone hit. He was so tired that he'd probably sleep completely dreamless. Well, except for maybe dreaming about Kenzie's bare ass. Yeah, now that he'd seen that again, he'd most likely dream about it for a good many hours.

Days.

Years.

"Aidan."

Hell. Tommy was leaning up against Aidan's truck, a file in his hands, mouth pinched tight, looking as if he had plenty of things to say, and all fantasies about Kenzie's ass vanished. "What now?"

"I wasn't aware that you knew her personally."

"Who?"

"Come on, Aidan. Don't play with me. Mackenzie Stafford. You didn't say that you knew her."

He sighed. "So?"

"So it felt to me like maybe you knew her...*well*."

"Yeah. Once upon a time."

"Okay, and so once upon a time, did you know she was Blake's sister?"

Getting into tricky territory here. No one had known he and Kenzie had dated in the past. It'd been a quick, hot thing, *very* hot, and he certainly hadn't been in any hurry to tell Blake he'd gotten his sister in bed. Kenzie hadn't told Blake, either, for her own reasons, and then when Kenzie had gone off to Los Angeles, it hadn't mattered anymore.

Did it matter now, with Blake dead? He couldn't see how it did. "Yeah, I knew she was Blake's sister."

"Did you know that boat was Blake's?"

"Where are we going with this, Tommy?"

"Did you?"

Aidan let out a breath. "Not until we were in the water and she told me."

Tommy nodded. "Because you always sit around with someone you're rescuing and chat about property ownership."

"I asked her why she was there, on that boat. I was under the impression that she was in Los Angeles."

"Yeah?" Tommy's eyes studied him, considering. "So just how well do you know her?"

"Irrelevant."

"I wonder if Blake would have thought so."

Aidan fished his keys out of his pocket. "I'm going home to sleep. For many, many hours. When I'm back on duty you can drill me all you want. Maybe I'll be able to think more clearly."

"Maybe I don't want you thinking more clearly."

"And what the hell does that mean?"

"It means I need answers now. Did you know she was staying on the boat? Did you maybe visit with her there before the fire?"

"I told you. No. And no."

"Ms. Stafford thinks Blake is innocent. That he was not only framed but possibly murdered, and she intends to prove it."

Sounded right. Kenzie might look like a pretty ball of fluff, but she had sharp wits and was loyal to a fault. She also had the tenacity of a bulldog. Once she got her brain wrapped around an idea, there was nothing anyone could do to change her mind. Not about falling in love with him, not about being an actress and most definitely not about believing that Blake couldn't be guilty of arson.

"So the question stands," Tommy said quietly. "How well do you know her?"

"Did." Well enough that when he'd looked into her eyes, he'd felt an odd stirring, a sensation almost like coming home. Yeah, once upon a time he'd known her well. As well as he'd known anyone. "Past tense."

"Good enough."

"For what?"

"To get you to tell her to stay the hell out of this investigation and not interfere."

"People don't tell Kenzie what to do."

"You're going to. Because the chief has put out the word. If anyone hinders this investigation, we'll have them arrested, Blake's sister or not."

Great. Perfect. If Aidan told her that, she'd jump in with both feet, because one thing he remembered and remembered well—nothing scared her. Nothing. "Seriously. It's not a good idea for me to tell her anything."

"Well, then, I hope she has bail money."

Shit. Aidan watched Tommy walk away, then he turned to his truck. Needing sustenance before he passed out cold for at least the next twelve hours straight, he stopped at Sunrise, the café that was the perpetual hangout for everyone at the station. The two-story building was right on the beach. Downstairs was food central, while the second floor was the living quarters for Sheila, the owner. The rooftop was the place to go to view the mountains, the ocean, the entire world it seemed, and to think.

Stepping inside, his sense of smell immediately filled with all the aromas he associated with comfort: coffee, burgers, pies... Sheila smiled at him, and as the sixty-two-year-old always did, fawned over him as he imagined a mother would.

His own mother wasn't too into fawning, at least not over him. She'd divorced his father when Aidan had been two, and he'd spent most of his childhood years being shuffled from family member to family member while she'd relived her wild youth. Granted, he'd been more than a handful of trouble, purposely going after it in a pathetic bid for attention, so in hindsight he didn't blame anyone for not keeping him around for long.

Eventually, he'd ended back up at his dad's, where the two of them had spent a few years doing their best to tolerate each other until, when Aidan had been fifteen, his dad had remarried and promptly given his new wife three babies in a row.

Aidan had landed at his mom's once again, a little bit rebellious and a lot angry, but by then his mother had settled down some, remarrying as well.

Now Aidan had five half brothers and sisters, and didn't quite belong on either side of the family.

Not that he'd had it as rough as Blake and Kenzie had. He knew exactly why the brother and sister had been as close as they had, and exactly why Kenzie would fight tooth and nail to prove her brother's innocence.

What he didn't know was how to convince her to let the law handle things, or if he even had a right to ask such a thing of her.

Between a rock and a hard place.

He ate his fill, and by the time he set down his fork, he felt halfway human. He still needed his bed, badly, but with Tommy's words echoing in his head, he knew he had to try to talk to Kenzie again first. He needed to warn her to let Tommy do his job. For old times' sake.

Or so he told himself.

He pulled out his cell phone and called the hospital, but was told she'd been released.

Where would she go? Back to Los Angeles? No, she wouldn't leave Santa Rey, not until she did what she'd come to do, which was prove Blake's innocence, so he asked Sheila for the local phone book and a slice of key lime pie, both of which he took up to the roof. Sitting facing the ocean, he began calling. But as it turned out, Kenzie wasn't registered at any of the three hotels in the area, probably because there were two conventions in town and everything was fully booked. He looked at the remaining list of several dozen motels and B and Bs, and sighed. He'd made his way through the most likely candidates when Sheila came out on the roof with a fresh mug of coffee.

"What's up for you tonight?" Even with her bouffant hair, she barely came up to his shoulder. "You planning on saving any more damsels in distress?"

He didn't bother asking her how she knew about last night's fire—the gossip train in Santa Rey was infamous. "No damsels, distressed or otherwise. I have a bed in my immediate future."

"You sleeping alone these days?"

Unfortunately, yeah. The last woman he'd gone out with had found someone else, someone with more money and more time, and he'd gotten over her fairly quickly but hadn't yet moved on. He couldn't tell that to Sheila, though, or she'd set him up with her niece, as she'd been trying to do all year....

"My niece would be perfect for you, Mr. 2008."

He winced. "You saw the calendar."

"Honey, I saw, I bought, we all drooled. Now about my niece…"

Her niece was divorced with four kids, and while she was a very lovely woman, a waitress at Sunrise, in fact, he wasn't anxious to help create yet another fractured family. "I'm sorry, Sheila. But at the moment, I'm—"

"Enjoying being alone," Sheila finished for him with a sigh. "Yeah, yeah, I've heard it before."

Standing, he handed her back the phone book, then gave her a hug. "How about you? You could marry me."

She cackled good and long over that one, and walked to the roof door. "If I was thirty years younger, you'd be sorry you said that…."

He laughed, but his smile faded fast enough. With no idea how to track down Kenzie, he left and drove home, thinking he'd just go horizontal for a little while and then figure it out, but as he drove up to his house, he saw a red convertible Mercedes Cabriolet in his driveway.

And the outline of a woman sitting on his porch, lit from behind by the setting sun.

She was wearing two hospital gowns layered over each other and a pair of hospital booties, reminding him that her clothes had gotten sliced and diced pretty good and probably any luggage she'd had on the boat was long gone.

Her hair, wild on the best of days, had completely rioted around her face in an explosion of soft waves, the long side bangs poking her in one eye and resting against her cheek and jaw, where she had a darkening bruise that matched the one above her other eye, accompanied by a two-inch-long butterfly-bandaged cut. She was cradling her splinted left wrist in her lap. Her good hand was cut up as well, and so were both her arms—nothing that appeared too deep or serious, but enough to make him wince for her. Her legs were more of the same.

She was alone and beat up, and hell if that didn't grab him by the throat and squeeze. Then there were those melt-me eyes that lifted to his and filled.

Jesus. He thought he was so damn tough but one soft sigh from those naked lips and he was a bowl of freaking jelly.

She had a plastic bag beside her, and one peek at it tugged at him harder than he could have imagined given what he did for a living and how often he'd seen this very thing.

Her clothes from the fire.

Probably all that she had left here in Santa Rey. In her unsplinted hand she clutched a small prescription bottle, most likely pain meds. *Hell.* He was such a goner.

"I haven't taken any yet," she whispered, shaking the bottle. "Couldn't, because I took a cab from the hospital to the docks where I had my car, which I drove here."

"Kenzie—"

"You had a package. It was torn, so I looked in." She

lifted one of a stack of firefighter calendars, with his own mug and half-naked body on the cover.

"Nice," she said, a ghost of a smile crossing her lips. "Mr. 2008."

He bit back a sigh. "It's for charity."

"And you definitely contributed." She waggled her eyebrows, then winced. "*Ouch.* I'm not allowed in Blake's house—evidence. And the hotels are all booked up, just my luck. Did you know you have a convention of dog trainers in town? Why are there five hundred dog trainers in Santa Rey?"

"Because we let dogs on our beaches."

"Oh." She sighed. "So we let dogs on our beaches, but not me into a hotel. Kinda makes sense when you think about it."

How that made sense, he had no idea.

"Because my karma sucks."

"Okay, come on." Gently, he pulled her up, taking the bag. Letting her hold onto the medication, he led her inside, telling himself he was going to give her Tommy's warning and that was it.

Other than that, he was going to stay out of it entirely.

But holding onto her, he realized she was trembling, and as he took her into his living room, she went directly for his couch, which she sank onto with a grateful little sigh. "I think she went on vacation."

"Who?"

"My karma." She gave him an exasperated look, like he wasn't listening to her, and then very carefully leaned her head back and closed her eyes.

"Hey." Squatting down before her, he put his hands on her thighs, looking into her eyes when she opened them. "You okay?"

She let out a sound that might have been a laugh, or a sob.

He hoped to God it was the first. "Rough twenty-four hours," he murmured.

Another nod, carefully slow and precise, giving her away. She definitely wasn't laughing. In fact, she was in pain, lots of it; rising, he went into the kitchen for a glass of water. Bringing it back to her, he pried the prescription drugs from her fingers, read the label— yep, painkillers—and shook one out.

"I'm okay."

"You don't look it. You look like hell."

"You say the nicest things."

With another sigh, he once again hunkered down at her side. "Look, you've been through a lot. I know you're alone and…"

"If you say helpless, I'll slug you with my good fist."

Once upon a time she'd been the most amazing thing in his life.

The. Most. Amazing. Thing.

On the outside she'd been so mind-blowingly, adorably, effortlessly sexy. Inside, she'd been pure warmth and sweetness, loyal to a fault, always believing the best in everyone, willing to defend what she believed in to the death if necessary.

From their very first moment together, she'd wreaked havoc with his common sense. Before her, nothing in his world had been warm or sweet or particularly loyal. She'd brought lightness into the dark.

Until he'd sent her away. "Not helpless," he said a little thickly. "Never helpless."

"Okay, then." She hugged herself and shivered.

With a frown, he moved to the fireplace. For late summer, the evening did have a chill to it, and she probably was still in some shock. He set up kindling and held a lit match to it until it flamed with a low *whoosh*.

With a startled cry, Kenzie shrank back from the small flames, covering her face.

Yeah, still in shock. He should have thought about how she'd feel about a flame of any kind, and cursing himself, he rose and went to her.

"I'm okay," she whispered, peeking out from between her fingers, very carefully not looking at the flickering fire. "It's the crackling." She grimaced. "And, okay, the sight. I don't know what's wrong with me."

"It's normal."

"I don't feel normal."

He didn't feed the small fire, letting it burn out. "I'm sorry. Let's go with the heater instead, okay?"

Once again she leaned her head back, carefully not moving a single inch more than she absolutely had to. "Thanks."

She was killing him. "Kenzie—"

"Could we not talk? It's threatening my head's precarious perch on my shoulders."

"Take the pill."

"I guess I could use a little oblivion. Okay, I could use a lot of oblivion...." Turning her head, she eyed the fireplace as if it were a spitting cobra. "You know, they don't call me Kenzie in Los Angeles."

"Or in the gossip rags."

Without moving another muscle, she arched an eyebrow, appearing to be genuinely surprised. He'd given himself away.

"You read them?"

"Hard to miss when you're going through the grocery store," he said defensively. "They're right next to the candy bars."

The smallest smile crossed her lips.

"You dated that underwear model. The one who danced naked on all the commercials. Chad."

"Chase. And he wasn't naked. He was wearing the underwear he was marketing. Which isn't that much less than what you're wearing in that calendar, Mr. 2008." She gave him a long look.

"Last year you went out with a European prince."

"Now that was just publicity."

He didn't know if he believed her, or cared.

Strike that. He cared. "Take the pill." He watched her chase it with the glass of water he offered.

Yeah, he cared.

Dammit.

"Problem," she said, and licked a drop of water off her bottom lip.

He dragged his gaze up to hers. "What?"

"Even if there were no dogs. I still couldn't get a

room. I have no money—my purse either burned up or is below several yards of water, probably both." Kenzie winced. "The hospital had to give me an emergency taxi voucher to get to my car. I'd be really screwed right now if my keys hadn't been in my pocket. Luckily, I also left my cell in the car, so I called my financial manager and he's overnighting emergency funds. But your address was the only one I could think to give him, and I have no place to go until it arrives. And now I can't drive." She shook the bottle of pills. "It's not recommended."

Their eyes met as the implications of her little speech sank in.

"Apparently, I still trust you," she whispered. "At least a little."

Damn if that didn't cut right through everything to the heart of the matter. For better or worse, she trusted him, and he had to admit, that meant something to him. Plus, there was the other truth—there was no other place she could go. Like it or not, he was her only contact in town. Which meant…

She was staying here.

With him.

5

KENZIE SAT ON AIDAN'S COUCH absorbing the awkward silence. Her eyes were closed but she could feel him close. Thinking. Probably panicking. "Or if you loan me a few bucks, I'll call a cab."

"And go where?"

Right. Well, dammit, if he'd just give her some room, she could just sit and try to ignore him—*try* being the key word.

It wasn't his good looks that held her interest. She'd had her fill of good-looking guys on a daily basis at work and she would have said Aidan wasn't that pretty, at least not soap-star pretty. Until she'd seen the calendar. Because holy cow, he'd looked pretty damn fine in eight-and-a-half-by-eleven color glossy, there was no doubt. But he was also tough, and far more rugged than that. There was just something about his eyes and mouth, and the laugh lines lining both that suggested he could be dangerous or outrageous, sweet or maybe not so much so, sheer trouble or the boy next door….

She knew all to be true.

What she didn't know was why she'd come *here,* to his house.

Okay, she knew. He was the only familiar thing in her entire world. She'd gotten his address easily enough by calling his station, where some friendly firefighter had recognized her and cheerfully offered up direction. She'd driven here on auto-pilot, having no trouble remembering her way around Santa Rey, getting spooked only when she'd thought she was being followed by a gray sedan.

Which was ridiculous and paranoid. God, she needed a nap.

Aidan's house was tiny, and definitely old, but cozy. From the looks of things, he'd been remodeling it. The living room had lovely hardwood floors and gorgeous wood trim on all the windows, which looked out to the ocean and the rolling hills surrounding it.

He'd always been handy—with tools, with his mind, his words.

His body…

Yeah, he'd been really good in that department. In fact, it was fair to say he'd been her willing tutor, and she a most apt pupil.

But that thought led to others, including the fact that she'd once been young and stupid enough to believe in fairy tales. Aidan had been her prince, her happily-ever-after.

Until he hadn't been.

Luckily she was no longer young or stupid. She no longer dated men while dreaming of that white picket fence and two point four kids. Nope, she dated simply to have fun, and once in a while, to have good sex.

Easy come, easy go.

Too bad she and Aidan weren't having a go at things now, because she was finally with the program, she finally got the rules. They'd probably have a hell of a time.

An evening breeze came through an open window and she drew in a fresh breath. Her pain pill had begun to kick in, and she sank a little deeper into the very comfortable couch. The last time she'd been in Aidan's place, which back then had been an apartment, he'd owned a bed, a TV, a stereo and a box of condoms.

That'd been all they'd needed.

She hadn't been the only one to change. His needs had apparently upgraded. His couch was extra large, and double extra comfortable. There was a TV, triple extra large, and the perennial stereo. But he also had a desk with a computer on it, and some beautiful prints on the walls, which were painted in muted beachy colors.

No condoms in sight. That was undoubtedly for the best. But she liked the house. Low maintenance, calm, even warm and clean. Her place wasn't so different, which meant she felt far more at home here than she would have ever admitted out loud.

How ironic that she'd come back into town to handle Blake's affairs, and to raise hell on the arson charges, intending to stay as far out of Aidan's path as possible, only to end up here in his house, with nowhere else to go.

High on meds...

From the windows she could hear the waves slapping against the shore. Next to her, he was still, just sitting there breathing, soft and even, but she didn't look at him. Wasn't ready to look at him. Yet apparently her nose didn't get that memo because her nostrils quivered, trying to catch a quick whiff of the man—except all she could smell was herself and the smoke and soot stuck to her skin. "I stink."

"It's stress."

"No, not like that." She rolled her eyes, which hurt like a son-of-a-bitch. "Like smoke."

"You could take a shower." His voice was low, a little gritty, and a whole lot suggestive, although she knew that last was all her own imagination.

She couldn't help it, the guy had a voice that brought to mind slow, hot sex. Seriously, if he could bottle the sound, he'd have been rich.

"Kenzie? Do you want to take a shower?"

Yes, please. In her own place with her own things and her own thick, cozy, warm bathroom and fuzzy bunny slippers. And then she'd like a good DVD and a bag of popcorn, something to give her mind a mini-vacation from its current hell. "That would be nice, thanks."

He offered her a hand. She stared at it, and then into his face, which was solemnly watching her. "Just a hand," he murmured.

Knowing she was a bit wobbly, she put her hand in his bigger, warmer one and let him pull her up. She staggered into him, and for a moment he held her, and caving in to her own yearning, she pressed her face to his throat and was immediately overcome with memories.

But she didn't do memories, at least not anymore, so she forced herself to step free of him.

He led her down the hall and into what must have been his bedroom. The walls were a soft cream, which went beautifully with the cedar ceilings. But what caught her eye was the biggest bed she'd ever seen, piled high with a thick navy-blue comforter and a mountain of pillows. It was made, sort of. It was *boy*-made, which meant the covers had been tugged up. His hamper appeared to be a pile of clothes in the corner, but other than that, the room was as warm and clean and welcoming as the rest of the house.

She shouldn't have been surprised. The Aidan she'd known had been rough-and-tumble tough, always cool and calm and impenetrable no matter the circumstances, which she imagined served him well in his field. She'd seen that in action on the boat and in the water.

But much like his house, he had a warm, soft, welcoming center. It was what had made him so damn likeable.

Now, with the dubious honor of a few years and some maturing, that likeability had turned into an undeniable sex appeal she discovered while standing there staring at his bed, feeling a rather inexplicable stirring deep in her belly.

"Here." With a hand to the small of her back, he gently nudged her all the way into the room, then passed by her, his arm brushing hers as he moved into the bathroom, which was all cool, white tile and more wood trim. He flipped on the shower, which was nearly as big as his entire kitchen.

"Wow," she said, staring at it.

He shrugged. "I like showers."

"I remember." The words slipped out of her mouth before she could stop them. *Damn,* she really needed a script writer for this real-life thing.

His gaze slid to hers. Very slowly, he arched an eyebrow.

She turned away to blush in peace, but he turned her back toward him with a careful hand on her arm. "Kenzie?"

She stared at his chest, her vision a little compromised by the nice little pill she'd taken, but not so much so that she couldn't appreciate the view. "Yeah?"

"Do we need to talk?"

Absolutely not. "No."

She didn't want to discuss her carnal knowledge of his love of showering. Not when she remembered, in vivid Technicolor, taking more than a few with him. She remembered, for instance, the time he'd backed her up to the shower wall in his apartment, lifting her legs around his waist, thrusting into her until she couldn't have told him her own name. She remembered the feel of him, hot and thick inside her, remembered how it felt to be pressed between the hard wall and his harder body, the water pounding down over the top of them until she'd cried out so loudly his roommate had pounded on the bathroom door to make sure she was okay…. They'd laughed so hard they'd barely been able to finish, but they'd managed.

They'd always managed.

The humbling truth was, once upon a time, he'd been able to make her come in less than three minutes, using nothing more than his mouth and his portable showerhead.

God.

Just the reminder had her beginning to sweat and her knees wobbling. And if she was being honest, there were some other even more base reactions going on. She firmly ignored them all and lifted her chin. "No. We don't need to talk."

He nodded very solemnly, but she would have sworn his eyes had heated, and along with that heat was a sort of wry humor.

Oh, perfect. Now *he* was remembering, too.

But what really cooked her goose was while she was squirming, nipples hard, thighs trembling, he was amused.

She ought to slug him. She thought about it, but just then, from the plastic hospital bag came the muffled sound of her cell ringing. Since it could only be someone she didn't want to talk to, like her agent wanting her to get in line for auditions before everyone else from her show snatched up all the jobs, she ignored it.

He gestured toward the steaming shower. "It was the first thing I redid in the house."

Thinking about his shower was infinitely more appealing than thinking about being unemployed. Thinking about him *in* the shower? Priceless. But he was still looking just amused enough at her interest that she shrugged lightly. *Look at me not caring...*

But on the inside she was caring big-time, wondering how the hell to get him *un*-amused and hot, because dammit she wanted him hot.

Why the hell she wanted it made no sense to her, none whatsoever, but she couldn't stop thinking about it. *She* was hot, so *he* needed to be the same. Call it petty revenge on the guy who'd once walked away from her. Call it desperation for a diversion from her real reason for being here. But she wanted him to want her. *Needed* him to want her. She wanted that more than her next breath, and she wanted him to suffer for it.

Around them the steam started to rise, but instead of declaring his undying lust for her, he turned and walked back into his bedroom, vanishing from view.

Kenzie let out a breath. Weary, tired of her own smoky stench, she removed her splint and reached for the tie on her hospital gowns, then went still in surprise when Aidan reappeared.

His broad shoulders filling the doorway, his dark eyes met hers as he held out two folded towels. "You still like to use two?"

She blinked as he set them on the counter by the sink. "Yeah." She cleared her throat. "Thanks."

Jaw a little tight, he nodded, and very carefully didn't come any closer.

Huh. He didn't look that amused now. He looked, dared she think it, a little…hot.

Interesting.

He was going to give her some privacy. Privacy that, shock of all shocks, she didn't actually want. But there he went, turning away again.

"I'll be in the other room if you need anything," he said. "Just call for me."

Wow. He was being considerate, sweet and sensitive, none of the traits she would have associated with him. "You know, this would probably be a lot easier on me if you could continue to be the asshole that you once were."

"Yeah, there's a problem with that."

"Which is?"

"I'm not the same guy I was then."

She opened her mouth, not sure what she planned on saying, but it didn't matter because he walked away, shutting the door quietly behind him.

Kenzie stared at the closed door before stripping and then getting into the shower. Once there, she hissed when the water hit her various cuts but she stood beneath the spray anyway, for a very long time, before finally soaping up. It took five shampoos to get out the smoke smell and even then she wasn't sure she managed completely. By the time the hot water was gone, her skin was wrinkled like a prune and she smelled like Aidan. It was ridiculous but she kept lifting her arm to her nose so she could inhale the scent of him.

When she'd wrapped herself up in the towels, one

on her head, one around her body, she opened the bathroom door and found Aidan sitting on the bed, his legs spread, his hands clasped between them, his face pensive. "Better?" he asked, looking for himself.

"Almost human."

A brief smile curved his lips as he held out bandages and antiseptic cream for her injuries. "I was wondering if you planned on drowning yourself in there."

"I'm angry and frustrated and devastated, but not stupid."

He let out a slow nod, his gaze dropping from her face to her body, studying the towel covering her from just beneath her armpits to mid-thigh. She was gratified to see an absolute lack of humor now.

Slowly he stood up, and something surged within her. Lust, which she beat back. Triumph, which she let take over. *Want me...* Yeah, that worked for her, him wanting her. Because when he admitted that out loud, she was going to lift her chin, flat-out reject him and maybe feel just the tiniest bit better.

She hoped. God, she hoped. Because *something* had to ease this knot in her chest. *Knot, hell.* It was a ball, a huge ball, and it was suffocating her. If she gave too much thought to it, it swelled even bigger and threatened to overcome her.

Then he walked toward her, and she shivered in anticipation because here it came, the him wanting her portion of the evening.

But he simply held out her cell phone. "It went off again when you were in the shower. Local cell number."

"Oh." She flipped it open and looked at it, having no idea who would be calling her locally. Blake had been her last tie to Santa Rey. In any case, whoever it was hadn't left a message so she set the phone down.

Aidan strode right past her, going to his dresser.

Okay, she could work with this. Maybe he was going for a condom. Which of course he wasn't going to need—

He held up a shirt. "You still like to sleep in just a T-shirt?"

She stared at the shirt in his hand, at the hand that had once been able to make her purr. She lifted her head, met his gaze, and smiled.

He gave her a little smile in return, and it was all the more sexy because it was a little baffled, a little bowled over, as if he was surprised, pleasantly so, to find her finally smiling at him.

But she wanted more than that. Needed more than that, and she thought maybe she knew what to do.

If she dared…

But she'd always been bold, especially in front of a camera. And if she closed her eyes, she could be bold here as well.

Doing just that, she then reached up, pulling out the end of the towel from between her breasts, and let the thing drop.

It hit the floor with a soft thud.

Naked as a jay bird, she opened her eyes.

Aidan, unflappable, cool, calm as the eye-of-a-storm Aidan, had gone still as stone, his only movement his Adam's apple when he swallowed hard.

She held out a hand for the proffered T-shirt.

He didn't let go of it, seemingly frozen into place, as he looked her over from head to toes and back again.

She'd never thought of herself as particularly vengeful, and especially didn't wish him harm after he'd saved her life, but he'd once been able to walk away from her without a backward glance, and that had not only broken her heart, but destroyed her confidence.

The look on his face took a good part of that remembered pain away. "Thank you," she said, tugging on the T-shirt, practically having to pry it out of his fingers.

He didn't say a word, he didn't have to. The bulge behind the button fly of his jeans said it all, and with a little shimmying movement, she pulled the shirt over her head, letting it cover her body, before turning and walking out of the room, a real smile on her face for the first time since she'd heard about Blake's death.

6

THE MOMENT HE WAS ALONE in his bedroom, Aidan let out a long, slow breath. He needed to go after Kenzie to tell her she could have his bed to sleep in, but after the past sixty seconds, he needed a moment.

Or ten.

Or maybe a cold shower.

Bending for the towel she'd dropped, he winced. Still hard as a rock, but who wouldn't be? She had the body that most red-blooded males fantasized about— all soft, warm curves, and then there'd been her tan lines, outlining what looked like a string bikini.

God bless tan lines.

Yeah, he was going to need another moment. He calculated a few multiplication problems in his head, and then went after her. She stood in his living room with her back to him, facing the large picture window that looked out on a darkening sky. She wore the T-shirt he'd lent her, which thanks to the show she'd given him a moment ago, he now knew she had nothing on beneath it. Her shoulders were ramrod straight, her hands at her sides.

And he had no idea what she was thinking.

"I wanted to spread Blake's ashes into the ocean," she said softly to the window. "Off the bluffs. He would have liked that."

He let out a low breath, knowing what was coming next, hating what was coming next.

"Only there are no ashes."

The pain reverberated in her voice, and somehow bounced off his own chest, rolling over his heart. *Dammit.* He headed toward her.

"All I can do is put a marker next to our parents' graves." Her voice wobbled at this, but she didn't lose it, just stared out at the night. "He's innocent, Aidan."

The Kenzie he'd known had always believed the best of everyone, to a fault. Seemed that hadn't changed, only this time it was going to bite her on the ass.

"And I would have thought you'd think so, too," she said with more than a little accusation in her voice. She sighed, the sound soft and heart-breaking as it shuddered out of her.

"Look," he said. "Why don't you go to bed and get some sleep. You'll feel better if you do."

"I doubt that." But she finally turned from the window. The last of the day's light slanted in through the glass behind her, casting her in its soft glow, rendering the T-shirt just sheer enough to stop his heart.

Not sure how much more of her glorious body he could take without dropping to his knees and begging for mercy, he stayed right where he was instead of getting any closer to her.

Closer would be a mistake, especially with those hugely expressive eyes on his, and that look of grief all over her face.

"Sleep won't change anything that I'm feeling," she whispered. "He'll still be innocent."

"Kenzie, they found a scrapbook of all the fires in Blake's house. He was keeping track of them."

"That doesn't mean he's guilty."

"What *does* it mean?"

"Something else." She hugged herself, looking miserable and alone, and hurting. "I wish we were friends," she said very quietly. "I wish that you hadn't hurt me, and that I didn't have the urge to hurt you back."

Feeling bad, feeling a whole host of things he shouldn't be feeling at all, he took her hand. "I'm sorry I hurt you back then. I'm sorry I let you go. But I was young and stupid, Kenz. I was a complete ass."

She lifted a shoulder, tacitly agreeing with him.

"I'd like to think that if we were seeing each other now," he said softly, "and one of us wanted out, that we'd do better. That we'd make the friendship work."

Another lift of her shoulder, with slightly less temper in it this time.

Okay, that was something, a step at least. Pulling her toward him, he turned to lead her back to his bed, where he was going to tuck her in and then walk away.

Be the good guy.

Only she tugged him back, and suddenly he was holding onto her and she was pressing her face into his throat and breathing in deep, and…and *hell*. He was in trouble, sinking fast. "I showered at the station," he murmured into her hair. "But I need another. I still smell like smoke, Kenz, and—"

"Right." Pulling free, she turned away. "Sorry."

And now she thought he didn't want to hold her, when that was *all* he wanted. "Kenzie—"

"No, you're right. Absolutely right. Let's not go there." She smiled, and anyone who'd ever seen her smile for real would have recognized it as a first-class fake, but he didn't dare say a word about it because he had the feeling she was barely hanging on.

As was he.

She turned away. "You're right. Sleep might be best. But I'll take the couch—"

"No, don't be ridiculous. I—"

"Make no mistake, Aidan. I still want to hurt you. It's immature and extremely juvenile of me, but it's fact. So, no. I'm not sleeping in your bed." She walked back to the couch.

"Kenzie—"

"Please," she said, sinking down to the cushions and closing her eyes. "Could I have a blanket?"

"Of course." He went and got several, came back and spread them over her.

She didn't speak, or for that matter, move.

"Call me if you need anything," he finally said.

She gave no response to that, either, and he nodded even though she wasn't looking at him. "Okay then… night." He paused, but she still didn't say anything to release him from the strange torment he felt. In the end, he did as she seemed to want, and left her alone.

A FEW MINUTES LATER, Kenzie heard the shower go on, and in spite of herself, pictured Aidan stripping off his clothes and climbing in.

Soaping himself up…

Standing there beneath the steamy hot water all naked.

And unintentionally sexy.

Behind her, from somewhere else in the house, a phone rang. A machine clicked on and she heard Aidan's voice saying, "You know what to do at the beep."

Then came a "Hey, you" in a low, Marilyn Monroe–like purr. "It's Lori. You didn't call me back. I've been lonely for you, baby. Come over sometime soon, okay? I'll be waiting…"

Kenzie listened to the click as the machine went off and silence filled the house.

Seemed Aidan was still the guy who left women feeling lonely for him. She should return the favor. She should go…somewhere.

But as she listened to the shower running, she let out a long breath and admitted to herself—as silly as it seemed—there was something undeniably consoling about being here with him. She'd told him she trusted him a little, and that was as truthful as it was unsettling. Yes, she had nowhere else to go, but it was far more than that. At the moment, he was the only familiar, comforting presence in her life. At the moment, she wanted to be there, she really did, even knowing that the longer they spent together, the more they would grow closer, whether she liked it or not.

Only, she was afraid she would like it. A lot more than was wise.

AIDAN SURFACED from a deep, deep sleep, aware that something had woken him, but not sure what. He opened his eyes and saw his dark bedroom lit up in black and white by the faint glow of the moon slanting in through his horizontal blinds.

There, by his bed, stood an angel.

An angel in his T-shirt, in the same white swaths of moonlight as his room.

She was hurting, sad, scared…and why the hell hadn't he given her a suit of armor instead of just a T-shirt? Had he been looking for punishment? Because there it was, in flesh and blood and glorious curves and wild hair, and a face so hauntingly beautiful she took his breath. He was in trouble, deep trouble, because although he'd managed to resist opening his heart to her that first time, he wasn't quite sure he would be able to manage it this time.

Without a single word, she lifted his covers and scooted into the bed.

With him.

He was exhausted, beyond exhausted, and was afraid he didn't have the self-control to deal with this. *"Jesus,"* he gasped as she pressed her icy feet to his.

"Sorry."

But she didn't pull them back. Nope, she tucked them beneath his, sucking the warmth out of him.

"Don't look at me like that," she whispered.

He had no idea what she was talking about. There was no way she could clearly see his expression, she couldn't see any more than he could in the strips of moonlight. He could see her eyes, not her nose. He could see her mouth, not her chin...

"I'm not sleepwalking, or pain-pill walking." She pressed a little closer, so that her legs entangled in his.

Now would probably be as good a time as any to remind her that he slept naked, but as he opened his mouth, she spoke first.

"And I'm not here for another broken heart like I got the last time." She poked a finger into his chest. "In fact, if anyone's going to have a broken heart this time, it's going to be you. So you can just wipe that look of pity off your face."

"Pity is the last thing I've got going on," he assured her. He lay there achingly close, freezing his ass off thanks to her feet. "So you're going to break my heart?"

"Going to do my damnedest."

"I never meant to break yours."

"At least let me think I'm getting my revenge, okay?"

Her toes were killing him. So were her legs, the ones all caught up in his. And somehow he had a thigh between hers...

She propped her head up with her good hand, staring at him in the oddly lit room. Now he could see her forehead and her nose, but not her eyes or her mouth.

"It really is going to be you nursing the heart this time," she whispered.

That could very well be. But honestly, he wasn't sure his bruised heart functioned enough to break. Hell, it was probably dried up from misuse. And yet…and yet lying there with her in his arms seemed to jump-start the organ. It ached, and not just because of their past, it ached for the here and now, for the woman she'd become.

"You," she repeated softly, even a little smugly, and for some reason, some sick reason, it was a turn-on.

And because he was weak and maybe just a little bit stupid, he put his hand on her hip and leaned in to see her better, which he couldn't. She was still in slatted black and white. "I meant what I said, Kenz. I'm sorry you got hurt."

"Good. I *want* you sorry. Very, very sorry."

Yes, but did she want him aroused? Because he was. Her T-shirt had risen up enough to remind him she wasn't wearing panties.

Yeah, colossally stupid.

By now it had to be crystal clear to her that he was butt-ass naked. In the name of fair warning, he pulled her in a little closer.

"What are you doing?"

What was he doing? No idea. Bending his head, he rubbed his jaw to hers, bumped the tip of his nose to her earlobe.

With a shiver, she clutched at him and arched her neck, giving him better access.

Which he took.

"I can't remember what I was saying," she murmured.

He let out a breath in her ear and she shivered again, which he liked. He liked that a lot. "You were telling me how you're going to break my heart."

"That's right." Her fingers dug into the small of his back as she moved, the black and white shadows shifting over her. "I am. Aidan?"

"Yeah?"

"You're naked."

He'd been wondering when that would come up. Seeing as he was already quite "up"...

She gulped, and then did something he didn't expect. She rolled to her back and pulled him on top of her, allowing him to settle between her thighs, which were not cold like her feet, but warm and cushy and very, very welcoming.

"You should know," she whispered in his ear, making sure her lips brushed his flesh, causing a series of shivers of his own. "I plan to make you beg for mercy this time."

God. "I'm close to begging right now," he admitted.

"Really?"

She sounded breathless as hell, which was another big turn-on. So many... "Really."

He was hard. She was soft, so soft, and pressing all that softness up against him. "If you're not sleep-walking, or having a bad dream," he wondered, "why are you in here?"

"No hotels, remember?"

"Why are you in bed with me?" he clarified.

Her hands glided up and down his back, going lower on each pass. "My feet were cold."

He pressed his feet to hers, and then his mouth to her throat. "Is that all?"

"Absolutely. That and the begging."

He let out a huff of low laughter against her skin, and then because his mouth was right there against her neck, and because she was touching his butt, and because she smelled good, he took a little nibble.

Her fingers dug into him, telling him how much she liked it but she shook her head. "No more touching until you beg."

"I wasn't touching, I was kissing."

"No kissing until you beg. No anything until you beg."

"I've never begged for this before."

"No? Well, it's good for your character to try new things."

He laughed again. Laughed while trying to get laid. That was new. "Okay." Lifting his head, he cupped her face between his hands and looked into her eyes. She was smiling, too, and it was good to see her doing so. It was good to see her period; his smile slowly faded. "Can I kiss you, Kenzie?"

"Is that the best you got?"

"Can I pretty-please kiss you?"

"Well, I *suppose...*"

That was all he let her get out before he lowered his mouth to hers and kissed her. She let out a little murmur of surprise and what he sincerely hoped was pleasure, because *holy shit,* it was like taking a time machine back in time, back to that sweet, hot, most amazing summer he'd once spent in her arms.

She made the sound again, the one that drove him crazy with wanting, and then she entwined her arms up around his neck, gliding her fingers into his short hair and tightening them, as if she didn't want him going anywhere.

Fat chance.

When he slid his tongue to hers, it was another homecoming, and this time her shuddery sigh was pure, hungry delight with a sprinkle of unadulterated lust on top.

Oh, yeah. Pulling back just enough to look into her eyes, he found the same sense of bewildered wonderment across her face that he imagined was across his. Because, yes, they were attracted to each other because of their past, but suddenly it was much, much more than that. Then the next thing he knew, they'd lunged for each other again, trying to climb into each other's body, just like old times.

Only it was new, all so damn new, and all the more heart-wrenching and gripping for it. They were no longer young and stupid. They were old enough to know better, old enough to know exactly what they were doing, old enough that he knew that this time, there would be no escaping unscathed.

It didn't stop him.

7

OH. MY. GOD.

Kenzie struggled to think, but Aidan had taken her breath away And, as he surged up to his knees between her spread thighs, his hands fisted in the hem of his own shirt, his intention perfectly clear, he nearly stole her sanity—but she held on by a thread. "Wait," she gasped, putting a hand to his chest. "Hold it."

Still kneeling between her sprawled legs, his hands on the big T-shirt, about to strip her as naked as he was, he looked into her eyes. "Wait?"

She could have drowned in his gaze. Happily drowned. "You stopped begging."

He arched an eyebrow, which was highlighted by the slants of moonlight across his face. Stripes of light and dark, and in them, he was beautiful. "I mean it," she managed. "Absolutely nothing else happens here without some serious begging."

He stared at her, then lowered his head for a moment. When he lifted it again, she expected him to tell her he never begged for anything. That this—she—wasn't worth it. After all, she hadn't been once.

But he surprised her. "When we were together," he said quietly, "I dreamed about your body on the nights we didn't sleep in the same bed. Did you know that?"

"No." She shook her head. "You never said." He'd never said a lot of things. He'd held back so much.

And to be honest, so did I....

"I'd get off on it," he said, not holding back this time. Which did exactly what she hadn't wanted—it opened her heart to him.

"On you," he murmured. "For years afterward, I'd get off thinking about you."

She stared up at him. "You mean you…"

"Uh-huh. I jerked off." Leaning over her, he was nothing but a shadow until he bent even closer. Through the shutters, rectangles of light slashed over him as he let her look into his eyes, which were dark and scorching. "So much I'm lucky I'm not blind."

She laughed but also swallowed hard, surprisingly aroused at the thought of his touching himself while picturing her. "Oh."

"Yeah, oh." His eyes glittered with heat and memories and suddenly both the heat and memories were making her feel awfully warm from the inside out.

Actually, they were making her hot.

Very hot.

"Tonight, just looking at you…" He let out a long breath and shook his head. "It brings it all back, but it's even stronger."

His mouth was in the shadows. She couldn't see his lips moving but his voice washed over her, as did the images he evoked. He was bringing it all back for her, too.

"You were beautiful then," he said. "But you're even more beautiful now. I want to take this shirt off of you, Kenz. Please let me."

At his words, she nearly turned the tables and begged *him*. She could feel the T-shirt caught high on her thighs. His hips were holding her legs open to him, and with just a little nudge of the shirt, he'd be able to see all her god-given goodies, along with the fact that she was already wet.

"Please," he murmured. "Please let me."

Oh, God. "Yes."

He shifted, and then she could see his mouth, which rewarded her with a smile as he made his move, his fingers closing around the hem of the shirt, slowly tugging it up, revealing her body.

She'd wanted this, sought it out under the guise of getting her long-needed revenge, but that was really just a lie, and her first flicker of doubt hit.

Just who was going to get hurt here…?

The night air brushed over her breasts as he pulled the shirt all the way off and over her head. Her nipples hardened. Goose bumps spread over her flesh, and it wasn't because she was cold. There were five stripes of moonlight across her body, one across her eyes, her throat, another highlighting her breasts, her belly and her crotch. He couldn't have lined her up more perfectly for his perusal, and he definitely perused.

"Aidan—"

His hand stroked over her hip, and her breath backed up into her throat. She opened her mouth to say maybe she'd been hasty about this whole breaking his heart thing, but before she could, he'd put a hand on her inner thigh and pushed, further opening her to him.

The slants of shadows hampered his view, but he didn't seem bothered, not with his front row seat.

The only sound in the room came from him as he let out a groan. "God, Kenzie. You're so pretty." He lowered his head, then paused, his mouth a hairsbreadth away from her trembling belly. "I want to kiss. I want to taste. I want that more than I want my next breath. Please let me…"

As far as begging went, it was pretty good. "O-okay," she managed, and almost before the word was out, he'd nudged her legs open even wider, wedging them there with his broad shoulders. He slowly lowered his head. "Pretty please," he whispered across her flesh.

Her wet flesh.

"Yes." Her heels dug into the mattress as he "pretty pleased" his tongue over her, and then his teeth, and then his warm lips, over and over again leaving her a panting, gasping, quivery mass of sensitized nerve endings, and when she exploded for him, he surged up, produced a condom and slid into her with one sure, powerful thrust.

"Oh," she gasped, reaching up to hold onto him because her world had just spun on its axis. The feel of him deep inside her—and he was deep, as deep as he could get—had her spiraling. Gone were all thoughts of hurting him, or revenge. She could think of nothing but this, but him. Not that she would admit such a thing. "You...you didn't beg for that."

Cupping her face, he tilted it up to his. "Pretty-please may I drive you out of your living mind?"

Oh, God.

"Kenzie? May I?" His voice was thick with the same hunger and need that was driving her.

"Yes."

"Good. May I also pretty-please make you scream my name?"

In answer, she arched up, her breasts pressing into his hard, warm chest, her legs wrapping around his waist.

He groaned, a low, rough sound that scraped at all her good spots but he didn't move. "Can I?"

"I don't usually do much screaming."

He just smiled, and then took her mouth as he took her body, indeed driving her out of her mind with all too disturbing ease, and when she exploded again, she cried out his name.

Loudly.

She might have even screamed it.

As the blood finally slowed in her veins, as the roar of it lowered to a trickle in her head, she became aware of the fact that she was gripping him tight, holding him close with her arms and her legs, not letting him escape.

He didn't say a word, just nuzzled lazily at her neck as his breathing slowed.

Hers wasn't slowing. Embarrassed at how tightly

she was holding him, she forced herself to let him go, certain he'd roll away.

But in perhaps the loveliest thing he'd done all night, he didn't. Instead, he remained right where he was, turning just his head to press his lips to her jaw, murmuring her name on a sigh.

It was one of those defining moments, where she suddenly knew the truth—she'd not exacted a single ounce of revenge. In fact, she'd made things worse.

She'd risked her own heart.

But for that one moment at least, she didn't care, because maybe he'd changed. Maybe things could be different this time, and—

"You screamed my name." He lifted his head, revealing a strong smile. "You begged." He out-and-out grinned then, not broken, not even a little bit. "We still work hard."

"There's no *we*." She pushed him off her, suddenly and irrationally irritated. "No we at all."

Completely oblivious to the picture he made sprawled out on the bed, buck naked, he put his hands behind his head and continued to smile like an idiot. "Are you telling me you have no desire to do that again?"

"None."

"Ah, Kenzie. You're such a pretty liar."

Yeah. Yeah, she was. A pretty liar, and a good liar. But she had no idea how else to hide the fact that she still had feelings for him in spite of their past—or maybe because of it. *God.* She needed to get out for a while, needed to clear her head. Get some answers. *Alone.*

"Stay," he murmured.

"Okay." She looked at him. "I'll stay if you tell me this. Why did you really dump me?"

At that, his amusement faded. "I told you I was an idiot back then."

"Granted. Why else?"

He looked at her and she nearly backed down; she certainly held her breath, but he touched her face. "Because I didn't know what I had."

AIDAN SLEPT like the dead. Or like a man who'd been far too close to serious exhaustion. When he opened his eyes, he felt the various aches and pains from the fire, and from the mattress gymnastics he and Kenzie had executed, and was grateful to know he had two days off, because more sleep was on his To Do list. Much more.

So was more mattress gymnastics.

Considering that Kenzie was wrapped around him like a pretzel, that shouldn't be too difficult to manage. As he looked into her face, taking in each of the cuts and the bruises there in the light of day, he felt a tug in his belly.

He wished like hell he could say he was just hungry, but he knew the truth.

He was a goner.

She was as cut up and bruised as he was, more so, and if *he* hurt like hell, he could only imagine how she felt. He was used to such injuries. She wasn't.

"I realize I've spent my days on a television set,

where my worst injury was a paper cut from that day's script," she whispered, eyes still closed. "But I'm not feeling as bad as I probably look."

Her face was relaxed now; and he realized it hadn't been before—not on Blake's boat, not when she'd crawled in bed with him, not even when he'd stripped her out of his shirt and proceeded to make her scream.

That he'd undone her so easily didn't stroke his ego. She'd undone him just the same. It'd always been like that for them, a virtual explosion of need and lust and hunger.

But he'd attributed much of that to being young and horny. He hadn't anticipated a resurgence of those feelings, And he doubted she had either. But that's exactly what they'd gotten.

With a sigh, she slid out of his arms and off the bed. He enjoyed the view as she walked to the bathroom, but when she shut the door, his smile faded. She needed sustenance, and a bandage change. Getting up, he pulled on his jeans and went into the kitchen, where he grabbed a pan and eggs and went to work getting them both some protein so that they could go back to bed and burn it all off again.

His doorbell rang and Aidan stopped dicing peppers long enough to sign the clipboard of a pudgy guy in brown shorts, who handed him a slim package.

When he heard the shower go off, he finished the eggs and then grabbed his first-aid bag and knocked on the door. "Bandages, aspirin and breakfast. And your package from L.A. is here."

"Perfect timing—I've got to run."

"You mean back to Los Angeles?"

The door opened and steam came out. As did Kenzie wrapped in another of his towels. "Not back. Not yet."

The towel was tucked between her breasts, which pushed them up and nearly out, a fact he'd have taken the time to thoroughly enjoy except for the nasty bruise arcing along her left collar bone. "You need rest."

"I need clothes." She moved past him and into his bedroom. "Can I borrow a pair of sweats?"

"Sure." He opened his dresser and handed the clothes over.

"Thanks. I've really got to go."

She was going to go snoop. Get in Tommy's way. Get herself arrested. "Kenzie, listen to me. You need to stay out of the investigation. The chief doesn't want you digging—"

"I don't work for him. He can't tell me what to do."

"If you stay—"

"No. Thank you, but, no."

Usually in the light of day, with a woman in his bedroom, *he* was the one who had to go. Usually.

Okay, always.

It felt odd to have the shoe on the other foot. Especially given the magnitude of what they'd shared last night, and he wasn't alone in feeling it, dammit. He knew he wasn't.

But Kenzie moved carefully away from him, slowly, as if still in pain, but with conviction. She was set on going, leaving him with a disconcerted feeling in his gut.

Was this how he'd made women feel? Like they'd

already been forgotten? "Let's change your bandages—"

"I can do it on my own."

Seemed she was used to doing stuff on her own. That was new.

So was his unsettledness over the way this was going down.

"Yeah," she said at his quiet surprise. "I'm not the same helpless little thing I used to be."

"I never thought you were helpless."

"Well, I was. But I've grown up. I've changed. In many ways. And I don't need anyone's help. For anything."

He arched an eyebrow. "You needed me when we—"

"No. Well, yes, *yes,* I needed you to save me from the fire, but—"

"That's not what I was talking about." He pointed to his bed.

"Oh, no. That was just me, breaking your heart. I warned you, remember."

Bullshit. That hadn't been just revenge. "Kenzie."

"Sorry. Got to go. Have to go." Once again she dropped her towel, which had the same magical effect on him as it had last night. While he stood there taking in the glorious sight of her naked body, she pulled on the sweats, kissed him on the cheek, then walked out of the room.

And, given the sound of the front door opening and then closing, out of his house.

And, most likely, out of his life.

Fitting justice really, as he'd once done the same to her. Moving to the living room, he looked out the window in time to catch her taillights as they vanished down his driveway.

I've changed, she'd said, and she had.

But as the blood once again began a northward flow from behind the zipper of his pants back up to his brain, another thought managed to get his attention.

He'd changed as well. And he was going to prove it.

8

SOMEONE WAS KNOCKING on Aidan's door when he turned off the shower. *She'd come back.* With his pulse kicking, he grabbed a towel and wrapped it around his waist, heading for the door at a speed far faster than his usual get-there-when-I-get-there saunter.

Only it wasn't Kenzie at all. "Dammit."

His best friend and partner Zach just looked at him. "Nice to see you, too." Without waiting for an invitation, he pushed past Aidan and walked in.

Fair enough. Aidan had let himself into Zach's house plenty of times. Aidan shut the door behind Zach and shoved his fingers through his wet hair. "Sorry. Thought you were someone else."

Zach took in Aidan standing there dripping wet, wearing only a towel. "Clearly. Who is she?"

"How do you know it's a she?"

"Because if you're meeting a guy dressed like that, we have a whole different issue to talk about."

Aidan rolled his eyes and left Zach to go get some clothes. In his bedroom, he looked at his bed as he pulled on a clean shirt. The covers were tossed half on the floor, and on his nightstand were two empty condom wrappers.

And though it was crazy given that Kenzie had used his shampoo, his clothes and his soap, he'd have sworn he could smell her scent, some complicated mix of soft, determined, sexy woman. He stared at the bed, remembering how he'd felt when she'd crawled in with him, remembering how natural it'd been to kiss and touch her, to sink into her body and go to a place he hadn't been in a long time.

Then they'd slept together, and that had felt good, too, being all tangled up in each other again. Familiar, but new. Even better, if that was possible. Things hadn't been complicated in the dark.

Things had been amazing.

But she'd left.

When he walked back into the kitchen, he found Zach staring at the breakfast he'd made for Kenzie.

"You made breakfast," Zach said. "As in got out a pan and cooked something."

"Yeah. So?"

"You put out napkins."

"Let me repeat myself. So?"

"So you never put out napkins. Not when it's me or the other guys."

"Do you want to split the food with me or not?"

"You didn't cook this for me."

"You're right."

Zach raised an eyebrow.

"You're going to question a plate of food?" Aidan said. "Really?"

Zach didn't have to be asked twice. He grabbed a plate and pulled up a chair.

"I thought you and Brooke were going away for a few days since you haven't been cleared to go back to work yet."

"We are. We're leaving tomorrow morning. Wanted to see you first."

"Ah, that's so sweet. You're going to miss me."

"Actually, I'm not." Zach shoveled in some food, and looked at him. "I heard about the explosion. I should have been there."

Aidan looked at the cast on Zach's left wrist, remembered how close he'd come to losing him along with Blake, and felt the food get caught in his throat. "You're not healed yet."

"It's coming along though." He squeezed his fingers into a fist, then stretched them straight out. "I could be back at work, dammit. I have no idea why the chief's being so hard-assed about this. I'm willing and able."

"Enjoy your few days off. You and Brooke deserve it."

"Yeah." Zach sighed. "So is the boat a complete loss?"

"Unfortunately."

"Kenzie all right?"

"Heard about that, too, huh?"

"Yeah." Zach paused. "Was it awkward, considering your past with her?"

"To be the one rescuing her?"

"What else?"

Yeah, genius, what else. Maybe sleeping with her... But that hadn't been awkward. Not one little bit.

Zach was looking at him. "What am I missing?"

Aidan shook his head. "Nothing."

"Come on."

"Okay, nothing I want to talk about."

"That I buy," Zach said, and like the good friend he was, changed the subject. "I heard that Blake must have kept his accelerants on the boat, which is why it blew like it did."

That was one theory, Aidan was sure.

But he had another. "Well..."

"What?" Zach asked.

"You're going to tell me I'm crazy."

Zach stood up and went to the refrigerator for the milk. "All those times I thought those fires were arson, you were the only one who believed me. I'll be the last one to tell you that you're crazy."

"Yeah, but now we know that Tommy was behind you the entire time, he was just in the middle of his investigation. Still is, with the chief riding his ass to put an end to this."

"Yeah." Zach pushed away his plate. "So I wonder what they'd say now."

"About...?"

"About your not buying that boat fire was any more accidental than the other fires. Or me not buying it, either."

Aidan looked into his best friend's eyes and let out a breath. "That boat was blown up for a reason and I think that reason was to hide something. Something that someone didn't want found."

"What?"

"I don't know. And I'm betting Tommy and the Chief don't know either but they want to."

"It doesn't make sense," Zach said. "Blake's dead."

Aidan pushed away his plate. "Yeah." Goddamn, but he wasn't going to get used to that any time soon, the fact that Blake, a friend, *one of them* for Christ's sake, was not only gone, but accused of arson. "Which means that he wasn't working alone and whoever the other person is, they're running scared of something."

"Or someone," Zach said. "Kenzie shows up out of the blue after what, six years? Seems kind of odd, doesn't it?"

Aidan's gut tightened. "Her brother's dead, Zach."

"Yes. Her arsonist brother. They were close, right?"

"What are you saying, that she's his co-felon?"

"Look, I don't want to think about Blake doing the things they've accused him of, either. And I really don't want to think about the fact that if he was still alive, he'd be in jail. But those are the facts."

Aidan scrubbed his hands over his face. "She *just* got into town."

"You know that for sure?"

Actually, no, he didn't.

"Why was she on his boat?"

"Going through his things." Listen to him defend her. "Missing him."

Zach closed his eyes and rubbed them hard. "If that were true, wouldn't she have come sooner?"

"I don't know. I don't know anything except that Blake was all she had." Aidan got to his feet because he had to move, had to pace the length of the kitchen. "She's…devastated. Horrified. And pissed off that we all believe that Blake's guilty. I think she's going to go digging on her own and find out what she can."

"Which should make Tommy oh-so-happy."

"He's going to have her arrested if she hinders the investigation," Aidan admitted. "And she's going to hinder. It's in her nature. She intends to prove Blake innocent."

Zach raised a brow. "You got all that from pulling her out of the water?"

Well, shit. Aidan picked up his fork and shoveled some food in.

"You saw her after the fire. At the hospital."

"Yeah."

Zach paused. "And after that as well, I'm thinking."

"Yeah."

Zach peered around Aidan and into the living room, pointedly looking down the hallway.

"She's not still here."

"But she *was* here? Jesus, Aidan. What would Tommy say?"

"Since when does that matter?"

"Since we both now know that he was on our side about the arsons all along. He'll be on this, too, you can guarantee it."

Yeah. In hindsight, sleeping with Kenzie been a pretty stupid thing to do. And yet, what else could he have done but given her a place to stay?

Except for that using up two condoms part. He probably could have not done that.

"We've got to let Tommy do his thing here," Zach said quietly.

"I can't believe you're suggesting I stay out of it, when you did the very opposite."

"And paid for it," Zach reminded him, lifting his casted wrist.

"She was hurting, Zach. And alone. Her purse had burned in the fire and she had nowhere else to go so I let her stay here. End of story."

"You could have lent her money. She's a famous soap diva—I think she'd have been good for it."

"The hotels were all booked up."

When Zach just looked at him, Aidan lifted a shoulder. "It was just bad luck on her part."

"Just bad luck, huh? Funny, you don't look so put out."

"Don't you have a fiancée to go home to?"

Zach grinned dopily. "Yeah."

"So go already."

Zach got up, then paused. "Look, Aidan, I know she meant something to you once, but—"

"She's Blake's sister."

"And *your* ex. I'd think that'd be reason enough to stay away from her."

Yeah. One would think…

OPENING THE SLIM ENVELOPE she'd scooped from Aidan's kitchen table on her way out the door, Kenzie practically kissed the credit card she found inside. She needed some personal items, like clothes of her own, not to mention underwear. Not that she didn't love Aidan's sweats, because she did. They smelled like him. They felt like him.

Which was exactly why she had to get *out* of them.

She did her best not to pout over the loss of her Choos, which she wasn't going to find at Wal-Mart, but the store was still one of God's greatest creations. When she'd bought and put on a peasant skirt, two layered tank tops and a pair of sandals, she got back into her car. She'd missed two calls on her cell, both from that same local number as before, but no messages, so she put it out of her head and drove to the docks. Then she sat in the parking lot nursing a hot chocolate and a blessed box of donuts, staring at the charred remains of Blake's boat.

She was alone except for the occasional car. One was a light-gray sedan that slowed as it passed her, the windows so dark that she couldn't see in. Probably another looky-loo like herself, except…except she'd seen a car like it before, somewhere…

She ate a donut.

Until a couple of weeks ago, before Blake's death, she hadn't had chocolate or donuts in months. Maybe years. She'd been on a strict eighteen-hundred-calorie diet, combined with a workout every single day, without fail. All to look good.

That's what TV stars did. They looked good. She was paid to.

Except she no longer had a TV show to look good for. Back in L.A., she knew the job-finding frenzy had already begun. All her co-stars were busy auditioning, and what was she doing? Eating donuts instead of facing the fact that she was unemployed.

Her cushy, easy, comfortable, fun job had come to an end.

Life over.

She looked at *Blake's Girl* and felt the last donut congeal in her throat. No. Her job was over, not her life.

Blake's life was over.

God. Brushing the sugar from her fingers, she got out of the car. She wasn't looking her best, but then again, there were no paparazzi in Santa Rey. And thanks to no one in the press making the connection between her and *Blake's Girl,* there were no reporters to take pics of her pale, makeup-free face, or all of the bruises and cuts she'd sustained in the fire. Her wrist wasn't bothering her, but the splint was a pain in the butt. She hadn't been able to corral her hair into a ponytail, which meant it was flying wild around her face and in her eyes.

She could have asked Aidan for help but she'd rather have the wild hair than have his hands on her again.

Okay, that wasn't true, wasn't anywhere close to true, but she could pretend it was.

Dammit.

For those few hours last night in his arms, she'd not

been alone and lost and hurting. She'd been transported, taken out of herself.

And along the way, she'd forgotten to make him regret dumping her. *Nicely done.* Rolling her eyes at herself, she moved closer to the docks. The charred remains of *Blake's Girl* were taped off with yellow crime scene tape.

She didn't know what that was about.

They thought Blake was a criminal? Fine. But they couldn't pin this one on him, he was already gone.

Gone...

Chest tight, she walked along the yellow tape, getting as close as she could, which wasn't close enough. No one was around, on the dock or otherwise, and she couldn't stop the thought—what if she ducked under the tape? Surely, as Blake's only living relative, she deserved to have a look.

The two boats on either side of *Blake's Girl* were still there. Barely. One was nearly burned black, and in fact looked as if it might still be steaming. The other was half gone, and half untouched.

And between them? A shell of a boat, blackened and charred beyond recognition.

Blake's boat was completely destroyed.

Looking at it, she could see it as it'd been two nights ago, when she could stand on it and still feel her brother's presence, when his things had still been okay. She wished she'd gotten something of his, something, anything...

Maybe she could crawl beneath the tape and get onboard to comb through the torched remains, and thinking it, she bent down, but at the sound of an engine, stopped and turned.

It was the gray sedan again, making another pass of the parking lot.

Goose bumps rose on her arms as she got that same sensation of being watched she'd had at the hospital.

Who was following her?

It wasn't Aidan. No way. He'd make himself known, that was for damn sure. He had a way of making himself known...

Someone else then.

Tommy?

No. Tommy didn't have the resources to have her followed. She doubted anyone in Santa Rey did.

Then she remembered her earlier missed calls, and pulled out her phone, hitting the number.

No one answered.

She ran her hand along the yellow police tape, but the truth was, she didn't quite have the nerve to boldly defy the law.

At least not during the daylight hours.

But tonight...

Yeah, tonight.

Under the cover of darkness.

Turning away, she squeaked as she accidentally bumped into a hard wall.

A hard wall that was really a warm, hard chest she recognized all too well, along with the big, warm hands that settled on her arms.

9

THE COLLISION SET KENZIE back a step, but Aidan held her upright.

She tilted her head up, up, up...and looked into his face, which was unfortunately indecipherable.

"You okay?" he asked, his voice low and calm, and concerned.

Okay, concern was good. Concern implied that he hadn't noticed what she'd been about to do. But was she okay? *Hell, no.*

Not even close.

"Are you?" His gaze swept down her body, then up again, as if categorizing her injuries, which reminded her of last night, when he'd also been categorized her body.

With his tongue.

"Yes," she managed. "I'm fine."

"Good. What the hell are you doing here?"

"Funny, I was going to ask you the same thing. Are you following me?"

"No."

"You're not driving a gray sedan and going everywhere I go?"

"I drive a truck, a blue one and I didn't follow you here. I got lucky on the first try. I figured you'd come here and try to do something stupid."

"I did nothing of the kind."

"You don't consider ducking beneath that yellow tape stupid?"

"Only if I'd gotten caught."

"Hello," he said, still holding on to her. His fingers tightened. *"Caught."*

"Yes, but you don't count."

He looked both boggled *and* irritated. "And why is that?"

"Because what are you going to do, arrest me? Last night you were kissing me, touching me, fu—"

"Okay," he said with a low laugh. "Now just hold on a second—"

"I'm just saying." She narrowed her eyes and went for bravado, even though she could hardly breathe while looking at the big blackened sailboat that less than two days ago had been *Blake's Girl*.

Aidan had saved her.

He'd saved her and she was poking at him because she was all twisted up inside. So she let out a breath and looked into his face, where she found a surprising blend of sympathy and old affection mixed in with the frustration and fear.

"I came here to talk," he said. "Not arrest you. Jesus. Now what the hell is this about a gray sedan?"

"Nothing."

He just looked at her for a long moment. "What aren't you telling me?"

"Nothing."

"More like everything." He let out a breath. "Tommy expects you to let him do his job."

"I'm not going to get in his way. I'm going to help him."

"Now see, I don't think he likes help."

"Too bad for him."

"It's going to be too bad for you if you piss him off. He can and will have you arrested if you don't stay out of his way."

"Believe me, I plan to stay out of his way."

"Okay." He nodded. "New subject then."

Uh-oh.

"Last night…"

Kenzie didn't know how she felt about last night. And because she didn't, she absolutely didn't want to talk about it. "Yeah. Now's not a good time for me."

"You don't think so?"

She shook her head.

His eyes lit with something that might have been wry humor. He'd been just as beat up as her yesterday, but unlike her, today he did not look like something the cat dragged in. No, he looked tall and fit, and in his loose cargoes and T-shirt, he seemed very in charge of himself and his world.

She, on the other hand, was in charge of exactly nothing at the moment. "Maybe later." And maybe not.

He hadn't taken his hands off of her arms, and if

asked she'd have said she wasn't sure how she felt about that, but that would be a lie. At the moment, his support felt like a lifeline.

Her only lifeline. "Tell me something," she said very quietly, her eyes on his so she didn't miss any little nuance, because this was very, very important to her. "Arson. It's a well studied crime, right? The people who do it, most of them belong to a particular character type. Aggressive. Violent. Repeat offenders."

"Yes," he agreed. "How do you know this?"

"We did a whole plotline about an arsonist last year. Would you characterize Blake as aggressive or violent?"

"Not even close."

"Exactly," she said.

"Which doesn't prove anything. There's physical evidence—"

"Okay," she agreed. She knew about the evidence. "But most arsonists *want* their work admired. Isn't that correct?"

"Yes, but—"

"*But* Blake maintained his innocence. Tommy told me that much."

"Yes," Aidan agreed, his expression reflecting his worry for her, whether he wanted it to or not.

Which she didn't want to face. She meant to do two things when it came to Aidan, especially after last night. First: keep her distance. And second: leave *him* pining for *her*.

It was going to be nearly impossible to handle the second while doing the first but she would give it her best shot. "So can't you concede that it's possible that you're wrong about Blake?"

"I'm not the one accusing him of anything."

She looked at him, really looked at him, and understood something she'd missed before. He didn't want to believe the worst of Blake any more than she did, and that was so much more than she expected from him, from anyone, that it was like a balm to all her fear and grief.

He wasn't against her or Blake. She wasn't completely alone, at least not in that moment, and she found herself closing the gap between them to wrap her arms around his broad shoulders, hugging him hard, so damn relieved to have him there with her.

With a rough sound, his arms came around her, too, and he pulled her in, letting her lean on him. "Kenzie," he whispered, bowing his head over hers. "It's okay. It's going to be okay."

Yeah. Keeping her distance from him was going to be damned tough.

So would be breaking his heart, but she was still going to do it. It was that, or see hers crushed again, and that was simply not going to happen.

Aidan had never been a hugging sort of guy. He loved physical contact, especially the naked kind, with the fairer sex, but touching just out of sheer affection and nothing else? That hadn't really been a part of his life. Having been the sort of child who'd made it difficult for others to like him, much less love him, he hadn't inspired a lot of affection growing up. And working with mostly guys all the time...well, they tended to shove and wrestle rather than hug.

So this, with Kenzie, should have felt awkward. Alien. At the very least it was an intrusion of his personal space that he would have thought would make him squirm to be free.

But it didn't. Even though a piece of her hair was poking him in the eye and she was stepping on his toe, and her nose—pressed against his throat—was icy enough to make him wince, he didn't move.

In fact, he tightened his arms on her, pressing his face into her hair, inhaling her as if he didn't want to let go.

Because he really didn't.

She was warm and soft and sweet, and when her fingers slid into his hair he nearly purred. His hand skimmed down her spine, pressing low on her back, urging her even closer as he just continued to breathe her in.

Just down the dock, two seagulls argued over some found treasure. Water slapped at the wood pylons. Beyond that, the devastation of the fire sat right before their eyes. Aidan didn't want her looking at it. "You need to get out of here."

"Yeah." She stepped back. "I know. I'm going."

He caught her hand, and when she looked at him questioningly, he saw the truth in her eyes. Wherever she was headed, it was to make trouble.

"I'm a big girl now."

Yes. She was a woman who could more than take

care of herself. Which in no way eradicated the need within him to protect her. "Have you eaten?"

She stared at him, then let out a low breath. "I tell you I can take care of myself and you want to feed me? Even after I also told you that I only wanted to be with you in order to break your heart?"

"Yeah, see, about that…" He stroked a loose strand of hair off her face, letting his finger trace the rim of her ear, absorbing her little shiver. "I don't really believe you."

"Oh, it's true," she said with utter conviction. "I'm going to break your heart."

"That wasn't the only reason you stayed with me last night. Slept with me."

"Okay, true. You saved my life. I owed you."

He shook his head. "That wasn't it, either."

"What was it then, smart guy?"

"You like being with me."

A helpless laugh escaped her at that.

"I like being with you, too, Kenz."

She shook her head. "You're off your rocker."

"Already established. So. Food?"

She stared at him, then caved. "I guess I could eat."

She followed him in her car to Sunrise Café. Aidan had no idea why he took her there, other than that taking her back to his place, where they'd be alone, seemed like a really bad idea.

Sheila was thrilled to see him and gave him a huge hug, smiling with some speculation at Kenzie. Even though it was afternoon by then, Aidan ordered a large breakfast. When Kenzie tried to get just coffee, he merely doubled his order, and then took her up to the roof.

There was a long bench against the far wall, where they sat to watch the surf. It was rough, which didn't stop the surfers from enjoying it.

Kenzie stared out at the waves. "It's nice up here. A good place to think. You come here a lot?"

"I do."

"Sheila's fond of you."

"Very," he agreed.

She smiled at him, and just like that, melted his heart. "You've made some good ties," she said softly.

He got a little lost in her eyes, and leaned in with some half-baked idea of kissing her, and—

"Come and get it!" Sheila yelled up from the bottom of the stairwell.

Sighing—what else could he do—Aidan led the way down to the crowded dining room. Sheila seated them, then brought them their plates, winking at Aidan before leaving.

Kenzie looked down at her loaded plate. "I'm not that hungry."

"Uh-huh." He nudged her fork closer to her fingers. "That's what you always used to say. You'd tell me you weren't hungry and then you'd eat everything off my plate, remember?"

Humor lit her eyes. "What I remember is that you were my boyfriend. You were supposed to share."

"So, what are you saying? That you wouldn't, say, eat off Chad's plate?"

"Chase. And he's vegan and doesn't eat anything that isn't completely raw, so, no, I wouldn't."

Aidan leaned over and stroked another stray strand of hair off her cheek. He had no idea why he kept finding excuses to touch her, other than she looked sad and just a little lost. She wore no makeup, and all those gorgeous blond waves had rioted around her face, a few long strands curling around her jaw. It was just Kenzie. No smoke and mirrors, no pomp or celebrity. Just the woman who'd once touched his heart.

And, apparently, still did.

So he did what he'd wanted to do on the roof—he leaned over their food and kissed her, just once, softly on the lips. When he pulled back, she gave a baffled little smile and touched her fingers to her mouth. "What was that for?"

Before he could answer, Zach walked up to their table. "Hey."

"Hey," Aidan said in surprise. "Kenzie, this is Zach. Zach, Kenzie is—"

"Blake's sister." Zach's eyes softened as he looked at her. "I miss your brother."

"Thank you," she murmured. "Me, too."

Zach turned to Aidan and handed him a file.

"What's this?"

"I wanted you to have it while I was gone. In case you need it for anything."

Aidan opened the file and instantly knew what he held. All the evidence Zach had gathered over the past few months on the mysterious arsons. Zach had been the first one to suspect something was going on and the first to go to Tommy for answers. Closing the file he met Zach's steady gaze. "Thanks. Want to join us?"

"Can't. Brooke's waiting for me. I just talked to Eddie and Sam. Did you know there was another explosion last night? The hardware store on Sixth."

"Injuries?"

"Several, and one death. Tracy Gibson."

Aidan's stomach dropped. The woman Blake had had a crush on for months before his death.

Kenzie divided her gaze between them. "Who's Tracy?"

"She was an employee at the hardware store," Zach told her. "Same setup as *Blake's Girl*," he said to Aidan, tapping the file with meaning. "So keep this."

Aidan understood. Zach thought he might need the info in the file when he was gone.

"Nice meeting you," Zach said to Kenzie. With a squeeze to Aidan's shoulder, he left.

"So what does that mean?" Kenzie asked. "If there was a similar explosion, maybe Blake's boat wasn't an accident."

"Maybe."

"A new serial arsonist?" she scoffed. "What are the chances of that in a small town like this?"

"I don't know."

"I know," she said. "Next to nil."

She was watching him with sadness still in her eyes, along with a sense of sharp intelligence that said she wasn't going to let this go. The brash tilt of her chin alluded to a strength of will, of passion, he knew first-hand, and suddenly he was afraid for her.

For her, *of her,* and of the feelings she invoked inside him. Damn, not again… Not falling for her again, he told himself. But it didn't matter that he was seated across from her in a crowded café, surrounded by people.

She was all he saw.

He watched her push her food around the plate for a few minutes, then wrapped his fingers around her wrist, guiding her fork to a large bite of eggs and bringing it to her mouth.

She took it into her mouth, chewed and swallowed, all with her gaze never leaving his. "You keep looking at me like you care."

"I do."

"You shouldn't."

"Why not?"

"Because I'm not going to care about you back." At that, she broke eye contract and stared down at the food. "At least not like I did before."

"So you've mentioned."

"I mean it."

"I believe you." He also believed that she just might get her big wish, because looking at her sitting there, knowing *she'd* be walking away from *him* this time, caused a strange sensation deep inside him. He'd have sworn it was his heart rolling over and exposing its underbelly.

Kenzie took another bite of food as his cell phone

buzzed. It was Dispatch. "Sorry," he said, standing. "I have to take this."

"No problem." She was suddenly engrossed in her food, not even looking up when he went outside to get good enough reception to hear that two firefighters had come down with the flu. They needed replacements for the next shift. So much for a day off—he was going back on duty, starting now.

He turned to go back inside the café and nearly bumped into Kenzie. "Sorry," she said, flashing a smile that didn't quite meet her eyes. "I've got to go."

Huh. That had been *his* line.

"I paid the bill—"

He reached for his wallet. "Let me—"

But she put her hand over his and shook her head. "It's on me. Consider it a very small down payment."

"For what?"

"For what I owe you for saving my life."

"Kenzie—"

"Thank you," she said softly, looking into his eyes, making his head spin. "I'm not sure I said that enough. I am extremely grateful."

Wait. That sounded like a good-bye. "Okay, hold on a second. Are you—"

Going up on tiptoes, she put a hand to his chest, leaned in and kissed him on the jaw. She added a smile to the mix, one that went all the way to her eyes this time as she touched her fingers to her lips and then blew him another kiss.

Then she turned and walked away.

As he'd once done to her. "Kenzie."

But she'd already gotten into her car. Where the hell was she going? She revved the engine and was gone, out of the lot, perhaps out of his world. He stood there a moment, absorbing a barrage of emotions, starting with regret and ending with a surprising hurt, and then he shrugged it off and walked inside to say good-bye to Sheila. That's when his head stopped spinning and it hit him.

Kenzie had stolen his file.

10

UNFORTUNATELY FOR KENZIE, the doggie convention was still in town. She tried a couple of B and Bs and got excited when a cute front desk clerk recognized her and said he'd stir up a room. But then he picked up his phone and yelled, "Ma! Get out of the room, I've got a girl!"

Kenzie shouldn't have been surprised, since her karma was clearly still on vacation. She made the clerk leave his mother in the room and escaped. Back in her car, she sighed, feeling very alone.

She missed Blake.

And dammit, she already missed Aidan, too. Missed his voice, his smile, his touch.

How was that even possible? She'd just left him. She'd stolen his file for God's sake. No doubt he was cursing her right this minute.

And definitely *not* missing her.

She pulled into the library and made herself comfortable on a large chair in a far corner, then opened the file. Almost immediately she felt an odd prickle of awareness, and then the hair on the back of her neck stood up.

She was being watched again.

She craned her neck left and then right, but no one in her immediate area was so much as looking at her. Behind her was a set of shelves, and she shifted, trying to see through a gap to the aisle on the other side.

Nothing.

Clearly she was still in the process of losing her mind. Determined, she went back to the file. Zach and Aidan had been thorough. There was a list of fire calls from Firehouse Thirty-Four over the past six months, five of them highlighted. The questionable fires, she realized.

The arsons Blake had ultimately been accused of starting.

Attached were details of those five properties: architectural plans, permits, a history of ownership, purchases and sales. Each had been plotted out on a map, and scrutinized up one side and down the other, including everything that had been found on site after the fire.

Zach had noted finding a metal mesh trash can at each site, and even had a picture of one, from the fire just before the one at Zach's own house. As she was looking at it, her cell phone vibrated. She nearly ignored it until she saw it was the same local cell phone number as before, and she grabbed it. "Hello?" she said breathlessly.

When several people in chairs nearby glared at her, especially one older woman going through a stack of history books, Kenzie hunched her shoulders, mouthed a "sorry" and whispered "hello" much more softly.

An equally soft voice spoke in return. "Forget about it, forget about *all* of it, and go back to Los Angeles."

Kenzie clutched the phone. She couldn't tell if she recognized the speaker because the voice was purposely being disguised. "Is that a threat?"

"You're going to be stubborn. Goddammit."

"Who is this?" she demanded.

"It doesn't matter. Just get the hell out of Santa Rey."

"So you *are* threatening me."

"If I said yes, would you go?"

"No."

"Shit." There was a beat of silence. "Okay, listen to me. There's only one way out of this."

"What?" she said, forgetting to whisper, receiving more glares for that. With effort, she lowered her voice. "What do you mean?"

"Your laptop was destroyed in the boat fire?"

"How do you know that?"

"You have backup."

"What does that have to do with—" She went still as it hit her. She and Blake had shared files. Music files, movie files…they'd e-mailed and IM'd each other regularly. And once a week he'd send her a large backup file from his laptop so that if it ever crashed, she could just send him back what he needed. She'd done the same. She'd saved all her stuff, *and* Blake's, in her Yahoo account. All she had to do was get to another computer. *"Who are you?"*

"Check the demos. That's the key."

"What?" Kenzie clutched the phone. "What does that mean? Who are—"

But she knew before she even finished her sentence

that he was gone. But who was he? A friend of Blake's? *"Dammit."*

"Shh!" everyone around her hissed.

Yeah, yeah, fine. But the prickle in the back of her neck hadn't gone away. She got to her feet and moved to the end of the aisle, peeking around the corner just in time to catch sight of the back of a guy running away. No red shirt this time but she knew it was the same guy she'd seen at the hospital. She hightailed it after him, but when she got to the other end of the aisle, she plowed directly into the librarian.

"No running in the library!"

"Sorry." Kenzie stepped around her, but it was too late. Her helpful mysterious caller was gone. She turned back to the librarian. "Can I use an online computer?"

"You have to sign up."

"Okay, where?"

"We're closing in half an hour, and the computers are in use until then. How about the morning?"

"Fine." She'd spend tonight going through the boat and Blake's place for anything that could help her. Then she'd borrow Aidan's computer—if he let her—or come back here to prove that Blake had been set up. Because that was the only answer she was willing to accept.

Someone had framed him, was *still* framing him. And she was going to find out who.

AT THE STATION, Aidan was run ragged by one call after another. Near the end of the shift, his unit was called out to a secondary fire at the hardware store, where the explosion from two days ago had killed Tracy. Looking at the scene woke Aidan right up. The new fire wasn't from any smoldering spark left over from the explosion. No way. This fire had been set.

Purposely.

In a wire mesh trash can.

Tommy was already there, and at the look on Aidan's face, shook his head. "Don't start."

"Arson."

"I said don't start."

"Let me guess. We're not going to have this conversation."

"Bingo." Tommy sounded extremely tense. "And this time I'll tell you why." He got up in Aidan's face. "Because I'm close, okay? I'm very, *very* close to finishing this. So you need to let me do just that. Got it?"

Aidan didn't see that he had a choice. Later, back at the station, he stretched out on the station couch, closing his bleary eyes, needing to think.

Somehow it was all connected, he just knew it... He fell asleep trying to piece it all together, and then dreamed of a certain hot, curvy, sweet woman. A hot, curvy, sexy woman who happened to also be a *thief.*

He woke up when someone sat on him.

And then bounced on him.

Opening his eyes, he met Cristina's frowning ones. "Trying to sleep here."

"No, you're not. Your eyes are open."

"Watch this." He closed them again.

She bounced again, a maneuver that threatened to break his legs. "How's Blake's sister?"

"Why are you asking me?"

"Because you're sleeping with her. Is she okay?"

He shook his head. "How? How do you know what I barely know?"

"Rumor mill." Her derisive humor hid her misery. Cristina was hurting. Hurting over losing Blake, her partner. Hurting over somehow blowing it with Dustin. She was so hard on the outside that they all forgot how soft and sensitive she was deep inside. She'd loved Blake like a brother, and cared about Kenzie by default.

"How is she, Aidan?"

"I don't know," he answered honestly.

"What do you mean you don't know?"

"She hasn't returned my phone calls."

"So you're losing your touch, too." She broke off, momentarily distracted when Dustin walked into the room.

The tall, tough-bodied, soft-hearted EMT pushed up his glasses, glanced at Cristina and a muscle jumped in his jaw.

Cristina didn't appear to breathe. Five agonizing seconds passed, and finally, she looked away first.

Dustin merely sighed.

The two of them had been doing some kind of emotional tap dance for weeks now. Dustin said he wanted more. Cristina said she didn't.

Now the tension in the room was so thick Aidan could hardly even see them anymore. "Hey, here's an idea. You two could lust after each other in secret and then ignore each other in person. Because it's not awkward at all."

"Shut up, Aidan." Cristina sent a glare in Dustin's direction, one that said *you're an idiot*.

Without a word, Dustin walked away, into the kitchen.

Cristina expelled a low breath.

"Looks like I'm not the only one losing my touch," Aidan noted. "What did you do?"

"How do you know I did something?"

"Please."

Cristina sighed. "He's got his panties all unraveled because I went out with an ex."

"Ouch."

"No. No ouch. It was just dinner for God's sake. No biggee."

"Yeah. But it was dinner with a guy you've gotten naked with."

She shrugged, but dejection had settled over her pretty features. "Whatever."

"Cristina."

"I told you, it was just dinner." She got off of his legs, making sure to get an elbow in his gut. "And if he can't see that then screw him."

"Why don't you just talk to him? Tell him the truth?"

"Talking isn't what I want." She headed outside, slamming the door as she went.

Aidan's cell rang and he leaped for it, hoping for Kenzie, but he got Tommy instead.

"Might want to get down to county," the inspector said in an undecipherable tone.

"Why?"

"Because I had your girlfriend arrested."

"You arrested Kenzie?"

"You have another girlfriend I don't know about?"

"She's not my—" He pinched the bridge of his nose. "What the hell happened?"

"She's in for trespassing and interfering with a crime scene, so you figure it out. You don't control your women very well."

"She's not my woman!"

"Either way, I'd hurry. Oh, and get your checkbook. This date's going to cost you big."

11

JAIL WASN'T NEARLY as adventurous as it'd been that time Kenzie had been arrested on her soap. Then she'd had a costume director and a makeup artist. Oh, and nice, soft, flattering lights. Plus she'd been able to walk off the set when the director had yelled "cut", and had sipped her iced tea and laughed it all off.

No such luxuries today.

Real life sucked.

She was given her phone call—which went to her attorney, who promised to work on getting her out. With Kenzie's own checkbook, of course.

After several hours in a holding cell, during which she contemplated the odd and unwelcome turn her life had taken, and also chewed on a few nails, she was handed her see-through baggie of personal belongings—that was twice in two days—and shown the door.

Standing in front of it wasn't her attorney, but her own gorgeous, personal savior.

Aidan was dressed in his firefighter uniform, which told her he'd come right from the job. He still wore his firefighter badass expression, too, and was looking more than a little bit temperamental as well.

Yeah. Not exactly thrilled to see her.

Nor was she thrilled to see him.

Okay, so a little part of her was. The bad girl part of her, which reared its horny head and begged *Oh, please can we have him just one more time?*

She ignored that and her quivery belly, and tried to brush past him.

"What, no thank you?" He shifted so that she was forced to bump into him.

Backing up, she put her hands on her hips and sent him a glare as mean as she could conjure up after a few hours spent in jail. "I didn't call you."

"Yeah. I noticed."

There were several people milling around, all from a different part of society than she was used to. The guy closest to her might have been fifty, or a hundred and fifty, it was hard to tell with the multitude of hats and coats he was wearing, despite it being summer. He pulled out a cigarette and a match, and even though she saw it coming, when he struck the match to the matchbox and the little *whoosh* hit her ears, she cringed.

Aidan was there in a second, holding her steady, which only further embarrassed her. "Easy."

"Damn." She let out a shaky breath. "What *is* that?"

"Post traumatic—"

She waggled a finger in his face. "Don't say it."

"—stress. Why didn't you call me, Kenzie?"

"Who did?"

"Tommy."

"Rat-fink bastard." It was coming back to her, her childhood here—the small town mentality, the utter lack of secrets, the way everyone stuck their nose in everyone else's business. She'd had enough of that from her early years to last her a lifetime.

She and Blake had been kept together as they'd gone into the child care protective services, where they'd landed in a total of three foster homes, each as kind and as warm as they could possibly be, and for that she was more than grateful, she was also lucky— but she'd never really settled into any of them. She didn't tend to settle, didn't tend to get comfortable; it was what had made her so certain Aidan was the one.

Look how that had blown up in her face.

When she'd gone off to Los Angeles and begun acting, she'd found heaven. Pretending to live someone else's life, already all scripted out? Perfect. She'd loved it. *Still* loved it.

But a small part of her knew that she couldn't always rely on a script. That at some point she would have to wing it. She'd eventually need a life, a *real* one, and she'd always figured that life would somehow be entwined with her brother's, maybe even right here in Santa Rey....

But now there was nothing for her here, nothing except proving Blake's innocence.

Aidan caught her arm as she stepped outside. She yanked free and he put up his hands, letting her step away from him as they walked outside. He leaned a hip against a tree, looking big and tall and attitude-ridden as he eyed her like she was a lit fuse.

His hair had been finger-combed at best. She could smell soap and man, and the potent mix of testosterone and pheromones boggled her mind. If she lived to be two hundred years old, she'd never understand her attraction to him. Back in her L.A. world, she had access to dozens of gorgeous men. Hundreds.

But while some had been nice dalliances, none of them had ever really gotten anywhere. Probably because a good number of the men she met were like her.

Pretend.

Not Aidan. He lived life with his eyes wide open, no script needed. His job demanded a lot of him, and he was tough because of it, but he hadn't ever shied away from something just because it was hard. Except for her.

"Thanks for bailing me out," she conceded.

"Need a ride to your car? Or are you going to manage that on your own, too?"

The sun was warm and bright, and she stood still in it for a moment, tilting her head up to it, inhaling deeply. Then she turned to the man who had once been her everything. Whether she liked it or not—and for the record, she didn't—he could still stop her heart, make her pulse race, and worst of all, make her hormones stand up and shimmy. "Yeah. A ride would be great, if you don't mind."

He let out a sound that told her what he thought of that, and took her to his truck.

"About that ride…" She slowed, dragging her

feet. "Everything's still booked. Maybe there's something—"

"You know where there's something." He turned on the engine and pulled out of the lot. "At my place."

"Yeah." She shook her head. "No."

"Yeah no?"

She sighed. "It's just that staying with you seems like a whole lot of trouble I don't want to face."

"Why?"

"Because I don't want to lead you on."

"I thought you enjoyed exacting your revenge on my body."

With more than a slight twinge of regret and, *dammit,* guilt, she avoided his gaze.

"Come on, Kenz, be honest. You're not afraid of hurting me. You're afraid *you'll* get hurt."

Wasn't that the plain ugly truth.

"You made sure I understood that you'd changed," he said softly, looking over at her for a beat before returning his attention to the road. "Now you have to understand something. I've changed as well."

Yes. Yes, he had.

"Look, you wanted to know what happened all those years ago?" he asked. "I got scared, that's what the hell happened. I'd always lived my life without letting people inside my heart, where they could hurt me. But you got in, and, yeah, that terrified me. You're doing it again, by the way, getting in, and I'm not any more thrilled about it now than I was then."

Something warm slid through her at his words, and

the low, rough tone in which they were spoken. Warm, and dangerously seductive.

He pulled into his driveway and shut off the engine, turning in his seat to face her. "You'll have to make do without the five-star rating." He paused a beat. "Although there are certain five-star services I *do* offer."

When she met his gaze she saw the sparkle of pure wicked trouble in his eyes. *Oh, boy.* "Aidan—"

"I'm talking about my breakfasts, which you happened to miss out on. And then there's my massage specialty." He didn't add any obvious eyebrow waggle or other suggestive gesture, but his eyes crinkled and she knew he was *thinking* suggestively.

Yup. Dangerously seductive. She already knew how erotic his touch could be, just how earthy, how naughty, and she wasn't ready to go back there. Not if she intended to be the one to walk away this time.

And there would be walking away when this was over...

Even while she was thinking it, he took her hand and led her to his door. Her instinct was to make a smartass comment to piss him off, chase him away, and yet she didn't do anything but allow him to open the door for her. Once she started to step inside, he stopped her. When she met his gaze, he asked, "You planning anything else I should know about?"

"Like?"

"Shit. Anything. It could be anything."

The sun was bright. The surf behind them loud and choppy. She loved the scent of the ocean. She'd missed that, working long, long days on set in the middle of Los Angeles. Now that she'd been cancelled, she could see taking a laptop out on the beach and just writing to her heart's content if she wanted. "My immediate plans involve a shower."

"That's all?" he asked so warily that she smiled.

"Yeah. That's all."

He touched the corner of her smiling mouth. "That's a good look for you."

"What are you talking about, I smile all the time."

"On TV, maybe. But I haven't seen much of it here."

"Well, maybe that's because I was in a fire, then facing the fact that my brother's dead, and then…" And then she'd been in his bed, naked, panting, sobbing his name, holding onto his head as his mouth and then his body had taken her to heaven—

"*That* look," he said, pointing at her. "I want to know what you were thinking just then to put *that* look on your face."

She crossed her arms over her suddenly aching breasts. "Nothing."

"You are such a liar," he chided softly.

He gestured her inside his place, and she took a better look around than she had when she'd been fresh out of the hospital, and then fresh out of his bed. She saw the pretty windows, the wood floors he'd done himself, and felt another ache, this one in her chest.

She knew that growing up, Aidan hadn't had much of a stable home life, either. He'd been shuffled around as much as she had. Going into the fire academy had changed his life, given him a team, but more than that, his first *real* friendships. The kind of friendships that would last, the kind of friend that had his back no matter what. He still hadn't had any real understanding of what that meant when she'd gone off to Los Angeles, but she could tell it had come to him in the years since. There was an easy confidence about him, an air that said he'd been well liked, well taken care of…

Well loved.

Her heart did a little flop at that because she hadn't given herself the same. Oh, sure, she was liked. She'd been taken care of. But loved by someone other than Blake?

No.

And if she took away the fame, leaving just small-town girl Kenzie Stafford, what would actually be left?

The answer was as unsettling as the thought, especially given that now she really was without that fancy job. "Aidan?"

He'd headed for the kitchen, but stopped and turned to her. "Yeah?"

"Thanks."

"For?"

"For bailing me out. For waiting to make sure I was okay."

He leaned back against the wall and studied her. "So why did you do it, Kenz? Why did you go back after I'd warned you not to—" He broke off and shook his head. "Never mind. I just heard my own words and realized *exactly* why you did it. *Because* I warned you not to."

"Am I that stubborn?"

"Hell, yeah, you're that stubborn."

She rolled her eyes, then caught the flash of humor in his. He was laughing at her, and not with her, which should have made her defensive and possibly bitchy, but in spite of herself, she let out a laugh, too. "Okay, so it wasn't the smartest thing I've done. But it was the right thing."

"How about stealing my file, was that the right thing, too?"

She let out a low breath. "I was wondering when we were going to get to that."

He just looked at her, big and bad and…patient. So damn patient. She pulled the file from her bag and handed it over. "Thanks."

"I'd say you're welcome, if I'd given it to you."

"You'd have done the same thing in my position."

"You think so?"

She looked into his compelling eyes and felt her breath catch. "Okay, no. You would have asked. But maybe you're a better person than I am."

His eyes expressed his surprise at that statement. They both knew she hadn't always considered him such a great guy. "People change," she whispered, mirroring his words back to her. "Right?"

"That's right." The smile hit his eyes before his lips slowly curved, and there was an answering quiver that began in her belly. *Oh, boy.* Not good. He was standing too close, and not being annoying or antagonistic, and suddenly it all seemed too intimate.

She started to turn away but that was cowardice, and if she was going to learn anything while being back here in Santa Rey, it was not going to be that, so she faced him again. "I really am sorry for dragging you into this. For getting arrested and you having to bail me out. For driving you crazy. Pick any of the above."

"You didn't drag me into anything."

"Maybe not, but I'm about to." She let out a breath. "I need to tell you something."

"Okay." When she didn't go on, he raised an eyebrow. "Is it something that's going to get you arrested again?"

"No. I'm kind of hoping to avoid repeating that experience."

"Good."

"But there are things you should know. Things you're not going to like."

"Try me."

"Okay. I've been getting calls from someone I think is trying to help me."

He stared at her. "Your local cell caller?"

"Yes. He told me the key, whatever that means, is in Blake's computer files."

"He?"

"I think so. But I can't place the voice, he's disguised it."

"How the hell does he know the key's in Blake's computer files?" Aidan asked her.

"I don't know."

"Blake's laptop was never found. I'm betting it went up in *Blake's Girl*."

"As did mine. But with a computer, I could access my backup files, which would include Blake's backup files."

"I have a computer." He was close enough that she could see the green swirling in his light brown eyes. The scar bisecting his left eyebrow, the lines on his face, only added character, and a sexiness she couldn't have explained to save her life.

His mouth was slightly curved and she knew if she leaned in and touched hers to it, his lips would be warm and skilled, and most of all, giving.

"I didn't think I'd be happy to see you," she murmured, stepping closer. "But I've been proven wrong on two accounts now. When you saved me from the fire, and when I came out of jail and saw you standing there."

"Just the two?"

"Well, *maybe* one other time…"

Leaning close, he let his mouth brush her ear. "Try a couple."

At the reminder of how he'd made her come *several* times, easily she might add, as if he knew her body better than she did, a little shiver of awareness went down her spine, chased by another one, this one pure anticipation.

He could do it again. He could take her there again, to heaven, to oblivion… Only this time it wouldn't be adrenaline. This time she'd go in with her eyes wide open. His needed to be as well.

"I was worried about you," he murmured. "You've got to stay out of this one, Kenzie. Stay out of Tommy's way."

Somehow her face was nuzzling his throat, and she was trying to breathe him in. "I'm going to prove Blake's innocence in all this," she told him, liking the feel of her lips against his skin. "No matter the cost."

"Even if the price is my friendship?"

Her throat actually tightened at the thought and she pulled back to look into his eyes. "Is it going to cost me that?"

"Depends." He took her hand, put it on his chest and offered her a smile. "You still intending on stomping all over my tender heart?"

At that, and the crinkles at the corners of his eyes, the ones telling her he was teasing her, she out and out laughed, feeling much of tension drain away. "Yes."

His hands went to her hips, pulling her closer, and she stared into his face, feeling so at home in his house that she found herself hesitating, not for the first time that day, and wishing she had a script for what came next.

"You're thinking again," he murmured.

"Yeah."

He leaned back against the front door, unexpectedly giving her space. Space she thought she'd wanted, but found she didn't want at all. "I really did intend to stomp all over your heart, you know. When I first saw you again, I wanted to hurt you the way you'd hurt me. But then we kissed."

"We did a lot more than kiss."

She flashed back to that night, when she'd climbed into bed with him, pressing her icy feet to his, then her body. She remembered realizing he was naked and warm and strong and hard...*God*. He'd been so utterly irresistible, she'd lost her head. And, yeah, they'd done a lot more than kiss. "Fine. We kissed, and then I decided I should sleep with you and then walk away. Perfect, neat revenge."

"Neat, maybe. But not perfect." His eyes were glittering with knowledge, hard won. "Because it wasn't as easy as you thought, was it?"

No, it hadn't been. Because it'd been amazing between them. So damned amazing. "Maybe I've been looking at this wrong."

He didn't move from the door, just kept looking at her, his eyes warm, his mouth curved, his body big and bad and so gorgeous she could hardly stand it.

She wanted him.

Again.

Still.

"Maybe it's not about sleeping with you once and walking away," she heard herself say. "Maybe it's about letting this thing take its own lead for as long as I'm here."

"'This thing'? You mean the way we apparently can't stay out of each other's pants?"

At the huskiness in his voice, her nipples hardened. "Yes."

12

AIDAN PUSHED AWAY from the door and came toward Kenzie, all easy, loose-limbed confidence, yet radiating an intensity that made her breath catch. He didn't stop until they were toe-to-toe, and she slowly tipped up her head to look into his inscrutable eyes.

"You want to have sex," he said silkily. "Here. Tonight. Now."

Her breath caught at his bluntness. "And then maybe again later."

"Later," he repeated, as if trying to process this.

"Maybe even until I leave Santa Rey. At which time we both walk away, eyes wide open."

He just stared at her for the longest moment. "What happened to trouncing on my heart?"

"It seems you were right. I don't really want to hurt you."

When he shot her a not-buying-it look, she caved. "Okay, so I want to hurt you less than I want to sleep with you again."

"You know, you'd think I'd be tough enough to walk away from such an overwhelmingly romantic offer," he said drily, sounding both intrigued and baffled. "But apparently..." He put his hands on her hips. "I'm not."

She offered a smile that was sheer nerve. "So...yes?"

His eyes never wavered, holding hers, leveling her as he pulled her in. "I don't know, Kenzie. I'm a little afraid..."

"Be serious."

His smile was crooked and impossibly endearing. "I am. This time you could really do it, whether you're trying to or not. This time, you just might take out my heart."

"Come on," she quipped, even as a part of her was afraid he was right, for both of them. "If we're just having a physical relationship and nothing else, how can we get hurt?"

With a soft laugh, he slid his hands up her spine, and then back again, low enough now to cup her butt and squeeze.

He was hard.

Bending his head, he put his mouth to her ear and let out a breath that made her shiver in longing. "Just a physical relationship, Kenzie? Is that all this is? Really?" He sank his teeth into her lobe and she shivered again.

"It—it's all it *should* be," she managed.

Another soft, deprecating laugh rumbled through his chest, this one aimed at the both of them. "Okay, well as long as we're being honest, you should know..." His hands glided up her spine again, this time beneath her shirt to touch bare skin. "Even though you *are* going to hurt me, it's not enough to make me say no. Truth is, nothing could..."

She opened her mouth to say something, but then he kissed the spot he'd just nipped at, soothing the ache as his fingers stroked over her skin. Her eyes drifted shut, and she slid her arms around his neck, pressing close. "No pain, no gain," she whispered, and he let out another low laugh as he lifted her up and carried her to his bedroom.

To his bed.

He settled over her, looking down into her face for a beat before lowering his head and taking her mouth with his demanding one.

If simply walking into his house had felt like a homecoming, then this, here, now, felt even more so. He felt like home, he smelled like home, and he tasted even better; she hesitated, thinking, *uh-oh*.

His hands came up to hold her face. "What?"

She stared up into his eyes and saw herself reflected there, as if they were one, and although it was deeply unsettling to realize that this time she could fall even harder for him—if she let herself—she also couldn't imagine walking away, without being in his arms again.

"Kenz?"

"Nothing, it's nothing." And she pulled him down for another kiss as the heat of him seeped into her bones, warming her with a sensual promise of what was to come. Those big, warm hands slid along her arms, lifting them up over her head, entwining their fingers as his mouth continued to plunder hers, delivering on that promise.

It was familiar, and it was comforting, and yet it was so, so much more as well. Not since being with Aidan six years ago had she given any thought to what it would be like to be with a guy long enough that he felt…like home. She was a woman who liked change, who liked the new and exciting, who lived off the lines someone else wrote for her each day.

But with Aidan, she knew what he felt like, what he tasted like, exactly how crazy he could drive her with a touch of a single finger, and yet being with him felt almost unbearably *right,* and far more arousing than she could have ever imagined.

Still kissing her, he pulled off her top, then her skirt. Her new bra was a front hook, which didn't slow him down at all, and when he had her naked except her panties, he hooked his fingers in the thin strip of cotton on her hips and let his gaze meet hers. Then he tugged, slipping the underwear down her legs and off, sailing them over one shoulder. Towering over her, fully dressed while she was as naked as she could get, he let out a low breath. "You're so beautiful."

"And you're overdressed." Still in his fire gear, in fact…

"In a minute." He was kneeling between her legs. He spread his, which in turn spread hers, and his gaze took her in, in one fell swoop, heating her skin everywhere he looked. He traced his fingers over her breasts, her belly, her thighs.

Between.

When he bent his head with fierce intent, she sucked in a breath, a breath that clogged her throat when he replaced his fingers with his mouth.

"Aidan," she managed, hardly recognizing her own voice. "I—"

His tongue encircled her tender, sensitized flesh, making her quiver from the inside out, and she promptly forgot what she'd meant to say. While his tongue and fingers circled and teased and stroked, she gripped the sheets and stared down at him. His hair stood up, from her fingers, she realized. His eyes were closed, his expression dreamy as he brought her such bliss she could hardly even see, much less think.

But she didn't close her eyes. She watched him concentrate on her pleasure as if it were his own, took in his moves, the moves that were driving her right out of her ever-loving mind.

It was as if he knew what made her tick, inside and out. That was a terrifying thought, really. Because the girl he'd once known no longer existed, and since then…well, she hadn't really let anyone know her.

An ever-changing script.

That was her life.

A life she was no longer sure about. But having him take her apart the way he was, *that* she was sure about.

He opened his eyes, so molten hot that they were nearly black, and looked up at her. He was sure, too, which should have stopped her cold, and she stirred. "Aidan—"

"Shh."

Then he swirled his tongue in a precise rhythm over ground zero, and she lost it.

Completely.

Lost.

It.

Panting for breath, arching up off the mattress and into his mouth, she dug her fingers into the sheets, throwing her head back at the peak, sobbing out his name.

Slowly he brought her back to planet earth. She closed her eyes, savoring the pleasure, still quivering and pulsing as he kissed his way back up her body, his tongue stroking a rib, a nipple, her throat...and then he cupped her face and smiled at her.

"You shushed me," she said, her voice sounding weak and raspy.

"It was for a good cause." He rocked his hips into hers.

"I'm going to get you back for that."

He smiled wickedly. "Should I be scared?"

"Terrified." Rolling him over, she sat on him and tugged his uniform shirt off. She could have spent a year lapping him up with nothing but her tongue. He had a tight body, toned from years of physical labor. His chest was broad, hard, his belly rippled with sinew and rising and falling in a way that assured her she was in no way alone in this almost chemical-like attraction they shared, which transcended both time and logic.

His hands went to the button on his pants to help speed up the process, and she ran her fingers up the taut, corded muscles of his abs. He unzipped, she tugged, and then nearly drooled at the sight of the part of him so happy to see her.

She licked her lips.

He groaned.

She kissed him, on the very tip.

"Kenz—" he choked out, tunneling his fingers through her hair.

Since her mouth was now full, she couldn't answer, and he said something completely unintelligible anyway, which, she had to admit, only egged her on. God, she loved rendering this big, bad, tough man completely incapable of speech. Loved the power that surged through her at the way he was breathing, saying her name.

Loved so much about it that it scared her. Scared her into being even more bold and brazen so that she didn't have to think about how much being with him meant to her.

How much he meant to her.

Using her hands and mouth, she drew him to the edge. "Two-minute warning," he groaned out, his hands fisted in the sheets at his sides as she ran her tongue up his length. "Okay, thirty seconds. *Maybe.*"

She kept going until he swore and grabbed a condom, nudging her to her back, his hands running up the undersides of her arms until they were over her head. His knee spread her legs, his thigh rubbing against the core of her.

"In," she gasped, arching into him. "In me now."

Lowering his body to hers, he nipped at her lower lip, then kissed her, hard and deep, his tongue slipping into her mouth at the very moment he slipped into her body. "Like that?"

She couldn't answer. Hell, she could hardly breathe.

"Kenzie?"

"Yes," she managed, then shuddered as he withdrew, only to thrust into her again. And again. *"Like that."*

The feel of him, thick and hot and filling her to the brink, had her gasping his name, wrapping her legs around his hips, leaving her unable to remember exactly what she was supposedly paying him back for. Her toes were curling, her skin feeling too tight for her body, which seemed to swell from the inside out. "Aidan—"

"Come," he demanded, grinding his teeth in what looked like agony. "I want to feel you come before I—"

She burst in mindless, blind sensation, and barely heard his strangled answering groan as he exploded.

For long moments afterward, they lay there entwined, panting and damp, and powerless to move, their breathing echoing loudly through the bedroom.

"Is it just me," she finally managed, "or does that get better and better?"

"Oh, yeah."

She fell quiet a moment, but then couldn't resist. "You think it'll keep happening? You know, until I leave?"

"If it does, it's likely to kill me."

"Yes." She sighed dreamily. "But what a way to go."

His soft huff of laughter was the last thing she remembered before she drifted off to sleep.

AIDAN WOKE UP SOMETIME LATER with a smile, his body ready for another round. In the pitch-dark, he rolled over for Kenzie.

And got nothing.

With a very bad feeling in his gut, he sat up. "You're gone, aren't you?" he said into the night.

When he got no answer, he tossed back the covers and got out of bed, but it was too late. She had left. He told himself he wasn't her keeper, and she could go wherever she wanted, but he'd been lulled into the impression that she hadn't been done with him yet.

She *wasn't* done with him, not yet. Which meant she was probably out there looking to poke her nose into the arsons. Aidan hurriedly got dressed. He had no idea where she was but he needed to find out, because with whatever information she'd get, she'd go snooping into things that were guaranteed to piss off Tommy.

Hell. They'd just spent hours in his bed. And in his shower. And then his bed again. Hadn't he tired her out?

His stomach was grumbling and his head starting to pound when he picked up his cell phone and called hers; he was shocked when she answered.

"Hi," she said in that soft, breathless voice that had only a few hours before made him come.

Just hearing it stirred him halfway to life. He was little better than Pavlov's dogs. "Where are you?"

"Oh, out and about." She still sounded breathless.

"Kenzie, what are you doing?"

"Um…exercising?"

"That's a bad word to you."

"Not anymore. Do you have any idea how much work it takes to stay in TV shape?"

And then he heard it, the unmistakable sound of a sliding door either opening or closing. "Where are you?"

"Whoops, bad connection," she said.

He gnashed his teeth together. "We have a great connection. What are you up to?"

"Wow, I can hardly hear you…"

"Kenz—"

"Gotta go."

He didn't have to hear the click to know she'd shut her phone. Nor did he bother with swearing. Instead, he grabbed his keys and went after her, figuring her options were severely limited. She wouldn't have gone back to the docks because there were no sliding door there. So she was probably at Blake's house. He supposed she could also be at any one of the arsons Blake had been accused of, but most of them had been demo'd, and plus it seemed likely that if she was butting her nose in, she'd start at the top.

So would he.

He hit the jackpot on his first try. Pulling into the small house Blake had claimed as his own, he parked right next to Kenzie's flashy Mercedes. He got out of his truck and felt the hood of her car.

Still warm.

So she hadn't been there long. She was just damn lucky she hadn't gotten herself arrested again, considering the yellow tape surrounding the house. Just thinking about what Tommy would say, and how long he'd jail her this time, had him sweating. The front door was shut and, as he discovered, locked.

Aidan moved around the side of the house. His plan was simple. He was going to scare the hell out of her. And then he was going to kiss the hell out of her.

And then…and then he had no idea. Spanking her seemed like a good option.

The sliding back door on Blake's deck was unlocked and opened an inch. This was where she'd entered, and following suit, he slipped inside. The place was dark, but there was a light on upstairs, and he headed in that direction. At a sound behind him, he whipped around just as two hands smacked him in the chest and shoved. As he fell back, he reached out and hauled his assailant with him. He hit his ass on the bottom step and Kenzie landed on him.

"What are you doing?" she demanded.

The stairs biting into his back, her full weight over the top of him, he hissed out a breath of pain. "What am *I* doing? What are *you* doing?"

"I'm—" She bit back whatever she'd been about to say, crawled backward off of him and stood up.

"No, it's okay, I'm fine, thanks," he muttered, getting up on his own and brushing himself off. "How did you get in here?"

"Blake gave me his spare key a long time ago."

"Okay, so back to my first question. Why are you here?"

"Looking for clues to Blake's innocence." She glared at him, then pointed to the door. "You need to leave."

"So do you."

"Oh, no. This is my brother's place. I'm his beneficiary. I get to be here."

"Not with the caution tape still blocking the front door, you don't."

She was breathing fast, her voice thick and husky as if she'd been crying. Or maybe she still was. He couldn't see her clearly enough to decide. "Ah, Kenzie. Don't—"

"Go," she said, crossing her arms over her chest.

"Fine. But you're coming with me."

"No, I'm not."

"Yeah, you are." Wrapping his fingers around her arm, he headed toward the sliding door, toting her with him, until she yanked free. Then, lifting her nose, she stalked out in front of him, going willingly but not happily. "Kenzie," he said as she got into her car.

"I don't want to talk right now." She tried to shut the driver's door on him but he stepped closer, holding it open.

"Isn't that convenient."

"Dammit, Aidan. Get out of my way."

"Just tell me where you're going."

For the first time, she hesitated.

"You could try my house," he suggested. "My computer."

She paused another beat. "I wouldn't want to impose."

"Imposing would be getting your pretty ass arrested again, goddammit. Meet me there."

"Fine." Putting the car into gear, she peeled out, leaving him little choice but to hope that she would.

13

WITH LITTLE TO NO TRAFFIC in the middle of the night, it took only five minutes to get home. Aidan pulled into his driveway next to the little red sports car, watching Kenzie storm up the walk to his front door, looking irritated and frustrated.

Just as irritated and frustrated, he followed. Did she have no clue what she was doing to him?

How could she not?

"Wait," she said, stopping so fast he plowed into her, staring back at the street. "Did you see that car?"

"No."

"It was gray." She chewed on her thumbnail. "Look, I'm not trying to change the subject here, because trust me, I'm pissed and enjoying being pissed, but I think someone's following me."

Reaching past her, he unlocked the door and gestured her in ahead of him, keeping his body in front of her back as he turned to eye the street.

He didn't see the car—at the moment, there were *no* cars—but he didn't doubt her. "You've seen it before?"

"Yes. Truthfully, I'm beginning to feel sort of

stalked." She whirled to face him. "Okay, so back to being pissed off."

Oh, no. Not yet. He'd anticipated her, and was standing so close she bumped into him, squeaking in surprise, but when she tried to take a step back, he held her still. Christ, she smelled good and the way her hair framed her face… "How long have you suspected someone's been following you?"

"Since the boat fire, I guess."

"Have you told anyone? Tommy? The police?"

"I wasn't really sure. I'm still not sure. It's just a feeling."

He let go of her to pull out his cell phone.

"What are you doing?"

"Calling the police."

Kenzie stepped close and shut the phone, stuffing it back into his pocket. "Aidan, listen to me. We both know that you and I don't do *real* relationships, especially not with each other. Now sex, we do that just fine. And in case you're confused, the biggest difference between the two is that with just sex, there's no sharing of personal information."

He was not liking where this was going. At all. "Meaning?"

"Meaning I don't have to account to you, and you're not responsible for me."

He stared at her, more stung than he'd like to admit. "Well, shit."

"I mean it, Aidan."

"You don't want me to call the police."

"And scare off the guy? No, I don't."

"Fine."

"*Fine*. Now where the hell is your computer? We have some files to access."

"My bedroom."

They were nose-to-nose, now. Breathing in each other's air. He could feel the heat of her radiating into him, and for whatever reason, his hands ran down her arms and then back up again, squeezing a little, more moved by the close proximity than he'd like to admit.

The very tips of her breasts brushed against his shirt. Her thighs bumped into his. Sparks were flying from her eyes, her mouth grim.

A mouth that suddenly he couldn't stop looking at.

Her hands had come up to his chest and she dug her fingers into his pecs, hard enough to have him hissing out a breath. Her eyes were on his, but then they lowered to his mouth.

She was thinking about kissing him.

Leaning in, he took care of that little piece of business for her. Covering her mouth with his, he swallowed her little moan of pleasure and promptly lost himself in her when she melted against him, entwining her arms around his neck so tightly he couldn't breathe. Since breathing was overrated anyway, especially when kissing her, he just hauled her up tighter against him and kept at it. Her hands were in his hair, his molded the length of her body to him, until suddenly, she shoved him clear, turned and stalked off, heading down the hallway and into his bedroom. He stared after her, breathing like a misused race horse, warring with himself. He could go after her. Or *he* could walk out on *her* for a change of pace.

Yeah, right. He went after her.

WHEN AIDAN OPENED THE DOOR of his bedroom, Kenzie held her breath. She hadn't turned on the light, so he was silhouetted from behind by the lamp in the living room, looking tall, dark, and so sexy she could hardly stand it.

And attitude-ridden. Don't forget that. Stalking past her, he opened his laptop and hit the power button. While it booted up, she just stared through the dim room at him, wishing…hell.

Wishing things were different. That's all. If only she could call the writers and complain about this particular plotline, and maybe get it adjusted. Or get a new script delivered. Yeah, that would be best. One with a happy ending, please. With a sigh, she moved to the laptop. "Should I download it to your desktop?"

"Yes."

She accessed her mail, and the files she'd saved, clicking on the first of Blake's. "It's going to take a while. It's a big file. And it'll take even longer to flip through it all and see if there's even anything in it that we can use."

"Your caller suggested there was."

"Yes, but how did he know? *What* did he know?"

"Let's find out. Kenzie—"

"I'm not ready to talk."

He stepped closer, a big, tall, badass outline. "What *are* you ready for?"

"How about the only thing we're good at?"

With a low sound that might have been an agreeing groan, he came even closer. "Kenzie—"

"No. I mean it." He was hard. She could feel him. Could feel, too, the tension shimmering throughout his entire body. It matched hers. "No talking."

"Fine." With a rough tug, he hauled her up against him. His body was warm and corded with strength, his hands hard and hot on her. And his mouth...

God, his mouth.

He was the most amazing kisser, his lips warm and soft and firm all at the same time, his tongue both talented and greedy and generous.

So generous that she moaned into his mouth and held on for the ride until she couldn't stand it anymore. "Clothes," she muttered, and yanked off her own top, gratified to see him doing the same. She stared through the dark at his bared torso as she worked the buttons on her jeans while simultaneously kicking off her shoes. God, he was gorgeous. Sleek, toned and so damned yummy she wanted to gobble him up on the spot. She shoved down her jeans, watching him do the same, but unlike her, his underwear went bye-bye with his jeans, and her mouth actually went dry.

Riveted by the sight, she stood there in her bra and panties and socks. Staring.

He stood there in nothing. In glorious, mouth-dropping, heart-stopping nothing. Yeah, she'd seen it before, all of it and more—*but, damn.*

"You cheated," he said, reaching for her bra.

His erection nudged her belly, and forgetting to finish stripping, she wrapped her fingers around him. He hissed out a breath.

"Too tight?" she asked as she stroked.

"No, your fingers are frozen."

For some reason that made her laugh. How the hell that was even possible with all the sensations crowding and pushing for space in her brain was beyond her but she stood there, her fingers wrapped around a very impressive erection and laughed.

"Yeah, see, you're not really supposed to hold onto a guy's favorite body part and laugh."

Which, of course, made her laugh harder.

With a shake of his head, he just smiled, clearly not too worried because he remained hard as a rock in her hand…

As his fingers worked their magic and her bra fell to the floor at their feet.

When he stepped even closer, her nipples brushed his chest, and it was her turn to hiss in a breath as they hardened.

And then she couldn't breathe at all because he dropped to his knees, hooked his thumbs in the edge of her panties and tugged.

At the sight he revealed, he gave a low, ragged groan and slid his hands up the backs of her thighs, cupping her bottom in his big palms. "God, look at you."

"Aidan—"

"You're so pretty here." He ran a finger over her. "All wet and glistening. For me." There was a deep, husky satisfaction to his voice that made her thighs quiver.

"Spread your legs," he murmured, skimming hot, wet, openmouthed kisses up an inner thigh. "Yeah, like that." He pulled her forward, and right into his mouth.

At the first unerring stroke of his tongue her knees nearly buckled but he had a grip on her, one hand on her hip, holding her upright, the other exploring between her legs, working with his tongue to drive her out of her mind. "Aidan—"

"You taste like heaven," he whispered against her. *"Heaven."*

And he felt like it. She strained against him, her fingers tunneled into his hair, her head thrown back as he took her exactly where he wanted to her to go, which was to the very edge of a cliff, so high she couldn't see all the way to the bottom, couldn't speak, couldn't do anything but feel.

And she was feeling plenty. Mostly a need for speed at this point, but he purposely slowed her down, dancing his tongue over her as light as a feather. She tightened her fingers in his hair, silently threatening to make him bald if he didn't get back to business. Her business. "Aidan, dammit."

"I could look at you all day."

"Look later. Do now."

"Always in a hurry." He tsked, but obliged.

Oh, God, how he obliged, skimming his hands up

the front of her thighs, gently opening her. For a moment he pulled back, admiring the sight before him, wet from his tongue, wet from her own arousal.

Standing there so open and vulnerable, she let out a growl of frustration and need, and he leaned in, this time sucking her into his mouth hard, giving her the rhythm she needed to completely lose it.

When her knees gave out, he let her fall, catching her, rising to his feet, spinning toward the bed, his mouth fastened to hers. His hands moved over her body, thoroughly, ruthlessly, ravenously kissing her as they went, until from somewhere behind them, from the pocket of her pants, her cell phone went off. She couldn't even think about getting it. Hell, the entire place could have gone up in flames right then and there and she doubted she would have thought about it. "In me, in me."

He let out a rough laugh.

"Now."

Because now was the only thing that mattered, and this was the only thing that registered, the feel of his hands on her body, molding, sculpting, flaming the wildfire flickering to life inside her.

Aidan crawled up her body. He'd found a condom, and made himself at home between her thighs. Then he stared down into her eyes, his unwavering and fierce. "This is not just sex." His voice was low and rough. "It's not. Not for me."

She blinked, trying to clear her fuzzy head.

"And if that's all it is for you, I want to know it now."

He lifted her hips, his strong callused fingers gliding over her flesh, making sure she was ready for him.

She was.

Beyond ready.

"Tell me," he demanded, holding still, waiting on her word. She stared up at him, her heart swelling at the truth. "It's more," she admitted, which—*ding, ding, ding*—was the right answer because then he spread her thighs wider and drove himself into her, hard and fast, the way she'd wanted, and took her right where she needed to go.

Halfway there, with her breath sobbing in her throat, with their bodies straining with each other, she cupped his jaw and looked into his face.

He was damp with sweat, hard with tension, and so damned sexy she could scarcely speak. "Aidan."

"Don't stop me."

She shook her head at his rough plea. Stop him? Was he kidding? She wanted him to never stop.

Never…a terrifying thought. "Aidan…"

His mouth nuzzled at her ear. "Yeah?"

"I missed you," she whispered, letting him in on her biggest secret, giving it to him without reserve, letting him look deeply into her eyes.

She absorbed both his surprise and his next thrust, and then that was it.

She burst.

And so did he.

14

AIDAN LAY ON HIS BACK, a hot, naked, still quivering Kenzie in his arms, and let her words soak in.

She'd missed him. "Kenz?"

"Mmm." Her face was pressed against his throat, her mouth sending shivers of delight down his spine even now, when his bones had turned into overcooked noodles and he couldn't have moved to save his life.

Well, except a certain part of his anatomy, which appeared to have segregated from his brain. That part moved. That part wanted round two.

And possibly round three, please.

Kenzie lifted her head and looked at him, all sleepy-eyed and still glowing. Waiting for him to speak.

He found himself cupping her face, and bringing it in for a kiss that lingered.

And deepened.

"I missed you, too," he whispered against her lips.

She pulled back and closed her eyes.

Staring down at her, he let out a breath. Okay. So she hadn't meant it. It'd just been the heat of the moment talking. He supposed he could understand that. Had to understand that. After all, the moment had gotten pretty damn heated. "It's all right." God, listen to him lie. "I get it."

Across the room sat his laptop, with answers. Or so he hoped. "We'd better get up." He was relieved to note that his voice seemed to sound normal, that he was still breathing and that the heart she'd just stabbed was apparently still in working order.

Even if it was bleeding all over the place. Internal carnage…

But he had no one to blame but himself for opening it up to her in the first place. She'd warned him, hadn't she? She'd warned him and he'd been cocky enough not to believe it possible.

"Aidan?"

He managed to look at her.

"I *did* miss you. I missed this. But…"

"But life intrudes. I get that, too."

She looked into his eyes, sighed, then slipped from the bed. Gloriously naked, she walked to his computer. Lit only by the glow of the screen, she afforded him a particularly fine view. "Huh," she said, and bent over a little so that her fingers could move over the keyboard.

She was absolutely clueless about the picture she made in green glowing profile, with her hair wild around her head, a whisker burn from his face across a breast and her ribs, and her very sweet ass looking good enough to bite.

"That's odd," she muttered, her fingers moving

faster, the furrow between her eyebrows deepening as she frowned.

He opened his mouth to ask what was odd, but she bent a little farther and he couldn't gather enough working brain cells to do anything but stare. Her spine was narrow and pretty, and his gaze followed it down past the indention of her waist and the gentle flare of her hips to one of his favorite parts of a woman's anatomy. Her legs were spread slightly, her thighs taut, allowing him a peek of the treasure between—

"Aidan?"

At the tone, he managed to squelch the lust. *Barely.* Rising, he walked up behind her. Also naked. Curling his body around hers from behind, a good amount of that lust came barreling back, hitting him like a freight train. He couldn't help it. His chest was against her back, her world-class ass pressed into his crotch. His hands went to her hips, one slipping around to her ribs, his fingers just brushing the underside of her breast. Pressing his lips to the side of her neck, he let his hand skim up, gliding over her nipple, which hardened gratifyingly in his fingers.

Oh, yeah.

His other hand slid to her belly and began a southward descent—

"Look." Catching his hand, she pointed to an opened Excel worksheet. She had brought up an interesting list. "My mysterious caller said to look at the demos," she told him. "I didn't know what he meant, but all the burned buildings have been razed to the ground. I saw the photos in Zach's file—not all of those buildings were severely damaged."

With great difficulty, he frowned at the computer and not at her nude body, his hands still full with warm, sweet, sexy-as-hell woman. "It's true," he said. "But the properties were demolished anyway. Except for the last two."

"On whose orders?"

"The records have been sealed."

"Why?"

"That's the question. Zach tried to get the answer to that and it cost him."

Forcing his concentration from her body, he took in the worksheet in front of him. "Pretty impressive information here." Blake had been busy.

So had he been keeping track of his own handi-work, along with what happened to each property after the fires?

"Who has the power to order a demolition of a burned property?" Kenzie asked him.

"The owner, anyone acting on the behalf of an owner or the fire department, if the property is deemed unstable or unsafe for any reason."

She pulled free and went for her clothes, which were strewn across the room. He watched with great regret as she found the pieces one by one and covered up that gorgeous bod.

With a sigh, he reached for his jeans and slid them on. Back to the grown-up world apparently... "How is it you've never looked through Blake's files before?"

"I never thought to. We regularly sent each other files, just in case. It was our backup system."

"What did you send him?"

She lifted a shoulder. "Rough drafts of stuff."

"Stuff?"

"I've been writing. Scripts." Another lift of her shoulder. "For the day I finally ate too many donuts and didn't get asked to audition anymore."

"I bet you're a great writer."

"Really?"

He thought about how deeply she felt things, how good she was with words, and nodded.

Looking touched, she smiled. "Thanks."

"How long ago did he send you this file?"

"He sent me a backup file every week. We were supposed to keep only the latest version for each other, but I was always too lazy to go back and delete the week before, so I should have them all—" She stared at him for a beat before whipping back to the computer. Her fingers raced over the keys as he bent his head close to hers, looking at what she brought up.

An entire list of arson-related backup files from Blake, starting shortly after the first suspicious fires, until the day before he died.

"So," she said slowly. "Either he was a damned stupid felon, or he was investigating the arsons himself."

Her tone made it clear which she believed.

"Or," he said softly, knowing she was going to hate him. "He's keeping track of the arsons for a partner."

She looked at him again, her eyes cooling to, oh, about thirty-five degrees below zero.

"Open the first file."

Without a word, she clicked on it. It was a Word document, a diary of notes with a running commentary. The first read:

Hill Street fire:
Second point of origin mysteriously vanished on day of cleanup. Wire metal trash can, unique enough in design that it should be traceable. When I mentioned this to the chief, he said I should stick to fighting fires.

Kenzie read the entry out loud, twice, then scrolled down to the next entry, several weeks later.

Blood is thicker than water. I was told that today and apparently need to remember it. If I want to live.

Kenzie whipped her gaze to Aidan. "What the hell does that mean?"

"Sounds like a threat," he said grimly.

"Blood is thicker than water," she repeated. "Who is he talking about? We have no family. At least no family who cares about us, anyway."

He hated the look on her face, the faraway, distant, self-protective look she got whenever she had to talk about her past. There was no doubt, she and Blake had had it rough growing up, being shuffled from one foster home to another. The saving grace was that they'd been kept together. It was what had made their bond so strong—they'd been all each other had had. "Is there possibly a blood relative somewhere?"

"A few, scattered here and there across the country. A great-aunt in Florida, an uncle in Chicago, a cousin in Dallas…" She crossed her arms, closing him out mentally and physically. "Just no one who wanted us."

Gently he turned her to face him. "Could he be talking about you, then?"

"Definitely not. We were in touch all during that time, but we never had a conversation about any of this."

Aidan went back to reading the entries, one of which mentioned employee hours. Copies of the schedules were attached. So was Blake keeping track of *his* alibi, or someone's whereabouts?

Blake had somehow gotten Tommy's first official reports on the arsons as well. Aidan and Kenzie discovered that he hadn't been on duty at any of the suspicious fires, a fact that Tommy had apparently considered evidence since it left Blake without an alibi for when the fires had been lit. Aidan scrolled down the list.

"Whoa, stop." Kenzie pointed to the second fire. "There. That one can't be right. He had an alibi for that one, he was with me. He'd come to Los Angeles that week. I remember because he was my date for the Emmys. He flew home immediately after, catching a red-eye because he said he had to be back at work for an early shift."

"Okay." Aidan pulled up the employee schedule for that day. "But he's not listed as on duty."

Kenzie stared at the screen, shaking her head. "He wouldn't have lied to me."

She said this with utter sincerity, and Aidan was inclined to absolutely believe because *she* believed. But if Blake *hadn't* lied to Kenzie, then there was only one other explanation.

"The schedule got changed?" she asked.

"It could have happened. Someone traded. Or—"

"Or something physically changed the schedule after the fact," she said flatly. "And Blake isn't here to defend himself."

"No, but we are." He was looking at the screen, until he realized that she wasn't. She was staring at him. "What?"

Her eyes were shimmering brilliantly with anger and something else, a deep, gut-wrenching emotion. "I didn't think it was possible." Her voice sounded thick. "I didn't want it to be possible. Oh, God." She covered her face. "This is so stupid."

"What?" He looked at the screen again, trying to figure out what she was talking about. *"What's stupid?"*

"That I could like you more than last time."

The words reached him as little had in all these years. "Kenz." Melting, he pulled down her hands. "I—"

She put a finger in his face. "Don't get excited. I

don't want to feel this way, and I'm telling you right now I *am* going to fight feeling this way."

His heart was squeezed tighter than a bow. "We were just kids, Kenz."

"And now we're not. It doesn't change anything except we're older, and *actually,* it's going to hurt more." Jaw tight, she shook her head again and looked at the screen. "This first. Blake first. He's far more important than rehashing old emotions that I don't really want to have." She worked the keyboard. "There. He's not on the schedule there, either, but he called me from the station. I know because it was my birthday, see? And he called me at 6:00 a.m. to catch me before work, but I didn't have an early morning shoot that day, and I was irritated that he woke me up. I'd been up late the night before celebrating."

"With Chad?"

She swiveled her eyes in his direction. "Actually, Teddy. Teddy White."

"Wasn't he on *People's* Most Beautiful list?"

"How do you know that?"

He knew it only because someone had stolen the porn out of the station bathroom, and Cristina had left her *People* magazine in there in its place, and— And Christ. He was crazy. "Never mind."

"It was just a one-night thing."

Oh, great. Even better. Now he could picture them having one-night sex, and—

"He's a friend."

A friend, as in someone who'd pulled her out of a fire? Someone who'd bail her out of jail?

"Yeah," she said softly. "I realize the word *friend* is a loose term, especially in Hollywood. Not like here."

"Do you miss it? Hollywood?"

She opened her mouth, then closed it and sighed. "I almost said yes, out of habit. The job is fun and the pay is amazing, but…" She lifted a shoulder. "It's empty. And I didn't really get that until I was here, either."

He tried to sort out his feelings regarding this revealing fact.

"And, anyway, it no longer matters." She turned back to the screen. "It's over."

"What do you mean?"

"My soap got cancelled."

"It did?"

"Yeah, and there are auditions for new parts but I've been eating too many donuts, so…"

"So…what?"

"So I'm going to get fat."

He let out a low laugh. "You look great, Kenzie. So great I haven't been able to keep my hands off you, as you might have noticed. But I'm very sorry about your job." He couldn't believe he was going to say this. "You could always stay in Santa Rey."

"I thought about it." She sighed and faced him again. "But staying seems like a comfort thing. You know, like going back to the last place where I was happy. It's a cop-out. And I was only happy here because of Blake."

He held his breath. He'd made her happy, too. Until he hadn't. "Maybe it was more than that."

"I don't know." She sighed without giving away her exact feelings on the matter, although he suspected she didn't know her exact feelings. "I wouldn't be able to get a job here."

"I know they don't film TV or movies anywhere close, but you could do something other than act."

She scoffed, then looked at him with heart-breaking hope. "Like what?"

"You know what. You could write. And eat all the damn donuts you want."

She just looked at him for a long moment, until he nearly squirmed. "What?"

"I'd have thought you'd be holding open the door for me to get the hell out of Dodge."

"Yeah, well, that was the old me."

"Well the new me is here to get Blake's name cleared. That's it."

"And also to stomp on my heart. Don't forget that part."

"I won't." She sighed. "Except I'd really rather get out of here without hurting you at all." With no idea that she'd just stunned him to his core, she leaned in close to see the screen better. A strand of her hair got stuck to the stubble on his jaw. It smelled good.

She smelled good.

It was all he could do not to bury his face in the rest

of her hair and say things that would lead her back to his bed but not really get them anywhere. In fact, he'd opened his mouth to do just that when she spoke.

"Look." She pointed to where Blake had entered another note:

Not noted in any of the official investigation reports is the fact that the source for the wire mesh trash cans is the hardware store where Tracy works.

Kenzie frowned and turned her head to look at Aidan, who had gone still in sudden shock. "The Tracy who…"

"Died." Aidan managed to find his vocal cords. "Yeah. They dated a couple of times. He really liked her."

"Really? He told me he'd gone out with Tracy, but he never said how much he liked her."

"Maybe he didn't tell you everything."

"He did," she insisted. "We told each other everything."

"Kenzie, you didn't tell him when *we* were going out. Maybe—"

"No." She shook her head. "You're going to say he kept secrets. That he kept the arsons a secret, but he wouldn't have— He wouldn't have done this, Aidan. Tracy being killed, well that's got to be a terrible coincidence."

"I'm beginning to believe that nothing's a coincidence. Look at the next entry."

Tracy's going to get me a list of people who've purchased the trash cans, but she has to wait until the weekend when her boss isn't in.

The next entry didn't clear anything up, but made it all worse.

Got the list, and holy shit. Blood is thicker than water. Got to remember that...

Kenzie's fingers dug into Aidan's arm. "What does that mean, 'blood *is* thicker than water'? He's written that twice now."

Aidan frowned and shook his head. "I wish I knew."

He's onto me. Need to be damn careful now.

"*Who's* onto him?" Kenzie stood up and paced the length of the bedroom. "God. Whoever he's talking about, do you think...?"

Yeah. Yeah, he did. Blake had gotten himself into hot water with someone. And that someone had either been his partner in crime, or, as Aidan was coming to believe, it was the person whom Blake had been privately, quietly, investigating on his own.

And if *that* was true, and Blake had been a victim, then this other person had not only been an arsonist, but also a murderer.

Aidan's cell phone chirped with a message that he was needed at work, ASAP.

"Go," she murmured. "It's okay. I'm just going to go through all of this and see what else I can find."

"Stay here."

Her gaze slid to his.

"Kenzie…" How to say this without sounding like a complete idiot? There was no way to sugarcoat it, so he decided to just let it out. "I have a bad feeling."

She arched an eyebrow. "You, the most pragmatic, logical, cool person I know, have a bad *feeling?*"

"Go with me on this."

"You think I'm in danger," she said flatly.

He didn't just think it, he knew it. Only he couldn't explain how or why, and that was going to drive him crazy, along with worrying and wondering where she was and if she was okay.

And safe.

And alive.

"Aidan, I'm not going to hole up here. That's ridiculous. Besides, no one knows what I'm doing."

"You were arrested, Kenzie. Everyone knows what you're doing."

"I'll be fine."

Short of tying her up, which had a *most* interesting vision popping into his head, what could he do? "Promise me you'll be careful."

She looked at him for a long moment, her hair still crazy from his fingers, her shirt crooked, her feet bare, looking like a hot mess.

A hot mess he wanted in his life.

"I thought we weren't going to do the promise thing," she said. "Not ever again."

"Promise me," he said again.

"Don't worry." She backed away from him, her face so carefully blank. "I intend to be careful and smart, and I intend to get out of here unscathed, on all counts."

What the hell did that mean?

"See you, Aidan."

Okay, that was no simple *"I'll see you later."* It seemed like a we're-done-doing-the-naked-happy-dance see-you. The get-over-me because I'm-over-you see-you.

Which didn't bode well for his heart, the one that in spite of himself, had gotten attached. Again. More attached, if that was even possible. "I'll be back."

"Okay."

"I will." He paused. "Will you be here?"

She met his gaze. "I don't know."

Well, hell. That didn't bode well.

15

IN BETWEEN CALLS, Aidan slipped into the office of the fire station. He'd never spent much time in there, always preferring to be outside or working, or just about anywhere else.

But he made himself comfortable now. He told whoever gave him a strange look that he was working on his taxes, and given the sympathetic grimaces that got him, it was a genius excuse. Left alone, he went through the daily fire reports and employee schedules, pulling the dates that matched the arsons.

Which is where he discovered that those schedules did not match the ones Blake had saved on his computer.

In fact, according to the office reports, Blake *had* been scheduled on each of the days of the arsons, whether by coincidence or design, Aidan had no idea. Dispatch didn't always need all available units to go out on the calls. On two of the fires, Blake's unit hadn't been called to respond at all and yet he'd been placed on scene by witnesses.

Had he been the arsonist, or simply trying to stop him?

The door to the office opened and Aidan turned around, the excuse already on his lips about being late getting his receipts together—

"Save it," Tommy said, and dropped a disk on the table.

"What's that?"

"A copy of the surveillance tape I got out of the camera I had at Blake's place."

"You had Blake's place under surveillance?"

"I'm an investigator. It's what I do, investigate."

"What were you looking for?"

"There's a bigger, better question. What was *Kenzie* looking for?"

"I couldn't tell you."

"Couldn't, or won't?"

Aidan didn't respond to that.

"You're doing a shitty job of keeping her out of my hair."

Yeah. He was doing a shitty job keeping Kenzie out of *his* hair as well.

"Okay, here's how this is going to work," Tommy decided. "You're going to tell me everything you've discovered about these arsons and Blake, and in return, I'm not going to charge you with interfering with my investigation."

Aidan didn't care about the underlying threat in Tommy's voice. What he cared about was discovering the truth. For Blake. For Kenzie. And as big a pain in his ass as Tommy was, Aidan believed them to be on the same side.

"Yes?"

"Yes."

With a nod, Tommy locked the door and pulled up a chair.

KENZIE HAD NO PROBLEM keeping herself occupied. She spent the day reading Blake's files, poring over them, analyzing each of her brother's entries.

She slept in Aidan's big, wonderful bed all by herself, which wasn't nearly as much fun as sleeping next to the big, wonderful man usually in it. Her dreams were wild, vacillating between nightmares about being trapped in a fire and hearing Blake scream for her, and another type of dream entirely. A dream where Aidan slowly stripped her naked and used his tongue on every inch of her body, a dream she woke up from damp with sweat, panting for air, her own hand between her thighs.

Damn, the man was potent.

In the morning, she went back to *Blake's Girl*. She couldn't help herself. She stood on the end of the dock staring at the shell that used to be Blake's sailboat, a huge lump inside her throat, wondering what the hell she was supposed to do next when her cell phone rang. Her local caller.

"Did you get the backups?"

"Who is this?"

"You need to stay away from the boat. There's nothing there for you."

With a gasp, she whirled, searching her immediate

area but seeing no one. "*Where are you? Are you watching me?*"

"Don't be scared."

The parking lot had only three cars in it, no people. No one was on the docks, and the neighboring boats seemed deserted. "Don't be scared? Are you crazy?"

"Listen to me," he said urgently. "It's time for you to back off. Time for you to go home, Kenzie."

The hair at the back of her neck prickled and she once again turned slowly. Behind one of the three cars was another.

Gray. Tinted windows.

Eyes narrowed, she headed toward it, needing to know who the hell she was talking to and why his voice made the hair on her arms stand up, as if she could almost recognize him, but not quite.

"Don't come any closer," he warned.

She kept walking. "Do I know you?"

The car's engine started up.

"No," she cried, breaking into a run. "*Wait—*"

The gray sedan squealed forward and to the right, giving her only the briefest glimpse of the driver behind the wheel. But it was enough to have her gasp in shock as her chest tightened beyond all bearing.

The car ripped out of the lot. She hardly even noticed as she hit her knees on the concrete, her hands fanned over her chest to hold her heart in because she'd have sworn, she'd have laid her life on the line, that the driver of that car had been none other than her dead brother.

Blake.

SHE SPED ALL THE WAY BACK to Aidan's house before re-membering he was at work. Still shaken, she turned around and headed to the station. Zach was there, standing in the middle of the main room. He wore jeans and a T-shirt and a rueful smile as he stuck a pencil down the cast on his arm.

"This thing is driving me crazy." He tossed the pencil to a small desk against a wall. "You looking for Aidan?"

"Yes." Because she wanted to tell him her brother wasn't dead. Or that she was losing her mind. One or the other.

"He's on a call." Zach took a closer look at her and frowned. "Are you okay?"

No. "I saw the file you put together on the arsons." The fires had cost Zach his house, which in itself would have given him a good reason to hate her brother. "When Blake died, there wasn't a body."

A shadow crossed his face. "The fire was hot. Nothing survived it."

She begged to differ. "Anything survive? Anything at all?"

"A portion of the shell of the blow torch Blake had been holding, and his hard hat."

"But no physical evidence of *him?*"

He paused a long moment. "Why?"

Oh, because maybe he hadn't really died... "Do you know when Aidan'll be back?"

"No, but I can have him call you. He was worried about you."

"I'm fine." She smiled to prove it, but truthfully, she was worried, too. She left the station, got into her car and pulled out her cell. Taking a deep breath, she dialed her mysterious caller's number.

"Hello."

Kenzie went utterly still at that voice, still disguised, but it didn't matter. She now knew who she was talking to. "Blake?"

Click.

Oh, God. Heart pounding, she drove straight to Tommy Ramirez's office. He opened his door at her knock, raising a single eyebrow at the sight of her, then simply sighed when she pushed past him and let herself in.

He had three unopened Red Bulls on his desk. She grabbed one, cracked it open and drank deeply. Eyes closed, she stood there until the caffeine kicked in. "God, I needed that."

He shut the door, leaned back against it and just looked at her. "That was my Red Bull."

"Thanks for sharing."

"You know, most people are afraid of me."

"Yes, but most people don't know that once upon a time you paid for my dancing lessons."

"Keep it down, will you? I don't want that to get out."

She shook her head. "Always the tough guy." Back when Blake had been in the academy, she and her brother had made some financial mistakes. Lots of financial mistakes. Tommy had known Blake's situation and had lent him some money to see him through fire school, and Kenzie enough to cover her dance lessons.

Not many knew the investigator had such a soft side; he didn't like to show it. He hadn't shown it to Kenzie since, but she'd never forgotten. Nor had she ever even briefly considered that it could be Tommy framing Blake. Blake had trusted Tommy, and she did, too.

Tommy tossed the files in his hands to his desk and grabbed one of the remaining Red Bulls. "I put you in jail to keep you safe. I didn't intend for you to bail yourself out. I wanted to keep you there until this was over, but it's taking longer than I thought."

"You put me in jail to keep me safe?"

"Trust me, it made sense to me. Look, I know this has been hard on you."

"Yes," she agreed blandly. "It's been hard on me having my brother blamed for something he didn't do. It's been hard on me knowing that all his friends, his coworkers, *everyone,* believes he committed arson. It's hard on me knowing that he can't defend himself. But it's even harder knowing that you're not."

"You don't understand."

"Then help me to."

He opened his mouth, and then shut it. "I can't."

"Would you like to know what the hardest thing of all is?" she whispered, her throat tight with a sudden need to cry. "I know he's innocent and I know that you believe it, too."

"Kenzie—"

"You can't talk about it, I get it. But I think I saw Blake alive. Can you talk about that?"

He stared at her. *"What?"*

"I think I saw him at the docks, in the parking lot."

Tommy sank to his chair. "What were you doing at the docks?"

"Blake. *Alive.* Did you hear that part?"

His eyes filled with sympathy. "Kenzie—"

"No." She let out a low laugh. "Listen to me. *I saw him.* Plus someone's been calling me, giving me clues. It's him, he—"

"What kind of clues?"

"I don't know, that the key is in the demos, which I don't get. And that blood is thicker than water. I don't get that either, honestly."

Tommy went pale. He came to her, taking her arm and leading her to the door. "I need you to listen to me, okay? Listen very carefully. Go back to Los Angeles. I'll call you—"

"No." She pulled free. "I'm not leaving."

"Yes, you are. If I have to have you arrested again—"

"On what charges?"

"I'll find something."

She looked into his face, where his emotions were clear. "Okay, you're scared for me. I get that. I'll stay back, I'll stay clear."

"Promise me."

She took a long look at him. "What did I say? Was it the blood is thicker than water thing?"

"Promise me."

"I promise," she said very quietly. "Now you promise me this. You'll come to me as soon as you can with answers."

"Deal."

DURING THE SUMMER MONTHS, Santa Rey swelled to upwards of three times its normal population, which was reflected in the increased volume of calls the fire station received. In the past twenty-four hours alone, Aidan had fought a restaurant fire, a storefront fire, a car fire and two house fires, each caused by human stupidity. Then, it happened.

Another explosion.

It thankfully occurred in an empty warehouse this time. No one was injured, except Cristina, who fell off a ladder and hurt her ankle.

Dustin wanted to take her to the E.R. for an X-ray, but in typical Cristina fashion, she wanted to tough it out.

Aidan left them alone to their silent battle of wills, and let himself inside the burned shell of a warehouse.

Tommy was there, with his bag of equipment, his camera out. When he saw Aidan, he jaw ticked. "I've got it from here."

Aidan's eyes went to the wall in front of Tommy, where the burn marks on the wall indicated a hot flash, and most likely, the point of origin. "I never did get onto *Blake's Girl* after the explosion. But I'm going to take a wild guess that you found something like this there, and also at the hardware explosion that killed Tracy."

Tommy clearly fought with himself, and then finally sighed. "Look, I'm not going to insult your intelligence the way I insulted Zach's, okay? That was a mistake, shutting him out, because it only made him all the more determined to prove he was right—"

"He *was* right—"

"Yeah, but I was on it. I told him that, but he didn't listen, and then he dug harder and got himself targeted by the arsonist."

"The arsonist? I thought you were so sure it was Blake."

"I'm not going to insult your intelligence," he repeated tightly, "by letting you think what we want the general public to think. So know this. I'm going to nail this guy. So when I say back off, *do it*. Don't pull a Zach and get yourself hurt."

Aidan stared at him. "You know there's someone else."

"I'm close."

"You've always known."

Tommy acknowledged this with a slight nod. "So now all you have to do is stay out of my way. And keep Kenzie out of the way as well. No one else dies."

"Blake's innocent."

"That's one theory."

"Is it the right theory?"

"Jesus, Aidan." Tommy scrubbed a hand over his face. "Are you just playing with that girl?"

"No. And how is this any of your business, anyway? A few days ago you were arresting her."

"Just don't hurt her. You hear me? Don't even think about it."

Aidan let out a low, mirthless laugh. "Trust me, if someone's getting hurt, it's going to be me."

THE MINUTE AIDAN GOT OFF WORK, he went straight home, hoping Kenzie would be there waiting for him. It was with great relief that he pulled in next to her car. Letting himself in, he called out her name.

No response. Dropping his keys on the small desk in the living room, he moved through the house and heard the shower running. Things were looking up if he had a naked, wet, hot woman in his shower. And at that realization, all the myriad things he'd wanted to say to her flew out the window, replaced by memories of how she looked standing under a stream of water.

She hadn't left…

Weak with relief, he knocked on the bathroom door. "Kenz?"

When she still didn't respond, he cracked open the door and found her sitting in his shower, face to her knees, arms wrapped around herself.

"Kenzie?"

"I'm fine."

Yeah. She was fine, he was fine, so they could just all be fine together.

She lifted her head when he opened the shower door but didn't say a word as he stepped into it with her.

"You're dressed," she finally said, inanely.

Yeah, which sucked. "Tell me what's wrong."

"You're not going to like it."

He already didn't like it, or the clothes now sticking to him like a second skin. "Try me."

"I saw Blake."

He blinked away the water in his eyes. "You…saw Blake." He crouched before her. "In a dream?"

"No."

"You saw Blake," he repeated, trying to understand, and failing. "Not in a dream. What does that mean?"

"It means he's alive."

16

KENZIE WATCHED AIDAN try to absorb her news while the shower rained down over top of him, soaking into his hair, his clothes. "I know, it's a shock," she said.

The water ran in rivulets down his face. His shirt was plastered to his broad shoulders and arms, his pants suctioned to his legs. There was something about the way he'd rushed in there to save her from her own demons that got to her. More than got to her. He devastated her.

She wasn't sure how it'd happened, especially when she'd set out to keep her heart safe, but she'd fallen for him all over again.

"You saw Blake," he repeated.

"He's alive. He's the one who's been calling me." She stood up. "He's been alive and didn't tell me. The men I love suck."

Aidan hissed out a breath and straightened to his feet as well, towering over her, his broad shoulders taking the beating of the water. "The men you love?"

"Go away."

"The men you love?" he asked, staring down at her. "Kenz—"

"No." She shook her head. "Not doing this." She put her hands on his chest to shove him away but somehow ended up fisting her hands in his drenched shirt and yanking. Surprised, he lost his balance as he came toward her, slapping his hands on the tile on either side of her to hold himself upright. "Kenz—"

She stopped whatever he might have said with her mouth. It made no sense, none at all, but she wanted to have him, needed to have him, right there, right then, if only for this one last time before all hell broke loose.

"God," he managed on a roughly expelled breath as she kissed her way over his jaw while she fumbled with the buttons on his Levi's.

His hands left the tile and squeezed her arms. Water was running down his face. "I thought you'd said good-bye to me."

She'd tried. After all, she had a life to get back to. Too bad she had no idea what that life would entail— but that was a worry for tomorrow. After she figured out the Blake being alive thing. "So I said good-bye. Now I'm saying hello." Still squished between the wall and Aidan, she slid her hands up his chest, her fingers entwining in his hair as she arched back, her breasts sliding along the material of his wet shirt.

Her nipples hardened and she felt the rough grumble of the groan in his chest. Almost as if acting of their own accord, his hands moved down her sides, to her hips, her bottom, which he roughly squeezed while letting out another of those incredibly arousing groans. "Is there another good-bye coming my way after this shower?"

"Maybe not right after," she panted because something was happening to her, something that had nothing to do with lust or hormones or getting an orgasm, but far deeper. Far more dangerous. Tightening her fingers in his hair, she lifted his head from her breast and stared into his eyes. There, she could see the reflection of her own. And in that reflection was her heart and soul, her very life.

She loved him. And if they did this, if she let him inside her body again, she'd never recover. She knew it, but like last time, it wasn't going to stop her. Small wonder when he was against her like a second skin, holding her to the wall. Closing her eyes, she hugged him close, pressing her face to his throat.

Her name tumbled from his lips in a harsh whisper, and then their hands were fighting to get his clothes off, pushing off his shirt, shoving down his jeans. Then he was reaching for those jeans, and the condom in his pocket. He pressed her back against the wall, freeing his hands to skim down her bare, trembling thighs, which opened and wrapped around his waist, bringing him flush to her. In one thrust he was deep inside, and she was…lost?

Not lost.

No, when she was with him, she was found.

AIDAN'S HEART was still thundering in his ears in tune to the water pounding his back when Kenzie slid free of him. Drained, he watched her lean past him and turn off the water. She tossed him a towel, grabbed one for herself and left him alone in the bathroom.

He had no idea what had just happened.

When he managed to dry himself off and walk out of the bathroom, on legs that still quivered, he found her dressing in his bedroom. "Did you get the license of that truck that just hit me?"

She didn't smile. "I really saw him."

When he just looked at her, she slipped into her shoes. "And I'm going to go find him."

"Kenzie," he said gently. "Blake is—"

"Dead. I know. But he's not." She left the room.

With a sigh, he headed to his dresser for clothes. He'd gotten into a dry pair of jeans when he heard her keys jangling. "Kenzie," he called out. *Dammit.* "Wait." He grabbed a shirt and headed down the hallway just as she opened the front door. She hesitated when her cell phone beeped an incoming text message.

"Is it…him?" he asked.

"Yes, it's him. Texting me from the dead." She opened her phone and let him read over her shoulder.

Go home. I'll find you there when this is over, when you're safe.

As they stood there in his open doorway looking down at the screen, a huge trash truck lumbered down the street, making the earth shudder as it went past—
Boom.

Kenzie's bright red sports car vanished in a cloud of smoke and flames and flying metal as it exploded.

KENZIE SAT ON AIDAN'S CURB looking out at the street, which was littered with cops and various other official personnel, including Tommy and the chief. And lots of red car parts.

Everyone was trying to figure out what the hell had happened.

Her car had gone boom, just like *Blake's Girl,* that was what had happened.

"Kenzie." Aidan's athletic shoes appeared in her peripheral vision, and then the rest of him as he sat at her side.

"My insurance company isn't going to be happy," she said. "I blame the trash truck."

"The trash truck saved your life. You car had been rigged to blow when you got into it, but the truck vibrated the street so much it went up early."

"Oh." She winced. "I wish I didn't know that."

"Give me your cell phone."

"Why?"

"So I can call whoever's been calling you."

"Blake. Blake's been calling me."

"Whoever it is." His mouth was grim as some of his clear frustration and fear for her filtered into his words. "I just want him to stay the hell away from you."

"This wasn't him."

"Then who?"

"I'm working on that."

He looked down at her. "By yourself."

"It's how I work best, apparently." She stood up. During the time she'd been gone from Santa Rey, she'd closed herself off, both her heart and soul. It was a hell of a time to realize that. But no matter what happened here—whether she left and went back to Los Angeles, or whether she stayed—whatever she settled on for herself, she couldn't go back to closing herself off.

"Kenzie."

"I didn't mean to get so good at being alone. I didn't realize, living in L.A., the land of pretend, that I'd never built myself any real relationships." She let out a long breath and met his gaze. "But that changed when I got here. When I was with you. I love you, Aidan. Again. Still. I love you."

And while that shocking statement hung in the air, someone called for Aidan. But he just stared at Kenzie. "You—"

"Aidan!"

With a grimace, he looked over his shoulder. "Shit, it's the chief."

"Go."

"Kenzie—"

"*Go.*"

A muscle ticked in his jaw. "Don't move, I'll be right back."

Nodding, she watched him walk toward a tall man whose back was to her, stretching out a dark blue shirt that said Chief across the shoulders.

Then she walked away. She didn't have a car, so she had no idea where she thought she was going, but she had to leave.

In her pocket, her cell phone buzzed with an incoming text.

Another half block. Gray car.

I LOVE YOU. Aidan muttered the three little words that Kenzie had said to him. She'd said them, and then she'd vanished, and he had no idea where she'd gone. One moment he'd been talking to the chief, and the next… She'd been gone. It'd been hours, and not a word.

He was at the station now, and she still hadn't answered her damn cell phone, and he was starting to lose it. He shouldn't have walked away to talk to the chief, he should have dragged her with him.

"Hey, Mr. 2008." Cristina came into the station kitchen and went straight for the refrigerator. "What are you pouting about?" She helped herself to someone else's lunch.

"You could bring your own."

"I could." Cristina pulled out a thick turkey sandwich. "But I don't."

"Hey, that's mine," Dustin said, joining them from the garage. "What did I tell you about stealing my sandwich?"

Cristina spoke around a huge mouthful. "If I was still sleeping with you, I'd bet you'd *give* me your sandwich."

Dustin's eyes darkened. "You slept with me once."

"Your point?"

"My point is that if we were *still* sleeping together, I'd *make* you your own damn sandwich."

She took another bite, chewing with a moan. "You know, I should give that some thought, because you do make the best sandwiches."

Dustin tossed up his hands and walked back out of the room.

When he was gone, Cristina dropped her tough girl pose, watching him go with a naked look of longing.

"You could just tell him the truth," Aidan said.

"What, that he makes crappy sandwiches?"

"No, that you're scared. He'd understand fear." Hell, he understood it all too well.

"Are you kidding me? I'm not scared." Cristina tossed the sandwich back in the fridge. "I'm not scared of anything." But as she shut the fridge, she pressed her forehead to the door. "Ah, hell. I'm scared. Everything's messed up. Dustin's mad at me. Blake's gone. There's no good food. Blake's gone."

"You still miss him."

"Hell, yeah, I still miss him. He was a great partner. And now even the chief, his own flesh and blood, wants to make him out to be a monster that we know he wasn't."

"Wait." Aidan grabbed her arm. "What?"

"He wasn't a monster."

"The flesh and blood part. What did you mean about that?"

Cristina's lips tightened. "Blake asked me never to tell."

"He asked you never to tell what?"

She sighed. "That the chief's his uncle. They were estranged, though. Blake's parents were—"

"Dead. They died years ago."

"Yeah. But his father was the chief's half brother."

Blood is thicker than water... Good God. "If that's true," he asked hoarsely, "why did Blake and Kenzie spend their childhood in foster care?"

"Because the chief didn't want kids. Or something like that." She shrugged. "Not sure on the details."

Neither was he. Except that somehow...*Christ.* Somehow the chief—

His cell phone rang. When he looked down at the screen, his heart skipped a beat. "Thank God," he said to Kenzie in lieu of a greeting. "Listen to me. I just realized—"

"Aidan, I need you. I'm sorry, I know I don't really have the right to say that to you, but I do. Can you come meet me? Now? Please?"

"Just tell me where."

AIDAN BURST INSIDE the Sunrise Café and looked around the tables.

No Kenzie.

"She's on the roof," Sheila told him, standing behind the bar drying glasses.

"Thanks."

"Something about Tommy being on his way, and having all the answers you need..."

Aidan had the answers. He just didn't have the girl,

which he intended to rectify. He headed for the stairs as Sheila turned her attention to someone else. "Hey, there, good-looking," she called out with a smile of greeting. Aidan took the stairs without looking back, coming to a relieved halt on the roof at the sight of Kenzie sitting on the bench.

"Tommy's on his way," she said, standing up. Someone stepped out from the shadows behind her and Aidan's heart stopped.

It was Blake, who by all logical accounts should be dead.

Only there was nothing logical about any of this. Not the arsons, and not the way Aidan knew he loved the woman standing in front of him like he'd never loved anyone before.

"Listen to him," Kenzie said quietly. "Listen to your heart."

He *was* listening to his heart, which had kicked back to life and was screaming, demanding that he pull Kenzie close and tell her he loved her, too. That he was sorry it'd taken him so long, but like Cristina, he'd been afraid, was in fact *still* afraid but would no longer run from how he felt.

He'd never again run from her.

But that would have to wait. He looked at Blake, who was thinner than ever. And he walked with a cane. "I know, it's crazy," his old friend said, his voice low and urgent. "You thought I was dead and I'm not. I…faked my own death."

"I'm getting that."

"When I found out who the real arsonist was, I realized no one was safe." Blake's face was twisted in tortured misery. "He killed Tracy right after he blew up my boat."

"I know. I know all of it. I even know *who* we're talking about. I just don't know why."

"Oh, I can tell you why," said the man who came through the roof door to stand in front of them. The chief nodded in Aidan's direction. "If you really want to know."

Shit. Aidan pulled out his cell, hit Tommy's number and put the phone to his ear.

"Nearly there," Tommy said tensely.

"Hurry. Bring backup."

"Oh, it'll be too late," the chief said conversationally.

"Uncle Allan?" Kenzie breathed, staring at the chief. She looked at Aidan. "He's the fire chief? I thought…" She turned back to her uncle. "I thought you were in Chicago."

"I was. I came back here a year ago. A shame we lost touch or you'd have known."

"We lost touch—" Kenzie took a step toward him, or tried to, but Blake grabbed her hand and held her back "—because you didn't want us."

"Now, now. That's not entirely true. I just didn't want to be responsible for raising kids. I never wanted kids."

"But it's okay to be responsible for *killing people?*"

"*One* person," he corrected. "Not people. And that was an accident."

"You killed Tracy and that was no accident," Blake ground out. "You murdered her."

"Ah, now, see *murder* implies intent, and I don't have intent. I have an addiction." He smiled sadly. "It means I can't help it."

Kenzie again tried to charge him, but this time it was Aidan who held her back, not trusting that asshole with her.

"If I was an alcoholic," the chief asked, "would you still be looking at me like that? If I had a drug problem? No, you'd be trying to get me help."

"I *tried* to get you help," Blake told him. "When I figured out you had started that second fire all those months ago, you begged me to understand. You lied and said it was your first time, and that you'd stop, that you'd get help. Instead a child died and when I tried to turn you in you threatened me."

The chief slowly shook his head. "Tommy was getting close. You wouldn't leave me alone. I had to do something. I had to keep you quiet."

Blake gave Aidan an agonized look, as though pleading for forgiveness. "By then he had implicated me. He'd changed the schedules, he'd planted evidence. He discredited me so that even if I did tell, *I'd* be the first one they'd lock up. And once I was in jail, he threatened to hurt Kenzie.

"Then Zach started asking questions and the chief tried to kill him by burning down his house. I had followed him, Zach saw me, and I didn't know what to do. I panicked and faked my death. If I was gone, he had no reason to harm Kenzie."

"And I didn't."

"You killed Tracy!"

"But not Kenzie," the chief said calmly. "Look, Tracy was going to put together a list of people who'd purchased those metal trash cans. I would have been on that list."

"You didn't have to kill her," Blake shouted.

"He had to set more fires," Aidan said grimly.

"That's true." The chief nodded emphatically. "I can't help myself. I tried like hell. I couldn't stop, but at least I went for old and dilapidated properties, or overly insured buildings." He paused. "Like this one."

Aidan stared at him. "What?"

"Sheila is getting ready to renovate," the chief said.

"She has to," Aidan said. "The building has structural problems."

"Yes, and now she's over insured to protect it. It's a situation that cries out to an arsonist. It needs to burn."

"Ohmigod," Kenzie breathed, looking horrified. "You're a very sick man."

"Agreed." Her uncle smiled without any mirth. He clapped his hands together. "Well, it's been nice clearing all this up but I've got to end this now."

"You're not walking away," Aidan said. "Not from this. You have to pay for your crimes."

"I'm not paying for anything. You didn't get hurt. None of you died."

"Are you kidding?" Aidan asked incredulously. "Blake nearly died trying to stop you. You nearly killed Kenzie on *Blake's Girl,* and then again when you blew up her car."

"*Nearly* won't hold up in a court of law. I was just trying to scare her out of town, anyway. The car was supposed to blow an hour earlier, but a fuse failed me. And the boat was an accident. I was just trying to get rid of Blake's laptop. I didn't know she was there that night."

"There's something else you don't know," Aidan told him. "Blake e-mailed Kenzie backup files."

The chief's mouth tightened. "I'm not going down for this, for any of it. I'm the chief."

"Not for long you're not," Blake said. "You're going to be stripped of that title and put in jail."

"Not happening," the Chief declared. "I won't go to jail—I've made sure of it. I've risked my life to save people for almost thirty years. I *won't* be remembered as an arsonist."

Aidan's gut clenched. There was only one reason the chief would come out in the open like this and confess his crimes. And that was if he didn't intend for them to live to tell the tale. "Whatever you've planned, *no.*"

"You're too late." The chief looked first to Kenzie, then to Blake. "I'm sorry. Truly sorry."

"What did you do?" Blake demanded. "Oh, Christ, you didn't—" Without finishing that thought, he whirled and limped to the roof door, yelling as he took the stairs, "Evacuate! Everyone out—"

Which was all he got out before a thundering explosion hit. The entire building shook, throwing Aidan and Kenzie to the ground.

17

AT THE EXPLOSION, the world seemed to stop, or at least go into slow motion. Kenzie managed to lift her head just as Aidan rolled toward her, his face a mask of concern. Her uncle, ten feet away, wasn't moving at all. Pushing to her knees, she stared at the doorway where her brother had just disappeared. "Blake!" she screamed.

He didn't reappear, no one did, nothing except a plume of smoke that struck terror in her heart. "Ohmigod. *Aidan*—"

"Are you okay?" He was on his knees before her, running his hands down her sides, pushing her hair from her face, looking her over, his expression calm, only his eyes showing his fear. "Are you okay?" he demanded again hoarsely.

Shaken, but all in one piece, she nodded and pointed to the doorway. "Blake—"

His eyes and mouth were grim. "I know. He's down with the others. We'll get to him." He glanced at the chief.

"Is he—"

Aidan checked for a pulse. "Just out cold." He

pulled her to her feet, yanking his cell phone out of his pocket. From far below, they could hear screams and yelling over the whooping sound of smoke and car alarms going off.

All of it brought Kenzie back to the night on *Blake's Girl,* back to that irrational terror. Then they'd been able to jump into the water. Now there was nothing down there except concrete.

Three floors down.

"Call 9-1-1," Aidan said to her, shoving the phone into her hands as he ran past the very still chief to the edge of the building and looked over the side. "Dammit, I can't see if people are getting out of here."

The café hadn't been full to capacity, but there had been at least twenty people inside when they'd entered, and then there was Sheila and her staff.

And Blake. God, Blake. Could she really have found him only to lose him again, for real this time? "Aidan—"

"Listen to me. There's no way off of here except for the stairwell. No outside fire escape or ladder."

They both looked at the dark doorway, emitting smoke now. "Ohmigod." She felt frozen. Logically she knew she had to go down to get to Blake, not to mention to safety. But there was nothing logical about the fear blocking her windpipe. She'd thought Blake had died in a fire. *She'd* nearly died in the boat fire. Instead of seeing the roof's doorway, she kept flashing back to *Blake's Girl,* the black night and blacker water. She could feel the heat from that fire prickling her skin even as she could feel the iciness of the water closing around her body—

"Kenzie."

She blinked Aidan into view. He had his hands on her arms and he was frowning into her face.

"I can't go in there," she said, unable to catch her breath. "I just can't."

"Okay." They both looked at the chief, who still wasn't moving. Again Aidan went to the edge of the roof and looked over. Whatever he saw made his jaw go tight and his eyes, grim. Then he backed Kenzie to a corner and gently pushed her down until she was sitting there, her back to the wall, facing the opened door to the only exit. "I'm going—"

"No." She gripped his arms, digging her fingers into the muscles there.

"Kenzie—"

"No!" Icy, terrifying fear overcame her as she stared at the smoke now pouring out through the opened door. "There's a fire down there!"

He didn't say it, he didn't have to.

"I already hear sirens. They're coming to put out the fire. It's going to be okay. But I have to go help. This roof won't be safe to be on for long."

"I know."

With his eyes reflecting the torment he felt at leaving her, he pried her fingers from his arms.

"Come right back," she ordered.

"Okay."

"And stay safe, you hear me?"

"I will."

"And Blake. Bring me Blake."

"I promise." He held her gaze for one beat, letting her see into his heart and soul. He never made promises, never, and yet he did now, to her, which meant more than anything he'd ever done. Pretending to be brave, she nodded and then sagged back, covering her face with her hands so she couldn't see the smoke pouring out of the doorway as he vanished into it.

Dammit, she really needed a new script. Aidan was probably worrying about her instead of completely focusing on the fire—and that was dangerous. She forced her eyes open, glued her gaze to the black doorway. He had saved her life on Blake's boat, and that had been amazing, but she could have saved herself. She knew how to swim.

And she could save herself this time.

All she had to do was get past her fear. Any second now…

The sirens were louder now, and that reached her somehow. Tommy was probably nearly here, too. She got to her feet, wiped the sweat from her eyes and headed to her uncle. He'd hit his head on the A/C vent. Turning her back on him, she headed toward the door. "You're a coward," she told herself. "You're fine, you're fine…" She kept up the mantra as she entered the dark doorway. Unable to breathe through the smoke, she pulled her shirt up over her mouth and took another step.

And then it happened. The floor beneath her rumbled, the walls shimmied and shook, and she froze as a second explosion hit, flinging her against a wall. Then the power flickered and went off, leaving her in complete darkness.

Oh, God.

Sitting up, she felt for the railing and pushed herself upright. She was okay. Relatively speaking, anyway.

Just as she began heading down again, the stairs beneath her began rumbling, but not with yet another explosion. This time it was pounding footsteps as someone ran up the stairs, and then reached out toward her. "Kenzie?"

"*Blake?* Ohmigod, Blake, you're okay—"

"Where is he? The chief?" he demanded.

"On the roof."

"Stay here," he commanded. "Stay right here!" And then he rushed up and out.

Like hell. She was going to be proactive this time, dammit. She was rewriting this script her way. And when it was over, she was going to write scripts all damn day long to her heart's content. And eat donuts. Yeah, lots of donuts. Heart pounding, she stumbled after her brother. Bursting back out on the roof, she was horrified to see that part of it had begun to cave in, with flames flickering out from underneath. And standing far too close to that area was Blake, facing off with the chief.

"No," she cried, just as Aidan came out the doorway behind her, looking as if he'd been in a car wreck, all torn and bloody, calling her name hoarsely.

"You're hurt," she cried, rushing to his side.

"The explosion kicked me down the stairs." He

hugged her tight, not taking his eyes off the chief and Blake. "I'm okay."

It was like a bad movie, playing in slow motion as the chief leaped for the edge of the roof, and Blake leaped for him the best he could, wrestling him to the ground.

Flames shot up through the floor at all of them and Kenzie screamed, trying to get close to her brother, but Aidan had a hold of her, even though *he* was the one with torn clothing and blood seeping from his various injuries, all covered in soot.

On the ground now, Blake rolled with the chief, the two of them still throwing punches.

"Stay back," Aidan told her, holding onto her. "The flames—"

They were licking at them from all angles now, but suddenly, from below, they were hit with water. Streams of it, coming up from the street.

The fire trucks had arrived, and none too soon as the flames forced Kenzie and Aidan back from yet another cave-in.

"Hold still, you son of a bitch," Blake growled out to the chief, who was trying to crawl free and get to the edge of the roof.

Aidan tried to move around the flames to help Blake with the chief, but suddenly he wavered, then sank to his knees.

"Aidan!"

"Yeah. Think maybe I hit my head before." He blinked at her face as she dropped to her knees in front of him. "There's three of you."

"Oh, God." She touched the gash along his temple, which was bleeding freely. "Hold still!"

"Not a problem."

A ladder and bucket came into view over the roofline, lifted by a crane from below. It held two fire-fighters, who took one look at Blake and staggered to a shocked halt.

"Later," Blake yelled at them. "I'll explain later! Aidan's down and we need Tommy and some cuffs. Tell me someone has some cuffs!"

IT ACTUALLY WASN'T THAT EASY, nothing ever was, Kenzie thought. Hours later, they were all sitting around Aidan's hospital bed, where he was being held overnight, thanks to a concussion.

The chief had been taken to jail, which was such a huge town scandal that Tommy had left to prepare for a press conference. Sheila was sitting in a chair, her wrist in a sling. It was her only injury, but the café was a complete loss. Dustin was next to her, his arm around her shoulders. Cristina was there, too, holding a bucket full of money from emergency personnel on the scene who'd already poured some of their support into it for Sheila.

"I could go to Hawaii with all that." Tears were thick in Sheila's voice.

"Or you could rebuild," Aidan said from flat on his back.

At the sound of his voice, Kenzie's heart squeezed. He'd been so damn quiet, and she'd been so damn worried.

On the other side of Aidan's bed, Blake stirred. "The chief's in custody," he told Aidan. "And he's not going to get off easy."

Aidan's gaze tracked to Kenzie. "I don't want to get off easy, either." He reached for her hand. "Not tonight, or any night."

She gripped his fingers tightly and pressed them to her aching heart. He was talking, but not making any sense. She hadn't taken a full breath since they'd taken him for X-rays and she didn't take one now. "I'll go get your nurse—"

"No." His grip was like iron. "I'm not crazy."

"I know—"

"Listen to me. You pulled it off, you broke my damn heart. We're even."

Oh, God, and now he was delirious. "Aidan—"

"Maybe we should give them a moment," Dustin said, guiding Sheila out of the room. Cristina followed.

Blake did not leave. "What's going on?"

"I love you back, Kenzie." Aidan managed a smile, although it was crooked. "But I think you already knew that."

"No." She shook her head, finding herself both laughing and crying. "I didn't. I hoped…"

Blake was staring at the two of them, mouth grim. "Wait. Love?"

Aidan, who still hadn't stopped looking into Kenzie's eyes, nodded. "Definitely love."

And just like that, Kenzie took a full breath. God, it felt good to breathe. Breathe and live and love.

"Okay, somebody talk to me," Blake said.

"Well you've been dead, or I'd have told you before now," Kenzie reminded him. "I've been busy trying to make Aidan pay for breaking my heart all those years ago."

At this, Blake blinked, then sent a glacial stare at Aidan. "You broke my sister's heart?"

Aidan winced. "Yeah, but if it helps, I was an idiot."

"He really was," Kenzie agreed.

"And trust me, she got me back," Aidan said. "Her evil plan worked. I fell hard. I love her, Blake." He broke eye contact with Kenzie and looked right at Blake, his smile gone, eyes dead serious. "I love her with everything I've got."

Blake looked as if a good wind could knock him over. "You put your heart out there? *You?*"

Bringing his and Kenzie's still joined hands to his chest, Aidan nodded. "Yeah."

"And then she stomped on it?"

"In boots, with spikes on the soles," Aidan assured him.

Blake took this in and considered, then relaxed. "Okay, then. As long as you're even."

"Not even," Kenzie whispered. "Not yet."

Uncertainty twisted Aidan's features. "Kenzie—"

"We're not even until I get my happily-ever-after." Her throat was so tight she could barely speak. "But since I'm going to be writing, I'm pretty sure I can plot it out for myself."

Aidan's eyes registered both surprise and pride.

"You're going to be great at writing. But about that ending… Am I in it?"

"I can guarantee it."

He smiled, and right then, Kenzie knew. She didn't need a script for this, her life, not anymore. The real thing was so much better. Taking the first step, she cupped Aidan's gorgeous face and kissed him.

* * * * *

*Delta Force operator Ransom Bennett is used to
handling anything that comes his way. But debilitating
combat injury has almost put him out of action.
Luckily, his new neighbour, Hannah Hartwell,
knows how to handle his pain...and him, too!*

Turn the page for a sneak preview of

Ready For Action
by
Karen Foley

the second book in the UNIFORMLY HOT!
*mini-series, available from Mills & Boon® Blaze®
in February 2010*

Ready For Action
by
Karen Foley

HEAT LICKED at her skin, made her shift restlessly and moan softly in distress. Her breath came in soft pants. She was hot, feverish with need. The man's hands moved over her body, touching and stroking her in all the right places. His mouth trailed moistly along the length of her neck and he took her earlobe between his teeth and bit gently, then soothed the sensitized flesh with the tip of his tongue.

She wanted desperately to see his face, but with his lips working magic along the whorl of her ear, she couldn't focus properly. He moved over her, his shoulders impossibly wide. She stroked her hands along the long, firm muscles of his back, and lower. She cupped his lean buttocks, loving how they flexed beneath her fingers, loving how he drove forcefully into her, pushing her higher and higher. Her thighs clenched around his slim hips, striving for the release that was so close. The inner muscles of her sex gripped him, reveling in his size and power. He stroked her, filled her, the rough silk of his flesh demanding a response. With a soft cry, she arched against him, rubbing her breasts against his chest. She was so close….

His movements quickened, became stronger. Her fingers fisted themselves in the sheets as the force of his thrusts caused the headboard behind her to thunk against the wall. Faster now, harder…if she could just see his face, look into his eyes…her climax was so close now.

Thunk, thunk, thunk.

The headboard reverberated against the wall as he filled her, stretched her, pounded into her.

Thunk. Thunk. Thunk.

Oh, no, please no. She was losing the feeling, moving back from the brink of what promised to be an exquisite explosion of pleasure. The surge of intense sexual need was receding. Even the hard masculine heat stroking between her thighs was vanishing, leaving her with only a throbbing, unfulfilled ache, and the thunking of…what *was* that noise?

Slowly, Hannah Hartwell came awake, disoriented and very much alone, still clinging to the vestiges of the erotic dream she'd been immersed in. It had seemed so real. She could still feel the hard length of her dream lover as he'd plunged into her, still feel the moist sweep of his breath against her ear and the weight of him pressing her down into the bed.

The abrupt ending of the dream left her bereft. Maybe, if she closed her eyes tightly, she could go back. She knew if she were to touch herself, she'd be wet and swollen with desire. It would take no more than several quick strokes of her fingers to ease the throbbing ache that still tormented her. How long had it been since she'd had good sex? Too long.

Thunk. Thunk.

Rolling onto her side, Hannah groped for the bedside clock, peering at it through the darkness. Jeez. Two-thirty in the morning. God, it was hot. Even the fan whirring softly in her open window did little to ease the sticky heat that had gripped the region for the past week.

Flopping onto her back, she stared at the ceiling and listened to the sound of something hard and dull striking the floorboards overhead. What the hell were they doing up there? Without central air-conditioning, the building was oppressively warm. It was probably even worse in the apartment upstairs. While she understood how the heat could make sleeping uncomfortable, if not impossible, it wasn't an excuse for being disruptive.

She'd moved into the first-floor apartment just six days earlier, and had yet to get a full night's rest, thanks to whoever lived in the apartment above her own. Every night, at nearly the same time, she was awakened by the strange thumping noise. She was beyond exhausted. She didn't know how many more interrupted nights she could handle. If it wasn't her neighbor keeping her awake, it was her own vivid imagination.

Despite telling herself that Sully had no idea where she was and wouldn't come after her even if he did, she couldn't quite convince herself of that. She'd heard rumors that he was connected to the mob, although at the time she hadn't believed them. He was a police officer, after all, sworn to serve and protect. In the weeks following the break-in at her South Boston shop, he'd come around every day to check on her. She hadn't suspected that he had an ulterior motive until the day he'd tried to pressure her into having sex with him in the back room of her shop. She'd been shocked and insulted, knowing the officer had both a wife and kids at home.

She'd refused, of course, but her life had taken a downward spiral as a result. She still had nightmares about the day he'd arrested her in a petty attempt to get back at her for rejecting him.

She'd been acquitted of any wrongdoing, but she'd been too afraid of reprisals to stick around. She knew what Sully was capable of, and the knowledge terrified her. Even now, the slightest of noises made her jump. Several times, she'd caught herself glancing over her shoulder as if expecting to see him bearing down on her, his eyes filled with gleeful retribution.

She was safe. She just had to keep reminding herself of that.

She'd put eight hundred miles between herself and Sully. Cliftondale, North Carolina, was a far cry from South Boston, and while she missed the brownstones and cozy pubs of East

Broadway, and the eclectic mixture of Irish locals and the artsy college crowd who had patronized her little New Age shop, Hannah didn't miss the anxiety she'd lived with.

She'd actually encouraged Sully to come around, at least in the beginning. She'd sensed a conflict within him and had hoped to perform a Reiki treatment on him. Her intuition had told her that if anyone needed spiritual balancing, it was Sully. But she'd quickly learned he wanted more than energy healing. Hannah still couldn't believe she'd misread him so completely. But all that was behind her now. She was making a new start.

In conjunction with the tiny furnished apartment, she'd also leased the first-floor storefront of the quaint little clapboard building, hardly able to believe her luck in finding two perfect rentals available under one roof. For a summer resort town, the combined rent was incredibly affordable. The fact that Labor Day had passed and Cliftondale was heading into its off-season didn't deter Hannah at all. The shop was hers.

Her parents had tried to dissuade her from using her "gift," convinced that doing so would only bring her trouble. Hannah understood their reluctance; her aunt had also inherited the ability to feel and soothe the physical pain of others through the touch of her hands. Aunt Elle had joined a nationally televised faith-healing ministry and her healing abilities had become legendary. At least, until the day the founder and minister of the church was arrested for solicitation. Overnight, Aunt Elle was decried as a charlatan. She had returned to Boston to live with Hannah's parents, but the press had been relentless in hounding her. It had been more than a year before their lives had returned to normal and Aunt Elle had had to give up her energy healing.

Which was why Hannah had chosen a more subtle venue in which to use her own healing abilities, because despite her parents' misgivings she couldn't deny her skills. Helping others was a physical imperative, a calling that she was unable to ignore. She was a master Reiki practitioner, and most of the time she restricted her treatments to just Reiki. But occasionally, if she sensed a client might benefit from her unique healing touch, she would use her skill to help ease a particularly painful joint or muscle.

The past week had been an endless cycle of moving furniture and boxes into both the apartment and the shop. Only ten days remained before the grand opening of her holistic health and wellness shop, and she had a laundry list of things to do before she could open the doors to the public.

Her muscles ached from the physical demands of moving, and she felt ill from a lack of sleep that no amount of meditation or yoga could restore. She knew the erotic dream she'd had was her body's way of releasing the stress and pent-up anxiety she subconsciously harbored, and now even that pleasure had been denied her.

Lingering frissons of sexual arousal still teased her, and Hannah briefly considered satisfying herself. In the same instant, there came another thunk on the ceiling overhead.

With a groan, she sat up and swung her legs to the floor. Perched on the edge of the bed, she scrubbed her hands over her face and then tucked her hair behind her ears, debating what to do. She could ignore the disturbance, bury her head beneath her pillows and hope to get at least a little more sleep. She could make herself a strong cup of coffee and tackle the unpacked boxes stacked throughout the apartment. Or, she could go upstairs right now and confront her neighbor. One thing was clear—she couldn't go on like this. Something had to be done, and since it seemed her neighbor was as wide-awake as she was, now was as good a time as any.

Determinedly, she made her way across the dark bedroom. A full moon streamed silver light through the windows and illuminated the storage boxes stacked haphazardly along the perimeter of the room. She'd get around to unpacking them eventually, but not until after her business was up and running.

Unlocking her apartment door, she peered cautiously into the shadowed hallway. The staircase that led to the second floor was dimly lit by an overhead light. From where she stood, she couldn't see the upstairs apartment door. She'd been curious about who lived there, but mostly in terms of whether they were strong enough and willing to help her shift her heavier pieces of furniture around her own apartment.

She'd spotted an old, black Land Rover parked in the narrow driveway alongside the house. Two mornings in a row, she'd been awakened early by the engine throbbing to life, but she hadn't been quick enough to catch a glimpse of the driver as the vehicle reversed out of the driveway. She was always plugged into her iPod when she worked in the shop, and hadn't heard the Land Rover return, or its owner climb the stairs to the second floor.

Twice, she'd crept partway up the staircase, intending to introduce herself, but each time the sight of the closed door had unnerved her. In the end, she'd decided against asking for help and had done the majority of the work herself.

She'd spent most of the past week in the shop and hadn't seen anyone enter or leave the building. Aside from the late-night thumping, there'd been no other sign of life from whoever occupied the second-floor apartment. There was no name on the mailbox secured just above hers beside the front door; nor had she seen any mail being delivered to it.

She'd even snooped around the building a little, stepping into the tiny backyard to stare up at the second-floor balcony. But the sliding doors had been closed, the curtains firmly drawn, and there was nothing on the balcony itself to indicate who might live there. No flowers, no table or chairs, no wind chimes, no nothing. In fact, if it weren't for the late-night disturbances and the Land Rover sitting in the driveway, she'd be convinced the apartment above her own was empty.

Glancing down at herself to make sure she was adequately

covered, Hannah decided her tank top and men's boxer shorts were more than conservative enough. The tiny coastal town of Cliftondale was an artists' haven, and during the hot summer months the narrow, winding streets swarmed with college students and tourists who wore less clothing than she did right now. She wasn't wearing a bra, but then she barely filled a B-cup, so it wasn't like she had a lot going on in that department to worry about.

It didn't matter. She was going upstairs, regardless.

Hannah drew in a deep breath, striving for a calm, serene manner. This wasn't a confrontation. It was an opportunity to make a new friend, to connect with another human being and extend herself. She had a natural gift for communing with others, and she had no reason to think this occasion would be any different.

She climbed the staircase, her hand running along the cool, chunky balustrade. Her bare feet moved silently on the worn treads. The air was even warmer on the second floor than it had been outside her apartment. Reaching the top of the stairs, she hesitated and some of her positive self-talk deserted her. Confronting a total stranger at two-thirty in the morning no longer seemed like such a great idea. Maybe she should just forget it; she could always do this during the day.

In the next instant, she chided herself for her cowardice. What was the worst that could happen?

Hannah strode over to the apartment door and, before she could change her mind, knocked firmly—three brief, sharp raps of her knuckles against the wood panels. She waited, aware that her heart was beating faster. She was being ridiculous. It was probably a sweet old lady who suffered from insomnia. She might even own one of those foot-driven antique spinning wheels. That could be the source of the thumping that woke her up each night. Even as she conjured up images of an apple-cheeked grandmother, the apartment door was yanked open and

Hannah found herself staring at a solid wall of hard, muscular, very ungrandmotherly maleness.

She took an involuntary step back.

Good Lord. He was close to six-and-a-half-feet tall and wore nothing but a pair of boxer shorts, the stretchy kind that hugged a guy's hips and outlined his masculine assets. Above the waistband of his briefs, he had acres of bare, tanned skin. His arms were an incredible mix of bulging muscles and lean sinews. Her hands would probably be incapable of spanning those impressive biceps.

Her gaze drifted upward, past the hard ridges of his stomach to the flat planes of his chest, where a set of black military dog tags dangled from a slender chain and nestled in the shallow groove between his pectorals.

Hannah swallowed and forced herself to meet his eyes. They were dark and fathomless, and so completely bloodshot that she suspected he'd slept even less than she had during the past week. By the dim, overhead light, she could see the vivid scar that bisected one eyebrow and slashed upward into his dark hair.

She shivered, unable to shake the sense that she stood at the leading edge of a dark storm front. The very air around them seemed to tremble with turbulence. Hannah could almost feel a shift in the air pressure as she stared at him.

His face was lean and hard like the rest of him, all thrusting cheekbones and square jaw, covered in what must have been several days' growth of whiskers. Lines of weariness had etched themselves into the grooves alongside his mouth, and his eyes were red-rimmed with fatigue. His brows were drawn fiercely together as he swept her with a look that was both contemptuous and speculative.

"Who the hell are you?" His voice was low and deep, with a rasping quality to it, as if he'd just inhaled smoke. As he spoke, something resonated within Hannah, responding to the timbre of his voice and making her long to hear more.

2 FREE BOOKS
AND A SURPRISE GIFT

We would like to take this opportunity to thank you for reading this Mills & Boon® book by offering you the chance to take TWO more specially selected titles from the Blaze® series absolutely FREE! We're also making this offer to introduce you to the benefits of the Mills & Boon® Book Club™—

- **FREE home delivery**
- **FREE gifts and competitions**
- **FREE monthly Newsletter**
- **Exclusive Mills & Boon Book Club offers**
- **Books available before they're in the shops**

Accepting these FREE books and gift places you under no obligation to buy, you may cancel at any time, even after receiving your free books. Simply complete your details below and return the entire page to the address below. You don't even need a stamp!

YES Please send me 2 free Blaze books and a surprise gift. I understand that unless you hear from me, I will receive 3 superb new books every month, including a 2-in-1 book priced at £4.99 and two single books priced at £3.19 each, postage and packing free. I am under no obligation to purchase any books and may cancel my subscription at any time. The free books and gift will be mine to keep in any case.

Ms/Mrs/Miss/Mr ——————— Initials ———————

Surname ————————————————————
Address ————————————————————

———————————————— Postcode ———————

Send this whole page to: Mills & Boon Book Club, Free Book Offer, FREEPOST NAT 10298, Richmond, TW9 1BR